EATEN BY THE NIGHT

Barbara Unković

www.barbaraunkovic.com

Barbara Unković has asserted her right to be identified as the author of this work in accordance with copyright

First published 2021

Barbara Unković is of Croatian and English descent. She is a cousin to DH Lawrence and holds a Master of Creative Writing with honours from the University of Auckland in New Zealand

Barbara is a freelance editor and manuscript assessor

Other titles by Barbara Unković

Moon Walking

Adriatic Blue

Overheated

Lady Chatterley's Enemy

Croatia Blue

The Ship of Death (under pen name BG Lawrence)

Dedication

For descendants of the people of the Former Republic of Yugoslavia and refugees who fled the Balkans in 1991 at the beginning of the war, arriving in a foreign country with nothing but a suitcase of possessions, to start a new life in a strange distant land.

Author's Note

Real characters flit through the pages of this novel and a number of the events described are based on true occurrences with a writer's licence for dialogue. Against this factual setting I have woven my fictional characters who bear no resemblance to any person living or dead.

Glossary

ajvar – roast red pepper sauce

baba – grandmother

baka – crone or old hag

BiH – Bosnia and Herzegovina

blitva – silver beet or swiss chard

Borba – struggle, combat

brodetto – fish stew

burek – filled pastry of Turkish origin

čevapcići – spicy sausage

cro juda – traitor

crni rižot – black risotto

dida – grandfather

Djido – nickname for Milovan Đilas

draga – darling or dear

frendica – female friend or pal

HDZ – Croatian Democratic Union

hobotnice – octopus

HOS – Croatian Defence Force

ICTY – International Criminal Court for Yugoslavia

jebati – shit as in swear word

JNA – Yugoslav People's Army

kladionica – betting shop often found in cafés in Croatia

koke – chicken or little chicken as in endearing nickname

kolači – cake

konoba – wine cellar

koristi – used

Krištof – nickname for Edvard Kardelj

kroštule – sweet pastry knots

krumpir – potato

kukuriku – cock-a-doodle-doo

kulen – hot spicy salami made in the north of Croatia

kumulonimbus – heavy, dense storm cloud

kurac – prick as in swear word

kupus – a type of cabbage which grows on a tall stalk

Leko – nickname for Aleksandar Ranković

majka – mother

nemoj me jebati – don't fuck with me

nespretan – clumsy

Operacija Bljesak – Operation Flash

Operacija Ulja – Operation Storm

oprostite – pardon me

peka – bell-shaped dome used to cook food over an open fire

pomoć – help

rakija – fiery alcohol often home brewed

SDP – Reformed Communist Party

selo – village

Sretan Božić – Merry Christmas

SRS – Serbian Radical Party

slušati – listen

Stari – Tito's nickname which means old or old one; only used by those close to him

šumadija – weak plum brandy

tata – father

UDBA – the Yugoslav secret police in operation from 1946 to 1991

ulica – street

Vlad – Vladimir Dedijer

vukejebina – the middle of nowhere (the place where wolves fuck)

zastava – flag

zdravo drug – hello friend

za dom spremni – for the homeland – Ustaše equivalent of the fascist or Nazi salute *Sieg heil*

zlata – gold

Zagreb 1941

Part One

Chapter one

Anđa and Ivan pushed ahead hoping to gain a better vantage point. It was just as well they were both slight, otherwise it would have been difficult to insinuate their way forward through the throng. Drizzle had begun to fall from clouds that were the same grey as the shadows under Anđa's eyes.

He couldn't believe the number of people who had come to see the unwholesome spectacle. People lined the main thoroughfare, the side streets and the square. The mass of humanity stretched as far as his eye could see. While he could cope with the crush of bodies, he was not prepared for the mood of the crowd — everywhere he turned ecstatic people were laughing, smiling and cheering. There was no opposition to the arrogant soldiers marching into the city as if they were a shock of cassowary in disguise. The jubilation was deafening.

'Are they mad?' Anđa said into his son's ear as a renewed wave of merriment rang out when a group of soldiers on horseback followed by several tanks went past. 'Anyone would think Hitler's soldiers were liberating the city,' he added.

Ivan shook his blond head in disgust. 'Look over there,' he said pointing to the opposite side of the street where women were throwing gifts to the soldiers and children were waving paper flags. When the chanting started and they heard cries of, 'No war and we have a state.' They looked at each other with horror.

'It's time to go,' Anđa said. 'Thousands and thousands of fools are gathered here. It's no place for us.' Anđa knew he shouldn't be making such bold statements in public, even though he'd kept his voice down, in case someone heard him. Yet he couldn't stop himself. Inside he was churned up with a mixture of fear, anger and hatred.

As she listened to the broadcast Mara stared out of the kitchen window at nothing as she repeatedly ran her hands through her blonde hair in a nervous gesture as she swept her overgrown fringe out of her eyes and leant her plump body against the kitchen bench. She had become fearful; it was time to turn off the radio. She'd heard enough. When Belgrade was invaded four days ago she knew it wouldn't be long before German soldiers entered her city.

Mara had lived her entire life in Zagreb. The only home she had ever known had once belonged to her parents who had died not long after her marriage. Both had been taken by cancer within a year of each other. Although she missed them, in a way she was glad they were gone, she couldn't imagine how they would have coped with the war that was about to envelop her country. What would happen next? The thought that her home could be taken over by Nazis was distressing and abhorrent. She tried to shut it out of her mind.

Built from pale-cream magnificent stone, the most outstanding feature of the traditional building in Maksimirska Cesta where she lived was the hand-carved stone columns on either side of the main entrance. Her home was spread over two floors while Jelena Petrović, a widow, lived in the small apartment above.

The apartment wasn't big, only large enough to house her family. Mara and Anda's three boys slept in the largest bedroom upstairs, while she and her husband occupied the middle-sized one and their daughter Zlata slept in the small room, which was scarcely large enough to accommodate a single bed.

Downstairs, the kitchen with its green Formica bench and walk-in pantry, was combined with the living room. In comparison to the upstairs there was more space. The rectangular dining table was large enough for everyone to squeeze around on the assortment of battered-mismatched chairs. The oak dresser and the two brown sofas were cumbersome and took up most of the remaining space. While a wood-burning stove in the far corner presided over the room as if it was a silent monster. A narrow wooden staircase beside the pantry led to the *konoba* where wine and firewood were stored. The interior walls, as in most homes in Zagreb, were white, while the timberwork was varnished a sombre brown.

Mara's mouth was clamped shut with resignation in a face the colour of putty. She was thinking about her beloved country and the predicament it was in. So many aspects were a riddle to her — the disparities between the *Ustaše,* the Nazis and the Communists. Was the difference between them caused by their cultures or their ideologies? She found it too difficult to understand. It was easier not to dwell on it because she had no answers. It was too much of a complex conundrum.

She turned her attention to the potatoes she had dug earlier from her garden around the corner in the next street. As she cleaned off the soil in the stone sink she wondered what her husband and their eldest son Ivan would have to report when they came home after spending the day in Central Zagreb. She wasn't concerned about their welfare. Her husband was more than capable of looking after himself. After all he'd survived detection by the authorities for five years after he'd joined the communists — an illegal group.

Yet again Mara stared out of the window above the sink. It could have been a bright, sunny, spring day. It wasn't. The ominous, dark-grey clouds that scudded across the sky matched her mood. Her mouth was a permanently grim-thin line. She had just listened to Slavko Kvaternik, one of the *Ustaše* commanders, proclaiming the establishment of the independent State of Croatia. She knew she shouldn't have turned on the radio.

At the end of their school day, three of her children, Zlata, Damir and Zoran burst in the door. The boys came in ahead of their younger sister, who was more reticent. Almost immediately they began to gabble at their mother.

'Did you know there are German tanks in Trg bana Jelačića?' Damir said with such a pronounced frown that his eyebrows knitted together.

'Has the war started?' Zoran said as he folded his arms in an attitude of defiance.

'Slow down, slow down,' Mara said. 'One question at a time. 'I don't know what it means.' She almost added *you're safe*, but stopped herself.

'Nothing will happen to us, will it?' twelve-year-old Zlata asked as she leant against the kitchen door frame looking thoughtful and twisting a lock of shiny auburn hair around her forefinger as she looked from one to the other while she followed the conversation.

'I can't answer your questions. You'll have to wait until your father and Ivan come home. They've gone to see what's going on. Right now I'd like you to get on with your jobs.'

'Boys, we need more wood brought inside before it gets rained on and Zlata go and pick some broad beans for dinner please.'

'But *Majka* ...' Damir said.

'No! Not now. Off you go.'

'I only wanted ...'

'I said, not now.' Mara's voice was firm as she pushed her short yellow hair behind her ears. She never shouted at her children, although they knew by her tone that they must do as they were told or suffer the consequences — usually a paddle on the behind with the hand-carved wooden spoon she kept on top of the oak sideboard.

By the time Anđa and Ivan came in the door it was dark. Mara had expected they would be home earlier and when she smelt alcohol on her husband's breath she knew they'd stopped off somewhere for a drink. She didn't comment. Nagging wasn't something she indulged in and now wasn't the time to start. She knew life was on the verge of becoming difficult for him — in fact, difficult for the entire family.

After he'd taken off his well-worn hat and coat Anđa sat in his usual seat on the sofa. When Mara glanced at him, his long-thin face was pale, there were leaden marks under his eyes and he looked distracted — he wore the same frown as their son Damir. Zlata sat next to her father — so close she was almost in his lap. A small smile twitched the corners of Mara's mouth when her husband draped his arm around their daughter and ruffled her hair with his other hand. Ivan had gone upstairs and Zoran and Damir were sitting opposite their father on the other shabby sofa looking at him expectantly.

When his father didn't speak and the silence became too much for Damir he had to say what was on his mind. '*Tata,* what did you see? What's going on?' he blurted out as he moved to the edge of his seat.

'I'll get to it in a minute son, as soon as your mother's brought me a drink. Is there any wine left?' he called to his wife who was stirring a pot on top of the stove.

Flushed by the heat from the stove, Mara walked across the room and handed him a half-empty glass.

Mara looked on in dismay as her husband stared at the contents before he knocked it back in one go. The red wine was no longer bright and clear and when the glass was empty there was sediment in the bottom.

Anđa grimaced as he handed the glass back to his wife. 'Is that all there is?' he asked as he looked at his wife's eyes — the twinkle he loved was absent and there was no trace of her usual smile that showed her missing teeth.

'Yes, there's no more anywhere. I tried several shops yesterday.' She shrugged as she sat down next to her sons and twirled the stem of the glass round and round in her fingers as she too waited anxiously for her husband to speak.

When at last Anđa spoke, Mara knew he'd thought carefully about his words as he looked at his sons.

'Well, there wasn't much to see. We caught a glimpse of soldiers and a few tanks.' He stopped speaking. Mara was certain he was reluctant to mention the magnitude of the invading force.

'How many soldiers do you think there were?' Zoran asked.

'I couldn't say. We had a bad view.' She was certain he could have given an estimate based on what he'd been told at the Party meeting he'd attended yesterday, even so he wasn't prepared to say.

'What does it all mean?' Damir asked. 'It can't be a good thing?'

'I expect not, but there's no point in worrying about it because there's nothing we can do to stop it.'

'Fools,' Mara muttered under her breath.

'What did you say, *Majka?*' Zoran asked.

'Nothing,' Mara replied. 'It's dinner time.' She stood up, went to the kitchen and began to set the table with plates and cutlery. She didn't want her children picking up on her troubled frame of mind.

'What were the explosions we heard this morning? They were loud,' Zoran asked.

'We saw planes overheard too,' Damir added.

'They were bombing the roads leading into Zagreb so they could get their tanks in,' their father said in a resigned voice.

'Yugoslavia's become another notch in Germany's belt,' Ivan said as he descended the staircase with his hands jammed as far as they would go into his pockets.

Mara looked from father to son as her husband gave Ivan, their eldest child, a look to stop him elaborating.

'That means war for us now, doesn't it, *Tata?* Damir said.

'We'll see,' Anđa replied.

Mara knew it did, and she also knew her husband didn't want to vocalize it to their children. Mara was well aware that her children knew Hitler's planes had been bombing London for the last ten months and that German forces had occupied France a year ago.

'War? Will they kill us?' Zlata said as she gulped and her eyes filled with tears.

'Goodness me no! You'll be fine as long as you do what your mother and me tell you. Anyway, enough of that. Your mother is waiting for us to come to the table.'

That night in bed Mara discussed the implications of the German invasion at greater length with her husband and listened as he told her about the elated seething mass of people he'd suffered earlier in the day.

'What I didn't say in front of the children was that the Italians attacked Istria and the Dalmatian coast today and they're in control there. Ivan knows, but I told him not to tell the others. It'll only make them more unsettled.'

Mara was wide awake lying on her back staring at the ceiling. 'I know. I heard it on the radio. Didn't our troops even put up a fight to stop the Nazis?' she asked.

'A token resistance from what I heard. In Belgrade they were more hostile towards them, even though it didn't do them any good. Krištof and Vlad were there. They weren't injured, thank God. Krištof said the first bombs were dropped before seven in the morning. The markets were crowded as usual because it was Sunday and extra revellers were in the streets celebrating the non-agression pact that's just been signed between the USSR and Yugoslavia. The second attack came at eleven and according to Krištof it was worse than the first. The German airforce methodically bombed the whole city. Vlad thinks several thousand were killed and that's not counting the ones who were buried by rubble. All things considered we were spared what they went through. Anyway, it's probably just as well Zagreb capitulated. What could our pathetic army do against Hitler's Wehrmacht?'

'So, we're surrounded? Germans and *Ustaše* on one side and Italians on the other,' Mara said as she rubbed her temples to try and stem the headache she'd had since the middle of the day.

'Yes and of course Pavelić and his *Ustaše* mongrels are bleating on about bringing new race rules into force. He wants an ethnically pure state. And we know what that means.'

'Yes,' Mara said in a quiet voice. 'What'll we do?' She turned towards Anđa and he put his arms around her. His hip bones were sharp. He'd always been thin with no spare flesh, but these days he seemed thinner.

'I don't know yet, but depending on what happens next I might have to leave.'

'No!' Mara's body went rigid as tears spurted from her eyes.

'Ssh! You don't want the children to hear you, do you? We'll worry about that if and when it happens.'

Chapter two

Only days after the invasion by the Germans, as Anđa had predicted, Pavelić formed a new government.

It was always in bed at night when he and Mara discussed the plight of Yugoslavia.

'As I knew he would, Pavelić has created abhorrent rules and began to enforce them immediately. Jews, Serbs and Gypsies are being rounded up,' he told his wife.

'I thought Jews only had to wear yellow armbands. Aren't they safe either?' Mara asked.

'No, they're being massacred. Thousands from all three races have been put in prison, executed at sites around the city, and in the forests, while others are sent to concentration camps.' Anđa paused. The Party meetings were his source of information. 'I'm not sure why I'm telling you this dreadful stuff. Do you want me to go on?'

'Yes, I need to know. I have to keep informed.'

'Pavélic's foremost rule is, kill a third, convert a third and expel a third,' Anđa said as he thought about telling his wife that Pavelić collected human eyes — he kept a basketful in his office — that was something she didn't need to hear.

'Are you serious? What kind of depraved individual would invent a rule like that? Are you sure it's true? I don't know much about him. What's he like?'

'It's true alright. The Party isn't prone to receiving or spreading false information. He's been in exile for the last thirteen years because he was wanted for murder and treason. He's been hiding. First in Hungary, then in Italy and Germany and keeping a low profile. He's a nasty son-of-a-bitch,' Anđa said as a shudder shook his thin frame.

'I don't think I know what he looks like.'

'He has a jowly-square face. In my opinion he's quite faceless and he seldom smiles. Anyway, you'll be seeing him soon enough because I hear that his ugly mug is going to be pictured on anything he can find starting with postage stamps.'

'Yes, I've heard he has a thing about stamps. He collects them, doesn't he?'

'I guess you could say that,' Anđa replied. 'He's particularly interested in the ones he steals from dead people.'

'That's disgusting.'

'As I said, he's a nasty son-of-a-bitch.'

'What do you imagine all those idiots are thinking now after they welcomed the

Germans with open arms?' Anđa asked because he felt he had to change the subject.

'Many of them'll be happy. There are plenty who don't like living with other races.' Mara paused. 'I found that out when I went shopping this morning. I was almost home and I had just turned the corner into our street when I was spat at and called scum. One of them shouted, 'It's only a matter of time before they get you.'

'Who were they?'

'The Tomić brothers.'

'That's rich coming from them. Their mother's a Serb. Hope you told them where to go.'

'No, I crossed over and tried my best to ignore them.'

'I'll speak to their father,' Anđa said with a vexatious look on his face.

'I'd rather you didn't. It could cause trouble for the children. They'll most likely be taunted at school if you do.'

'I expect you're right.' It was Anđa's turn to pause and a short silence fell between them as he pulled the coarse brown blanket over his chest. 'It'll get worse from what I hear. In the areas under the control of the Third Reich they're forcing Yugoslavs to sign statements saying they're German and if they won't then they get twenty-four hours to leave. The only belongings they can take are those they can carry.'

'Is ours one of those areas?'

'Not yet, but if they come and ask you to sign while I'm not here, do it. We'll have to hope like hell they don't commandeer this part of town and make us move out.'

'It couldn't get much worse, could it?'

'Well yes … they're imposing a seven p.m. curfew and they're talking about us needing permits to move from one area of town to another. And the form of the permit will change every three days to prevent forgeries.'

'Yes, I know. You don't have to tell me. It was on the radio this morning and the loud speakers are bleating about the curfew. You'd have to be deaf not to hear them.' Mara's voice was blunt, blunter than she intended.

For a time they lay side by side in companionable silence.

'I don't want you to go,' Mara said as she moved over to her husband's side of the bed put her arms around him and hugged him. Anđa knew she was afraid and there was nothing he could do or say to alleviate her fear. He ventured into the heart of the city often, there were meetings he had to attend. Every time he was about to leave Mara's words were always the same.

'Do you have to go? What if they arrest you?'

And everyday his reply was the same, 'I must, you know, I must.'

At least Mara didn't ask what the meetings were about, but he knew she had a fair idea. Five years ago he had become involved with the group of anti-fascists led by Josif Broz Tito. They were in the throes of forming a resistance group, but that was all he had told her.

'The less you know about it the better,' he said.

It was a week later when Zlata came home from school in tears. Mara looked up with alarm when she dropped her school bag on the kitchen floor, sank on to a chair and buried her face in her arms on top of the kitchen table. Sobs racked her small body.

Mara hastily wiped her wet hands and rushed over to her daughter.

'What's the matter?' she asked as she put her hand on her daughter's shoulder.

Zlata dashed the tears from her cheeks as she looked up at her mother with stricken eyes.

'The Serbian boys in my class — Matija and Vlado — they've gone. Someone said they've been killed. What if I'm next?' Zlata disintegrated into another bout of weeping.

'The Tomić brothers?'

'Yes!'

Mara grimaced. 'Come here,' she said as she pulled Zlata to her feet and held her close. 'You mustn't think things like that. Your brothers will look after you, don't worry,' she said even though she knew her daughter would continue to fret. Zlata was an anxious child and she certainly didn't need incidents like this heightening her nervousness.

'Do I have to go to school tomorrow?' Zlata asked.

'I'm afraid you must. As I said, your brothers will look after you. I'll speak to them and make sure they do.'

Zlata put her hand to her mouth and began biting her nails — a habit Mara had never seen her daughter indulge in before.

'Keep your eyes straightahead and don't stop to talk to anyone on the way,' Mara told her three children the next morning before they left for school. 'Walk as quickly as possible, and boys, make sure you look out for your sister. Don't dawdle and use the back streets so you can avoid any soldiers or tanks.'

'What if I'm asked about *Tata?* What do I say?'

'Ignore them, pretend you didn't hear and walk away, but don't run. And remember you were born here — you're not Serbian.'

It wasn't long before the food shortages grew worse. Mara had been hoarding supplies for months as well as drying seeds and growing rotational crops of broad beans and potatoes. Ivan helped her by digging over the soil, a task which she was finding increasingly difficult because of the arthritis in her right ankle.

When a feeling of menace and fear invaded the city as the stock of essentials declined, Mara dreaded going shopping. When basic necessities such as flour, oil, sugar and coffee became scarce Mara implemented a rationing system in her household to conserve what they had.

The next blow descended when Ivan came home early from his job as an apprentice baker. Without saying a word, he walked into the kitchen and placed a bag of flour on the bench. His mother blinked when she saw it and turned to look at him. His round face was downcast below his overgrown thatch of yellow hair.

'What is it?' she asked.

'I've been laid off. The flour shortage means Stefan can't bake many loaves, there's not enough work and he can't afford to keep me on. He gave me this as a parting gift.'
Mara put her arms wordlessly around her eldest son. What was there to say? She couldn't blame Stefan. He was a good man and if she'd been in his position she'd probably have done the same.

It was Ivan who broke the gloomy silence. 'I'll be able to help you with the garden from now on. It's not likely I can get another job. Certainly not one as a baker anyway. The shortages are already starting all over the city from what I hear.'

'Oh son!' was all Mara said as she stepped away from him and took her lace-edged handkerchief out of her housecoat pocket and pressed it against her mouth.

Chapter three

Three months after the German invasion Anđa attended the last meeting of the Communist Party that was held in Zagreb. It wasn't easy getting all the members together because by then the German command had implemented the special permit process. Most of those who attended the meeting required permits and it took time for these to be forged.

When Anđa set out for the meeting a strong sun had appeared in a bright-blue sky. It was the middle of summer. Inside the vacant flat in a backstreet he looked around the sparsely furnished, dreary room at the assembled company and noted Tito, Krištof, Leko, Djido and Vlad, who was as usual already busy writing, even though the meeting had yet to start.

Vlad, a law graduate from Belgrade University was an athletic, burly man in his mid-thirties. He was the notetaker and the editor of *Borba,* the official communist newspaper, and there was nothing that escaped his attention. He was never without his fountain pen or his supply of ink.

Anđa took a seat as others entered the room.

Tito began by giving a detailed report on Yugoslavia's situation before opening the floor to a discussion that lasted all day. Anđa took note of the serious look in Tito's blue-green eyes. He had always been intrigued by them. It wasn't to do with the colour. Although that was unusual — it was about how the look in them changed. Often they were elusive and sometimes menacing and occasionally joyful, but on this occasion they were nothing other than solemn.

One of Tito's opening lines stuck in Anđa's mind — *We are the first party to call for a fight against the invaders.* Anđa was certain he had to be part of this — come what may.

By the end of the day several decisions had been made and the foundation for the National Liberation Front, had been laid. Tito had plenty to say for himself and Anđa listened eagerly.

'The people harbour bitter feelings towards the king and the former government because they betrayed our country and failed to make the necessary provisions to defend it against invaders. For that reason, the feeling against those collaborating with Hitler and Mussolini is strong. Our struggle against the invaders must be a determined one and preparations for the uprising must be stepped up immediately,' Tito said in his Croatian peasant-like accent that was tinged with a trace of Russian.

It was 1927, when Anđa first met Tito, a sturdy physical specimen with thin lips and a strong jaw. Anđa found him spirited yet nervous with blunt, strong hands that matched the bone structure of his face. Anđa supposed Tito was best described as handsome, but didn't all men look handsome to their admirers once they became leaders?

They'd met at their place of employment — a factory outside Zagreb that manufactured railway carriages. Not long after he had started working there, Anđa, along with Tito and four others were arrested and accused of plotting a revolution. By then Tito had become secretary of the metalworkers' union and when he protested about the men in the factory having to work sixteen hours a day in freezing winter weather, Anđa supported his cause. All six were found guilty, Tito and Anđa escaped after three months in custody. A year later, Tito was arrested for being a member of the illegal Communist Party of Yugoslavia and although Anđa was also a member he was lucky and escaped. When Tito was sentenced to five years' hard labour, Anđa watched from a discreet distance as Tito was led from the courthouse. He would never forget Tito shouting, "Long live the Communist Party of Yugoslavia." It was then that Anđa began to admire Tito's courage and conviction.

Anđa was aware that Tito had gone to St Petersburg in 1917 and joined the *Reds* to fight in the Russian Civil War that lasted until 1921. He also knew that Tito had visited Russia on three subsequent occasions, the last one being 1939, when he changed his name from Broz to Tito.

The discussion moved on to talk about setting up groups with commanders in various areas of the country, collection of arms, nursing and first-aid courses. Anđa was to be part of Tito's Supreme Command.

At the end of the meeting Tito, of course, had the final say. 'This will be our last meeting here. It has come to my attention that I'm under surveillance by the *Ustaše*. It's time to move. Our new headquarters will be in Belgrade. You will be advised when and where our next meeting will be convened.'

It was a matter of days later, the day before Zlata's thirteenth birthday, in fact, when Anđa made his announcement. He had already told his wife the night before and once the family sat down in the living room she struggled to keep her composure.

Anđa's expression was sombre as he broke the news to his children.

'I must leave … I'm going to fight for our country.' He got no further before Zlata, who always sat next to her father, let out a harrowing cry and clung to him. Zoran and Damir's mouths dropped open although they remained silent. Neither had any idea this was coming. Ivan was the only one to speak.

'I want to go with you, *Tata,*' he said.

'No Son, you can't, you're too young and besides I need you to stay here and look after the rest of the family while I'm away.'

'But *Tata,* I know how to fire a gun.'

'You may well do, but your place is here. You'll be in charge of the family while I'm away.' Anđa was trying to make his son feel important even though Mara would in reality be head of the household.

Ivan hung his head in disappointment. He knew there was no point in aguing with his father.

'Where will you be going?' Damir asked.

'I don't know. Wherever I'm told, I expect.'

'When are you leaving?' Zoran, who was absentmindedly picking at the scab on a graze on the back of his left hand, asked.

Anđa paused before he imparted his unpalatable answer. 'Tonight, once it's dark.' He didn't say he was joining the resistance because he was well aware that giving information such as this to any of his family could put them in danger.

'But *Tata,* tomorrow is my birthday,' Zlata, who had been sitting with a brooding expression on her face, wailed.

'I know sweetheart. I can't help it. It has to be tonight.'

'But *Tata* we always go for a walk in Maksimir on my birthday and you promised you'd teach me more of the names of the trees.'

'I know. When I come back we'll go, I promise.' The renewed promise resulted in a fresh flood of tears from Zlata. Anđa looked at the stricken face of his daughter. He knew walking hand in hand through the park with him was one of Zlata's favourite pastimes.

When Zlata's sobbing became uncontrollable Anđa was surprised when his wife got up and tried to prise her away from him. But Zlata wouldn't have it, and when her crying increased in volume, he was astounded by his wife's outburst.

'Enough!' Mara shouted. 'You're not the only one distressed about your father leaving. We're all miserable and you're making it worse for the rest of us.'

Anđa had never heard her speak so harshly to their daughter.

'Ssh Zlata! I won't be gone forever. With a bit of luck I might be back sooner than you think.' Of course Anđa had no idea when he'd be back or if he'd be back, but it was all he could think of saying to try to calm his daughter.

Much later that night he did indeed depart, but not before Zlata clung to his leg and tried to stop him.

'*Tata* don't go, please don't go,' she stammered through her tears.

In the end, after she ignored both her mother and father, it was Ivan who picked her up and held her as Anđa slipped out of the door into the darkness.

Chapter four

Anđa pulled his cap more firmly on his head and turned up the collar of his coat before he set off. He wasn't cold. He just didn't want to be recognised. It was a mild summer's night with a sickle moon hanging in a deep-violet sky. With his head down he stepped up his pace. Because of the curfew the streets were deserted and it was easy going.

His mind was working overtime as he strode along quickly. As yet he had no idea of his destination and he wondered where he was being sent. He felt both excitement and trepidation in equal measure. He was happy to be on the verge of defending his country, although he couldn't suppress his fear of dying in the effort. Then there was his family. Even though his wife was a strong woman he was well aware that might not be enough to protect her and their children. His family was always in his mind.

In a street behind Groblje Mirogoi he withdrew into the doorway of a vacant building and checked his watch. He'd got there in forty minutes. He was pleased. So far, so good. He looked up at the sickle moon; the sky had changed to what Anđa thought of as dark tank-grey. Trees across the road were quivering as a light breeze ruffled the thin boughs that were covered with new growth.

Two minutes later, when he spotted the glowing tips of two cigarettes he knew Djido and his brother Aleksa where already there. They shook hands in silence and after Djido and his brother extinguished their cigarettes they set off. Further along the street a dirty-green, battered Albion truck was parked. Djido waited until they'd clambered into the cab before he spoke.

'We're headed to Belgrade for a meeting. Stari and most of the others should be there already and all going well we'll be there in about four hours, maybe less depending on what we have to avoid on the way,' Djido said as he tugged on his left ear lobe. It was a habit he indulged in whenever he was talking.

'I take it we're not travelling on the main road,' Anđa said.

'No, I've mapped out a different route. One that's not well used. It might take a bit longer, but there'll be less chance of running into German patrols,' Aleksa said as he extracted a roughly drawn map from his jacket pocket and put on his spectacles.

'What's the meeting about?' Anđa asked.

'Strategies, I think and a discussion about negotiations with the *Četniks*. From what there was, or should I say wasn't, in Stari's communiqué, it looks likely that me and Aleksa will be going to command the offensive in Montenegro and I imagine you'll be part of the negotiating team meeting Mihailović. That's just my guess and until we're given our orders we won't know for certain.'

'Who's heading the negotiations?' Anđa asked.

'Leko, I expect or at least that's what Krištof thinks. I spoke to him yesterday and since he advises Stari on strategies, if that's what he thinks then that's probably who it'll be,' Djido said. 'Best do as Aleksa has and try to get some sleep,' Djido added as he changed gear.

Anđa glanced at Aleksa who was dozing with his head back and his mouth wide open. He slouched in his seat and closed his eyes. Sleep didn't come easily. The cab was full of cigarette smoke and the potholes on the unsealed road were relentless plus his mind was alive with questions. *What makes Tito and Krištof think that the Četniks will be prepared to do a deal, and if they are, will they honour it?* He'd always seen them as an untrustworthy bunch. Mihailović had defected from the 2nd Army deployed in Bosnia by King Peter II's Government in exile after he had failed to follow orders from the king's supreme staff. And besides who could trust any of them when *Četnik* meant to plunder and burn down. Anđa saw them as a group of rebels who claimed allegiance to the king and pledged restoration of the monarchy. Yet Anđa believed that at the end of the day they would side with whoever they thought would be the victor in the struggle for power.

Anđa glanced across at Djido who was puffing on a cigarette. 'When's the meeting? You didn't say.'

'Tomorrow.'

Anđa grunted acknowledgment and once again shut his eyes.

At one-thirty a.m. they were met by Mitra, Djido's wife, at a house belonging to Vladislav Ribnikar, a journalist who was the founder of *Politika*. When she greeted them, at first Anđa didn't recognise her — her dark hair had been dyed blonde and cut exceptionally short. He knew she had recently escaped from prison and he guessed she'd dyed it to avoid detection by the police.

'Stari will be expecting you tomorrow at eleven,' Mitra said.

'Is he here?' Djido asked.

'Not yet.'

Because Anđa knew he would be expected to spruce himself up for the meeting the following day, he intended to buy a better-looking coat.

He set off on foot for Lower Dorćol on the right bank of the Danube about 700 metres from the central town square of Terazije. He knew it wouldn't take him long to get there. He was making for Cara Dušana Street, which apart from being the site of the oldest building in Belgrade, was also the location of Koristi, a shop that sold second-hand clothing. As he walked along streets paved with ancient cobblestones and lined with tall trees in the poor multi-cultural area of Belgrade, the absence of people was apparent. A significant number of Jews lived in the area and while he could understand that they were more than likely hiding, where were the other people who lived in the area? The only souls he encountered were dead ones lying in the gutters with flies swarming around them. The area had been bombed by the Germans when they invaded Belgrade and it wasn't long before he came upon piles of rubble and burnt out buildings that had caught fire after being bombed. Concerned that the shop he sought might have been obliterated, Anđa picked up his pace. Much to his relief it was still standing, and it was open, although the building next door had been bombed and was nothing but a heap of rubble. He shuddered as he pushed open the door and went inside.

He arrived at the meeting glad he was wearing a leather coat. Although those in attendance were not in uniform they were well dressed. Nearly every man was wearing a Royal Yugoslav Army cap, including Anđa. Tito was the exception. He was wearing a soviet pilot's cap, which instead of having a red star, it had an enamelled Soviet star with a hammer and sickle.

As soon as Tito arrived Anđa went over to him.

'Good to see you,' Tito said as he embraced Anđa. Below his cap Tito's hair was red. Anđa stared at it in surprise. He knew Tito had changed his name, sometimes he called himself Walter and at other times Rudi, but his vibrant hair was a shock.

'Comrade, your hair is not well dyed,' Anđa said and gave a small laugh. 'A smart policeman would spot you at once.'

Tito did nothing other than grunt and fix Anđa with a stare.

Shortly after the meeting started areas of responsibility were confirmed. Leko, the only man Anđa knew who had dimples when he smiled, would run operations in Bosnia, Djido in Montenegro and Krištof in Slovenia. But first and foremost, once they had moved their headquarters to Užice, Anđa would accompany Leko to negotiate with the *Četniks*. As he expected, Anđa found Tito industrious, if a little rash as he doled out duties.

'Shoot anyone, even a member of the provincial leadership, if he weakens or commits a breach of discipline,' Tito said to Djido. 'But take care not to launch an uprising. The

Italians are strong and well organised. They can break you. Start with minor operations.'

Tito disappeared for a short time after the meeting and was late for dinner. While the others waited for him Anđa chatted to Krištof, who, much to his delight, was sitting next to him.

'What's with these secretaries following party officials around like puppies? It seems like devotion beyond the call of duty,' Anđa said.

'Most of them have intimate relations with their bosses, including Stari,' Krištof replied.

'You as well? It's against party policy, isn't it?'

'Tito is always saying, "Do as I say, not as I do, and if you must do as I do, then don't let me catch you at it or I'll have you shot." You must have heard him. And by the way, I'm the exception. My secretary is ugly.'

Anđa nodded and laughed. 'Which one is your secretary?'

'Haven't you seen her? She's not here now. I sent her home earlier.'

'No, I haven't see her, but she can't be that bad.'

'When I tell you she's bad, I mean it,' Krištof said and laughed.

'I'll take your word for it, then,' Anđa said and gave a chuckle. 'I take it Stari is referring to his relationship with Zdenka when he says do as I say and not as I do?'

'Yes, I imagine so.'

'Where did he meet her?' Anđa asked.

'She was a radiotelegraphy student. He met her when she was studying.'

'So, she hasn't been his secretary for long then?'

'No, and the worst of it is she isn't well organised or diligent. Stari is infatuated with her beauty.'

'She's quite striking, isn't she?'

'Yes, it's those intense, dark-gleaming eyes and that flawless-olive complexion.'

'Zdenka isn't her real name though, is it? Why do they call her that?'

'By birth she's Davorjanka Paunović, but Stari calls her Zdenka, so now everyone does.'

'What's she like?' Anđa, who had only met her a couple of times and never had much to do with her, asked.

'Nervous, prone to panicking.' Krištof shrugged. 'Not brave, not well liked.'

'Why is that?'

'She causes too many scenes over nothing and picks fights, even with Stari. Do yourself a favour and keep away from her.'

'Does Herta know about her?'

'Not as far as I'm aware. Stari keeps them well away from each other.'

'Herta must be due to have Stari's child any day now.'

'Yes. Some of us are hoping that once it's born Tito will go back to Herta and extricate himself from his relationship with Zdenka.'

'Perhaps war gives him the excuse to have a mistress and a common-law wife,' Anđa replied. 'Herta was a student too, wasn't she? From Slovenia if my memory serves me correctly. I knew her back in '37 when Stari first met her. I remember how shapely she was.'

'Yes, quite a body, although who knows what she'll look like once the child is born.'

When the subject of Tito's infidelity was exhausted, silence fell between them for a time.

'Have you confirmed when the negotiations are starting?' Krištof asked as he broke into Anđa's thoughts about Tito's private life which, it seemed to Anđa, was inseparably bound up with his political life.

'A week's time,' Anđa said. 'We need to settle in at Užice first. We'll meet Mihailović at Čačak, if he keeps his word. Somehow I bet he won't. And what about you? There was no mention of when you're leaving.'

'I won't be going to Slovenia until the negotiations have been concluded. As you know Stari has decided Belgrade is too dangerous. I'll be going to Užice with the rest of you tomorrow. Don't forget I'm a strategist, not a fighter.' Krištof looked like a studious schoolteacher. He wore thick-lensed spectacles and was softly spoken. Anđa knew his eyesight was poor and his legs were feeble. He'd had rickets as a child and his legs continued giving him problems. Regardless, Krištof seldom mentioned his handicaps or used them as an excuse for keeping out of front-line action. Anđa liked Krištof and sadly he knew he would probably see less of him in the coming months. He felt an affinity towards him — he was comfortable expressing his inner-most thoughts to him, including his doubts, philosophies and qualms. Krištof was a good listener as well as a compassionate, logical thinker.

That night they gathered around a long table and partook of a meagre meal — mashed potatoes with *kupus* and a stew with onions and carrots and a trace of fatty beef. All things in moderation and no alcohol were party policies dictated by Tito. Those in command ate what their men ate — the meal was not lavish.

Anđa set out for Užice, the headquarters of Tito's Supreme Command, onboard a train overflowing with *Četniks*. The train, which travelled slowly, was not attacked during the journey, although it was already riddled with bullet holes after being assaulted by Stukas nine days earlier at Brdani. Anđa remained incognito, and he could do nothing other than stand by and watch when the train was stopped by German soldiers and one of his comrades Milan Blagojević was forcibly removed and shot.

Upon his arrival in Western Serbia at nine o'clock that night, though it was only early autumn, Anđa felt the cold. The wind was brisk and squalls of rain came through intermittently. He had not anticipated that the wind combined with the increase in altitude would mean his body temperature would drop. After all, Užice was no more than a hundred miles from Belgrade. Situated on both sides of the river Đetinja, Užice was surrounded by lush green countryside while in the distance the Dinaric Alps, with Mt Zlatibor as the jewel in the crown, circled the town.

Anđa shivered as he squinted at the façade of the National Bank building which was to be the new seat of command. This building along with several houses nearby was adorned with a hammer, a sickle and a red star.

He was tired after the nerve-racking journey and was happy to retire early and sleep in the gymnasium where three hundred German prisoners who had been captured by the Partisans were being held.

It was a cool morning on the first day of the negotiations when Anđa, accompanied by Tito, Leko and a small band of armed guards set out early, as Anđa suspected, for a different destination to the one that had originally been agreed. It was a peasant house in the village of Strugarik. The distance between the two towns was not far by vehicle along the main route; however, they could not use that route in case they were ambushed by Germans, Italians or *Četniks*. A circuitous safer route on horseback would take longer. The wind had begun to rise when they set out and leaves were constantly blown across their path. The greenish-brown leaves were heavy with moisture from the previous day's rain and they lolloped across the track in front of the horses like inebriated frogs.

There was nothing for Anđa to do once the talks got underway other than listen.

From the outset the two leaders did not take to each other. Both were tense and Tito grew tenser when Mihailović, with his long-pointed nose, sharp eyes and unkempt beard, offered them what Anđa thought was tea. He couldn't fail to see the sour expression on Tito's face when he picked up the glass and smelt it. As soon as he tasted it Anđa knew it was, in fact, *šumadija*. When Tito's expression turned to a grimace after he took his first mouthful, Anđa had difficulty keeping a straight face. He knew Tito was play-acting. He might have banned alcohol from his soldiers' camps, but Anđa was well aware that Tito enjoyed alcohol — strong alcohol. He was sure Tito's behaviour added to the uncongenial atmosphere. Did he actually want to cut a deal with Mihailović?

Anđa was not surprised when no agreement was reached. That night as they sat and smoked around a small campfire he relayed what had happened to Krištof.

'They'll never see eye to eye,' he said. 'Milailović thinks we should wait until the German forces have weakened before we attack, whereas Stari persists in suggesting that the *Četniks* and the Partisans must join forces and strike now. When the Germans have been defeated, Mihailović wants to hand Yugoslavia back to the king — there is no way Stari will agree to that. He wants to establish a communist state whereas Mihailović is solely trying to protect the Serbs because of his nationalist tendencies. I doubt they'll find any common ground on which to base a treaty. The negotiations are becoming more and more drawn out. In my heart, I'm certain that Stari doesn't want a workable agreement.'

'There are huge differences between us and the *Četniks,*' Krištof said. 'They're incredibly disorganised and lack discipline — and they're primitive. Their units are made up of old men — too many married peasants from wealthy families who aren't keen to take on the Germans.'

'Mihailović made that obvious when he said we were wasting the blood of the Serbian people mercilessly in an uneven struggle against the Germans.'

'So what happens now? Did Stari agree to another meeting?'

'Mihailović was particularly evasive and as a result, the only thing that was reached was a stalemate.'

It was after the meeting of the Partisan commanders in Stolica, where it was agreed that Tito should pursue further talks, that Tito contacted Mihailović about a second meeting. But once again Mihailović was difficult in pin down. Tito offered several sites for the meeting, but Mihailović rejected all of them.

'If he won't compromise then I'll go to his headquarters. I doubt he'll refuse to see me,' Tito said when he grew tired of being fobbed off.

This time Anđa accompanied Tito, Leko and Djido along with eight burly

Montenegrin Partisans. The contingent bound for Brajice on Ravna Gora mountain set out in two cars.

Once again the meeting was inside a peasant house — a larger one. Anđa surveyed the scene as the men took their places at a rectangular table in the middle of the room in a house built of rough-sawn timber with unlined walls. Tito and his men sat along one side while Mihailović and his associates were on the other. Tito's bodyguards, who were carrying sub-machine guns, stood behind Tito and his men, while Mihailović's stood behind him against the wall. The difference between the attendees was marked — Mihailović's men were older and wore long-straggly beards, whereas Tito's were much younger and mostly clean-shaven except for a moustache or two.

The negotiations were, as Anđa expected, protracted and at one point almost got out of control when the bodyguards from both sides began to express their opinions. This angered Mihailović and he scratched at his beard and glowered. 'Shut up all of you,' he shouted. 'Nobody wants to know what you think.'

It was then that the talks came to a temporary halt and Mihailović's special tea was brought in.

Anđa thought the tea was much sweeter than the last time they'd drunk it and sure enough when Tito took a large swig he started coughing and spat tea down the front of his uniform. Anđa knew this would upset him because he was so particular about his appearance being absolutely perfect. The incident was made worse when Mihailović burst out laughing as Tito dabbed at his uniform with his handkerchief.

That night after supper the talks carried on without much success. Mihailović would not agree to any of Tito's proposals and after an uncomfortable silence Mihailović dropped his bomb. 'I'll only fight the Germans if you supply us with weapons,' he said to Tito.

When Anđa heard this he was perturbed. He didn't trust the *Četniks*. As nationalists, they should have been opposed to invaders, yet they had already begun to co-operate with the Italians, who had given them weapons and supplies to fight the communists. Now they were asking for more weapons. Anđa was opposed to Tito giving Mihailović even one gun, but it wasn't his decision. When Tito promised Mihailović five hundred rifles and twenty-five thousand rounds of ammunition, Anđa was beyond shocked. It was all he could do to stay in his seat and keep quiet.

After spending the night in Mihailović's headquarters it was a warm, calm day when the Partisan contingent left early the following morning. Anđa was particularly quiet. He desperately wanted someone to talk to, yet he was uncertain whether the others agreed with what Tito had done.

In one of the houses adjacent to the bank, while he and Krištof enjoyed a cigarette before retiring there for the night, Krištof asked Anđa for more detail on the agreement.

'What was Stari thinking when he made that rash decision?' Krištof said in response to Anđa's comments.

'So you don't trust the *Četniks* any more than I do?'

'You know I don't. There's something shifty about Mihailović. He says one thing and does another.'

'Yes, you're right there, but there's nothing we can do about it. It's too late now,' Anđa said as he stifled a yawn. The day's events had exhausted and depressed him.

Anđa knew the Germans were close to Užice, but when the alarm sounded signalling an attack, he had not realised they were that close. It was dawn when he joined his platoon to drive back the invaders who were scarcely two miles out of town. Luckily, extra Partisan units had arrived in Užice two days before because of the heightened German presence. That meant that when the Partisans surrounded the attacking force they retreated in a hurry. It was then that Anđa noticed their beards and scruffy clothing and the realisation hit him. The men he had been fighting were *Četniks,* not Germans. He wasn't at all surprised that Mihailović had used the weapons given to him by Tito to attack Tito's stronghold. And he had chosen his moment with care and struck when a German offensive was threatening Tito's headquarters. What would Tito do when he discovered who their attackers were?

'But that's impossible,' Tito said when Anđa told him.

'What do you want us to do?' Anđa asked. 'We've surrounded Mihailović's headquarters. Should we kill him?'

'No,' Tito replied. 'I'll wait to hear what Stalin wants me to do.' He looked across at Vlad who was sitting next to the radio waiting to hear from Moscow.

'Anything yet?' Tito asked.

'No,' Vlad said as he rubbed a bite on the back of his hand that was itching. 'They're taking their time.'

'Is it such a difficult decision?' Anđa, who could no longer keep quiet, asked.

Tito and Vlad said nothing.

When Moscow's decision came it was not a palatable one. Tito was ordered to let

Mihailović go unharmed. Stalin foolishly believed he was leading the resistance against the Italians and the Germans.

'How could they possibly have come to that conclusion,' Tito said as he strode from the room in disgust.

The situation in Užice had begun to deteriorate. The Germans were advancing and the town was overcrowded by an increasing number of wounded Partisans.

It was a blustery afternoon with squalls of rain and dull-grey light sitting above the horizon, when Anđa hid behind the side of a building with the rest of his platoon and kept the Germans at bay. Tito had received information, the source of which Anđa was not privy to, that the attack on Užice had been ordered by the English and the Yugoslav Government in exile. Anđa knew that the bourgeoisie did not care about the liberation of the common people. Fortunately, the Partisans were alerted to the presence of the attackers when they were still a mile from town.

When he had stepped out of the cover provided by the side of an abandoned house and raised his rifle to finish off a wounded German at close range it was the first time Anđa had shot and killed a human being. His heart didn't miss a beat — he was protecting his comrades and he was prepared to die in the process. Moments later, he recoiled with shock and pain as he was shot in the leg. He soon forgot about the pain when Javorski and Ivanjica who had been standing on either side of him were shot and crumpled to the ground. He assumed they were dead because neither of them so much as twitched a muscle let alone cried out. Without bothering to inspect their bodies for signs of life, his heart hammered as he retreated as fast as he could into the dense undergrowth nearby. As soon as he was well covered by vegetation he inspected his leg wound. '*Jebati!* he shouted as waves of pain surged through him. He'd been hit above the ankle on the outside of his right leg. There wasn't much blood and he hoped that meant it wasn't a serious wound. He limped away in the direction of Užice to find a medic to attend to it. From now on it would be imperative to remain in a constant state of readiness — he intended to sleep fully clothed and keep his boots on.

When he was ordered to rest by the nurse who had dressed his wound, he lay on a make-shift bed covered by a leather coat, which had belonged to a dead man, in one of the tunnels attached to the munitions factory which was being used as a hospital ward. The coat kept the light out of his eyes so he could sleep. The bullet had grazed his leg without inflicting serious damage.

'Keep off your feet for the rest of the day,' the nurse said. 'Give the blood a chance to clot properly so the healing can begin.'

It was after midday when the explosion woke him. The ground shook and the brick wall next to his bed quivered. He had no time to run.

'Christ!' he shouted as smoke billowed in the doorway and smaller explosions echoed in his ears. He was sitting on the edge of the bed trying to gather his senses and work out what to do and where to go when the brick wall came towards him. He was struck by flying bricks and knocked to the floor.

Anđa was alive and conscious, but breathing was difficult and he couldn't see or move. *How long can I hold out?* He had no idea how much time had passed when he heard shouting ... he prayed they were digging him out.

'Here's one of his feet,' a voice shouted.

'Anđa! Can you hear me?' another voice shouted.

'The flames are close,' the first voice shouted. 'Hurry!'

Anđa could do nothing except wait and hope as he struggled to suck in air. But everytime he took a breath his airway felt clogged and his need to cough grew more urgent.

'Quickly! Get the bricks off his head or he'll suffocate,' shouted a voice that sounded like Leko.

Anđa passed out.

When he opened grey eyelids in a dust-covered face, he saw Leko and Vlad beside him throwing bricks in all directions. As soon as he was free of the bricks that had buried him, he tried to lift his right arm first and then his right leg. They felt like lead weights and no matter how hard he tried to focus on making them function, they stayed put.

'My comrades, you have saved me, but what about the other patients?' he croaked as Leko and Vlad lifted him and carried him outside to safety.

'There's no hope of the others surviving. The mountain of bricks covering them would take days to move. You were the only lucky bastard,' Leko replied.

'What the hell happened in there?' Anđa asked as Leko and Vlad supported him between them as all three headed towards Tito's headquarters.

'My bet is the tunnel in the munition's factory was sabotaged by Mihailović's spies,' Leko replied. 'There was a gunpowder dump in the tunnel that must have ignited and it looks as though the fire has spread to the adjoining streets and houses. Look at the smoke billowing in the air.'

Anđa looked up and saw great clouds of gun-metal grey smoke at the same time as he smelt the unmistakeable pungent reek of gunpowder.

'Civilians will be dead, most probably burnt alive judging by the size of the blast. I shudder to think how many. There'll be women and children who had no chance of escape,' Vlad added.

'Bastards,' Anđa mumbled. 'What about headquarters?'

'Not sure. There's smoke spiralling out of that building but not much. Hopefully it's only a small fire, and no one is seriously injured. We'll find out in a minute when we get there,' Leko replied.

Anđa had been shaken up; he was uninjured apart from small cuts and bruises to his face and arms.

It was four days later when another din erupted.

'What the hell is that?' Krištof shouted when he heard a rumbling sound and rushed to peer outside. Anđa joined him in the doorway and followed Krištof's line of sight. Whatever was creating the ruckus was too far away to be seen.

'Tanks!' Tito shouted. 'The sound is unmistakeable and they're too close for comfort. Get ready to evacuate … Anđa, go and see what you can find out while the rest of you prepare for departure. We'll carry the wounded on stretchers. If any of them can walk, then they'll have to. The printing press and several crates of silver will have to go into carts. How many horses have we got?'

When Anđa reappeared it was not with good news. 'There's at least fifty German tanks just outside town,' he said to Tito as he gasped for breath. He had run all the way there and back — as fast as his leg permitted.

'We'll head towards Zlatibor,' Tito said.

In the soft morning light Anđa and several other party members scurried like rats through the back streets as they kept an eye on the planes flying above them. They had mined the main road in the hope that it wouldn't be usable. Anđa, Leko and Krištof stood on a ridge immediately outside town and watched briefly as German tanks rolled along untouched by the mines.

'Bah!' Leko shouted. We'd better get the hell out of here. The mines are faulty.' Just then an aircraft swooped over them. When they dived for cover into the nearby scrub, they became separated. Anđa was cut off from the other two by machine-gun fire. Just before he set off towards the mountain peak he caught a glimpse of Tito. He had cleared the town when the tanks arrived and he was lagging at least a hundred and fifty yards behind.

Immediately before dark Anđa reached the summit of Mount Zlatibor where snow had been falling. He stopped and stared at his footprints in the unblemished white carpet. Vlad, who had arrived the day before, was sitting alone in the largest room of the house with one solitary candle burning in a saucer on the table.

'Where's Stari?' Vlad asked as soon as Anđa came in the door.

'I don't know. He was among the last to leave,' Anđa replied.

Vlad shook his head in despair.

When Leko and Krištof appeared moments later they too asked the same question. Nobody had an answer. They sat despondently around a rickety wooden table eating chunks of stale bread and thin beef stew that had been prepared by the cook who had accompanied Vlad.

It was well and truly dark when Tito's car arrived without him.

'Where's Tito?' Leko asked the driver.

'He told me to go without him,' the driver said as his face turned pink with embarassment.

'How did you think he was going to get here?' Leko snapped.

The driver looked down at his hands which were nervously plucking at his cap while his complexion deepened to red. 'I was just obeying orders,' he mumbled.

'Anđa, take the car and go and find him,' Leko said as he shook his head in frustration.

'In the dark?' Anđa asked.

'There's a moon. You won't need the headlights.' Leko's order was blunt.

Anđa looked up at an enormous whey-faced moon and set off reluctantly. They had gone no more than two kilometres when he heard the planes.

'Stop! We'll have to take shelter,' he said as he threw open the passenger door and leapt out. The driver was much slower to react. Anđa looked up from the snow-covered ditch beside the road as six, twin-engine bombers, probably Dorniers, peppered the road and the driver with machine-gun fire. It was moments later when the planes unleashed their bombs. Certain the driver was beyond help, Anđa scurried towards a group of dark shapes that were, in fact, oak trees. It was a short distance, but as soon as he took off, fragments ricocheted of the splintering rocks above his head as machine guns assaulted the air around him. He was trapped.

'*Jebati!*' he cursed. 'What a way to die.' As another bomb dropped metres from him, he covered his head with his arms and prepared for what he hoped would be a swift painless death.

Chapter five

In the weeks following her husband's departure Mara became increasingly concerned about Zlata when she refused to get out of bed or go to school. When she sat down on Zlata's bed and tried to persuade her to go, at first Zlata was silent, then she spoke in the stutter she had developed after he father left. 'Don't you know what they're saying?'

'Tell me.'

'They're all shouting, *death to fascism, death to freedom*. What does it mean? I'm frightened they'll kill me *Majka*.'

Mara too had heard that resistance slogan — it was on many people's lips — the lips of those who had the courage to express themselves. She gathered her daughter in her arms and held her. 'Shh! Shh! You'll be okay. I won't let anything happen to you,' she said as she stroked Zlata's auburn hair. When Zlata's breathing calmed down Mara told her to sleep.

In the end, Mara let her daughter stay home. Zlata needed time to come to terms with her father's departure and besides Mara had the rest of her family to take care of and the burden of that responsibility combined with worrying about her husband weighed heavily upon her. Her blue eyes were often bloodshot, her hair, which had gone from blonde to grey almost overnight, was thinning rapidly.

The months dragged by. Mara had received only one letter from her husband. She kept it in her housecoat pocket and she read it so many times that the paper had become thin and small holes had developed where she had folded it. Yet again she took the letter out and read it:

Draga Mara,

A quick few lines to let you know I am well. I have settled in and am enjoying the company of my comrades, so don't worry about me. Save your energy for more important things.

I hope you and the children are well.

I think about all of you every day as I wish for an end to all this madness sooner rather than later and a speedy trip home.

With love and affection.

Anđa.

Mara clung to it like a lifeline.

She had hoped seventeen-year-old Ivan would have been more help now that he was unemployed, yet instead of applying himself and doing what she asked, he was distracted and skived off at every available opportunity. She didn't ask where he went because she knew, though he never commented. She was certain he had joined the resistance youth organization who were raising money to help the anti-fascist fighters which her husband had joined. She had overheard Ivan talking to his father about it before he'd left. Her husband's words had stuck in her mind, *It's the best thing you can do to support me,* he'd said to Ivan.

It was winter when Mara began struggling to produce enough edible food for her children. The supplies she had been hoarding in her pantry were decreasing by the day and the produce she could grow during winter was limited. When she was least expecting it, a bright spot came — a bulletin was issued over Radio Zagreb saying that Red Cross food parcels would be arriving in Central Zagreb.

It was a bitingly cold day when she and Ivan set off for the church that was the distribution point for the parcels. Rugged up in their winter clothes they kept their heads down as they trudged through snowdrifts that had fallen the night before. As they plodded along she wondered where her husband was and hoped he was warm enough.

By the time they got there, they were too late. The meagre quantity of parcels had already arrived and been doled out.

'You must have got the time wrong,' Ivan said.

'No, I'm sure I didn't. Anyway, there's no point in going on about it, is there? We're too late and that's that. We'll have to hope there'll be others.'

After months of being inert Zlata was at last getting out of bed every morning and helping her mother around the house. It was December when Mara and Zlata set off in the hope of buying supplies.

Jelena Petrović, Mara's neighbour upstairs had come to visit Mara as she did from time to time. They didn't live in each other's pockets despite living in close proximity. Jelena, who was older than Mara, limped into the kitchen as if she had a stone in her shoe and sat down on a chair she'd pulled out from the kitchen table. A slight woman, with a hunched frame and steely grey hair in a bun on top of her head, Jelena had been a widow for some years after her husband died of a heart attack at the age of fifty-four.

'How are you?' she asked Mara.

'Coping,' Mara replied but my food stocks are getting dangerously low and with so many mouths to feed it's becoming more difficult by the day. And you?'

'Bearing up. I've come to tell you that the shop in Dubrava Street has stock. I was there yesterday morning.'

'It has? I'd better get there then. Thank you.'

'I'd go sooner rather than later. It'll run out quickly once word gets around.'

Zlata was carrying a basket over her arm when they set out on their shopping expedition and Mara was pleased to see that her daughter was more cheerful than she had been since the departure of her father. Much to Mara's surprise, she cracked a feeble joke.

'Do you think we'll be able to fit everything in this basket? It might be too heavy to carry,' she said.

They had just rounded the corner of the street when they came upon the grotesque sight that neither would ever forget.

Sixteen bodies hung motionless below a sky filled with rain-swollen clouds. Mara tried to shield her daughter's view with her ample frame, but she was too late. Zlata let out a piercing scream, dropped the basket, turned and fled. Mara dragged her eyes away from the corpses and silently beseeched God to banish the vision from her daughter's mind as she set off after her. Her arthritic ankle hampered her and all too soon she lost sight of Zlata.

If only she hadn't gone in search of provisions, but Mara had taken Jelena at her word when she said she'd been to the shop and found flour and oil.

By the time Mara arrived home Zlata was buried underneath her bed clothes with her bedroom door shut. Nothing Mara said or did could entice her out of her room.

For the time being Mara left her daughter alone. As she trudged out of her front door and went to visit her upstairs neighbour, Jelena, she hoped sleep would heal her daughter.

Jelena's door was locked. Gone were the days when she left it slightly ajar.

'It's me,' Mara called out in a shaky voice.

Toothless, spry Jelena, who looked and acted younger than her years, came to the door at once. 'What's wrong? You face is so pale.'

'I …' Mara stammered, unsure where to start.

'Sit down. Tell me. What is it?' Jelena she pushed her wire-framed spectacles up her nose.

'Bodies, at least a dozen hanging in Dubrava Street,' Mara blurted out.

'What? What are you saying?' Jelena's eyes opened wide.

'Just what I said. Dead bodies strung up on butcher's hooks. The most horrific thing I've ever seen. Zlata screamed loudly enough to wake the dead when she saw them and ran all the way home. Now she won't come out of her bedroom.'

'Oh my God!' Jelena took her handkerchief out of the sleeve of her cardigan and pressed it to her mouth. 'Who do you think they are?'

'No idea, but judging by their clothes they certainly aren't Germans or *Ustaše*.

'I'll turn on the radio. Maybe that will tell us.'

The women listened in silence to the report that came five minutes later on the news. Sixteen anti-fascists had been murdered by the fascists in retaliation for the death of Ljudevit Tiljk, a member of the *Ustaše*. The victims would be left suspended from the butcher's hooks for several days as a warning to others.

Mara and Jelena looked at each other when the news came to an end. Words were beyond them as their eyes filled with tears of anxiety. They knew the incident was designed to paralyse Zagreb's inhabitants with fear.

Over the next few days Mara took meagre meals to her, but Zlata hardly touched them. Most of the time she sat with unblinking eyes staring at the wall. When Mara spoke to her she didn't answer and the unchanged expression on her face suggested she hadn't heard her mother's voice. It was as though she was inhabiting another world. Days later when Mara had not elicited a word from her daughter she began to fear for her sanity. Not knowing what else to do, she moved Zlata into her bed so she could keep a close eye on her and try to encourage her to snap out of her trance. Every night she held her close and spoke gently to her. 'Darling it's over. You need to forget about it. Dwelling on it won't help. You must do your best the banish it from your mind,' Mara crooned as she stroked her daughter's forehead. Zlata was lying on her back as rigid as a board and staring blankly at the ceiling. When there was no change in Zlata's way of being, out of desperation Mara spoke to the doctor.

'What can I say? She may never recover. Medicine won't help. If she becomes agitated you can give her some barbiturates to calm her down, otherwise all you can do is lavish her with love and care,' he said as he stared at her with a grave expression on his kindly, well-meaning face.

Mara left his office feeling more distraught.

It was on the day that Mara had at last enticed her daughter to come downstairs when the unexpected visitors turned up. Zlata was mindlessly winding wool into a ball while Mara was washing clothes in the stone sink when there was a loud hammering on the door followed by a raised voice. Zlata reacted immediately. She dropped the ball of wool and fled upstairs.

Mara took her time drying her hands on her apron before she walked towards the door. Needless to say the first thought that came to her mind was her husband. She had not received any further letters from him. She thought it might have been someone coming to inform her that he was dead or perhaps the *Ustaše* coming to throw them out and take over her house. As she reached the door, the shouting came again. This time the words were more hostile. 'Open the door immediately or we'll break it down.'

Mara saw two pairs of shiny-black, knee-high boots on the snow-covered door mat first before her eyes travelled up to the faces of two unsmiling *Ustaše* with overconfident expressions. She stared at them. In the dead of night she had often imagined this moment and what she would do. But she did nothing other than gawp at them. Words failed her.

'We're here to speak to Anđa Milić. Is he here?' the taller of the two said.

'No.' Mara's voice was almost inaudible as she struggled to answer.

'When will he be home?'

'I don't know.'

'What do you mean, you don't know. Where is he?'

'I don't know.'

'What do you mean, you don't know? He is your husband, isn't he?'

'Yes.'

'You must know where he is.'

'I told you, I don't. He went away.'

'When will he be back?'

'He didn't say.'

The men looked at each other and the shorter one with the Hitler-like moustache spoke.

'Stand aside! You've declined to co-operate with us, so we'll search your house.'

Mara flattened herself against the door as they pushed past her.

They began with the downstairs and she looked on with dismay as they pulled open drawers and cupboards and rummaged through the contents.

'What's down there? the tall one asked as he pointed at the stairs that led to the *konoba*.

He came back quickly as she knew he would. The *konoba* contained nothing of interest.

Step by step Mara began edging her way to the stairs that led to the bedrooms. She had to get to Zlata before the *Ustaše* did. She had reached the foot of the stairs when the tall one shouted at her.

'Where do you think you're going?'

'Upstairs. My daughter is sick.'

'Stay where you are,' he said as he bounded up the stairs.

Mara held her breath.

The scream Zlata let out when he entered the bedroom where she was cowering in her mother's bed was piercing.

'I must go to her,' Mara said boldly.

When there was no reaction from the other officer she went up the stairs as quickly as she could.

She was at the bedroom door when Zlata's scream increased in intensity.

'Shut up,' the officer said as he raised his fist and slapped her face.

'Don't touch her! She's a child,' Mara shouted in desperation.

'Child! She's a madwoman. Shut her up or I will — permanently.'

Mara rushed to the bed, pulled her daughter close and buried her face against her ample bosom. 'No more Zlata. Do you understand? No more. You're safe now,' she said and then wondered why she'd made such an irrational comment. Mara and her daughter stayed huddled together on the bed as upstairs suffered the same fate as downstairs. Mara watched in horror as the room around her was trashed before they moved on. What were they were hoping to find? She knew Anđa would never have left anything to compromise her or their children. There was nothing but the sea chest. When the cold-eyed one opened the wardrobe and there was silence she knew he was looking at the chest.

'What's in here?' he barked.

'Nothing. It's not locked; you can look inside.'

Moments later she heard him slam the lid with a grunt. She breathed a small sigh of relief.

When they were about to leave, the tall one scowled at Mara.

'I don't need to remind you what the penalty is for harbouring anti-fascists — we'll be back,' he shouted.

After giving Zlata two of the barbiturate tablets prescribed by the doctor, Mara was in the kitchen making herself a cup of tea when her sons came in. She was so distressed about the visit from the *Ustaše* she didn't bother to ask where they'd been, instead she related what had transpired in their absence. Halfway through the explanation her voice dried up. It was as if the stress she had been under since her husband's departure had suddenly become too much. She burst into tears and covered her face with her hands.

'Sit down, *Majka*,' Ivan said as he pulled out a chair. 'Zoran make some more tea. We all need a cup.'

'What did they want?' Zoran asked as he set about taking cups from the dresser and putting them on the table.

'Your father, they wanted your father.' Mara's voice was croaky. 'They got angry when I said I didn't know where he was. I expect they didn't believe me.'

'Was that why they searched the house?' Damir asked.

'I don't know. I suppose so.'

'Well, it's over now,' Ivan said. 'The bastards! I hate the bastards.'

Under normal circumstances Mara would have reprimanded her son for speaking like that, but these were not normal circumstances. Damir and Zoran were silent. All that could be heard was Ivan stirring two large spoons of sugar, from the meagre quantity they had been eeking out, into his mother's tea.

'But that's not the end of it,' Mara said as she broke the silence. 'They said they're coming back.

'What for?' Zoran asked.

'If I knew I'd tell you. I've already told them he's not here.' There was an edge to her voice. Although she had pulled herself together, she didn't mean to speak to her son so harshly, yet she couldn't stop herself. 'My biggest fear is what'll happen to Zlata if she's here when they come back ... I don't know how to protect her.'

'Do you think they're going to harm her?' Damir asked.

'I don't know. Her screaming was so loud that the one with the cold eyes said he'd kill her if she didn't shut up. He slapped her face and it's bruised.'

'Christ!' Ivan muttered.

'And even if they don't touch her she probably won't stay sane if they come here again. I've given her two pills instead of one to calm her down. She'll sleep for at least twelve hours maybe longer.

For a time no one spoke. Zoran was picking at a rough edge of the table where the timber had splintered, Damir was staring into space and Ivan and his mother held each other's gaze. The lull was broken by Ivan.

'What if we ask Marija's family to look after her for a few days? I could talk to them in the morning and see if they'll help us.'

'Marija?' Mara said and the name hung in the air. Mara had never particularly liked Zlata's best friend, Marija. A mousy girl with a sulky mouth who, it seemed to Mara, with her small cold eyes, was always staring at anyone and everyone for too long and never knew when to look away. She was a taciturn, morose child who seldom smiled, and to Mara's way of thinking she coveted what others had. This showed in the way she always gaped at Zlata — envious of her beauty. Mara suspected that jealousy was an unfortunate part of Marija's personality. But she never said anything to her daughter about her thoughts. Zlata didn't make friends easily and Mara had never chosen her children's friends. She might not approve of their choices, but she never interfered because she believed it was not her place to do so.

Zlata's outward appearance was one of sullenness, when she was, in fact, shy. But it took a discerning person to work this out and most never got beyond Zlata's persistent frown.

'Yes, they're a good family,' Mara replied after a lengthy silence. She didn't know Marija's parents well. Her father was a school teacher and her mother was a seamstress who took in clothing alterations. They were decent and hardworking and their home was clean and tidy.

'Okay, that's settled then. I'll go across to their place first thing in the morning and see if I can take her there after she wakes up,' Ivan said.

Chapter six

Anda had misjudged where the bomb was landing and it turned out to be further away than he thought. Yet, it didn't lessen the seriousness of the predicament he found himself in. The ground shook when the bomb struck and although he was showered with heavy wet snow and dirt and the air was clouded with dust — he was unhurt except for minor cuts and scratches. He crawled towards a water pipe and hid inside it. As soon as the planes had gone and the machine-gun fire had ceased, he dared to come out to inspect the car. The roof was riddled with bullet holes, but the body looked intact, which was more than he could say for the driver. He got in and had a go at starting the engine. When it turned over and kept going he breathed a sigh of relief before he turned the car around and headed back the way they had come. The moon was huge and white and the sky was clear. He had no difficulty finding his way without headlights. He had gone no further than the next bend when he came across an overturned cart. It and the dead horses that had been pulling it were blocking the way. He was left with no choice but to abandon the car. He clambered out and began to climb the nearest slope and make his way towards the crest of a small hill. Halfway up, the sound of machine-gun fire came again and puffs of dust exploded around him. Positive he was going to die at any minute, he tried to run up the slope, yet his legs seemed paralysed with fear and patches of melting snow made the going difficult. He had a short distance to go to reach the apex and he went at it by zigzagging in the hope that the bullets would miss him. His heart was hammering as he let out a shout when he hurled himself over the brow of the hill into safety. From there he looked down on a convoy of German troops before he set off on foot through a clearing in the woods and on towards the summit. As he pressed ahead he made a mental note to send a letter to Mara. After his brush with death he had a need to let her know he was okay.

The floor was hard, Anda was cold and he couldn't sleep. Earlier, when they retired the group was sullen. Still, nobody knew what had happened to Tito.

Anda was wide awake listening to distant gunfire at two in the morning when Tito appeared covered in mud.

'Where've you been?' Leko asked as he and the others stared in shock at the dishelleved figure of Tito who was standing inside the door with a ferocious frown on his face.

'I was pinned down on the outskirts of Užice for hours on end with planes strafing the ground around me. I had to wait until it was dark before I could get away. It's been a hell of a night,' Tito said in a dejected voice.

At dawn the following morning after a hasty meeting, Tito ordered the group to retreat further. In doing so he countermanded the orders he had issued only days before because he believed the lives of the most important members of the Party were in danger — with the advance of the day would come the advance of the Germans.

Light rain was sifting down out of dull leaden clouds when Anđa set out on the back of an old truck in the company of Leko, Tito, Vlad and twenty crates of silver that they had taken from the vault in supreme headquarters in Užice. Krištof had departed for Slovevia while Djido would be heading to Montenegro. The rest of the men followed on foot.

'How far do you think we'll get in this decrepit wreck?' Leko said to nobody in particular.

'The terrain is too steep. We'll have to walk from now on until we can find horses,' Tito said as they came to a village and he banged on the roof of the truck. 'Stop here,' he shouted to the driver.

'What about the silver and the printing press?' Leko said as he stood up and surveyed the obscure village around them.

'We'll bury the silver in the garden where that woman is digging and we'll have to leave the press here too,' Tito replied.

'Leave it?' Vlad said with a grim look on his handsome face. 'We can't print *Borba* without the press.' Anđa knew that *Borba,* the communist newspaper was his pride and joy.

'I am well aware of that, but we've got no choice unless you want to carry it on your back,' Tito replied.

Anđa followed Tito's line of sight where an old woman with a scarf around her head and clothes as dirty as the earth, was tilling the soil in preparation for planting. Tito, Leko, Vlad and Anđa stood and smoked while they watched the contingent of men who had accompanied the truck as they dug a deep hole.

'Just remember where it is and we'll retrieve it later,' Tito said as he thanked the woman and they set off on foot.

For most of the day the Germans tracked them from one crest of a hill to the next as they were pushed into the mountains, closer and closer to the Italians. Ridges were unsafe and every time they reached one they were peppered with machine-gun fire. Anđa lay on his stomach and observed the German soldiers through his binoculars. Most seemed to be agile young men; this probably accounted for their relentless pursuit. He wondered if they'd give up and let the Italians continue the chase as he readied himself for the next inevitable slog.

It was a long day spent dodging bullets. Anđa was weary. In the late afternoon he and Leko, who were scouting ahead of the main group of Partisans, came upon a small band of Italian soldiers — about a dozen. They watched as the Italians dozed at the edge of a clearing — their sentry too had fallen sleep.

'Go and get a handful of our best men. We'll take these bastards before they have a chance to wake up,' Leko whispered.

'What if there are more of them in the trees?' Anđa asked.

'I'll check out the area behind them while you get the reinforcements. We'll take them alive. Quickly! Go!' Leko said in a hoarse whisper.

It wasn't difficult to surround and capture all twelve while they continued to snooze in the sun.

'We'll keep them and use them as servants and packhorses,' Tito said. 'They look fit and able and it'll save us using our own men.'

Anđa looked them over. Most were young, and Tito was right, they looked well-fed and fit. He hoped it was a good decision Tito had made and that the Italians would not cause trouble.

That evening he employed two of the prisoners to prepare the sleeping area for Tito and the influential party members.

'What are your names?' Anđa asked in Italian.

'Mario and Matteo,' the younger-looking one with jet-black hair which flopped across his forehead in a wave of greasy curls, said. 'I'm Matteo,' he added with an open smile.

From then on Anđa used these two for menial tasks. They were obliging and worked well enough. He assumed that was because they were relieved to be alive. They also turned out to be innovative at preparing different meals. They had roasted three small carcasses covered with wild herbs which were shared by the members of the supreme command when Anđa felt compelled to comment.

'This is good,' he said as he nodded and sucked the last of the flesh from a hind leg which was his allotted share. 'Is it the herbs that give it the flavour?'

'Yes and no,' Matteo replied.

'What sort of meat is it?'

'Cat.'

'Ugh! Cat!' Anđa shouted.

'Yes, we caught three in the village today and roasted them with oregano. We found some in an old lady's garden.' He didn't add that they'd stolen it without asking her.

Anđa was pleased he'd chosen these two to cook and carry out menial tasks. They seemed decent enough and they tried hard to please. Within a matter of days he gave them Yugoslav nicknames. He had called Matteo *Koke* because of his cackling laugh and Mario was *Frendica* because he had long eyelashes like a girl.

The next day Tito's group carried on trekking from before dawn until late at night. Before long Anđa lost all sense of direction and when the vegetation all looked the same he wondered if they were going round in circles.

After yet another day of prolonged marching Anđa thought he would drop from lack of sleep, but sleep was not on the agenda. Tito had called another meeting and issued new orders. They would be heading for Montenegro instead of Bosnia.

It was past midnight when Anđa was at last able to retire on the hard ground where he fell asleep immediately. It was just as well because he knew he was in for several hard days of marching.

It had rained during the night. The mountains were shrouded in mist and the path ahead was muddy and slippery. *At least there was no snow,* Anđa thought as he slogged ahead and the mud became thicker. Behind him were the vivid imprints of his boots and with each breath he took, the pungent smell of the mud assaulted his nostrils. He was pleased when they stopped at a village and borrowed half-a-dozen horses. They were about to go on their way when it became clear there had been a mix up over Tito's horse. They had miscalculated the numbers and he didn't have one.

When Tito set out on foot, Anđa was embarrassed and spoke up. 'Take mine,' he said.

'No,' Tito said. 'I don't need it.'

'Then we can give this one back, because if you won't ride it, then neither will I,' Anda said as he stood beside the horse and held out the reins to Tito.

Tito stared at Anđa long and hard before he took the reins and mounted the horse.

Anđa knew he'd done the right thing, but he was powerless to solve the next problem. They hadn't gone far when Tito's horse decided it needed a rest and lay down.

'What's up with this beast. Can you believe he just sank underneath me in the mud? Did you give it to me because you knew it was lazy?' Tito said with a chuckle and laughing eyes. It took a lot of urging to get the beast on its feet, but Anđa was relieved that Tito saw the funny side of it.

At last Anđa was able to pen a hasty letter to his wife. Although, little did he know it would never reach her.

Dear Mara,

The villagers here are some of the most hospitable I have come across. I would go so far as to say that they are proud to host us, and although the village is made up of only women, children and old people, nothing is too much trouble for them. All their young men have gone to join our cause. Just after we arrived we were presented with milk, cornmeal and meat from an old ewe that the women slaughtered in our honour. It was a generous gesture and I ate my share despite having reached the stage where I detest boiled mutton. My diet since I left Zagreb is lacking in vegetables and I'm concerned about my teeth. I suspect It'll only be a matter of time before they became loose and fall out. Although I sincerely hope that isn't the case, but it's a small price to pay for defending our homeland. I don't want you to worry about me. I am in good spirits as are the men with me.

I hope you are bearing up and the children are well. I will write again soon.
Your loving caring husband who thinks about you and our children every day.

Anđa left out his name just as he left out the name of the village in case his letter fell into enemy hands.

The following day Leko appeared while Anđa was standing in a small clearing near the village smoking half a cigarette he had been hoarding. Leko's face was without his usual dimples. His lips were pressed together tightly and his expression was grave. Anđa knew immediately that he was not about to impart good news. 'Our dispatcher has been killed by a German patrol. The scouting party have found him and his horse in the bottom of a ravine. The mail's been stolen. Luckily, his satchel didn't contain anything of importance written by Stari.'

'Bastards!' Anđa replied. 'The letter I wrote to my wife was in there.'

It was winter when the German offensive drove Tito and his party to seek cover deeper in the mountains where snow had already begun to fall. As they endeavoured to move into more mountainous country they were accompanied by the constant drone of planes and the rumbling of tanks. It was five-thirty in the morning when they set out for Sandžak in two cars. They had not travelled far when they came across a car blocking the road and were forced to continue on foot. From then on the day turned sour as they were constantly dogged by German soldiers and planes and machine-gun fire rained down with regular monotony. They were all on edge. Anyone could have been hit. As they pressed on Anđa watched as men fell. Some dead. Some wounded — one so seriously he decided to put an end to his own suffering. Anđa flinched when the gunshot went off. As the day drew to a close, Anđa was worn out and depressed as he watched more and more men die. At least sixty had crawled away across a snow-covered field. Many were missing limbs. But the field provided neither haven nor escape. The Germans ran over them with their tanks. Anđa felt helpless as he imagined the painful deaths many of them suffered. In his mind's eye he saw his helpless comrades being pursued by rumbling tanks, looking up at the great-grey hulks bearing down on them as they tried to crawl faster or veer off in another direction. He heard their agonised screams as the unstoppable monsters crushed their remaining limbs, bodies and finally their heads. Anđa shuddered, relieved that his fate didn't lie there. He'd rather be shot and die instantly than suffer like these men around him.

That evening after dark Tito sent Anđa, Vlad and twenty men on a reconnaissance mission.

'We need to know the exact positions of the enemy — Germans, *Četniks* and Italians,' Tito told them.

When they set off the moonlight was so bright it glinted off the dazzling white snow and turned night into day. It wasn't long before they came across a local boy wandering on his own. They stopped to talk to him.

'The Germans have been and gone,' he said. 'They've stolen our ducks, preserved fruit and my pillow.' Anđa was about to laugh but thought better of it when he saw the annoyance written all over the skinny lad's grimy face.

Just then Leko turned up. Anđa was surprised to see him and before he could ask why he had come, Vlad beat him to it. 'What are you doing here?' he asked.

'I have to watch your back. Not everybody gets to be Tito's biographer. He's concerned that if something happens to you then the story of the war will never be told. And Anđa, you're one of our key men. He's sent me to watch out for both of you.'

Anđa and Vlad grinned at each other.

'You can escort us back to camp then,' Anđa replied.

They set off straightaway and Anđa was so happy to be alive after the dangerous time they'd been through in the last few days that he began to sing in a melodious voice. Vlad and Leko joined in.

The steel hammer and sickle
give wheaten bread.
The wheat had ripened
Šumadija has spoken
Šumadija our pride
Full of Bolshevik ...

After three hours of ragged, restless sleep they were off again. Aware that Germans and Italians were lurking nearby they moved at a steady pace as they followed Tito who had already left.

In a small wood, they stopped, ready to face the Italians. Their wait was in vain. The peasant who had said the Italians were ten minutes away was wrong.

Feeling as if he'd been idle for too long, Anđa set about carving a hammer and sickle in the trunk of the tree he'd been leaning against. He had taken up carving in his childhood and he still enjoyed it. As a final touch he added the date.

When Tito gave the order to carry on, Anđa was struck by the look in his eyes. It was forceful. So much so that nobody would dare argue with him, or question his decision.

Dull, sleety weather had descended around them by the time they reached the village of Drenova. There was more than a little jubilation when shortly after their arrival a courier turned up from Sarajevo and they learnt that 3,500 Italians had been taken prisoner by the Partisans. Anđa thought a celebration would have been good, but of course, they had no alcohol.

After climbing a steep hillside in the dark, they found quarters in an abandoned group of houses. He had no idea when the previous inhabitants, who had taken only scant belongings with them, had left. He thought it must have been some time ago because vermin had invaded the rooms and there were mice and rat droppings everywhere as well as the occasional larger turd obviously belonging to a bigger animal. The odour of urine was strong as Anđa kicked aside the worst of the droppings and made a space on the hard-packed earth floor of what had once been the living room. He slept deeply for two hours despite the cold air seeping in the uncovered window on the other side of the small room.

He had woken up and was eating a bowl of barley porridge when a sentry burst in. 'The villages are on fire,' he shouted from the doorway.

Anđa sprinted outside and scaled the nearest ridge — a mile away three villages were lit up by bright yellow and orange flames. The Italians had gained ground. It was time to leave. In his haste to get back to the camp, pack up and get moving, Anđa wasn't watching where he put his feet and before he knew it he was sprawled on his back on the frozen ground. He had slipped on a patch of ice on the side of the slope. He knew immediately that he hadn't landed well and as soon as he stood up the pain in his knee confirmed it. *'Jebati,'* he swore as he limped the rest of the way back to the camp.

After gulping down the last of his porridge Anđa joined the rest of the party as they moved to higher ground and hid among the rocks. There they would stay until darkness.

Two nights later, they were on the move again travelling in extreme cold when a blizzard engulfed the supreme command and the attached platoons. Anđa was struggling to keep up when Tito insisted he take his horse.

'I can't,' Anđa said as he shook his head.

'Yes you can. I insist. That knee you injured yesterday has blown up like a balloon. You're limping so badly it's hindering your progress. You need to rest it. Here,' Tito said in a gruff voice as he dismounted and handed Anđa the reins. Anđa mounted the old nag with only a little reluctance. Tito was right, his knee had swollen to twice its normal size and it throbbed. Even the cold wasn't sufficient to numb the pain.

The blizzard became more intense and heavy snow was swirling around Anđa's head when he felt the girth on his saddle give way. Without warning the saddle slid sideways. When his shoulder hit the road, which had a coating of ice, Anđa slithered off the track and down an incline. When he came to a stop he found himself buried up to his neck in freshly fallen snow. It was all he could do to keep his head free. As he struggled to get out of the hole he was trapped in, he sunk deeper. When his mouth filled with snow he spat it out along with angry words. 'Get me the fuck out of here!' He was reluctant to move again in case he sank deeper.

'Where the hell are you?' Leko shouted. 'We can't see you.'

'I'm buried up to my neck, I can't move and I'm bloody freezing to death. What's taking you so long. Get me out!'

By the time Tito and Leko had dug Anđa out of the snow ditch, he was shaking with cold. His teeth were chattering and he couldn't keep his limbs still.

'Put on my coat until you're warmer,' Tito said as he took it off and threw it around Anđa's shoulders. Anđa struggled into it. He had never been so cold — ever.

'How far have we got to go?' Anđa asked as he battled to move his frozen face and form the words.

'Another half hour. I believe there's a village up ahead. Get on the horse again. Leko's fixed the girth. Some lazy bugger hadn't fastened it properly.' Anđa couldn't see Tito's eyes, but he knew they would be black with anger.

The village was small — a deserted group of ten huts perched on a hillside with precipitous snow-covered rocks overhanging the dwellings. The transparent icicles hanging from the eaves of the buildings, the trees, the rocks and anything else they could attach themselves to, told Anđa it was well below zero when he finally fell into a restless sleep on a damp pile of musty straw. The fall from the horse had resulted in him bruising his shoulder and twisting his other knee. He was feeling acutely cold and miserable.

Chapter seven

It was a week later — seven o'clock at night when the *Ustaše* returned. Mara and her sons had finished eating a watery vegetable soup for dinner.

The same two *Ustaše* were equally as unpleasant as they had been on their previous visit and Mara's negative response to the whereabouts of her husband did not satisfy them any more than it had last time.

'*You* are lying,' the one with the moustache and the piercing eyes said.

Mara said nothing. She had no idea if her husband was dead or alive.

'Which one of you is Ivan?' the same officer asked.

'I am,' Ivan replied.

'You will come with us.'

Mara stepped in front of her son to shield him as the officer reached out to grab Ivan's arm.

'You can't take him. He's only a child.'

The officer's reply was to spit in her face. 'In the absence of your husband and because you won't tell us where he is, we will take this one instead.'

When Ivan lashed out at the German with his feet, Mara threw her arms around her son. She held on to Ivan with a fierce determination and did her best to stop the German prising her arms away. As fast as the officer pulled them away Mara put them back. For a short time Mara was trapped between the two males as if she was the meat in a sandwich.

'You can't!' she screamed while Damir and Zoran stood by paralysed with dread. In the end, when the tall officer drew his gun and pointed it at her, Mara surrendered her hold on her son. As they led him out of the door he looked back and although his eyes were full of fear his chin was held high.

They were outside the door when Mara yelled at them. 'Where are you taking him?' When there was no reply she shouted again. Still there was no reply. As she closed the door she was grateful that Zlata was still at Marija's place.

That night Mara tossed and turned and sobbed into her pillow. At one point she stuffed it into her mouth to stifle the anguish rising up in her. She couldn't let Zoran and Damir hear her.

She got up early the following morning, and when her sons heard her clattering in the kitchen they came and joined her.

The ticking of the white-faced clock with the black roman numerals on the wall beside the oak dresser was loud as the three remaining family members sat in gloomy silence.

'What do we do now?' Damir asked.

'I'll have to see if I can find him and try to get him released,' Mara said.

'We'll come with you,' Damir said.

'No, I'll go alone in case they arrest you as well.'

The brothers looked at each other with resignation. Their mother had spoken and she would not change her mind — there was no point in arguing with her.

Mara spent much of the day traipsing from one police station to another, but nobody would tell her anything. Ivan had disappeared without trace and she didn't know where else to look. Regardless, she carried on searching and asking questions of anyone she thought might be able to help her. Three days later she was worn out and her feet had blisters from trudging along what seemed like the entire maze of city streets. She was reluctant to tell her sons she was giving up because her search was as futile as looking for a mongoose without fur.

'Perhaps he'll come home when we least expect it,' Damir said.

'Do you think so?' Mara replied.

Damir shrugged. All three knew the chances of finding Ivan alive were remote — extremely remote, but not one of them was prepared to say so.

'If he's not in any of the police stations then he could be in prison, but where is anybody's guess,' Damir said. 'It might sound like a stupid question, but did you try the prison in Savska Cesta?'

Or he could have been murdered or deported to a concentration camp. Mara was in a world of her own, traumatised by wretched thoughts. She was quite aware that Ante Pavelić's *Ustaše* were eliminating what they called the undesirable population with gruesome violence. She couldn't tell her sons this at the risk of upsetting them more than they already had been.

'Why don't you let Damir and I go to the Savska Cesta Prison and see if he's there, *Majka?*'

'No! I've already told you I don't want either of you putting yourselves in danger, it's bad enough that your father and Ivan are both gone …' her words trailed away as she struggled to keep her voice level.

'But he could be in that prison. Did you go there or not?' There was an edge to Damir's voice. His mother's inattention had begun to exasperate him.

'Did I go where?' she asked.

'Savska Cesta Prison.'

'No, why would I? That's for criminals. Ivan isn't a criminal.'

'If you won't go, then we will … tomorrow. I thought that would have been the first place you'd try,' Damir said.

'No, it didn't occur to me. If you think I should go there then I will … as soon as I can.'

As they sat at the kitchen table, each was preoccupied with their own thoughts.

'What will we tell Zlata about Ivan?' Damir asked in a shaky voice. 'We have to collect her tomorrow. She was only meant to stay there for a week and that was up two days ago.'

'I've already thought about that. We must tell her he's gone to join his father. If we tell her the truth she won't cope with it.' Mara's voice was subdued.

Both Zoran and Damir made no comment as they digested their mother's words.

'And if Ivan doesn't come back?' Damir asked in a voice so choked up it was almost unintelligible.

'I'll deal with that when the time comes,' Mara said as she blew her nose on a well-used handkerchief. 'We must try to be positive and not give up hope.'

At eleven in the morning on the day that Zlata returned home at first she appeared fine. However, when she noticed Ivan's absence the questions began.

It was lunchtime when she spoke up after being her usual quiet self. 'Where's Ivan? Why didn't he come home for lunch? Is he working again?'

Zoran and Damir looked at the mother as soon as the words were out of their sister's mouth.

'He's gone to join his father,' Mara said without looking at her daughter.

'But *Tata* said he was too young.'

'He changed his mind.'

'Did you hear from *Tata* while I was at Marija's? What did he say?' Zlata smiled for the first time since she'd come home.

'No,' Mara said. 'We received a message.'

'Who from?'

'One of your father's comrades.'

'Oh, so he must have spoken to *Tata*. Did he say where *Tata* is and how he's getting on?'

'No. I'm afraid not.' Mara's voice was diminished as she struggled to carry on eating her tasteless bowl of soup.

'So you didn't find out where Ivan was meeting *Tata* or where he was going?'

'No,' Mara said as the eyes of her three children continued to stare at her with scarcely a blink. 'I think that's enough questions for now, Zlata. Please, eat your soup it must be cold by now.'

Zlata seemed to accept the lie Mara had fashioned, but that night she brought up the subject again.

'Will they come home to visit us?'

'They're probably stationed too far away and it would take too long to get here and by the time they arrived it would be time to go back again,' Mara said. Lying didn't come easily to her and she felt sure that her face had gone pink, but if it had, Zlata didn't notice.

'I hope they write to us then.'

'You father has written. You know that. I showed you the letter. Remember? I'm sure we'll get another one soon.'

Zlata's response was a frown that was so intense it made her look angry.

Chapter eight

Anda and Leko temporarily parted company with Tito and the others in the early morning. The weather was gloomy and wet, snow remained underfoot and rain drifted down like spider's webs. Not long after they set out on their horses Anda tried to make conversation, but Leko was not his usual calm self. He was dejected and taciturn and answered with the occasional grunt. Anda too fell silent. Obviously Leko's mind was on other things and Anda felt it was pointless trying to engage him in conversation. It hadn't been that long since Leko had been captured and tortured by the Gestapo — a matter of months, in fact. Nonetheless, Anda didn't think he was dwelling on that. He was resilient enough to have moved on.

Anda had been lucky he too hadn't been captured. At the beginning of the war they had been trying to dynamite Radio Belgrade to stop the Germans using it to broadcast their propaganda after they had taken control of the city. Leko had gone on ahead to meet the technician who had agreed to help them. Anda, who was carrying the dynamite, was to follow minutes later, once the technician had given Leko access to the building. Anda had been hiding across the street watching from a concealed doorway as Leko approached the entrance and the technician came out to meet him.

'Don't come across until you see my signal,' Leko said.

So far, so good, Anda thought when Leko and the technician shook hands. Then, from seemingly out of nowhere four men jumped on Leko, punched him and knocked him to the ground.

'Is this the one?' one of the men asked the technician.

'Yes,' the technician replied.

Anda shrank back into the doorway out of sight.

'Who is he?' another one asked.

'Don't know,' the technician replied. 'I only know he was planning to blow up the radio station. He didn't say who he was and I didn't ask. I called you.'

Anda watched as they dragged Leko away before he followed at a discreet distance until they came to the Gestapo prison in Banjica. Leko was carrying an identity card in the name of Boris Stanišić and Anđa wondered how long it would take them to ascertain his real name. It was imperative that they rescue Leko before the Gestapo tortured him, discovered his true identity and that he was a member of Tito's staff.

Anđa continued his surveillance of the prison while he waited for Tito to come up with a plan to free Leko. It was evening when Leko appeared — walking, but barely. Armed men on either side supported him as they dragged and pushed him towards another building.

'*Kurac!*' Anđa swore under his breath as he stared at Leko. There were bruises on his face and the fact that he couldn't walk unaided said it all — he had been beaten. When Leko entered the next building Anđa knew it was the prison hospital.

He strode off to find the nearest telephone. Tito needed to know about the latest development.

'Come to the flat. I've called an emergency meeting. But before you do contact Dr Ukić in the hospital. Tell him who you are and see if he can give you a map of the interior so we know which room Leko is in.'

It was ten the next morning and the sky was clear and blue when Leko and thirty-nine Partisans dressed in civilian clothes and armed with hand grenades and revolvers descended on the hospital. They took up positions in groups of three at all the entrances while Anđa and nine other men entered the hospital with one man handcuffed to another as if he was a prisoner under escort. Anđa approved of Tito's cunning plan. They had no difficulty hoodwinking the police at the entrance, but when a policeman in the corridor shouted at them to halt, Anđa shot him with his revolver.

'Quickly! Anđa hissed. 'His room is next on the left.'

From the doorway Anđa saw four guards and a male nurse inside Leko's room.

'Hands up!' he shouted as he raised his gun.

Anđa wasn't sure Leko was able to walk unaided and while he kept his gun trained on the guards and the nurse, two Partisans helped Leko out of bed.

'Can you walk?' Anđa asked as Leko teetered momentarily beside the bed and tried to take a step unaided. When he pitched forward and came perilously close to nose diving into the floor his comrades grabbed his arms.

'Come, we must go quickly. There is no time to lose,' Anđa said as the other two manhandled Leko supporting him roughly by his arms and rushed out of the room as fast as they could with the injured man between them.

Once they were outside Anđa issued more orders. 'We'll have to go over that wall because the police will be waiting for us at the main entrance. 'Are you up to it, Leko?'

'I'll have to be,' Leko said as he mustered all his strength and followed two men who had already cleared it.

Just as Leko leapt at the wall, Anđa heard gunshots on the other side, by then it was too late to stop him; Leko had committed himself. With a boost from the men beside him he went up clutching as best he could at the jagged rocks protruding from the wall. He paused on the top before he fell down the other side where he landed heavily on the point of his right shoulder. He lay on the pavement winded and in pain and let out an audible groan that he couldn't suppress as air was expelled from his chest.

When Anđa followed him immediately and landed on his feet; he wasn't expecting to be greeted by the grisly site on the pavement. Two Gestapo were sprawled on their backs with sightless eyes staring towards the sky. He paid them scant attention. Two of his men were hit.

'We got both the swine,' the Partisan lying nearby, said.

Anđa crouched down beside him. 'How bad is it?' he asked the man who was struggling to stand up. 'Can you walk?'

'Yeah, I think so. It's my side, Luckily the bastard was a poor shot and missed my guts. Give me a hand to get on my feet and we'll see.'

'What about you Frano?' Anđa asked the other wounded man.

'Left arm. Bullet's gone straight through, missed the bone though, I think. Hurts like hell, but I'll live. Just need to stop the bleeding. Can you rip of strip off my shirt and bind it before we get the hell out of it? Here,' he said as he shrugged out his shirt. His mouth formed a grimace below the bushy moustache on his craggy face.

Meanwhile Leko had sat up. 'Give me a hand to get on my feet, will you?' he asked as he winced in pain.

Eager to get away, Anđa was dismayed when he looked up and down the street and found no sign of the car that should have been there to pick them up.

'These bastards must have hijacked the car. It should have been here by now,' he said to Leko. 'Come on, we're in for another walk, I'm afraid.' The group set off half carrying Leko and with one of them supporting the man with the wound in his side to the accompaniment of gunfire behind them at the hospital. The other Partisans had obviously encountered more resistance. There was a safe house not too far away and once they reached it, they would be okay.

Anđa wasn't surprised by Leko's aloof demeanour. Whatever was bothering him was his business.

It was the next morning when they received an order from Tito via a messenger on horseback that they were to move north instead of south towards the coast. Tito had decided their presence in Montenegro was no longer necessary. Anđa was surprised Tito had countermanded his previous instructions, yet he knew Tito was often impulsive, sometimes hasty and often changed his mind.

'We're to go to Foča,' Anđa told Leko. 'Djido is being withdrawn from Montenegro.'

'Did he say why?' Leko asked.

'No, but he'll be joining us in Foča. Something must have happened in Montenegro.

Close to their destination they came upon a young boy standing on the side of the road. As they came nearer to him he held his ground.

'Where are you headed?' Anđa asked the lad.

'I'm hoping to join the Partisans. Is that what you are? I'm Jovica,' he said as he stepped forward and held out his hand.

Anđa dismounted and shook the boy's hand. His handshake was firm and the look in his unblinking, golden eyes was sincere. He was handsome with jet-black curls, pale skin and a saddle of freckles across the bridge of his nose.

'Yes we are. I'm Anđa and this is Leko.'

'How old are you?' Leko asked.

'Fifteen … but I'll be sixteen in a month's time,' Jovica said as he tried not to cough.

'Family? Where are they?' Anđa asked.

'Dead. All dead. I'm the only one left.'

Anđa looked at Leko. Leko nodded.

'Okay. File in with the men behind us. I'll talk to you later about your duties,' Anđa said.

Jovica's face was one large smile as he hastened forward. 'I'll do anything to defend my homeland. Just tell me what you need me to do.'

'I couldn't turn him down,' Anđa said to Leko as they moved off.

'Yes, I know what you mean. He's homeless and those eyes … such an unusual colour, but there was a look in them that was too difficult to resist, and most of the time I'm a hard bastard.'

'You can say that again,' Anđa replied and laughed. 'Although I didn't like the sound of that cough and he's frail. It could be nothing more than lack of food; at least I hope so.'

It was springtime as Anđa approached Foča; light rain was falling and it was warm. When the road into Foča was deserted he felt sure this was ominous. The only sign of life was a stooped, wrinkled old woman, dressed in black rags trudging along the road with an ungainly bundle of sticks strapped to her back. When they caught up with her Anđa noted the defiant set of her thin-lipped mouth. They stopped to chat, hoping she would give them news from the town.

'Only old people and children are left — those of us who were able to hide or escape. They murdered Serbs and Muslims alike as if they were cattle. A blow to the head, then into the ditch or the river,' she said as she stabbed her walking stick rebelliously into the ground.

'Who was it? *Četniks?*' Anđa asked.

'Them and those *Ustaše*. I expect you know about the Orthodox priest in Rogatica?'

'No, we didn't stop there.'

'Well, they nailed horseshoes to his palms and knees and rode him through town until he died. The bastards!'

A look passed between Anđa and Leko as silence hung in the air.

'May God keep you safe,' Leko said as they moved on.

'God! Huh!' she called out as she stared after them with dark-knowing eyes. 'We've been forsaken by *him*.'

As they came closer to Foča, Anđa's first impression was of a peaceful haven where two mountain streams converged and orchards lined theis it was road. However, he flinched when they came upon corpses floating downstream in the clear-green water where rocks on the riverbed were visible in places. One in particular held his attention — a bloated, naked woman floating on her back, her dark hair, which was entangled with twigs and debris, was drifting along with her. Her eyes had been gouged out leaving gaping sockets and her breasts had been sliced off. There were abrasions on her body and her hands and feet. Anđa blinked as he struggled to stop staring at the body. He knew there would be worse to come. In the centre of town few people were about except the odd old man or woman and children dressed in rags. The inhabitants were mostly emaciated with dull-glazed expressions in their eyes.

After having a thorough look around, they eventually found what remained of the local resistance group holed up in a deserted house set apart from the main cluster of dwellings.

Anda and Leko were given a room in a house with blood splattered on the walls and bullet holes in the ceiling. Anda shuddered. The place had a dreadful atmosphere — the aura of death. He dared not contemplate what horrors the people who had once lived there had suffered before their deaths.

They were still checking out the house when Jovica appeared in the doorway.

'Can I stay here with you?' he asked looking at Anda. 'I can cook.'

'Can you now?' Anda said with a small smile.

'My grandmother taught me. And I'll fetch firewood.'

'What do you say, Leko?'

'Whatever you want,' Leko replied with a dismissive shrug.

'Okay. You can stay as long as you do what you're told.'

'Shall I make you a meal?' Jovica face was wreathed in a smile and his big golden eyes had lit up.

'Yes, that's a very good idea. We're hungry and you must be too. Provisions are low though, so I don't know what you are thinking we can eat.

'I have an idea. One of my grandmother's recipes. You'll see. But first I need wood for the fire. I'll be back,' he said as he scampered away.

A short time later Jovica had indeed succeeded in producing a meal — nettle soup and half a loaf of barley bread that he had scrounged from somewhere.

'It's good,' Anda said as he ate the thin watery, green-coloured soup. It had absolutely no flavour, but he knew Jovica was proud of what he'd created and he felt he must praise him for his effort. Once again Jovica's thin-pale face became wreathed in an enormous smile.

The next day Anda was amazed by Jovica's resourcefulness when he produced three small eggs that he proceeded to fry for their breakfast.

'Good lad. Where did you find them?' Anda asked. 'I can't remember the last time I ate an egg.'

'I'm a local remember and I have my sources. You just have to know where to look. But don't tell anyone because they'll want eggs too and there aren't anymore. And besides if anyone finds out where I got them I'll get into trouble.'

'Okay, we'll keep your secret, won't we Leko?' Anda ruffled Jovica's hair.

'What? Yes, yes, whatever you say,' Leko, who was distracted, replied.

Despite what the locals had endured they were hospitable and provided what food they could. Anđa would never forget the bread they were offered. It was made from pears and barley and it tasted revolting. He ate it regardless, because by then hunger was tightening its grip, on him and Leko as well as the peasants. Earlier that day he had come upon a family with nothing to eat other than a rotten cabbage and a boy who'd had nothing to eat for three days. Anđa gave him a meagre quantity of walnuts and dried wild pears. He knew times would get tougher — harvest was five months away.

Tito had yet to arrive and once they had dispatched a messenger with a report about what they had found in Foča, Leko and Anđa settled down to wait for further orders. The sky was heavy with dense cloud; there was no wind; the temperature had dropped suddenly and the cold was biting. Gone was the warmth they had encountered when they arrived in Foča. It had been a false spring. They lit a fire in the main room of their dwelling using furniture from a deserted house next door as fuel. Anđa was restless in the unfortunate, creepy aura that surrounded them. He had no desire to remain there.

'Tomorrow I think we should find somewhere else to stay,' he said. 'I don't know about you but I feel as though there are ghosts everywhere I turn.'

'You're right about that.' Leko nodded. 'I'll talk to the commander and see if there's somewhere else with a more congenial atmosphere.'

The surviving Partisans were a determined bunch and when Anđa told them they were to join forces with other battalions who were preparing to take Jablanica from the Italians they agreed readily.

'We'll be glad to have something to do. We've been milling round like a herd of cattle waiting to be slaughtered,' said their commander, a rugged-looking man in his fifties who had been shooting and come back bearing two lambs which he intended to roast to celebrate Tito's arrival.

Temporary respite from the war came the day after Tito's arrival when five couples were married by the commander of the Foča battalion. Thirty rounds were fired to commemorate the weddings, but this was cut short by an order from Tito. 'Every bullet is precious. That's enough,' he said with a look Anđa had not seen in his eyes before. Was it anger at the reveller's behaviour or despair that he'd had to reprimand them?

The following day was a mixed one. Anđa spent much of it trying to rid his body of lice. Everyone had them and if he didn't get rid of them then the risk of typhus would be serious. And for the first time in months he cleaned his teeth.

It was the middle of the night when Anđa heard Jovica moaning. He got up and went to him. The boy had been listless during the afternoon and Anđa had wondered then if he was weakening. As the night wore on he knew he had frostbite and he was sure he had tetanus. He had involuntary muscle spasms, a fever, he was sweating and he had trouble swallowing and his jaw kept clamping shut. Anđa sat with him until the early hours of the morning when his moaning began to subside. He held his hand as he grew steadily worse and thought about his own sons. And when Jovica could no longer speak and his face became fixed in a permanent grimace, Anđa picked up the frail boy and held him gently until he breathed his last breath. Tears rolled down Anđa's face as he closed Jovica's golden eyes which were no longer filled with light and emotion.

Jovica had only joined Anđa's platoon two weeks ago. His death had been swift and Anđa hoped painless, although he doubted it because of the contorted expression on his face. It was the middle of the afternoon when Anđa stood beside his grave as a group of youths sang in clear melodic voices: *We shall never yield our land ...*

Anđa would never forget Jovica's soulful eyes, which became so passionate when he talked about fighting for his homeland.

The next day it began to rain. Anđa stood in the doorway of his dwelling and watched sheets of water pouring out of the dark sky. He was hoping it would rain itself out by nightfall. The next day they were moving out to take on the Italians and heavy rain would be a huge inconvenience. However, so much rain had fallen that the river was now in spate and the remaining bodies were slowly being washed away.

The weather couldn't have been worse when Anđa accompanied the Partisans as they marched from Foča to the mountainous town of Jablanica where they hoped to liberate the town from the Germans. It was a twenty-nine hour slog on foot through rugged, beautiful mountainous country. The forest was dense and green with tall spruce and beech trees and every so often there were large irregular-shaped, moss-covered boulders. Although the rain had ceased, it had begun to snow, the temperature had plummeted and it was miserably cold. They were outnumbered by German soldiers and as Anđa stood with snow up to his calves while he fired his rifle incessantly he wished he could reload it more quickly. His only consolation was that he made almost every shot count.

He was jubilant when they won an unlikely victory by trickery. The bridge suspended between the cliffs was blown up by the Partisans in such a way that the enemy thought it was unusable, in fact, it was partly intact and the Partisans used it to deploy their forces to the east bank of the river where they staged a surprise attack on the unsuspecting Germans.

When the Partisans moved on to the Neretva Valley 4,000 wounded straggled behind them. After more than a day's march they encountered another battalion of German soldiers. Twice Anđa was knocked off his feet and pushed into the bright, emerald-green Neretva River. Bedraggled and freezing he struggled out of one of the coldest rivers in the world, stayed on his feet and kept fighting — without his rifle. When a German who'd also lost his weapon charged at him, Anđa already had his knife out. He lunged and stabbed the enemy soldier through the heart. Tito's Partisans where the victors of the resulting three-day battle which left the Neretva strewn with corpses.

There was no rest for the battle-weary men, when after beating off the Germans, they were attacked by a band of *Četniks*. They were few in number and it didn't take more than a few hours to deal with them before the Partisans headed back to Foča.

It was March when the snow began to melt. One sunny afternoon Anđa took a break and walked through the countryside on the outskirts of the village. Birds were singing and when he felt the sun hot on the nape of his neck he turned up his collar to protect it. He had no intention of getting burnt. March sun was danger sun. Winter lasted for so long that his skin had been covered up for six months. Vivid green grass was breaking through where the snow was melting and the willow trees were smothered with buds. Anđa was breaking off a branch to take back with him when he came upon a decomposing body — a giant of a man lying on his back with his hands chained together in front of his body. Abrasions covered much of his body as well as his wrists and ankles. His eye sockets were gaping holes, his genitals had been removed and patches of his skin were discoloured and seemed to have been nibbled by an animal or maybe the fish in the river. Anđa snapped off the budding branch and hastened away from the shocking sight.

Chapter nine

Mara couldn't sleep. She went over and over in her mind what she would say at the prison. She didn't know whether to grovel or risk their ire and demand to know if her son was being held there. When she finally decided to be respectful and she was almost asleep she heard a disturbance going on upstairs. She thought the shouting and thumping was coming from the flat above, yet that didn't make sense. Jelena Petrović never made noise even when her twelve-year-old grandson stayed with her, as he was now. Whatever was going on was quite out of character. After she had been to the prison Mara intended to investigate and see what the commotion had been about.

She got up early and drank a cup of weak herb tea. The thought of eating didn't enter her mind.

At seven she set out knowing she had a walk of an hour and a half ahead of her. The sky was a grey dome above her head and she knew rain was coming. It was spring and the trees were covered in buds and also the odd blossom. By the time she reached the prison she was footsore and weary. Her arthritic ankle always bothered her more in the cold weather.

She stopped and took in the drab, forbidding concrete structure. The mere sight of it make her apprehensive. She shivered with fear. Momentarily, she was rooted to the spot and couldn't move until she took a deep breath and forced herself to approach the guardhouse. Through the iron bars she saw a man in uniform — the dreaded *Ustaše* uniform. As she walked closer to the grill, he watched her with what she imagined were hate-filled eyes. Immediately in front of the enclosure she came to a halt. Neither of them spoke. She knew he wasn't going to make it easy for her.

'I'm looking for my son …' Mara's voice was a hesitant stammer. To her ears it sounded as if it belonged to someone else. 'His name is Ivan Milić.'

'What makes you think he's here?' the guard bellowed in such a loud voice that Mara jumped at the sound of it.

'Well … he was arrested and I've been all over the city looking for him. He's not a criminal though.' After she'd said that last sentence she wished she hadn't. It sounded inane.

The guard laughed sadistically. 'That's what they all say.'

'Could you check and see if you're holding him, please?' she pleaded.

There was a lengthy pause during which the guard looked Mara up and down before he replied. 'Since you've asked so nicely I'll see what I can find out. Ivan Milić, you said?'

'Yes.'

'Wait here.'

Mara waited for over half an hour. Had he forgotten her? She was on the point of giving up and going away when he reappeared.

'He's not here any longer. He's been transferred.'

For a brief moment Mara almost became excited. 'Transferred? Where to?'

'No idea. The register says transferred yesterday — nothing else. We don't keep a record of where prisoners are sent. We have too many and it would be too time consuming.'

'Isn't there anyone who would know?'

'No.'

'But I'm desperate. I have to find out where he is ... please.

'I've already given you all the information I have. Move along now ... please.' He eyeballed Mara with his insensitive stare and once again a shiver ran through her. With a ragged sigh she turned and walked away. As she plodded in the direction of home tears ran freely down her ravaged cheeks.

Upon her arrival her sons were waiting expectantly.

'Where's Zlata?' she asked.

'Still asleep. Did you find him?' Zoran blurted out as soon as she was in the door.

'No. He was taken there, but he was transferred somewhere else yesterday. I couldn't find out where. I did the best I could. If I'd pressed the guard any harder he would probably have arrested me.' Mara's eyes were glistening with tears as she stifled a sob. Zoran and Damir hung their heads in silent despair.

As it turned out she didn't end up going upstairs to Jelena's apartment. Her sons had already found out what had happened and gave her the bad news immediately after she'd told them what she'd found out at the prison.

'Mrs Petrović is gone,' Damir said. 'And her grandson. Looks like there was a scuffle in the kitchen. The neighbours in the house facing her living room on the other side said the *Ustaše* took them.'

'Why would they do that?' Mara asked. 'She's an old lady.'

'Since when did that stop them? They took Ivan. Nobody is exempt and Mrs Petrović was born in Serbia, wasn't she?'

'Yes,' Mara said quietly.

'What if we're next?' Damir asked as he voiced the thought that all three were having.

'Don't think like that. You're not Serbian. You were born here. I don't want to hear any more talk like that especially not in front of Zlata. Come on, you can both help me make a meal. I need to eat and so do you.'

'I've already started a pot of soup. We thought you'd be tired. There wasn't much to use, just those dried beans and some potatoes. What else shall I put in?' Zoran asked.

'Let's have a look,' Mara said as she lifted the lid of the pot which was simmering on the stove. 'Good, you put in some dried herbs. We'll make a chef out of you yet,' she said as she tried to lighten the mood after the depressing news they'd received.

Mara would never be the same again. The flesh had melted off her large frame and left jutting bones; her eyes were often red-rimmed from the crying she indulged in at night when she couldn't sleep. Her appearance and her personality were irreparably altered. She wore a permanently sad demeanour and when she smiled, which was not often, her eyes betrayed an underlying sadness that she didn't bother to hide. Her husband and her eldest son were constantly in her mind. And to add to her despair, she hadn't received any more letters from her husband. It was as if she was a robot when she mechanically put what food there was on the table for her children and continued to keep the house clean and tidy. Everyday she faced new challenges when it came to feeding her family. Some she could do nothing about while others left her enraged.

It was a Saturday when she sent her remaining sons to dig potatoes from her garden. They had not been gone for long when Damir returned on his own empty-handed. She was about to berate him when she noticed his swollen eye.

'Two dirty-rotten mongrels were digging up our potatoes,' Damir said.

'How many did they get?' Mara's anger was building.

'Only a few. They'd only just started digging when we got there. We let them have it. I hit one over the head with the spade and Zoran punched the other one. They scarpered. Do you want us to dig up the whole crop in case they come back?'

'Yes, I think you'd better. What a cheek. I've had that garden for so long and nothing like this has ever happened before. I suppose they must have been desperate. If they'd asked I might have given them some. Did you know them?'

'No, never seen them before.'

'You'd better let me have a look at your eye before you go.'

'It's not bad. You can look at it later. I'd better get back to Zoran in case they pluck up the courage to come back, although the one I hit over the head was staggering when he tried to run.'

'I shouldn't laugh,' Mara said, 'but it serves him right.'

As the war engulfed Zagreb, Mara and her family were no longer free to move about the city. Tanks and soldiers crawled over it like flies feeding on a corpse. At least once a month Mara and her family cowered in bomb shelters as their city was assaulted from the air. Mara continued to listen to the radio. It was her only link to what was going on in the rest of Yugoslavia. Belgrade and Split had been struck by German bombs and she assumed that Zagreb would soon suffer a similar fate. So far, the suburb they lived in had not received any direct hits. Other areas such as the airport were the targeted ones.

Chapter ten

After one hundred and ten days in Foča it was time to leave. Anđa was glad they would be leaving in the sunshine. That was the way it should be. The day was bright and a shining, pale-yellow sun had burst through the wispy clouds. Anđa believed the Partisans had brought freedom and new life to Foča — removed the corpses, stopped the slaughter and brought sun to one of the most backward places in Yugoslavia. The wounded had already left with an advance of able-bodied men while a further two hundred men were waiting to depart, despite the fact that they had no weapons and not much food. Anđa's last meal had been watery soup made with nettles and sour plum pulp — a variation of Jovica's recipe. But leave they must. The Italians were dangerously close. One last job needed to be done before they departed. They must set fire to their abandoned headquarters and any other buildings that the enemy could use.

Anđa lay in a ditch and took in the sad sight of Foča in smoke and flames as he said goodbye for the last time.

Their destination had changed yet again and they would be heading through southern Bosnia and on to Montenegro into another wild area of Yugoslavia.

They had begun their march when Anđa came upon one of the worst sights he had ever seen. Fifteen men who looked like unearthly ghosts were toiling along the road — typhus had claimed them. Their dusky-grey skin was almost transparent and tightly stretched over their gaunt, skeletal frames — as if they were already dead and it had begun to shrink. Anđa was certain that they would never make it through the almost impassable mountains.

Five hours later the column of men, with Anđa near its head, halted within sight of Mt Jahorina and Mt Maglić where they ate a meagre meal of hard maize mush. It was then that they were approached by two males wanting to join the Partisans — a sixty-year-old man and an eleven-year-old boy.

'I know how to shoot. I've fought the *Četniks,*' the skeletal boy said.

'I'll die for liberty,' the unkempt old man added.

Anđa's eyes filled with tears. He could not turn them away.

It was hours later, so many that Anđa had lost count, when they reached Montenegro. He was almost asleep on his feet as he mechanically continued to put one foot in front of the other. They spent the night in a disused school on the edge of the forest — an eerie place with caves, ravines and rocky cliffs. Anđa found the place strange and frightening. Perhaps it was the silence that caused his mind to imagine that sinister happenings had taken place here.

Just before bed Tito and his comrades crowded around the wireless and listened to a speech on the BBC by Winston Churchill. Anđa had no idea how Tito had managed to get hold of the radio, but he knew they were privileged to have it. Churchill talked about gaining a victory over fascism within the year and although Anđa wanted to believe it, he did not. It was too soon. Victory was not yet within their grasp with Germany showing no signs of weakening or surrendering. When the speech was over they retired to a bed of hay. Morale was low after the long march and it was decided that to boost it each of them would chose a song, which they would all sing ... but when Anđa's turn came he was already sound asleep.

That afternoon he made for the clean water of the Tara River. *If only there was food,* he thought as he dived in and bathed under a freezing cold waterfall. It was so refreshing he didn't care about the cold. All that concerned him was getting rid of his lice. As diligent as he was at removing them, it was only a matter of days before they reappeared. The worst infestation was always around his groin and upper thighs. They secreted themselves in among his body hair and it was not an easy task eradicating them.

That night he was sleeping well when Leko woke him and the others at three a.m. It was time to leave their warm beds and move on. Anđa was reluctant to get out of his warm nest in the hay; however, he would not miss the rat that ran over him not long after he'd gone to bed.

No matter what he did, Anđa could not warm up. The main party of twelve had been slogging uphill on a narrow mountain track for hours — five at least and their destination was still two hours away. They stopped briefly and took stock of where they were before moving on through more snow drifts and trees with copper-coloured needles. Under more cheerful circumstances Anđa knew he would have thought the place was scenic. When they reached a village called Nedajno, Anđa's face was lit by a brief smile for the first time in days. The word meant no surrender. The village was cupped in the side of a mountain among the natural beauty of nature. The inhabitants were friendly and welcoming. Sheepskins were stretched to dry on the outsides of houses and happy children ran amok. Tito decided they would spend a few days there. It was peaceful in a wild, untamed way.

The next morning Anda got up slowly and wandered outside. He was intending to take a piss. Once he'd rubbed sleep from his eyes, he turned his attention to his surroundings. It was then that he was greeted by a gruesome sight. During the night a wolf had attacked their packhorse, ripped open its stomach and killed it. The animal was lying on it's side and a jagged hole had been gnawed in its belly. What was left of its entrails were lying next to the beast. Anda shied away from the putrid smell of blood and intestines as he wondered how they would manage without the animal to carry their supplies. They would have to make use of the young Italian prisoners.

The quiet days were a refreshing respite as Anda welcomed the chance to rest and recover. For the first times in ages he was unable to hear gunfire. He gathered nettles for lunch and once he'd shared the watery soup prepared by the two Italians he went for a walk with Djido. A short distance away they came upon a peasant ploughing a field. Attached to the yoke were two skinny oxen and a woman.

'That plough belongs in a museum,' Djido called out.

The peasant was quick with his reply. 'I don't care. We will fight to the last man. Our children will survive and become men. I must provide them with food,' he said. He was a good man who was more than happy to give them a large quantity of wheat from the battered sack that he was carrying slung across his shoulder. He hadn't noticed the small hole in one corner of the old sack or the trickle of wheat that dribbled behind him as he walked. When they offered to pay, he wouldn't take their money.

'You're Partisans. This is the least I can do to help you,' he said.

They arrived back at camp in time to receive an update from Tito about casualties, prisoners and villages that had been won and lost. 'The few men we have available should not be used to capture empty, small towns. Instead we must attack the invaders communication lines where we know there will be weapons and munitions,' Tito said before he began to pace back and forth.

Anda wondered exactly what Tito was referring to when he didn't elaborate. No doubt they would find out in due course.

'There is more distressing news, I'm sorry to say. The Četniks have had a resurgence. The Italians have supplied them with automatic weapons.'

'If only we had their ammunition we'd beat them,' Djido said. 'They're in poor spirits. Their hearts aren't in it.'

That evening after they'd listened to more updates brought in by the courier and read aloud by Tito, Anđa watched him pace up and down again. This time in silence. In the end, the silence was broken by Leko. 'I take it we'll be leaving at four a.m?' he said.

Tito did nothing other than nod.

They made their way north after a breakfast of unsalted mutton which sat heavily in Anđa's stomach for most of the day. He almost wished he hadn't eaten it, but there was nothing else. He did his best to forget his uncomfortable stomach as he admired the fresh green forest through which they were travelling.

That night they slept in the open beside a fire. Anđa dropped off listening to the tinkling of the stream he'd swum in earlier in yet another attempt to rid his body of the inevitable lice.

He was woken from a sound sleep by the warmth of the fire. Someone had tended it and it was ablaze with cavorting yellow flames. It was then that the courier arrived with another report for Tito. He tore it open without delay. As he read he paced about with a frown on his face.

'How bad is it?' Anđa asked. He knew it was something catastrophic because Tito's eyes had turned almost black. Yet again Anđa marvelled at how changeable Tito's eyes could be.

'Goransko fell at midday ... the Italian swine. Hundreds have been wounded,' he said as he intensified his pacing around the clearing. 'We can't leave the wounded for the fascists to torture. I will reconsider our plans.'

The next day when Anđa got up Tito was already reading the latest report that had come in a few minutes earlier. The expression in his eyes was troubled.

'What is it?' Anđa asked.

Tito was silent for a long moment as he continued to stare at the paper in his hand. Then he looked up and glanced around at the members of his inner circle who were clustered around the fire, before he focused his attention on Leko.

'It's your wife Leko ... I'm afraid she's been killed by the Gestapo.'

Leko immediately turned white, slumped forward on his seat and buried his face in his hands.

'Another good comrade gone,' Anđa said as he stood up and was the first to embrace Leko.

'It's painful news,' Tito said. 'Your faithful comrade who loved you so much has died a heroic death. I cannot console you. Words are empty. You might find another mate in your life, but you will never find one who will be so devoted to you. Be strong. Your loss is also the Party's loss. We share your sorrow.'

Anđa's eyes glazed over with tears when Tito stopped speaking and bowed his head.

After hearing about one too many defeats Tito and his band kept retreating while each day they waited for the courier in the hope that better news would come.

In the early afternoon they were sitting in the open under a linden tree beside a small fire as they waited for Tito to read the latest dispatch while thunder boomed in the distance. Anđa couldn't make out whether it was gunfire or actual thunder. The sky was heavy with dark-rolling clouds and the wind had picked up. Anđa hoped it was the approach of a storm.

'We've captured one of Mihailović's couriers carrying forty letters from a government minister giving various officers instructions on how to attack us,' Tito said.

'Forewarned is forearmed,' Anđa said.

'If only we were armed enough … if only,' Djido said with a shake of his head.

'There's pleasing news,' Tito said. 'Krištof's Slovenes have killed 1,500 Italians.' Anđa grinned as he joined in the cheer that reverberated around the camp.

By two-thirty that day they were on the move trekking through wild country with cliffs that Anđa thought looked like gaping mouths. He was already cold, but he froze when they were pelted for over half an hour by a heavy hailstorm. It would be a difficult task drying his clothes and one that would have to wait until evening when they could light a fire — provided the enemy were not too near.

By now lack of food had become a real issue. The ripe strawberries they came upon late in the day did nothing to alleviate their hunger even though they gorged themselves. Anđa's stomach had long since given up asking for food and his teeth and gums ached. When he felt his teeth, several were loose and one had already fallen out. Given their diet of meat and gruel, scurvy was inevitable. As he thought back over his time since the beginning of the war, he knew there wasn't much he hadn't faced — cold, hunger, bombs, gunfire, typhus and starvation that never went away. Could there be anything yet to come? He gave himself constant, silent lectures about staying strong, and as he sat in front of the fire drying his clothes he gave himself yet another one. He didn't know what else he could do to keep his spirits up.

The next evening while he was out walking with Djido, they discussed their most pressing problem — hunger.

'I can't see a solution,' Djido said. 'The locals are starving too. I've lost so much weight I've had to tighten my belt four notches.'

'I've moved mine five and I'm having trouble keeping my trousers up. It's more than a bit of a hindrance,' Anđa added.

'God knows what we're going to do. We can't take food from the villagers. That would be unpardonable. We'll either have to buy it somewhere, but God alone knows where, or continue to go hungry,' Djido said.

'At least our horses aren't hungry. There's plenty of grass although why they persist in eating leaves off the trees I don't know.'

'Yes, strange, aren't they?'

'They certainly are. I've tried to reason with that stubborn packhorse and tell her not to eat the trees, but she won't listen,' Anđa said.

'Maybe she doesn't speak our language. Perhaps you should try German. Didn't we capture her from them?'

Anđa laughed.

By the time they were back at camp Anđa had begun scratching like a monkey. Yet again he was covered in lice and there was no river in sight.

As usual they forged ahead early the next morning. Breakfast was a piece of bread and a tiny morsel of bacon. Anđa savoured the meal as if it was his last.

In the moonlight he trudged on. He was thinking about his family hoping they were okay. He had yet to send any more letters home. He was waiting, although he didn't quite know what for. Was he afraid his next letter would suffer the same fate as the last one and not reach its destination? He knew that could put his family in danger. When he trod in a drift of rotten slimy leaves and stumbled down an incline he was jolted out of his reverie. Once again he was cold — exceptionally cold but not as cold as he'd been when he was trapped in the snow up to his neck. His fleshless body and his thin coat provided no protection against the harsh elements. When they stopped for a rest Anđa stayed standing. He was sure that if he sat down he'd never get up.

When they halted again Anđa was listless and overtired. He sat without stirring until Leko handed him a lump of horse meat. One of their horses had fallen and broken its leg and they'd had to shoot it.

'Eat it now while its warm and the juices are running,' Leko said. 'It'll give you a burst of energy.' They had gathered wild onions that afternoon and Leko had ordered Matteo to brown them and sear the slabs of horsemeat over a glowing beech coal. As Anđa chewed the meat blood ran down his chin.

'You look like Count Dracula,' Djido said as he bellowed with laughter.

'Thanks,' Anđa said. 'Glad I haven't got a mirror. I shudder to think what I look like … with or without the blood.'

Anđa's hunger gnawed at him without cessation. Yet he knew not every man felt that way. Anđa was what the Serbs called a white blackbird — a man whose belly spoke first. Day by day he was growing weaker. Once upon a time marching uphill for twenty kilometres had been relatively easy. Now he could barely manage three. He had no choice but to forget these problems — put them out of his mind. Around him men were singing. They seemed happy. What they could possibly be happy about he had no idea and neither did he have the energy or the inclination to ask. He had sunk into one of the worst bouts of depression he could ever remember.

It had been raining for twelve hours when they set off again. Anđa walked as if he was sleepwalking. He walked and he walked and then he walked some more until he could no longer stand. When he woke the rain had finally stopped.

Some days were worse than others. It depended on what the terrain was like — the further south they travelled the more mountainous it became. They encountered not only Germans, but Italians and *Četniks*.

At Mratinje, Djido and Anđa parted company with Tito and half of his staff. Tito was gruff when he made his announcement and as usual he paced up and down in the small clearing where they had stopped. 'It'll be safer if we split up. There are enemies in all directions no matter where we turn. If we stay together then we run the risk that all of us will be captured.'

They had reached the Tara river when Djido and Anđa faced their next dilemma. Where to cross? And cross it they must if they were to carry on. The bridges across the gorge had been mined and were unsafe and the river was flowing swiftly. The decision was a troublesome one made more difficult by the number of wounded they had with them. When Anđa looked back he experienced the greatest grief he had ever felt. A long procession of refugees continued to slog along behind the Partisans — starving, emaciated, barefoot, clad in rags — thousands were dragging one foot after the other except for a few who had oxen and wagons or carts. Fleeing the fascists were mothers, children and old men — few young men were among them. Most plodded with dignity; while here and there a child cried.

When a woman with four small children approached Anđa's group he thought his heart would burst open with pity. They were shivering, ragged and barefoot.

'Comrade,' she beseeched Anđa, 'put an end to these children's misery. Kill them. I haven't the strength to do it — please, I beg you.'

Anđa stopped, shed his shirt from under his coat and gave it to the biggest child while his comrades around him gave over their shirts and socks and the last of the food they were carrying. They moved on, only to be stopped again. This time by a mother walking barefoot on the ice that covered the track. She had one wailing child in a sack on her back and she was dragging a second one by the hand. A third was walking by itself crying. It's face was so encrusted with dirt and snot that Anđa couldn't tell if it was a boy or a girl let alone how old it was. When Anđa learnt that they'd had nothing to eat for five days, he spoke to his men and came up with another meagre quantity of food — bread that was stale and had gone hard and would need to be softened with water before it could be eaten.

Then there were the wounded who were now more than a serious issue — 1,000 with minor wounds and 420 stretcher cases. They were a sorry sight. Many wore clothes that were ragged, filthy and often covered with blood. Of those who could walk many staggered as if they were drunk. Audible moaning from the stretcher cases was the prevalent sound as most of the wounded and those transporting them plodded ahead in silence. The rest had gone with Tito.

On the edge of a high precipice Anđa asked Djido what he intended to do. 'We can't abandon them and you know the terrain better than I do,' Anđa said.

'Of course not, but the terrain is so difficult I doubt we can get them through. We couldn't be in a worse position.' They both fell silent as they surveyed the rugged, hostile ground around them.

'We're going to have to cross via that canyon over there,' Djido said as he pointed to his right.

'But there's no path. It could be hell on earth getting round those bluffs and slithering down the ravines,' Anđa replied.

'I know, but what choice do we have?'

'Less than none.' Anđa shrugged.

The route they chose was indeed tiresome because of the presence of the enemy. They came to a halt when they spotted a group of German soldiers close by.

'Wherever we go the Germans seem to follow us,' Anda said. 'Why are they so well informed about our whereabouts?'

'I've been thinking the same thing,' Djido replied. 'Do you think they've been intercepting our radio messages?'

'Yes, I do. But the question is how do we find out and what can we do about it?'

'I wouldn't be surprised if they've deciphered our code. It's too simple.'

'You might be right, although I hope you're not.' Djido pushed back his hair which had become overgrown. There never seemed to be time to get the battalion barber to cut it.

As the days passed, their situation grew more and more hopeless. Anda became acutely aware of it after one particularly horrendous day when they marched for over twenty-four hours with less than an hour's stop to eat a hastily prepared meal. They had been driven to this extreme out of necessity and to avoid danger. Anda knew that Djido was doing his best to keep up the morale of their men — men who Anda knew were sustained by nothing but their courage and beliefs. But there was only so much they could take and then, of course, there were the wounded. Anda did not envy Djido his command responsibility. Of the 4,000 men who had started out Anda estimated that less than 2,000 remained. Some had died in battle, while others had been taken by typhus and a few had perished from starvation. When the quandry of the fate of the wounded arose again, Djido asked Anda to send a message to Tito requesting permission to leave the wounded hidden in the woods and canyons.

Tito took forever to reply. Meanwhile the enemy came closer. Anda believed that Tito was a compassionate man and he imagined he was having difficulty making the decision to leave the men behind — they would face certain death one way or another.

Once again, they tried to cross into Sandžak — by night. But this proved too difficult. The road was choked with several hundred wounded being cared for by soldiers and peasants while at the end of the procession there was the never-ending, snaking bottleneck of refugees. The route was also littered with corpses — exhausted soldiers who had fallen and died on the spot.

The next morning they came upon a group of about thirty gravely wounded men resting around a pile of boulders. Some were sprawled on the ground and looked close to death while others were propped up against the boulders or each other. They had one element in common — their eyes were dull and their faces were etched with misery and despair. Djido asked Anda to halt their group because he felt he had to address them, but he had difficulty speaking. Their agony was almost his undoing. During a lull in his broken speech, a man with one leg missing took advantage of the pause.

'Give the order that we can keep our weapons. I beg you,' he said.

When Anda looked into the man's sorrowful eyes he understood. They wanted the option of committing suicide rather than being tortured by the enemy. On Djido's say-so Anda issued the order.

'We'll get help for you if we get through,' Anda said.

'Never mind us. Save yourselves,' another injured man replied.

Feeling powerless to offer any help Anda acknowledged his remark with a nod.

Later that day came the next obstacle — a clearing, which they needed to cross, and that was being shelled by German howitzers. They waited. Then came the respite. Mist drifted in and shrouded the clearing. There was no point in delay and Anda ran with the rest. When he reached the other side he threw himself so heavily on the ground that he was temporarily winded. He lay on his back gasping for breath as bodies materialised out of the mist while the guns remained silent.

It wasn't long before another river crossing came into view — a suspension bridge that appeared to be monitored by planes. They stood in the shelter of nearby trees and waited until the planes had gone. But as soon as Anda stepped on to the bridge, artillery sounded and planes droned. Feeling as if his heart had leapt out of his chest in fright, Anda ran, jumping over corpses as he went. He knew they were dead because they did not move. Some were sprawled haphardly with their arms outstretched while others had simply crumpled in a heap. Once he was across and sheltering in a grove of trees, he looked back as men who tried to follow his lead were cut down on the bridge or catapulted into the gorge below.

'By Christ, I was lucky to get across without being killed,' he said aloud. They suffered heavy losses including two of their experienced commanders who Anda had come to respect and admire. There was neither time to bury nor mourn them. It was imperative that they kept moving. Further along on the opposite bank Anda was aware of Germans watching them through binoculars. He scowled in their direction before he continued on yet another perilous journey. As he put one foot in front of the other he couldn't believe he and Djido were alive.

Hours later, when they believed they had distanced themselves from the enemy, they stopped to eat a meal of mutton and nettle stew prepared by the two young Italians over fires using dry sapless branches which did not give off smoke.

'This is good. Best meal we've had in a while,' Anđa said to Mario. 'We'll keep you on, provided you keep it up,' he added and gave a jovial laugh.

They had finished eating when the radio crackled into life. It was Vlad with new orders from Tito.

'He wants you to execute the Italians,' Vlad said in a flat voice.

'What Italians?' Djido asked.

'The ones travelling with you.'

There was silence while Djido and Anđa looked at each other as they absorbed Tito's unpalatable order.

'Why?' Anđa asked.

'One of them has betrayed your location to the Germans, so no more questions. The order is to be carried out immediately. Is that clear?' At that moment both Djido and Anđa knew it wasn't their codes that were being deciphered. There was a traitor in their midst.

Salty tears cascaded down Anđa's gaunt cheeks as he stood in silence and took aim with his rifle. He'd grown fond of Mario and Matteo. The Italians cowered together. All but one had no idea why their lives were being snuffed out. Neither Djido nor Anđa could see the point in giving them an explanation.

Anđa would never forget the look in Mario's wide-open, long-lashed eyes immediately before the bullet struck and killed him. It was a mixture of shock and disbelief. Anđa knew those huge, soft eyes would haunt him for the rest of his life. He lowered his rifle and swallowed to stem his tears before he shuddered and turned away — shocked and disgusted by what he'd been forced to do.

Yet again there was no time for Anđa to mourn, instead he thought momentarily about drinking an entire bottle of red wine to drown his sorrows. There was no chance of that either now, or in the immediate future. Alcohol was prohibited by Tito as was taking food or supplies from the local population. Payment was compulsory and taking anything by force was punishable by death with a bullet.

Once the bodies had been thrown into the ravine they broke camp and moved off.

Anđa lost track of time as his days blurred into monotony. Around him spring was turning into early summer and the trees were covered with bright-green growth. He scurried from one cluster of trees or mound of rocks to the next, dodging enemy fire as he went. Bullets hit trees and rocks close to him. Splinters of bark and shards of rock whizzed through the air and there was the constant whining of bullets. When his cheek was struck by a jagged chunk of rock, he winced in pain as his hand flew to his face and he cursed aloud. It was a superficial cut and although it had drawn blood, it wasn't serious. He took refuge behind the nearest boulder hoping the onslaught would pass. Some minutes later it did. Whenever he looked through his binoculars, German soldiers were always in sight — somewhere.

At Dragaš Selo, the platoon Anđa had become attached to since splitting up with the supreme command was joined by several others including the first Dalmatian and the Mostar Battalions, which had been reduced in number by half.

That night there was a small celebration which took the form of singing — for once no Germans could be seen in any direction.

The elation was short-lived when German soldiers attacked the right flank of their battalion the following morning. When the battle was over Djido called the commanders together for a meeting.

'We've sustained heavy losses. Our situation is dire. In case we are captured I want you to destroy anything you are carrying that would enable you to be identified,' he said. With a miserable feeling of numbness Anđa destroyed the last letter he had written to his family and was hoping to get dispatched. Unwilling to destroy the book given to him by his father with an inscription in the front, he stuffed it into a crevice in a rock. Perhaps he would be able to return under more favourable circumstances and retrieve it.

The following day morale was low and they moved out at a much slower pace. Anđa believed his death was imminent, and although he was resigned to it, he was angry. He hadn't lost the will to fight; it simply seemed hopeless because they were constantly outnumbered. As hard as he tried he could never see light at the end of the dark, depressive tunnel he felt trapped in.

It was not long after he'd had the premonition of his own death when he came upon a German soldier who had been disarmed by their advance scouts. Anđa scowled at him. 'Where's the rest of your battalion?' he shouted in halting German which he'd learnt years ago at school and until recently he hadn't had many opportunities to use. Much to his surprise he had remembered enough to make himself understood.

'All around you,' the German replied with a smirk.

The sneer on his over-confident face heightened Anđa's anger. He smashed the soldier over the head with the butt of his rifle. As he fell to the ground Anđa pulled out his knife, grabbed his hair, yanked back his head and slit his exposed throat. He hoped he'd feel better after venting his anger. He didn't.

The next day Anđa's spirits plummeted lower when he learnt that the Germans were murdering their wounded and there was nothing he could do about it.

He also became conscious for the first time of what he and the men around him had become — scrawny, fatigued and unkempt — hardly recognisable as men — more like wild beasts.

Yet another change of direction was called for when Djido received an order to meet up with Tito.

They carried on — nothing had changed except their direction. They were existing on meagre rations, mostly salted mutton, supplemented by wild berries. Vegetables remained non-existent and by then many men had developed scurvy. A significant number complained that their bones and gums ached, they had sores on various parts of their bodies that wouldn't heal, they felt weak and their teeth had fallen out. Every night they slept on hard ground now that the Germans were no longer persuing them so closely. However, within hours they found themselves avoiding Četnik and Ustaše patrols.

When at last they caught up with Tito, who was staying in a village, Anđa was relieved. Djido went shooting and came back with half a dozen rabbits and there was milk to be had in the village. Anđa wasn't expecting meat other than the rabbits, but when Tito's cow stopped producing milk they shot it and ate freshly roasted beef — much to Tito's horror.

'She was my favourite cow. Why did you kill her without my permission?' Tito's voice was full of outrage. Djido was ready with an answer.

'Didn't you know she had a broken leg?' She didn't, but Djido knew if he didn't find a good reason for the slaughter Tito would punish someone for her death.

'Well, that's okay then,' Tito said.

The other luxury Anđa enjoyed was coffee. Someone had given Tito a bag of beans and he was generous enough to share it with his inner circle. Anđa would never forget the smell as it was brewing. 'Come on,' Tito said. 'There's enough for everyone. Don't let it get cold.'

As he fell asleep in a real bed for the first time in months Anđa hoped the worst was over. It wasn't.

Chapter eleven

It was March when Tito announced that he wanted to engage in a prisoner exchange with the Germans. In a mill house beside the River Rama in Bosnia, they were gathered around a scarred, timber dining table when Tito mooted his idea.

'I want to exchange that German officer and others for some of our people,' he said.

Anđa knew that Tito's common-law wife, Herta Hass was one of the prisoners being held by the Germans. As Anđa listened to Tito outlining what he wanted, it soon became obvious that the deal was complex.

'Are you hoping to come to an understanding with the Germans? An alliance or a truce?' Anđa asked as he leant forward in his seat, almost unable to believe what Tito was saying.

'Yes, if we agree not to attack them then I would be expecting them to allow us to destroy the *Četniks* in the east. The way I see it, that's the only chance we have of moving forward into the safety of Montenegro,' Tito replied.

'And what about the British? If they land would we take a stand against them alongside the Germans?' Anđa asked.

'Yes.' Tito's answer was blunt.

'I can only speak for myself, but if the British keep supporting the *Četniks* then I believe we'll have no choice but to fight them too,' Djido added. 'We've already had three unsuccessful attempts at reaching Montenegro and we've lost too many men.'

'I want you to do the negotiating, Djido. I suggest you call yourself Miloš Marković because if they figure out who you are they certainly won't let you go. I think your German is up to it,' Tito said.

'It's fairly basic,' Djido replied.

'I am not expecting you to hold an academic discussion about Goethe or Kant, you know,' Tito replied. 'You can take Velebit with you too. We don't want him to be identified either so he can call himself Dr Vladimir Metrović. His legal knowledge will be useful and so too will Koča Popovic and Anđa Milić. Koča and Anđa both speak some German, I believe.'

Djido winked at Anđa as nods of agreement went round the group seated at the table.

'Are you going to tell Stalin what you intend to do?' Djido asked.

'Yes, I will,'

'He won't agree to it,' Leko said.

'Too bad. They always consider their country and their army before anyone else. In fact, the sooner I tell them the better, then we can get on with it.'

The following day a one-line unpalatable response was received from Stalin. Vlad read it out to Tito. "Is it possible you will cease the struggle against the worst enemy of mankind?"

'Tell the delegates to get ready to leave at dawn tomorrow,' Tito said without further deliberation. Anđa took in the expression in his eyes — it was black enough to rival a thundercloud.

The sun was high in a bright-blue sky when all four Partisans were blindfolded at the German guard post and transported to Sarajevo.

Anđa was stuck in the back of a Mercedes Benz with a mouthy German lieutenant-general. 'Look what you've done to your own country. It's a wasteland. Women are begging in the streets, typhus is raging and your children are dying of hunger. And here we are trying to bring you roads, electricity and hospitals. What a shame you're so ungrateful,' he said with self-assurance.

Anđa so wanted to smash in his teeth. Instead he clamped his mouth shut and clenched his fists. He hadn't wanted to be part of the delegation, but when Tito gave orders they had to be obeyed no matter what.

That night the four of them were billeted in a flat beside the Miljacka River. A Serbian woman, who was a prisoner of war, cooked them an excellent meal with *čevapćići*, mashed *krumpir* and *kupus*. There was also a side dish of homemade *ajvar*. And to cap it off there was a poppy seed roll that had also been homemade. It was the best meal Anđa had tasted since he'd left Zagreb, yet he couldn't do it justice. His stomach had shrunk and he was forced to eat slowly when nausea and a feeling of fullness struck him. He wished he could have taken what he couldn't eat with him.

After dinner the cook left the four of them sitting around smoking in the shabby living room and discussing tactics for the meeting the following day.

It transpired that Djido was not entirely comfortable with what Tito had asked him to undertake. 'If the Germans grant us a truce and we're forced to say where our units are stationed we could be in for big problems. What guarantee do we have that they won't take advantage of that knowledge and attack us?' Djido said.

'None,' Anđa replied. 'I'd already had the same thought and it was reinforced by that bastard mouthing off in the car today. I couldn't get over his arrogance.'

'It's how most of them are,' Koča said as he fiddled with his overgrown moustache. 'They think they're the chosen race who are superior to the rest of us.'

'Bah!' Velebit said as he hawked and spat on the floor.

The next day the negotiations took place in a nondescript building that had once been part of the town council's offices before they had been commandeered by the German Army. The windows were all closed and the room was hot, stuffy and airless.

Three Germans were seated behind a rectangular wooden table — Major General Benignus Dippold, one of his staff officers and a representative from Hitler Youth. Anđa did not take in the names of the two subordinates. Instead, he was fixated on Dippold's bony, stern face and his fat fingers that looked like uncooked sausages.

To save time and any confusion with language, Anđa's delegation handed over a written statement as soon as the introductions had been made. They identified their prisoners and indicated the ones they wanted in exchange. The exchange was to take place as soon as possible. If it was accepted then they would reciprocate. Their statement said they considered the *Četniks* their enemies and they also proposed an armistice during the exchange, which had to be ratified and signed by a higher authority. In other words by Himmler in Germany and by Tito. The last clause of their statement said that under no circumstances was Germany to consider that the Partisans were offering to surrender.

There was limited discussion and Anđa listened as Djido stopped short of expressing their concerns about the Germans setting a trap for the Partisans. He focused on saying that the Partisans would fight the British if they landed and continued to support the *Četniks*.

Dippold was a man of few words and the meeting did not last long. 'I must relay your terms to my superiors which may take some days.'

Two days later when an agreement seemed to have been reached, although it was without any official signatures, the Partisan delegation returned to their headquarters where Djido and Anđa reported to Tito.

'The Germans have agreed to the exchange and say they will refrain from attacking our Partisans in western Bosnia,' Djido told Tito.

Tito grunted.

Anđa wondered why Tito had nothing to say. What did he know that they didn't? He thought about asking, then changed his mind.

All was revealed a couple of days later when the exchange fell through because Hitler disallowed it. "I don't do deals with rebels. Rebels must be shot," was his response. Anđa knew then that Tito must have known this was in the offing.

'What will happen to Herta now?' Anđa asked Djido because he didn't want to ask Tito in case it was a sore point after the negotiations had fallen through.

'Don't worry. Velebit has pulled some strings and he's exchanging her for a high-ranking German officer as we speak.'

'And her son?'

'Yes, him as well. Poor little bastard is only two.'

'Is Stari pleased?'

'I suppose so, although he didn't show much emotion when I told him. He has Zdenka now. I guess he's moved on.'

The trap that Djido and Anđa had suspected the Germans were setting was sprung a month later during the middle of a dark night when they attacked and almost succeeded in destroying Tito's group of Partisans who were still staying in a village. Once more Tito and his men were forced to retreat into the mountains.

Chapter twelve

It was January when Tito issued the order to annihilate the railway. Anđa recalled Tito saying earlier that they should desist from attacking villages of no consequence. Clearly Tito had his eye on a far more substantial target — the railway.

'Our offensive has begun, but if we are to succeed then it's imperative we destroy the Sarajevo-Mostar railway. We'll utilize four brigades to attack thirty miles of track,' Tito said as his eyes flashed. It was some time since Anđa had seen them look so green and alive.

Anđa found the slog from Montenegro particularly difficult. It took days. Yet again, he lost count of how many. He slept as he walked, and from time to time he caught himself before he stepped off the path or over a cliff. When his platoon could no longer continue because of extreme exhaustion, they halted and Anđa dropped into a ditch beside the road and slept.

In the morning he woke to find it would only be another half day before they reached their destination.

By late afternoon he was lying in the long grass in the sun next to a cliff in the village of Lukovac where they stayed and rested for three days. Even so, their arrival had not been without incident. The *Ustaše* had been alerted about their imminent arrival just on dark. After a skirmish, which resulted in the Partisans arresting seven of the enemy, the rest scarpered and were never seen again. They did not encounter any other significant opposition.

Lukovac was a wild area where the village was situated on a plateau between three mountains. The scenery was mostly unblemished by humans and Anđa took in the different greens of the forest, the lush pastures and the sparkling water in the stream. By contrast the village was unsightly — ramshackle and dirty — a disappointment given the untouched beauty surrounding it.

On the fourth day Anđa and his platoon moved to the outskirts of Bradina — an all-Serbian village where Pavelić had been born. He preferred not to dwell on that thought. It was too repulsive. Bradina was also one of the main railway junctions and the location of a tunnel.

The rain had ceased by eight o'clock that night when Tito joined Anđa and other comrades at the head of the battalion.

'We've never seen Partisans before, but you're welcome. We've heard of you,' the spokesman for the first group of locals they came across, said.

While one group of men swarmed a goods' train, which had what Anđa thought of as glowing fascist eyes and wheels already moving, Anđa, Djido and half-a-dozen men from Anđa's platoon stormed the station. The two employees inside were dumbstruck when Partisans ripped open the door and burst in. Anđa thought their appearance alone would have been enough to terrify anyone. Most were unshaven and dirty and all were brandishing rifles.

'You have nothing to fear,' Djido shouted. 'We're Partisans, friends of the people. We're not here to harm you.'

Not a single shot was fired as they seized the contents of the first warehouse — wagons with vast quantities of flour, oil, maize and beans that had belonged to the Italians.

Meanwhile two other platoons commenced smashing the track leading to Sarajevo using dynamite, which they discovered in another warehouse.

The third warehouse they entered was full of goods, which according to the stationmaster, were being sent to Germany by Pavelić. Anđa's eyes grew wide when he saw motorbikes, cloth, honey, apricots and cherries.

'Half must go to our hospitals,' Tito said. 'And when we finish there'll be extra rations for every man from every platoon here today.'

Anđa was transfixed by the goods, especially the food. He couldn't help salivating. They had already unearthed so much he thought that must be the end of the booty. It wasn't.

'Open the buffet car,' Tito ordered. Inside were sacks of biscuits, bottles of liqueurs and oranges. Nobody touched any of it. Instead they looked at Tito.

'Send all of it to the hospital,' he said before he went outside to supervise the destruction of the turntable for the locomotives.

Meanwhile, Anđa and his men carried on destroying the station while the workers and conductors stood aside and watched. In the midst of the pandemonium the telephone began ringing.

'Should I answer it?' the stationmaster asked.

'Find out who it is and what they want. Then I'll decide what to do,' Djido replied.

'It's one of the neighbouring stations wanting to know why the goods' train hasn't started.'

'Stand back,' Djido ordered as he smashed the offending telephone with the butt of his rifle. 'Get rid of the rest of them,' he said to Anđa.

When Anđa laid into the other two, chunks of black bakelite flew in all directions.

'So you're not *Četniks?*' one of the conductors asked.

'Of course not! Don't insult us. We told you, we're Partisans,' Anđa replied.

'Well, that's okay then,' the conductor said with a grin.

By the time Tito had decided enough destruction had been carried out, including the detonation of a fascist locomotive inside the tunnel – it's eyes were dead and no longer gleaming — it was almost two in the morning. By then reports had come in saying that the other three platoons had finished their work and Leko had set fire to the *Ustaše* headquarters in Bradina.

It was seven in the morning when Anđa's platoon started singing. However, this came to an abrupt end when they were attacked by a band of *Ustaše*. Fortunately, the Partisans had been vigilant and the guards they had posted on the perimeter of their camp picked up the noise made by the invaders as they were in the process of surrounding the camp. They alerted the rest of the camp immediately. The fighting was fierce, partly because Anđa and the Partisans around him were on a high from the successful destruction of the railway. They won the battle and took one hundred and twenty prisoners.

Later, there was plenty to celebrate and Anđa eventually went to sleep with a full stomach.

Chapter thirteen

Tito's birthday on May 25, passed without being acknowledged when the Germans launched another attack against his headquarters. Anđa, Tito and the members of the supreme command were living in a timber cottage at the mouth of a cave above Drvar.

Anđa had had an inkling that something was afoot when planes had flown over several times in the preceding days. When no bombs were dropped he assumed the planes were carrying out reconnaissance.

The air raid began at dawn when bombs fell from a cloudless, pale-blue sky and airborne troops parachuted to the ground. Anđa hastily smoked a cigarette as he waited for Tito's orders. There was no wind and smoke flared out of his nostrils and hung in the still morning air. The town itself was not guarded by Partisans, and this made it easy enough for the German soldiers to secure it. On Tito's orders Djido, Krištof and Leko retreated to a plateau above the cave while Tito and Anđa waited at the mouth of the cave for the return of the courier Tito had dispatched to report on what he had found in the town. He was taking longer than expected and Tito was impatient.

'Where the hell is he?' he shouted as he paced around in small circles in front of the cave. 'He should be back by now.'

'The track up the ravine is treacherous. The grass is slippery from last night's rain,' Anđa replied.

'I'll give him treacherous when he gets here!' Tito bellowed. His eyes were full of green-gold fire. Anđa remained silent. He knew that was the best option when Tito became annoyed.

Just then the courier lurched up the path clutching the rickety handrail. Blood trickled down his forehead and he looked as if it was a struggle to stay upright. He staggered drunkenly towards Anđa and Tito, then dropped dead at their feet.

Before either of them could react a shot rang out. When Anđa felt pain in his upper arm he knew he'd been hit.

'Let's go! Into the cave. It's our only chance. How badly have you been hit?' Tito said as his eyes calmed down and he looked at the blood on Anđa's shirt sleeve.

'The bullet's gone straight through — a flesh wound,' Anđa said as he gritted his teeth against the pain. 'I'll need to stem the blood flow.'

They moved into the cave and as soon as they were out of sight of the entrance Tito took off his jacket, removed his shirt, tore a strip off the tail and bound Anđa's arm above the bullet wound.

'Are you okay?' Tito asked in a gruff but concerned voice.

'I'll live. Have you been in here before? Where does it lead?'

'Don't know, but we're about to find out.' Tito took a small torch out of his pocket and turned it on. 'I asked for some rope to be stashed in here in case it might come in handy and I have a feeling I was right.' He shone the light on a coil of coarse rope nestled on a ledge against the wall on their right.

Anđa advanced towards it and was about to heave it over his good shoulder when Tito stopped him.

'I'll take it,' he said in a brusque voice.

With the aid of a weakening torch battery they progressed deeper into the cave and as they did the sound of gunfire diminished.

'At least the stream is dry,' Anđa said as they passed an outcrop of slimy rocks.

'It may well be, but there's water dripping in from somewhere,' Tito said as he touched the nearest moss-covered rock and his hand came away covered with brown slime. 'I don't know if moisture is a bad thing or not. We'll go on. We have no choice.'

Seven minutes later they stopped. They had picked their way along the widest tunnel; the further they went the wetter the cave became. It was then that the path narrowed and divided into two.

'Which way?' Anđa asked. As soon as the words were out of his mouth he knew they were futile.

'Got any more stupid questions?' Tito snapped as he turned off the torch.

'What the hell are you doing?' Anđa snapped back.

'I'm trying to see if it's my imagination of not, but I think the path on the right is lighter. What do you think?'

In silence they peered down each dark tunnel.

'That way,' Anđa said pointing towards the path on their right.

Tito grunted as he turned on the torch again and they moved forward. When the light increased Tito turned off the torch to conserve the remaining battery. The path they had taken led to an empty grotto that smelt of dead or decaying animals. Anđa saw a pile of bones with dry, taut skin attached below a ledge that jutted out from one wall. He assumed some unfortunate animal must have fallen in and couldn't get out. The grotto wasn't as slimy as where they had come from and water trickled intermittently down the wall opposite where they were standing. They both looked up at the same time through the hole above their heads. The rope was all very well, thought Anđa, but there was nothing to attach it to.

'There's our escape route, but how the hell do we get up there? I'd suggest you stand on my shoulders, but you still wouldn't be able to reach the lip of the opening,' Tito said.

When the voices came, Tito and Anđa looked at each other and flattened themselves against the wall behind them. As they came nearer to the opening the voices became clearer.

'If I'm not mistaken it's Krištof and Djido,' Tito said with a grin. 'Hey!' he shouted. 'Down here. Can you see us?'

Anđa moved and stood underneath the opening and moments later Djido's bushy, dark head appeared above the hole alongside Krištof's solemn, bespectacled face.

'We have a rope,' Tito called out. 'I'll throw it up. You'll need to secure it and get us out. Anđa's been shot in the arm, so we'll get him out first.'

Thirty minutes later they were both standing on dry ground on the plateau above the cave. Anđa was lightheaded when Krištof took off the tourniquet on his arm to retie it.

'Here, sit on this rock before you fall over,' Krištof said as he steadied Anđa. The effort of hauling himself up the rope combined with the shock had taken its toll on Anđa, the wound was bleeding and he had broken out in a sweat. It had been impossible to climb the rope using only one hand and he'd had to grit his teeth, ignore the pain in his injured arm and use it. Every time he moved the wounded arm it was agony.

The attempt to capture Tito was unsuccessful. 'You know if the German's had dropped their men on the plateau above the cave they probably would have succeeded in catching Stari,' Anđa said to Krištof as he sat and waited for his strength to return.

The attack on Drvar continued for ten days and once it was over Tito decided to shift his headquarters yet again. The new the destination would be much more remote and secure — the island of Vis.

Chapter fourteen

At last Anđa was going home, if only for a few days. Once his leave was over he would liase with Krištof and Leko to coordinate the Partisans in Slovenia and Croatia in an attempt to free Belgrade from German occupation.

As soon as he arrived in Zagreb he went to a clothing store frequented by the central committee and bought new clothes. He couldn't turn up at home in his tattered rags. There was nothing he could do about his weight loss, but he could at least make himself presentable.

His mood was buoyant and he whistled a tune as he set out on his trek home. The sunny day matched his mood and he delighted in the sight of the immense-blue sky. He was two streets away from his house when he heard the first shout. It sounded as though someone was calling his name. He ignored it and sped up his pace. When the voice came again he ran. But it was to no avail. The *Ustaše* had set a trap for him and were waiting around the next corner — four of them with their weapons drawn. He halted.

'Milić, you prick! We've got you, at last,' one of them said. 'It's taken a while, but good things come to those who wait.' He bared his rotten teeth below his Hitler-like moustache.

'Get on with it then,' Anđa said. 'Put me out of my misery and shoot me.' His chin was up and his voice was strong despite knowing it was the end.

'Oh no! We have a different punishment in store for you. A long slow death in a place from which there is no escape.'

It was then that the other three lunged and grabbed him. With his hands tied behind his back they marched him away in the opposite direction. As he walked he wondered how they had found him. Somebody must have betrayed him. There was no other answer. Who it could have been, he had no idea. He would never find out and what did it matter. Ascertaining who it was wouldn't help him out of his predicament. As to where they were taking him — he knew, he just knew. Their words told him. He hoped he died swiftly — with a bit of luck his throat would be slit — like so many others who'd been taken there before him.

Chapter fifteen

When the Italians capitulated Mara dared to hope the war would end. Yet Yugoslavia was not free. Belgrade and Zagreb were still in German hands. Every night when she went to bed she prayed, while every morning when she got up she turned on her radio hoping and hoping for a catastrophic event that would end the war.

It came on the first of May — Hitler committed suicide. Once he was dead, Mara knew it wouldn't be long before the war was over. She was alone in her kitchen when she heard the news. 'Bloody good riddance — you murderous bastard!' she shouted and cheered. As each day passed she waited anxiously, while at night she lay awake with her fingers crossed for the safe return of her husband and her eldest son.

It was a week after the death of Hitler when Germany surrendered to the Allies and Pavelić's fascist government collapsed. Tito's men freed Zagreb first and then Belgrade. When Mara listened to Tito's speech on the radio and heard him say, "Glory to the fighters who fell for the liberation of Yugoslavia," she cried. Glory was no compensation for the loss of her husband and son.

Ecstatic that the war was finally over, on May 10, Mara and her family set out for Trg bana Jelačića to join the crowd to give the Partisans a rousing welcome. It was an unusually muggy day with a hot wind that had sprung up just after dawn. Dust devils danced along the streets as they walked.

The night before Mara hadn't been keen on going.

'But *Majka* you must come,' Damir said.

'If you don't then we'll go without you. It's a historic occasion. We have to be there,' Zoran added.

Mara looked at her sons. They might have been thin from lack of food, but at least for the first time in ages they were smiling. It was then that it occurred to her that Anđa and Ivan could be with the Partisans who were flooding into the city. Perhaps she would be able to find them. Then she realised the absurdity of the thought. It would be like looking for a white rabbit in a snowstorm. That didn't stop her harbouring a futile hope.

As the four of them stood sandwiched in the midst of the jubilant tide of people she was all eyes as groups of Partisans rode by on horseback or trudged along the thoroughfare with grinning, weather-beaten faces — none were familiar.

By the time she and her family were on their way home she was exhausted. The walking and her expectations had taken their toll, but notwithstanding, as she drew closer to home, hope sparked again. This time it occurred to her that Anđa and Ivan might already have arrived at home. For the duration of the war she had told herself that the authorities would surely have notified her if they were dead. Yet she'd heard nothing — less than nothing.

She turned her key in the lock and listened. Silence shouted at her. With weary steps she went inside.

As day turned into evening she became more and more miserable. She'd been certain that they would return now that the war was over. If Zoran, Damir and Zlata were thinking about their father and brother it wasn't obvious. That evening they were having a party to celebrate the end of the war. Zlata had baked a cake and Zoran had found some cheap wine, a drink they hadn't seen much of since the war began. They had invited a handful of their friends. Well mostly Zoran and Damir's friends plus Zlata and Marija.

Mara took herself off to bed early and left them to their fun. As she lay in bed listening to their laughter floating up the stairs she recalled the conversation she'd had with Zlata earlier in the day.

'When will Tata and Ivan be home?' she'd asked.

'Soon, I hope,' Mara replied.

'I know that, but which day?' she persisted.

'If I knew that I would have told you, wouldn't I? You'll have to be patient.' Mara's tone was curt, but if Zlata noticed she didn't comment.

'I'm so excited.' Zlata was bubbling over with expectation.

Chapter sixteen

Anđa didn't know how many months he'd been incarcerated. In the beginning he'd made marks on the wall beside his wooden bunk, but then as fatigue set in he couldn't remember whether he'd marked the current day or not; then sometimes he couldn't find anything to use to make the mark, while on other days he was too exhausted and depressed. He didn't dwell on it, but he couldn't believe he was still alive.

Everyday he was contained in the line of men who were marched out of the barracks to participate in forced labour. Carrying rocks to build a dam was the usual task he was compelled to take part in. He kept his head down and did his best to keep his pace steady in the hope he wouldn't be noticed, singled out, picked on and murdered. The authorities knew he was a communist — and a Serb. He imagined sooner rather than later that they'd kill him — one way or another. In his more miserable moments he wondered how he would die — it was possible he could drop dead from fatigue and overwork, but there were a number of other options — he could be hanged from the "poplar of sighs" at the mouth of the Una River, burnt to death, beaten to death with a cow-hide whip, trampled to death, bashed over the head with an iron bar or a wooden or metal hammer. He knew he wouldn't be struck on the head with a hoe — that was reserved for old people, sickly inmates and children. He'd seen prisoners die by all these methods. In earlier times he thought his time fighting with the Partisans had been the worst he'd ever endured but being incarcerated where he was now, far exceeded that. He was nothing more than an emaciated skeleton who had no idea how he continued to function from day to day let alone stay alive.

The first inkling he had that something had changed came when the camp was bombed by aircraft that he hoped were Partisan. He dearly wanted to rush outside to cheer, but an afternoon shift of inmates who had been been on their way to work in the labour camp had been struck by a bomb and were lying dead not far from his barracks.

'Poor bastards,' he mumbled under his breath as he watched the chaos from the doorway. *But maybe it's a blessing in disguise.* It was then that he momentarily thought about rushing outside in the hope that the next bomb would kill him. He didn't. Instead he trudged over to his bunk and sat down on the lumpy straw-filled mattress. Around him his fellow prisoners were in an agitated state.

'I'm going to make a run for it,' a man who had once been fat but now had a face that was a mass of hanging loose flesh, said.

'Where to?' another said as he cleaned the cracked lens of his battered glasses on the tail of his filthy shirt.

'Are you mad?' a third nervous character who always spoke with a stutter, said.

Anđa said nothing. He seldom joined in the conversations. He felt it was safer if he kept to himself.

'I've made up my mind. The guards are nowhere to be seen. I wouldn't be surprised if they've already left,' the first man said as he stood up and strode to the door. 'It's now or never,' he said as he walked outside. When he broke into a run he got no further than a few paces before a guard materialised seemingly out of nowhere and gunned him down.

Anđa hung his head when the shots rang out. The stuttering inmate who had gone to the doorway spoke and pronounced the would-be escapee dead. Groans and sighs erupted around Anđa.

It was the following day when inmates began leaving — not by choice. They were being transferred to other prisons. It was evening when inmates Simon Bittel and Silvio Alkalaj announced that they'd heard Belgrade had been liberated.

'They're talking about it in the kitchen,' Simon said as he scratched at the grey stubble on his chin with a grime-blackened hand. The time has come to plan our escape. How many of you are in with me and Silvio?' he asked.

The conversation that ensued sounded like the buzz of bees as the men in Anđa's barracks debated quietly what to do.

'Of course, there'll be reprisals when we go. Any of you who are left will be killed ... He looked around at the sea of faces from under the lock of lank, greasy hair that hung over his forehead. 'We have poison if you don't want to go. Simon has tested it on a dog. He licked it and died on the spot,' Silvio said.

Anđa looked around the room when he heard the sharp intake of breaths and saw jaws drop. 'I'll go,' he said as he stepped forward. 'What's the plan? I assume you have one.'

'We go tonight. The wire on the perimeter next to the tannery was cut this morning. We will make for the river and the boats they use to transport logs. The boats can only take twelve, so we need another nine. The rest of you can take your chances on foot through the forest or as I said there's the poison …'

Anđa dipped the paddle into the water as soundlessly as he could. He thought they'd got away undetected, but when he heard shouting he knew they had failed. He glanced over his shoulder and saw *Ustaše* guards following them in a boat which had a motor. They were gaining on the escapees and it would be no more than minutes before they were caught.

Anđa dropped his paddle into the bottom of the boat and slipped over the side into the oily-dark water. It was cold but not so cold that it chilled his body. No one followed his example and as he swam towards the shore he heard Simon urging the men with him to paddle harder. Anđa was crawling out of the water onto the river bank through slippery mud when the first shots rang out and he heard cries from the men in the boat. He could smell the pine trees and he stumbled as fast as he could towards them. The short swim had taken the last of his energy and his heart was beating fast. He had no idea where he was going, but he had to get off the river bank and out of sight. In a dense grove of trees he hesitated and looked about. A vast darkness surrounded him, although there was enough light to see where he was going. He paused and looked left then right. Which direction should he head? He had no idea. Voices close by made him decide in an instant. He shimmied up the nearest giant aleppo pine and climbed as high as he could and did his best to secrete himself behind a thick branch in the fork of the tree. He had only been there for a short time when the voices came closer and were audible.

'If you give yourself up we won't harm you,' one of the guards called out. Anđa recognised his voice. It was the one who had boils on his neck. 'We've killed all the other escapees. You don't want to suffer that fate, do you? Be sensible and give yourself up now — while you have the chance.'

Anđa could see the *Ustaše* mongrels — wandering in circles below him slashing at the vegetation — three cold-blooded bastards. He kept still and didn't move a muscle until agonising cramp struck his left calf and he was forced to change his position. As he did so he knocked loose a pine cone which clattered through the branches as it fell to the ground. He held his breath, aware that if they looked up, he'd be dead.

'What was that?' one of the men shouted.

'I didn't hear anything,' another said.

'You're deaf, so you wouldn't — you moron,' the guard with the boils on his neck shouted.

'It'll be the badger I disturbed. It's over there. Look at it's eyes shining,' the third guard said as he raised his rifle and blew the badger into bloody pieces.

Anđa shuddered and let out a small sigh of relief.

'Come on,' Boil Neck, who seemed to be in charge, said. 'We can't stay here all night to look for one miserable bastard. We'll tell the commander we shot the lot of them. He won't know any different and this guy will be caught sooner or later by one of our patrols or he'll starve to death.'

Anđa stayed put for what seemed like an eternity. His clothing was wet, he'd begun to shiver and his muscles had seized up. Once he was certain it was safe he took his time and made his way down the tree. When he reached the ground he spent time considering his location in relation to the camp. He knew there was a village called Ivanjski Bok in the north-west direction and without further delay he set off that way. He had brought nothing with him except a small carving he'd put in his trouser pocket for good luck before he'd left the barracks. He patted his pocket to make sure it was still there.

Four hours later it was the early hours of the morning when he saw the first sign of habitation. He stopped and surveyed the scene. The moon had come out and enabled him to see a group of rundown dwellings clustered together in among sparse-spindly vegetation. He crept forward — intent on doing so silently — he had no intention of making his presence known. The first house he came to had no window panes and appeared uninhabited when he peered through the window. In fact, it didn't look as if anyone had been living there for some time. He moved on and checked more dwellings. They were all abandoned. When he began to shake from cold, hunger and shock, all he wanted to do was sleep, but not where he could be found. He retraced his steps until he came to a barn he'd passed earlier. In the back corner away from the door, he made a nest out of hay behind a wooden plough and settled down to sleep.

He woke with a raging thirst and he felt hot. As he turned over he was dismayed to find that he had a fever. He touched his forehead — it was hot — too hot and his body was so hot that his clothes had dried and gone stiff. He lay still for some time listening to the sounds of birds until his thirst drove him out in search of water. He stumbled to his feet and on weak legs he staggered outside. The sky was an untarnished blue and the sun was warm. He shaded his eyes against the glare from the yellow orb which was high in the sky.

In the kitchen of the nearest house he came across a tap in a stone sink. He turned it on and rusty water trickled out. The tank it was connected to outside was riddled with bullet holes; fortunately they were only in the upper section. He ran the water until it was clear before he filled a tin mug and drank it, hoping like hell that the water wasn't poisoned. It was cool and felt good on his parched throat, so he drank another cup while he looked for a container he could fill and take back to the barn. He found a large empty ceramic jar with a wooden lid and filled it before he traipsed back to the barn. He was feeling weaker and assumed his temperature had risen because he had broken out in a renewed sweat.

In the barn he fell into a feverish doze as his temperature rose higher.

It was dark when he woke briefly before he lost consciousness with the untouched water container beside him.

Four days had passed while he'd been delirious. When at last he woke his temperature had gone down, yet he was so feeble he could barely sit up — however, he made himself. Propped against the wall he drank his way through the entire container of water before he broke out in an attack of the shakes and had to lie down again.

Hours later, he knew that if he was to survive he must have food. It was then that he recalled seeing a small quantity of wheat in a bin in the kitchen. With strength he didn't know he possessed he made his way to the kitchen where he found yellowed newspaper and wood and lit a fire in the old stove. When his pot of water was hot enough he added the wheat and cooked it until he had a pot full of gruel. He carried it back to the barn with unsteady hands, and over the next two days he ate the gruel a little at a time and continued to drink water. On the day when his hunger finally returned he knew he was on the road to recovery. All that remained was to get himself strong enough to make the journey back to Zagreb without getting caught. Yet, he knew it would be days if not weeks before he had enough strength to make the journey which was a hundred kilometres. Could he stay in the deserted village undetected for that long? He hoped so provided the smoke from his cooking fire was not seen.

It was early morning on a warm spring day when he ventured outside to explore. He was debating which way to go when he smelt a terrible stink. It didn't take him long to figure out where it was coming from — his body and clothes were putrid. He added washing to his list of jobs. He wandered the length of the track between the houses and when it ended he came to a small orchard where many of the trees were smothered with new growth and blossoms. He was about to turn back when he saw a pear tree. He fought his way through waist-high, lush-green grass and a closer inspection proved worthwhile when he found several pears that were half rotten but had partially edible flesh. He devoured three and as juice dripped down his chin, he made a mental note to come back and pick the rest.

He was on his way back to the barn when he encountered a splendid white goose. He stopped when it turned hostile and hissed at him. Unsure how dangerous it was he retreated a few paces and waited. It honked a few times and then lost interest in him and walked away between two dilapidated houses. Anda followed it at what he thought was a safe distance until the goose disappeared inside the window of a house. He peered inside and watched its plump body waddle over to a mound of straw. Anda smiled for the first time in days when he spotted the egg nestled in the straw. He licked his lips as he thought about frying it and eating it — then there was the goose. How many meals would it provide? He was salivating by the time he hoisted himself in the window determined to corner the big bird and wring its neck.

Chapter seventeen

It was a fine summer's day with a light breeze after the end of the war; Mara was hanging out the washing when she glimpsed a skeletal figure limping along the street carrying a battered knapsack. She ignored him. It wasn't until he opened the rickety-wooden gate that led from the street to the building where she lived that she knew it was her husband. She dropped the pegs and the sheet she was holding and ran.

After a long wordless embrace they walked inside hand in hand.

Although all she wanted was to ask him a hundred questions — she didn't. Instead, she went to find him clean clothes. Her husband followed her up the stairs and while she rummaged through the clothes in the wardrobe Anđa took the meagre contents out of his knapsack and stowed them inside the sea chest. After he had locked it, Mara watched as he prised up the loose board in the floor under the window and put the key inside the small wooden box secreted there.

Tears rolled down Mara's face at the sight of her husband's body as he got into the bath. He was so thin she could see his skeleton through his skin. The tip of the first finger on his right hand was missing and there was a bluey-purple lump on his right wrist where a bullet was lodged under the skin and there was a large, indented scar on his right bicep. Worse than his physical changes was the alteration in his personality. The gleam that had once been in his eyes was gone and they were so dead it was as though he was still inhabiting the far-away place he had recently left. Mara wondered what her children, particularly Zlata, would think when they encountered their *new* father.

While her husband was in the bath, Mara prepared a meal — boiled *krumpir* and *blitva*. She had nothing else to offer him. As she peeled the potatoes she wondered what to ask him first. Then she decided that perhaps it would be better if she just let him talk.

For a time Anđa did nothing other than occupy himself eating slowly. Mara knew he was savouring every bite. It was obvious that he probably hadn't had anything that substantial for some considerable time.

As she sat opposite and watched him eat, she opened her mouth to speak several times then shut it until at last she plucked up sufficient courage.

'They came looking for you,' she said.

'The *Ustaše?*'

'Yes. They searched the house.'

'Did they find the chest?'

'Yes, one of them opened it after I told him it was empty.'

Anđa stopped eating and looked at his wife. 'They didn't search it?'

'No, it seemed to be sufficient when I said it was empty.'

'It will stay locked from now on,' he said.

'They took Ivan when they couldn't find you.'

Anđa stopped chewing and looked at his wife. 'I know,' he replied in a quiet voice.

'You've seen him? Where is he?' she asked as she sat up straighter and leant towards him.

He looked up from staring into his cup. His eyes were dull and his right hand, which was holding his cup clumsily, was shaking. When he finished his mouthful and began to drink the second cup of tea she had poured him and he hadn't explained how he knew that they had taken Ivan, she had to ask. 'Where is he?'

'In an unmentinonable place that I can't talk about,' he replied.

'But where?' she persisted as she became more and more anxious and her eyes filled with tears.

Anđa ignored her question and instead began to talk about the night he left. She didn't learn much, his account was sketchy and brief before he stopped speaking. Mara waited as he sighed and rubbed his eyes.

'I feel as if I'm about a hundred-years-old.' He paused. 'Djido and Krištof are okay. Aleksa is dead.'

'Never mind them. Where's Ivan?' The look he gave her and the tremor that shook his body drove her on. She had to know. 'He's dead, isn't he?'

'Yes,' he said quietly and with hesitation before he paused and stared straightahead with a glazed look in his eyes. 'What time do the children come home?'

Mara couldn't move. She was as frozen as the ice on Lake Jarun as tears streamed down her face. 'Are you going to tell me about it?' she asked when she had composed herself sufficiently to speak. 'Tell me about it now, please,' she begged in an almost incoherent choked-up voice as she looked at the clock on the wall. 'Zlata should be here quite soon. I need to know before she gets here.'

'Later.' Anđa's voice was flat and he was staring into his empty cup as he spoke. 'Later,' he repeated and looked at her with a look that told her he didn't want to say more.

'No, now,' she said as she looked at him with beseeching eyes.

There was a long pause before Anđa spoke. 'He's dead. I've already told you.'

Mara stifled a cry by biting her fist. 'Please, what happened to him?'

'Isn't it enough to know he's gone? Why do you need to know more? That won't bring him back.'

'He's my first born. I have to know.'

'Woman! Don't you realise how hard it is for me to talk about this. You're making me relive it all over again.'

'I'm sorry, but I have to know. Don't you understand?' Mara's tears flowed unchecked down her ravaged face.

Anđa sighed. 'He was shot for disobeying orders. You know what he was like. Always had a mind of his own, like his mother …' His voice trailed away.

'Are you blaming me?'

'Of course not. I was proud of his defiance. He held his head up till the very end.' Anđa swallowed and broke out in a fit of coughing.

'Where is his grave?'

'Enough! Isn't it sufficient that I've told you your son is dead and he died a hero.' He paused. 'Look, I'm sorry for raising my voice. But I don't know where he's buried and there's no way I can find out.' He reached across the table for her hand. 'There's no more I can tell you. I'm sorry.'

They both fell silent and all that could be heard was Mara's anguished sobs.

'Where's Zlata?' Anđa asked at length.

'What?'

'I said, where's Zlata?'

'She's been at Marija's place for a couple of days and the boys should be here about six. They're working … in a factory that makes electrical parts … they've been there since

January.' Mara twisted her handkerchief around her fingers as she tried to compose herself before Zlata came in.

'Is Zlata still at Marija's?' he asked.

Mara nodded. 'She's not had the best health while you've been away. She helps me in the house most days. She's been at school off and on. She's had a lot of time off, but at least her arithmetic marks are good.'

She was surprised when Anđa made no comment, he didn't even ask what was wrong with her. He continued to stare at nothing. Her mind went back to her eldest son — she couldn't take in what Anđa had told her and a small part of her hoped he was wrong. 'How do you know he's …' She couldn't bring herself to say the word.

Anđa was slow to answer. 'Because I was there when he died.' He stood up and as he did so the legs of his chair made a screeching sound that jangled Mara's nerves as he pushed it backwards and it scraped on the floor. He walked towards the door.

'Where are you going?'

'To get Zlata.'

Mara watched his skeletal figure retreat. When the door closed she put her face in her hands and sobbed. 'Where are you Ivan?' she cried out.

It was a bittersweet evening as the family minus Ivan sat down to a dinner of vegetable soup and a loaf of bread that Zlata had been given by Marija's mother. It was at the beginning of the meal that Anđa put a stop to answering any questions about where he'd been.

'The last four years are in the past and I'm not going back there so don't ask me to. I won't talk about it — any of it. We need to look to the future now that peace is here.' His voice was halting and it required concentration to hear him clearly.

'But *Tata* … what about Ivan?' Damir said before his mother cut him off.

'You heard what your father said. Please respect his wishes. What about football Damir. Tell your father about your last game.'

'Yes *Tata*, where is Ivan? When's he coming home?' Zlata asked.

Silence descended over them as the rest of the family waited for Anđa to answer.

'Your mother will tell you,' Anđa stammered as he stood up hastily, strode out of the room and hurried upstairs.

As soon as he was gone the other children turned to their mother and implored her with their eyes.

'Is he ... coming back?' Zoran asked.

'I'm afraid not,' she said in a diminished voice, whereupon Zlata screamed.

'He's dead, isn't he?' Zlata wailed and promptly fainted.

When Anđa came downstairs almost an hour later he was greeted by his grief-stricken family. Zoran and Damir were sitting red-eyed in silence on one sofa while Mara and Zlata were huddled together on the other one. As yet Mara had not been able to stem the flow of her daughter's tears or silence her gasping sobs.

'Tell me about your football,' Anđa said to his sons as he sat down next to Zlata. The talk was half-hearted and Anđa hardly spoke. He gave the odd nod as Damir and Zamir talked lacklusterly about the defeats and successes of their team. Mara watched her husband and at times she wasn't sure he was listening. His eyes seemed fixed on something invisible and the dull expression in them unnerved her. Zlata was quiet during the rest of the evening as she clung to her father and he stroked her hair — at last she had calmed down. Perhaps it was temporarily sufficient that her father was home. Mara couldn't imagine the shock on her daughter's face when her father had turned up at Marija's house; she could almost hear the scream she would have let out when she recognised him.

Mara was anxious to retire and her husband had only just got into bed when she spoke.

'Tell me more,' she said.

'I can't.' He paused. 'I've told you all that I know. There's nothing left to tell.'

'Did you get to talk to him?'

'No, but he knew I was there ... at the end. He saw me and he raised his hand.' Anđa's voice cracked and his words ceased.

No sooner had he finished speaking when Zlata screamed.

Mara got out of bed hurriedly. When she opened Zlata's bedroom door Zlata was crouched in the corner of her room sobbing.

'Oh my dear. What is it?'

'A nightmare ... a terrible nightmare,' Zlata stammered.

Mara took her daughter's hand and forced her to stand up. When she turned her husband was standing behind her; they looked at each other wordlessly.

'You'll have to sleep in Zlata's bed tonight. Take her, please. Put her in our bed. I must get her something to help her sleep.'

Mara never imagined that on his first night back in their home her husband would sleep in his daughter's bed while Zlata slept drugged next to her, while she didn't sleep at all.

Chapter eighteen

Mara continued to live in fear regardless of the war being over even though her husband tried to persuade her that they would be safe because of his position in Tito's Central Committee.

'It's as if the war is continuing,' she said.

'You know it's over.'

'Then why are so many people still being killed. What if they come for us when you're not here?'

'They won't. I'll make sure of that.'

'I don't understand why so many are being accused of collaborating with the Germans when they didn't. Is it Tito's idea to kill them?'

'No,' Anđa said. 'It was not a decision made by Tito or the central committee. It's mass hysteria.'

'I wish you didn't have that job. It's dangerous. People know where you work and they look at me strangely.'

'Well, it's what I do. You'll have to accept that. Be glad you're not in my place.'

Mara was aware her husband seemed preoccupied, but what about she had no idea.

'Tito will be making an announcement to put an end to what's been going on, so things should get better,' he said.

Mara thought Tito's voice sounded strangely angry when his short speech was broadcast over the radio.

"Enough of all these death sentences and all this killing. The death sentence no longer has any effect. Too many have died. No one fears death any more," he said.

Mara couldn't grasp the meaning of his words. 'Surely everyone is afraid of dying, aren't they?' she asked.

'No. I can't explain to you what he means. You'd have to have gone through what I have to understand it.'

'It's a pointless statement anyway. Look at how many people have died. His words won't bring them back, will they?'

Anđa didn't answer.

Anđa had been anxious for days with thoughts about the man who had been taken into custody that morning. Aloysius Stepinac, the Archbishop of Zagreb, had been arrested and charged with high treason and collaboration with Pavelić's fascist government.

Taking part in his capture had been too difficult for Anđa. He had conflicting emotions. He was positive that Stepinac was guilty, and he was ashamed that a man of God had committed such heinous crimes. If he'd been given the opportunity he thought he could have easily killed Stepinac. Thankfully Tito hadn't insisted he take part in the arrest. Regardless, Anđa did attend Stepinac's trial in the Yugoslav Supreme Court.

In the silent courtroom, he stared at Stepinac's smooth face and the strip of thin hair that covered his mostly bald head. Obsequious was the word that came into Anđa's mind as he took him in and noted the dark panda-like circles around his eyes. Were they the result of fatigue or did he have a health issue?

When the questioning by the public prosecutor began, the defendant stared straightahead at nothing, declining to look at the prosecutor or anyone else in the courtroom.

'Accused Stepanic, do you know how many Serbs were rebaptised from the Orthodox to the Catholic faith during the occupation?' the prosecutor asked.

'I do not know,' Stepinac replied.

Anđa let out a loud sigh. The questions had only just begun and it was clear that Stepinac had no intention of cooperating. As the session progressed Anđa heard him repeat the words, 'I do not know' so many times he couldn't keep count. When he began to repeat, 'I fulfilled my patriotic duty and my conscience is clear,' Anđa wondered how long he could sit still. Then towards the end of the hearing when Stepinac read out his statement, this proved too much for Anđa. He got up and left. He was not present when the court sentenced Stepinac to sixteen years hard labour in the Lepoglava Prison.

Once Stepinac had been sentenced there was one man left who Anđa dearly wanted to kill — Pavelić. He had developed a fierce hatred for that fascist bastard and held him responsible for the death of his son. Unfortunately, he would never get the chance to kill

Pavelić or enjoy the spectacle of seeing him shot by firing squad or strung up. Pavelić, along with countless other fascists had escaped from Yugoslavia. Tito's men had come close to catching him when he went into hiding before his departure. They'd received a tip-off that he was secreted in a house in the interior of Bosnia near the village where he was born. By the time they got there someone had warned him and he had fled — apparently to Italy. He'd gone to Rome pretending to be a priest and travelling on a Peruvian passport in the name of Don Pedro Gonner. Tito tried to have him extradited but the Catholic Church were giving him protection and refused to give him up. If Mussolini had been alive, no doubt he too would have given him refuge.

'I've enlisted the help of the CIA,' Tito said when Anđa discussed the subject with him as only the two of them sat in Anđa's living room at the conclusion of a Communist Party meeting there. 'We thought we had him in Naples, but yet again the slippery fish got away. This time to Argentina. The worst of it is he is carrying on with his fascist activities.' Tito drained his tea cup. 'We'll have to keep an eye on him and bide our time.'

'Do you have someone tracking his movements?'

'I certainly do and if he goes anywhere where he's vulnerable we'll nab him.'

'Or kill him,' Anđa said. 'He's one bastard who deserves to die several times over.'

Tito didn't answer. Instead he gave Anđa one of his long intense stares — his eyes were compassionate.

Mihailović was still at large a year after the end of the war. In the last days of the Partisan offensive against the Germans he had escaped into Serbia with a few thousand of his men. The morale of his soldiers was poor and slowly but surely they deserted him. The Central Committee, which continued to meet at Anđa's house, if they were meeting in Zagreb, rather than Belgrade where Tito was living, received regular reports about him from his followers who had surrendered or been caught.

'He is continuously on the move, going from village to village searching for food and shelter,' one of his sergeants who had given himself in, said.

Tito gave explicit orders to Mihailović's pursuers. 'I want him captured alive. I have it on reliable authority that only four of his men are with him now.'

He was finally captured and taken to Belgrade after he left the foxhole where he was hiding.

As soon as Mihailović arrived Anđa and Leko went to see him in his prison cell. Anđa recoiled from the smell emanating from him as he stared at the filthy, half-starved, pathetic excuse for a man.'

'I know you,' Mihailović said as his alert eyes bored holes in Anđa.

'Yes, you do,' Anđa replied. 'I came to see you more than once to talk about you fighting the occupiers of our country. You declined and went on to become the worst traitor to the fatherland during the most dreadful days of our lives.'

Mihailović looked at the ground. He had nothing to say for himself other than to ask for a bath and clean underwear.

His trial was held in public and while Anđa attended it, Mara listened to it on the radio — it was broadcast from beginning to end. When he was condemned to death, Mihailović asked for a pardon. It was not granted. Anđa would never forget witnessing his execution.

That night he returned home with a white face. As soon as he came in the door Mara asked the question that she couldn't hold back. 'Was it ... you know ... bad?'

'He was a pitiful sight. Distraught, out of his mind and not at all courageous,' Anđa said in a quiet voice as he shook his head.

He didn't eat much of his meal even though Mara had cooked a splendid one using the Red Cross food parcel she had uplifted that day. She'd made homemade gnocchi using the flour and dried herbs from the parcel and she had made *kroštule* for desert. Although he thanked her for a splendid meal he was largely silent as he pushed food around his plate rather than eating it. It wasn't until they were in bed when Anđa finally spoke.

'I'm going to Moscow with Stari in a few days' time,' he said hesitantly because he was certain she wouldn't like it.

'Why you? You've never been sent there before.'

'Djido is unwell. I'm taking his place in the delegation.'

'Will you be meeting Stalin?'

'Yes, that's the idea.'

'Are you looking forward to it? I wonder what he's like.'

'We'll see ... we'll see.'

Chapter nineteen

The weather was gloomy and wet even though it was the spring. It was 1948 when after almost two days of travelling, Anđa, Tito, Krištof, Leko and their party arrived at the railway station in Moscow where they were met by Molotov and Stephanov, two of Stalin's highest ranking officials. Stephanov hovered in the background. Anđa had not met Molotov before and found him a stern-looking individual with his Hitler-like moustache and spectacles perched on the end of his nose. Neither did anything to enhance his appearance.

It wasn't long after they had arrived when it became clear that when Stalin received you, it was with virtually no notice. It was on the night that the Yugoslav delegation were attending an opera at the Bolshoi Theatre that Anđa met Stalin for the first time. One minute they were in the middle of watching the opera and half an hour later they were greeting Stalin.

In the Kremlin, Anđa walked the length of a wide hallway on red carpet that ran along the centre like a river of blood, while ornate chandeliers cast a light that tinged everything with a pale-yellow glow including the gold and white walls. He and his delegation were eventually led into a conference room with a long table and twelve chairs. This room had a plaster and gold elaborate ornamental ceiling, more chandeliers, faded strawberry-coloured fabric walls and a dazzling parquet floor. Anđa found it pompous yet menacing.

Stalin was much shorter than Anđa had expected. He'd seen photos of him which had led him to believe he was tall. He wondered if Stalin stood on a box when he had his photo taken. Stalin's shoulders were sloping — as if he had a physical deformity — this caused him to hold his arms away from his body. When he smiled his teeth were yellow, but then again who was Anđa to comment — half of his were missing. Stalin was dressed in a buttoned-up vest and his trousers were tucked into shiny boots. His clothing was made of fine quality beige fabric and there were prefect creases down the fronts of his trouser legs. When he shook hands with him Stalin looked him up and down. Anđa found it unnerving.

Once everyone was seated at the table Stalin began to doodle on the pad in front of him. Anđa thought it was an irritating, rude habit and wondered why he indulged in it. When Stalin began a protracted conversation about the delegation's journey to come to Moscow Anđa assumed it was a delaying tactic. But why did he need one?

Then Stalin asked about Djido. 'Why isn't Đjilas here?'

'He's unwell. Nothing serious. He needed to rest so Anđa is here in his place,' Tito said as Stalin fixed his beady eyes and yellow-toothed smile on Anđa.

Anđa listened as the conversation finally moved on to something of importance — joint stock companies in Yugoslavia. Nothing conclusive came out of that discussion before Stalin asked about the mineral deposits in Yugoslavia.

'You have oil, bauxite, copper and lead, but your bauxite is the best,' Stalin said.

Tito elaborated on the non-ferrous metals and also mentioned the sites of various mines. Again nothing decisive came from the conversation before it moved on.

This time it was political — Albania.

'What do you know about Ever Hoxha?' Stalin asked Tito. Anđa knew from the tone of Stalin's voice that he did not like Hoxha.

It was past midnight when Anđa stifled a yawn. He was growing weary and having difficulty focusing on a series of conversations that seemed to be going nowhere.

'What are your plans for tonight?' Stalin asked Tito and caused Anđa to pay attention.

'We don't have any,' Tito replied.

Stalin burst out laughing. 'Ha! Ha! A government without a state plan.' Stalin thought he'd cracked the funniest joke.

'We adapted our plans to suit you,' Tito replied.

'Then we'll eat,' Stalin said before calling his secretary and ordering him to get the cars ready. When Stalin carried on joking with the Yugoslavs, Anđa began to think he liked them, until all of a sudden Stalin changed. The cars were taking too long to arrive and this did not please him. He trembled with rage and his face grew red and distorted as if he was wearing a garish mask at a fancy-dress party. His thin-faced secretary, who was the major recipient of his anger, went pale and was visibly shaken. Anđa was agitated. In a flash he became so terrified of Stalin that he wanted to run — anywhere — he didn't care where.

The rest of Anđa's evening passed in a blur. They ate a meal in a dimly lit restaurant with oppressive dark-panelled timber walls, where there were no other diners. They were served by a stout woman wearing a white apron and a waiter in a white jacket. There was too much food, too much alcohol and too many toasts for Anđa's liking. He didn't know any of the Russian names for the dishes that were set out on the long table draped with a white cloth and set with crystal glasses and silver cutlery, which seemed out of character with the drabness of the place. He sampled cabbage soup, several types of fish including salmon and beluga, silver, orange and black caviar, blinis, spiced beef on skewers, buns filled with rice and mincemeat, thick sour soup and dumplings. At the end of the meal two layered honey cakes were placed in the centre of the table, but by then Anđa was far too full to try even a small piece. And of course everything was washed down and accompanied by heavy black bread and vodka. At the end of the meal vast quantities of food remained untouched. Anđa thought about the starvation he'd suffered during the war and how many Russian peasants' mouths these leftovers could feed. He doubted any of it would be distributed to the starving masses in Russia — a thought that left him feeling distressed and disgusted.

By the time Stalin had indulged in dancing by himself to Russian folk music, which he played on a gramophone in the corner of the room, it was five in the morning and at last the Yugoslav delegation was able to leave.

The following day Anđa spoke candidly to Tito. 'Were you satisfied with last night's meeting?' he asked.

Tito looked thoughtful before he responded. 'No,' he said. 'I believe the Soviet Union are trying to take advantage of us. Now that a new Yugoslavia has emerged out of the ashes of the war they want to exploit us economically. Last night merely served to confirm my feelings. I have other concerns too, but it's too early to voice them.'

Anđa listened in silence. He was in shock at the monster Stalin had turned out to be, and try as he might, he was unable to shake off the fear that continued to grip him.

Two days later another similar supper took place. The venue and the Russian attendees were different, but again there was an over abundance of food and alcohol and this time the Yugoslavs did not return to where they were staying until six in the morning.

It was in the middle of the evening when Molotov approached Anđa. At first he seemed friendly enough, but Anđa grew wary of him when his questions become invasive.

'Whereabouts in Zagreb did you say you live?' Molotov asked.

'I didn't,' Anđa replied.

Molotov ignored his reply. 'And you're married of course. How many children?'

'Enough.' Anđa's new self was in full flight and he detested quaking inside with fear. Once upon a time he would never have been so cowardly, but he was powerless to counteract it.

Chapter twenty

It was two months after he'd been to Moscow when the approach came. Anđa had not been expecting it and in the first instance he didn't understand what it meant.

'This is Colonel Ivan Stepanov. We've met before, I think,' the caller said in a heavily accented voice. 'Could we meet? My colleagues in Moscow have the highest regard for you. We're having some problems in the Bolshevik Party and we think you're the person to help us solve them.'

A brief silence ensued.

'What are you suggesting?' Anđa asked.

'That we meet for a drink and a chat. Nothing more.'

Anđa couldn't imagine what Stepanov was talking about; however, he was loath to say no to such a high-ranking Russian official.

'Okay. If you think I can be of assistance.'

'I do. I most definitely do. Until we've had a talk let's keep this between you and me, shall we? Does Kavkaz Kazališna Kavana suit you?' What about Wednesday night?'

When the date and time were agreed Anđa ended the call.

Wednesday was two days away and during this time Anđa mulled over the phone call. He wanted to mention it to Krištof or Djido, but Stepanov's words were stuck in his mind — *let's keep this between you and me*. When the day of the meeting dawned he had not mentioned the call to anyone.

It was a cold-calm evening when he made his way to Trg Republike Hrvatske. By the time he reached the café/bar it was snowing heavily and he was obliged to dust the white coating off his shoulders and shake his hat before he went inside. The interior was spacious and plenty of patrons were enjoying the warmth, the alcohol and the tinkling of the piano in the corner of the room. Anđa searched the room for Stepanov knowing he wouldn't be difficult to spot with his moustache and full beard both of which were quite black. When he saw him in the corner of the room already drinking vodka, Anđa instantly became apprehensive and took his time threading his way through the tables to meet him.

Stepanov stood up when he saw Anđa approaching and shook his hand warmly as if they were best friends. Given that Anđa had met Stepanov no more than a couple of times before he found the greeting rather too ebullient.

When their conversation began with a senseless chat about the snowstorm outside, Anđa wondered when Stepanov would get to the crux of what he wanted. It didn't take long for the topic to change and when it did Anđa's eyes were glued to Stepanov.

'Your leader Tito is a great man, almost as great as Stalin,' Stepanov said. 'You will realise of course that Yugoslavia is a small country which can only exist with the support of the Soviet Union.'

'What's that got to do with me?' Anđa asked.

'It was us, the Soviet Union and no one else who liberated your country, therefore we are entitled to request you to accommodate us and do as we ask.'

'There seems to be a misunderstanding here. Do you not give any credit to our Partisans for liberating our country?'

'Well, you helped, of course, but without us you would never have achieved the freedom you have now.'

'I beg to differ, but go on. Say what you have to say,' Anđa said as boldly as he could considering how churned up he felt.

'I'd like you to work for our Soviet Intelligence Service. It has come to our attention that certain of your central committee members are not loyal to your country or mine.'

'Who are you talking about, Kardelj, Đjilas, Ranković, Hebrang? Come on, out with it. Give me names.' Anđa's voice was growing louder and there was an edge to it.

'If you mean are they under suspicion then the answer is yes except for Hebrang,' Stepanov said as he drained his glass and sat back in his chair to watch the effect of what he had said on his companion.

Anđa stared at him until it was Stepanov who looked away. 'So, why the others and not Hebrang?'

'Hebrang works for us. He has done for some time,' Stepanov said with a sickly smile on his face.

'What would you want me to do?'

'Supply us with information about certain people.'

'And if I don't?'

'Then you will be putting your family at risk and, of course, there is the information I gave you about Hebrang. If we find that you have divulged that then we will have to tell Tito you are a traitor, and that you work for us and have done for some time.'

Anđa couldn't believe what he was hearing. He glared at Stepanov with a loathsome expression as he digested the threat he had been given.

'When do I have to make up my mind?'

'By the end of the month. Let's agree to meet here again on the last day of the month, shall we and you can give me your decision then?'

Two weeks — two weeks to decide whether to betray my country to save my family. Anđa stood up, put on his cap and walked out without saying goodbye or looking back.

Part Two

Chapter twenty-one

It was not long after she finished school when Zlata applied for a job as a teller in the bank at the foot of the Schlosserove Stube. In the days leading up to the interview she had been anxious and the night before she hadn't slept well.

The interview was conducted by the manager in his office, a small room with brown, wood-panelled walls. The tall, thin man was so waxy-faced, Zlata thought he was ill. As he went through her personal details she sat with her hands clasped together tightly. Her palms were damp and she struggled to keep her apprehension at bay. She hadn't been sure what the interview would consist of, but when it transpired that it would be an oral arithmetic test, she gave a small sigh of relief. Arithmetic was the one subject she had excelled in at school.

When the test was over, the manager smiled. 'Amazing,' he said. 'Not one wrong answer. The job is yours. Can you start on Monday of next week?'

Nineteen-forty-eight was a significant year for Zlata. It was the year she married Nikola. It was also the year that Tito split with Stalin, but Zlata had no idea of the significance of that historical event.

Zlata met Nikola the year before when her brothers brought him home one night after a football game that resulted in a draw. Both teams had gone on to a bar, drunk too much and lost track of time. When Nikola let slip that he would have to spend the night in the bus shelter because he didn't have enough money left for a bus ticket, Zoran and Damir brought him home where he spent the night on the sofa in the living room. Zlata found him there, sound asleep when she came downstairs the next morning. She might not have been aware of him stretched out on his back under the grey blanket if it hadn't been for his loud snoring, which gave her a fright when she walked through the darkened room on her way to the kitchen.

After that, Nikola became a regular visitor. At first, Zlata found him overconfident and loud, and to avoid him she left the room whenever he visited. Sure, he was handsome with his blond hair and blue eyes, but for her, this was part of his arrogance and she did her best to ignore him. Yet, it hadn't escaped her attention that the rest of the family appeared to enjoy his company, especially her mother. She remembered the day when Nikola was sitting with her mother and brothers at the kitchen table, they were all laughing and engaged in jovial conversation. She averted her gaze and looked at the floor as she made her way to the door.

'They haven't got a hope of winning.' She heard Nikola's animated shout before she slipped outside. At the time, she wondered what they saw in him.

It was the day she was dressed in her finest outfit, for the wedding of her best friend Marija's brother, when she saw Nikola watching her. She was about to leave when he walked in and looked her up and down. His eyes lingered on her waist, before moving on to her skinny ankles visible below her blue, full-skirted summer dress. Much to her horror, he let out a low whistle. She knew her face had turned bright pink, but it didn't stop there.

'Your sister's a bit of a looker,' Zlata heard him say to Zoran and Damir who were playing cards at the kitchen table. Zlata watched Damir raise his bushy eyebrows while Zoran rolled his eyes and pulled a funny face, using his fingers to stretch his eyes into slits.

Flattered by Nikola's compliment, the only attention she had ever received from a possible suitor, she had a sudden change of heart and began to admire Nikola's bright-blue eyes and blond hair from afar. She took pains to dress well all the time, in case he turned up unannounced. She surprised herself by overcoming her nervousness and remaining in the room when he visited. She sensed his eyes following her around the room often; she knew he was having difficulty concentrating on his card games.

Zlata was thrilled when he invited her to the cinema for the first time. She tried to hide it from the rest of her family, but it was impossible to prevent a smile spreading across her face when he came to pick her up.

Inside the cinema, she couldn't concentrate on the giant screen. Nikola held her hand for the duration of the film. She felt her palm growing clammy, but she was reluctant to remove it from his firm grasp. The film was a comedy, yet she couldn't remember the title or anything else about it. Nikola had laughed heartily all the way through while Zlata was more restrained.

It was a Saturday afternoon at the end of winter, five months later when Nikola, Zoran and Damir were ensconced in the kitchen next to the doorway of the pantry, whispering. When Zlata walked in they fell silent. She looked from one to the other, but their faces told her nothing. She felt left out even though she knew they often told smutty jokes behind her back. She surmised this was one of those occasions. *Childish boys,* she thought, turning to leave.

'Zlata. Don't go. Sit down, please,' Nikola called out, extending his hand towards her. His voice was animated and she sat down reluctantly as she self-consciously reached up to touch her hair. She hoped it didn't look greasy. She had wanted to wash it earlier, but it was raining and cold and according to her mother, it was not the kind of weather for hair washing.

'Wait a minute. I'll get *Majka* and *Tata,*' Zoran said as he winked at Nikola.

Her parents entered the room quietly and sat down at the opposite side of the table, which was covered with a green and yellow plastic tablecloth. Her mother was smiling while her father's sunken eyes were animated for the first time in ages. When Nikola stood up and took the red apple from his canvas bag, she knew; her fingers flew to her mouth and she let out a small exclamation. Nikola's eyes were shining when he stepped towards her and presented her with his *obilježje*. Excitement bubbled up inside her and tears of joy spilt down her cheeks. She turned the apple over. Embedded in the side was a ring. She gasped at the small cluster of diamonds winking at her from the cut in the apple's skin.

'Will you marry me?' Nikola asked in a formal voice. Zlata was choked up and incapable of answering, but it didn't matter. Her silence was filled up by whistling from her brothers. Damir began to sing as Nikola pulled her close and kissed her firmly on the lips.

Zlata had never imagined she would marry. On the morning of her wedding she thought back to how disrupted her family's life had been by the war. Then she thought about her brother, Ivan and remembered the terrible night that she'd found out that he was dead. She would never forget that — the night she almost lost her mind. Her eyes were brimming with tears as she wished more than anything that he was here.

Her wedding reception would be held in the paved courtyard at the rear of a restaurant near the family home. Starched, white-linen tablecloths would cover the scarred wooden tabletops, while porcelain vases with cascading pink rose buds would grace each table. In summer, when the dining area was covered by an ancient leafy grapevine, the setting was reminiscent of a lush vineyard. A few days before her wedding Zlata walked over to look at it again. The luxuriant green canopy would offer much-needed shade from the heat of the afternoon sun.

Zlata stared at her reflection in the mirror. For a moment, she imagined the image was someone else. When she ran her hands down her body before it was encased in the ivory gown her mother had worn on her wedding day, she was momentarily dismayed by her shapelessness. It was just as well the lace-trimmed gown had stays in the bodice. She was quite prepared to put up with the discomfort they would cause as they transformed her figure into something far more curvaceous.

Standing as still as she could, given her jittery state, she held her breath as her mother stood behind her and placed the veil with pearls handstitched around the edges onto her head. She smiled. How she wished she felt this confident all the time. She blinked when her musings ended abruptly, interrupted by the persistent honking of car horns below in the street. Her mother was waiting and so too was her fiancé and the wedding guests.

'Are you ready?' her mother asked as she admired her beautiful daughter.

Zlata had never seen Nikola so spruced up. His blond hair was slicked flat with Brylcreem. He was dressed in a suit tailored from coarse, dark fabric, while black patent-leather shoes, which he complained bitterly about having to wear, enclosed his large feet. He had arrived together with a boisterous group of his best mates, many of whom belonged to his football club. A band of four musicians wearing distinctive red and white costumes were clustered inside the living room entrance, tuning their instruments as guests filed in the door. As soon as Zlata entered, the band commenced playing. When Nikola offered her a glass of *rakija* the festivities began with him belting out a song. Zlata was struggling with nervousness and swallowed the *rakija* in one gulp. It seared its way down her throat; she coughed and spluttered, and for a moment she almost choked. However, no one noticed. All around her, everyone was intent on enjoying the wedding celebrations.

By the time the wedding procession, led by the jaunty flag bearer, one of Nikola's crazier friends, set out, Zlata was warmed by more *rakija*. With her head held high she walked in the bosom of her family, in the direction of the church around the corner. She strolled beside Nikola, behind a lively musician dressed in the colourful red, white and blue national costume, playing his *tamburica* with practised skill.

During the wedding ceremony, Zlata was oblivious to anything except the lean man standing beside her. Despite it being a long Catholic formality she felt as if it took no time at all. Once it was over, she turned to her husband and beamed.

'You look gorgeous, my darling,' he whispered. Never had he uttered such words of praise to her, and she was certain from the intensity of his blue-eyed scrutiny that he meant it. She smiled again. But all too soon, her smile disintegrated. On her way out of the church, she became aware that her friend Marija's face was suffused with a scowl.

By the time she arrived at the archway to the restaurant the *rakija* had done its work and she had erased Marija's sour countenance from her mind. As she stood inside the doorway, she watched guests greeted by ushers handing out stems of rosemary wrapped in red, white and blue ribbon. Zlata and her mother had spent two days making these pretty corsages and the fragrance of rosemary lingered in the air.

The evening progressed, yet she couldn't relax. She barely touched the wedding feast, which was a surprising banquet given that it wasn't long since the war had ended and some foods remained difficult to obtain. Zlata was delighted when her father made use of his contacts in the Communist Party and arranged delicacies, such as several spit-roasted lambs, and *hobotnice* cooked in a *peka*. She had dreamt of having these delights at her wedding feast and never imagined they would be there.

Zlata's stomach was unsettled and after drinking several glasses of wine her head felt fuzzy. Unsure how she would cope with the dancing that was imminent, she picked up her wine glass and drained the remaining quarter. She grimaced. She had never been much of a drinker. But it might calm her down, she told herself, especially if she was to survive dancing the energetic *kolo*.

Giddy from too much alcohol and twirling on the dance floor inside the restaurant, the next few minutes were reduced to a blur as she swayed on her feet. Renewed panic flooded over her when guests began to chant and her grinning brother Damir took her back to the bridal table, moved her chair and positioned it as if it was a throne. Zlata felt faint. Determined not to pass out, she took several deep breaths and blotted her face with her lavender-scented handkerchief. She dared not embarrass herself and her family and collapse in front of her wedding guests.

When Nikola led Zlata to her chair, she sank onto it with relief. This was the first time in her life she had drunk so much liquor and she vowed never to do it again.

It wasn't long before she began to tremble, knowing she couldn't avoid what was about to come. Without any preamble her husband flipped back the skirt of her wedding dress with a flourish. She gasped, aware that her skinny legs, encased in brown stockings attached to a suspender belt, were on show. When the cheering from the crowd stopped, it was an artificial calm. On her right leg, above her knee was the garter bestowed upon her earlier by her mother. A family heirloom, the once-white lace had yellowed after being locked up for years in a suitcase in the *konoba*.

Although she was familiar with the tradition of the groom removing the garter from his bride's leg, she was unprepared for the ear-splitting noise, which erupted when Nikola bent down and in one swift, rough movement, ripped the garter off her leg with his teeth. Her eyes blurred with tears and her face felt hot as the crowd whistled and applauded.

Chapter twenty-two

As soon as Anđa heard the incessant hammering on the door at five in the morning he knew what it meant. He woke up instantly as a shiver of fear shook his body. He looked across at his wife as she opened her eyes.

'Was that someone banging on the door?' she asked as she turned to face her husband.

Anđa ignored her comment, sat up and got out of bed.

'I'll see who it is,' he mumbled.

'Who has the cheek to knock on the door at this hour?'

Again Anđa ignored her question as he hastily put on his clothes. Just then the hammering came again. He was pulling on his shirt when he rushed down the stairs.

Two members of UDBA, the organisation, which had been set up after the war by Aleksandar Ranković on Tito's orders, were standing outside the door. Fortunately, they were not men Anđa knew.

'Anđa Milić?' the one with the swarthy complexion and three days of beard growth on his face, asked.

'Yes,' he answered with resignation.

'We have orders from Aleksandar Ranković to take you to the police station.'

At the sound of Leko's name Anđa flinched. 'Wait a minute I'll get my hat and coat and tell my wife.' He saw little point in asking questions or arguing. When he turned around Mara was walking towards him.

'What's happening? Where are you going?' she asked.

'To the police station.'

'What for?'

'I don't know,' he said although he did. As soon as he'd put on his jacket he hugged his wife.

'You'll be coming back, won't you?'

'Yes,' he said although he doubted it. 'Look after the children,' were his final words before the men insisted it was time to leave.

Mara stared at her husband's frail figure as he left the house. The door was closed when it suddenly occurred to her that she should have asked which police station. She hurried to the door and opened it hoping the threesome were still outside. She was too late. Their car was disappearing down the street. With a sigh she closed the door slowly.

'What's going on?' Damir asked as he stood at the foot of the stairs in his underwear. 'Was that someone knocking on the door?'

'Yes. Your father's gone with two men to the police station.' Mara was wearing a worried frown.

'What for?'

'I don't know. But, I don't have a good feeling about it.'

'Which police station?'

'I forgot to ask. I was too shocked by what was happening that I didn't think to ask anything. It all happened too quickly.'

'He'll be coming back, won't he? I expect it'll be about some prisoner they've arrested.'

'I certainly hope so,' Mara, who was on the verge of tears, said.

At the Central Police Station in Petrinija Ulica, Anđa was locked in solitary confinement. It was a dark, dingy, concrete cell, which contained nothing but a shit bucket in one corner and a wire-wove bed frame with a thin, stinking grey blanket decorated with holes — the bed had no mattress. He sat down on the bed and hung his head with only his thoughts for company. He'd known he'd be found out sooner or later. But what choice had he been given? None. At least his family were safe — for the moment anyway. For their sake he'd done the right thing. His life didn't matter any more. He had died before the end of the war. Since then he'd been marking time.

Twenty-four hours passed before they paid him any attention. He was given a chunk of bread and a bowl of strange smelling soup with specks of something grey floating in it — he assumed it was meat. Even though it tasted revolting, he forced down a couple of mouthfuls. He wasn't hungry.

'You're being transferred to Glavnjača Prison,' the officer, who came to collect his bowl, said.

'In Belgrade?'

'That's the only one with that name that I know of.' The officer's reply was contemptuous along with the look on his face.

Meanwhile Mara was struggling to cope with her tumultuous thoughts and her distraught family.

'You'll have to let us go and look for him, *Majka,*' Zoran said.

'We can't wait any longer,' Damir added. We'll start with the stations in Petrova and Antuna Bauera and if he's not there, then the central one in Petrinija. This time we're not taking no for an answer. There's no war on now.'

'I'll come with you,' Zlata's husband Nikola, said.

'Let's go then,' Zoran replied. 'We must hurry.'

Just then there was another loud knock on the door.

'I'll go,' Damir, who was buttoning up his coat, said.

On the doorstep were the same two officers who had come for Anđa the day before.

'Where do you think you're going?' the officer with the swarthy complexion asked.

'To find my father,' Damir replied.

'No, you're not. All the occupants of this house are under house arrest until further notice. This man here will be making sure none of you try to leave,' he said referring to the officer standing next to him. 'I am also here to inform you that Anđa Milić has been charged with being a spy.'

By this time, Mara, her children and Nikola were all standing next to Damir inside the door. Mara let out an involuntary gasp of shock while Zlata screamed and fainted.

'That's absurd,' Mara said. 'My husband isn't a spy. Spying for who?' she asked.

'I'm not at liberty to discuss this matter with you. I am merely here to inform you of his arrest and your detention until further notice,' the officer said before he turned and walked quickly down the path towards the gate.

Anđa was indeed transferred to the hideous prison called Glavnjača. His cell was smaller than the last one. There was no window and light bulb that was so feeble he could scarcely see three feet in front of him.

He had been in his cell for an hour when he was taken to the interrogation room and although it was larger than his cell, it was not much more pleasant despite the light coming in through the small, barred window high up on one wall.

He sat down on the chair opposite the small desk and waited. Would it be Leko who conducted the interview? He hoped not. He'd had a good relationship with Leko during and after the war. They weren't close, but then again nobody got close to Leko. He was a hard, cold man and not only because his wife had been murdered by the fascists. Anđa had seen the callous look in his eye when he had killed countless of the enemy. He knew he could not expect any mercy from Leko.

Half an hour later two UDBA officers entered the room and sat on the chairs behind the desk. Both unsmiling characters had noticeably short hair and were dressed in the UDBA uniform with long jackets belted at the waist, epaulets on the shoulders, a red star on the left jacket lapel and wide-legged trousers. Anđa had never made the acquaintance of either before although the one with the scar through his left eyebrow looked familiar.

'It has come to our attention that you have been meeting with a high-ranking Russian official — Colonel Stepanov. You are charged with spying for the Soviets. What have you got to say for yourself?' the officer with the scar on his face said.

Anđa stared at the wall behind the two officers and remained silent.

'Come on Milič! Speak up. If you don't, we'll extract a confession from you by other means — unpleasant means. Why don't you make it easy on yourself and confess your crime?'

'I have nothing to say,' Anđa said in an indistinct voice.

'Speak up! We can't hear you.'

'I have nothing to say.'

Scar Face stood up, walked around the desk and without pausing slapped Anđa's face repeatedly until he fell off his chair.

'We'll leave you here to think for a while.' Both men left the room and did not come back for three hours.

'Well, what have you got to say for yourself Milić?' Scar Face asked upon his return.

'Nothing.' Anđa's battered face was bleeding and swollen and talking was uncomfortable.

'Guard! Take him to the cellar,' Scar Face said as he opened the door and shouted at the guard who was outside.

Anđa knew what was in the cellar. He'd heard all about the torture chamber.

Hours later when Anđa was returned to his cell between two guards who were half carrying him because he couldn't walk unaided, he had bloody bandages on his feet where his toenails had once been. He lay on the bed frame with pain pulsating through his feet and radiating into his legs. He hadn't succumbed to the torture, but he knew he couldn't take any more. His eyes moved between the thin-grey blanket he had pulled over his body and the door handle. The blanket would tear easily and the door handle was sufficiently high on the door and there was no guard stationed outside his cell door. If there had been it wouldn't have mattered.

Chapter twenty-three

On the day that Mara and her family were released from house arrest, Anđa came home. However, it wasn't the homecoming the family were expecting. He was in a canvas body bag that was dumped on the doorstep.

'He took his own life,' the stony-faced officer who accompanied the two underlings who were carrying the body, said.

Mara and the rest of her family went into immediate shock.

'Nooo!' she shouted as Zlata let out a piercing scream and clung to her husband. After the boys had moved Anđa inside and put him on the sofa they clung to each other as they stared at the khaki bag. The room was filled with Mara's sobbing and Zlata's wailing.

'Why?' Zoran asked as he broke the silence with one word. When no one answered he repeated it.

'I have no idea,' Mara said. 'He was a good man. He fought for his country, he was so brave during the war and he suffered so much. I don't believe he was a spy.'

'I doubt we'll ever find out what went on and there's no point in asking. The Secret Police would never tell us a thing,' Damir added.

'It's best we remember *Tata* as he was in the good times,' Zoran said. After that there seemed nothing further to say. Again they all lapsed into silence.

My poor, dear husband, you never deserved this. For as long as I live I will never believe you were a spy. Mara wiped her eyes and looked around the room at her tormented family. *Ivan and Anđa are both gone. Who else will they take next? And what will become of Zlata? My beautiful Zlata with her golden-tipped curls and violet eyes. Look at her. Staring blankly at nothing and once again retreating into another world. She has none of the resilience of her brothers.* Mara let out a ragged sigh as she wondered how to summon the strength to help her children cope with the death of their father when all she wanted was to join her husband in a world where neither of them could come to any further harm.

The day of Anđa's funeral dawned fine and clear, but not long after sunrise a gusty north-easterly wind sprang up. The chill of the *bora scura* signaled the onset of an early winter.

Distraught with bottled up grief she could not share, Mara was frozen with despair as she stood next to the open grave in the small cemetery a few streets from her family home. There had been insufficient money to buy a plot for her husband in Groblje Mirogoj and Anđa wouldn't have wanted to be buried there anyway. There were few mourners. No more than immediate family and half a dozen neighbours.

Mara was transfixed by the gaping hole in the dark soil when a gravelly cough made her look up. Two men were standing apart from the other attendees — Kardelj and Đilas. Resentment rose in her. Why had they come when they had quite possibly been responsible for Anđa's death? Mara turned away and ignored them. When the gravediggers threw clods of earth on top of her husband's inexpensive, rough-sawn timber coffin Mara turned to walk away just as someone touched her arm.

'He was a good man and a good friend. I'll always think well of him,' Kardelj said as he pulled Mara awkwardly towards him in an attempt to embrace her. Mara stiffened, but when she saw the tears glistening in Kardelj's eyes she relaxed and allowed herself to be held. 'And I'll never forget him,' he added before he released her gently.

'Thank you.' Mara turned to leave as fresh tears filled her eyes.

In the back of Damir's dented, once-white Yugo, sandwiched between her son Zoran and a neighbour, Mara felt suffocated.

When they pulled up outside the gate and the concrete path that led to her front door, she walked slowly down the path and steeled herself for the inevitable gathering of mourners. Apart from not wanting to participate, she was curious about why her sons had bothered inviting people. It was doubtful anyone apart from family would turn up. No doubt they would all have heard the rumours. Shaken by the loudness of Damir's voice when he spoke in an accusative tone, anxiety attacked her.

'You didn't lock the door,' he said to Zoran whose dense eyebrows were knotted in a frown.

'Yes I did.'

Mara stared at the front door which was ajar and swinging in the breeze. On closer inspection, it was clear the lock had been smashed.

Before they left for church, Mara had set out plates of food on the table, but when she entered the kitchen, they were no longer there. Someone had broken into the house and trashed it. Food and crockery from the kitchen cupboards had been thrown on to the floor, trampled upon and smashed. The plate of *krafne* Damir bought from the bakery earlier, lay squashed at Mara's feet. Strawberry jam oozed from the doughnuts like blood from a bullet wound. Mara hurried from room to room. The trail of destruction was everywhere. None of the rooms had been spared, yet nothing seemed to be missing, although it was such a mess it was difficult to tell. She was angry and speechless with shock. What were they looking for? The chest? Anđa had asked the boys to hide it under the wood in the *konoba* not long after the end of the war. She descended the stairs to the *konoba* slowly and when she checked, the chest was still hidden and the firewood around it was undisturbed. She thought briefly about getting the boys to unearth it and open it. Anđa had obviously secreted something of importance inside. On reflection she decided whatever was in there could stay there — buried along with her husband — she no longer cared.

Chapter twenty-four

Zlata had never imagined herself as a mother. She knew it was inevitable, yet when she found out she was pregnant she was dismayed. As the months passed and her pregnancy progressed her mindset did not change. Her mother asked her often if she was feeling okay and as Zlata was reluctant to admit she wasn't looking forward to being a mother she always said she was fine.

'You don't look fine,' her mother, who had been overjoyed when Zlata told her she was pregnant, said.

'I'm fine. If you call being fat and uncomfortable and having to give up my job fine,' she replied in a sharp tone seven weeks before the birth when she was about to stop work.

When Zlata went into labour at nine o'clock at night, she was attended by two experienced midwives, but the baby was not born until twenty-four hours after the onset of her contractions.

'Get it out of me!' she screamed. 'I don't want it. It's killing me.'

Her mother who was sitting beside her holding her hand had done her best to pacify Zlata. Nothing she said calmed her down.

'Get it out!' she shouted again.

In the end, the child had to be pulled out using forceps. Zlata screamed the house down and then passed out. She was severely torn by the brutal birth and the doctor had to be called to stitch the tear.

Nikola came into the room as soon as he heard the baby emit it's first cry.

'It's a girl, a healthy girl,' Mara, who was holding the swaddled child, said. 'Would you like to hold her?'

With a hesitant smile on his face, Nikola took his daughter reluctantly. 'What if I drop her?' he said as he reached for the baby with clumsy hands.

'You won't,' Mara said. 'She's beautiful, isn't she? Look at her long eyelashes and her little button nose.'

'Yes,' Nikola replied, eager to hand his daughter back. 'Well done *Draga*,' he said to Zlata as he kissed his wife on cheek. 'Now it's time to celebrate.'

Zlata watched him leave. She knew he'd be gone for at least three days. In keeping with tradition, he would spend that time drinking with his friends.

Fortunately, Zlata forgot about the painful birth quite quickly. The traumatic event was eclipsed by her joy at the sight of her daughter and when her maternal instincts surfaced she began to delight in her good baby who seldom cried. Her shy smile had returned and at last she was happy. The child had her father's blond hair and Zlata thought her eyes were as blue as the sky on a sunny day. Zlata's days were joyful and although it was a tight fit with so many people squashed into her mother's house, she didn't mind. She and Nikola and the baby slept in the room her brothers used to share while they slept on bunks in the small bedroom that had once belonged to her.

The only veil to obscure her days came immediately before the baby's christening. Zlata and Nikola had agreed that Marija, who had been Zlata's best friend since they were children and who had yet to marry, would be the child's godmother and because they wished to bestow this honour on Marija in person, Zlata invited her for Sunday lunch. Mara cooked a special meal — two fat, roast chickens, fresh green beans and new potatoes from the garden. She also made individual *rožata* for desert. At the end of the meal, when the other members of Zlata's family had tactfully left the room, Zlata made her request with considerable formality.

'Of course I'll be godmother,' Marija said, although she didn't seem enthusiastic about the idea — there was no smile on her haughty face. Zlata was puzzled.

'What are you thinking of naming her?' Marija asked.

'We're not sure yet, but we have one or two names we like,' Nikola, who had not up until then, contributed to the conversation, said.

'You do know it's up to me to choose her name.' Marija's tone continued to be arrogant as she patted her dark hair to make sure no tendrils had escaped her ponytail. Zlata had never heard her sound like that before and she was dismayed. It was then that she remembered the ugly expression on Marija's face on her wedding day. Was Marija jealous? It was then that Zlata knew she should have paid more attention to Marija's behaviour back then. She'd dismissed her demeanour and hadn't thought about it in depth since then. Now it was too late.

As she cast her mind back she remembered what had happened when she first began going out with Nikola. Marija had turned up at her house far more frequently. She was always wearing the navy dress she saved for going to church on Sundays and whenever she could she sat as close to Nikola as possible. On one occasion, she had put her hand on Nikola's leg under the table. She thought Zlata hadn't seen her, but she had. Zlata knew she had been hoping to attract his attention and steal him away, but he had not given Marija so much as a second glance.

'She will be called Dunja,' Marija said. Zlata recoiled and stared at her in silence.

'Hmm,' Nikola said. The look on his face said he didn't like the name either, although he hadn't said so. 'Surely you must have more than one option for us to choose from,' he said.

'Why? It's a beautiful name,' Marija said before she looked at the clock on the wall and stood up.

'I have to go now or I'll be late.' She walked towards the door with a self-assured stride.

That night in bed, Zlata continued to agonise over Marija's choice of name.

'It's traditional for the godmother to choose the baby's name, you know that. There's nothing we can do about it,' Nikola said.

Zlata was upset — she hated the name with a passion. There had been a girl in her class at school with that name. Zlata found her loud and overbearing. Her level of confidence astounded Zlata given that she was quite unattractive with large sticking-out ears and buck teeth. She also thought that her friend Marija was getting inexplicable pleasure from choosing that name. Why would she do such an unpleasant thing? She knew how Zlata had felt about that girl at school. They had talked about it. Zlata couldn't understand it. Marija had, after all, been her best friend for as long as she could remember. Zlata had always been shy and lacking in confidence and never found it easy to make friends. When she was ten, she was nicknamed *Kumulonimbus* by her classmates. There were many occasions when she came home from school in despair. She had stared and stared at her face in the mirror, trying to erase the frown she exhibited when she was worried or anxious. In the end, she concluded she was ugly and that was why no one, except Marija, wanted to be her friend.

'Please, can't you talk to her? I hate that name and I know you don't like it either,' she said to her husband.

'It's not that bad. Anyway, what's a name? Does it matter that much?'

'How can you say such a thing? Of course it matters. I *hate* that name. Please talk to her?'

'No, I can't. If you detest the name so much, then *you* talk to her. She's your friend, not mine. Come on, let's get some sleep. It's late and I have work in the morning.'

Zlata was annoyed when he turned away.

It's not can't. It's won't — for the first time since she'd married him, she was cross with her husband. She couldn't talk to Marija. If anyone was going to challenge tradition, then it had to be her husband.

Zlata had difficulty falling asleep and when she did drift off, it was a bitter restless sleep. She blamed her husband for letting their beautiful daughter be christened with an ugly name — one that she would never use — as far as she was concerned her daughter would be called *Draga*.

Dunja was two when Zlata went back to work at the bank while her mother looked after Dunja during the day. When she wasn't working Zlata helped her mother with the food preparation. Nikola's birthday was coming up when Zlata told her mother she wanted to cook by herself.

'On Sunday I want to make his favourite *brodetto*,' she said. 'I'll go to the market tomorrow and buy a selection of seafood, not just fish.' In those days, because Zagreb is inland, seafood wasn't readily available; however, on Saturdays there was often a good selection. Zlata came home with *mol* fish, shrimps, mussels and calamari.

Zlata started preparing the meal as soon as breakfast was over and while she worked she hummed an old Dalmatian tune. When it was ready Zlata set the table with a white cloth embroidered around the edge by her mother. In the middle of the table she placed a small vase of white daisies. Just then Zoran turned up with his new girlfriend.

'This is Ljubica,' Zoran said as he introduced the slim, dark-haired girl to his sister. 'I bought you two loaves of bread as well.' Zoran was late but not as late as Nikola who had yet to arrive.

An hour later when he still hadn't turned up, they ended up eating in silence without him. Zlata's disappointment was bitter. Her husband had assured her he would be there. Zlata didn't know what time it was that night when he slipped quietly into bed beside her. She suspected it was the early hours of the morning. *Had he been playing cards all that time?*

Dunja was mesmerised by the tigers in the cage, but Zlata was transfixed by something more disquieting. She shook her head trying to clear it, but it didn't help — it felt as though it was stuffed with cotton wool. *What was wrong with her?* Most of the time she succeeded in holding back her tears, but deep inside she felt mixed up and confused and it took almost nothing to make her cry. Often, when these bad days came upon her, she wanted to hide under a blanket in the corner of the bedroom and shut out the world and everyone in it.

When her mother suggested they take Dunja to Park Maksimir, Zlata thought it was a good idea. It was warm and sunny and she knew how Dunja loved to watch the tigers. Before they set out, she had no idea the *feeling* would overcome her so swiftly.

She had been having these strange episodes off and on for some time. She did her best to ignore them and pretend they weren't happening, until the next one engulfed her. She had considered going to the doctor, but resisted the impulse. How could she explain her symptoms? There was nothing physically wrong with her and she was sure he would think she was being neurotic. She was also disinclined to talk to her mother. Sharing that kind of intimate problem with her would have been uncomfortable. Neither would she have considered discussing it with her husband. She had been close to her father, but that was before he went away to fight in the war. She thought about him often — her poor father.

Dulled by whatever she was suffering from, Zlata had lost all track of time and it wasn't until her mother called her in an exasperated voice that she came to her senses.

'Zlata! What's the matter with you? I've been calling you for ages. Didn't you hear me? It's time to go. I need to see to the evening meal … you seem distracted these days,' her mother probed. 'Is something wrong?'

'No, *Majka*, I'm fine.'

'Well you don't look it. Do you have problems at work? Or is something wrong between you and Nikola? Come on, it always helps to talk.'

'I said I'm fine. I'm tired, that's all. It's been a busier than usual week at work.' Zlata wished she would leave her alone.

'Well, if you're sure, dear. But you will talk to me if there's something troubling you, won't you?' Her mother's voice was full of concern as she gave her daughter an affectionate hug.

'Of course!' What else could she say? It was alright for her mother. She had all the self-confidence in the world, the same as Nikola. Zlata sped up her walking pace. She felt the need to put more distance between them.

The longer she looked at the doctor the more she detested him. She had resisted making an appointment to see him for so long, but her *bad patches*, as she thought of them, were becoming more frequent. She had made the appointment out of desperation because she had reached a point where she didn't know what to do. When she repeated herself for the third time she was frustrated when the doctor continued to misunderstand.

'It's normal to feel like this when you're pregnant,' he said as he pushed his horn-rimmed spectacles up his nose. 'In another four weeks, you'll feel better. Right now, your hormones are out of balance. That's normal when you're pregnant.'

'But I've had this feeling on and off for at least the last seven years. It's nothing to do with being pregnant.' She had no idea she was pregnant when she made the doctor's appointment. It came as a complete surprise when he examined her and told her that she was about twelve weeks. Although she and Nikola still slept in the same bed, during the previous six months they had been intimate only once. Zlata had never been comfortable or confident about sex and was unsure what was expected of her. She looked upon it as nothing more than her wifely duty. Although she feigned enjoyment she feared Nikola had seen through her façade. Now, he didn't appear to want her anymore. Could this be because he was disappointed by her inexperience? His behaviour saddened her, especially when he went out most evenings. Frequently, it was late when he came home and she was already asleep. Sometimes, instead of getting into bed with her, he got into bed with Dunja. He thought Zlata didn't know, but she did.

'Don't you want another child? Could that be why you're unhappy?' the doctor asked. Zlata knew she should be excited about expecting another baby, the way other women would be — instead she felt numb and empty.

'No, it's nothing to do with that. I don't feel right. As I've already told you, I've been having these patches where my head is cloudy and I'm always tired, despite hours of sleep. Maybe I have a brain tumour.'

The doctor leant back in his chair and laughed. 'Now you're being plain ridiculous. Come on, off with you and let me attend to my next patient. If you're unwell in a month, come and see me again. But for now, go home and share your wonderful news with your family.' He stood up from behind his desk and walked across the room to open the door for her.

On her way home, she felt a need to hide and covered her head with a paisley scarf, which she tied under her chin. Staring out of the bus window with unseeing eyes, she was more miserable than she had been before she visited the doctor. He wasn't interested in her problem. In a month's time, she knew she'd be feeling just as horrible — and she wouldn't be going back to consult him again. She'd have to learn to cope with her predicament and hide it. There was nothing else for it. If she mentioned it to anyone, they'd think she was crazy.

Her feet felt heavy and she was conscious of dragging them as she trudged from the bus stop. When a glimmer of hope surfaced that maybe being pregnant was the solution to her problem; she dismissed the thought as soon as it materialized.

Chapter twenty-five

Dunja was eight when her brother Dominik was born. At first she resented her baby brother. He was the reason they'd been forced to leave her grandmother's home because it had become overcrowded. But when his wide-open, innocent blue eyes seemed to be fixed on her rather than on their mother or anybody else, Dunja grew to love him.

Dunja's new home was in one of the newly built suburbs in an undesirable part of the city where the houses were soulless and lacked style or elegance. There were three apartments on each level of the new, three-storey building — hers was on the middle level. Although the rooms were spacious, Dunja didn't like living there.

All too soon, she began to miss her old home and the happy times there. Apart from the dreary interior, the atmosphere without her grandmother wasn't the same. She wasn't quite sure why it didn't feel like home. Perhaps it lacked the laughter that often surrounded her grandmother. Dunja's young eyes didn't focus on the institutional white-plaster walls, or the dismal brown that was everywhere — brown felt carpet, brown tiles in the bathroom and the kitchen as well as brown doors and window frames or the dull pink, floral carpet off-cut running the length of the hall, which was nothing more than a gloomy mismatch. The brightest room was the south-facing kitchen with its red Formica bench. But red and brown do not go well together. The floor and the bench tops clashed like two cymbals being struck. Neither could the huge rooms make up for the lack of light. The adjacent apartment blocked out the sun from two o'clock in the afternoon onwards.

Yet another problem about living in Savska Cesta was the unsavoury residents who lived nearby. Without jobs, these dregs loitered on the streets day and night, drinking, smoking and causing trouble. Dunja wasn't allowed to go outside because her parents considered it was dangerous, although her mother omitted to tell her that their new street had been the site of a prison during World War II. Admittedly, it had been further down the street.

Dunja had hoped she'd see more of her father when they moved and she was sad when he continued to spend all his time elsewhere as he had done when they'd lived in her grandmother's home. She knew it upset her mother too. She could tell by the miserable look on her face. She also wondered why her parents barely seemed to talk to each other and why her mother didn't seem to hear when she spoke to her.

Little did Dunja realise she was destined to call this unfriendly place her home off and on for many years.

The major highlight in Dunja's week was Sunday. Every Sunday without fail they went to her grandmother's home for lunch. Not only did Dunja savour her grandmother's cooking, but she also savoured her company and the happy aura that surrounded her. It was a wonderful family day. The entire family gathered around the table — her grandmother sat at the head nearest to the kitchen. Even her father was always there and often Zoran and Damir brought their girlfriends. The relationship between Zoran and the dark-haired Ljubica seemed to be a permanent one while Damir had recently brought along Lucija, a plump girl with a bubbly personality. When the meal was over the men usually played cards at the table while the women often went for a walk, weather permitting. Dominik always went with the women, in his pram when he was a baby, but once he could walk he was quite content to hold his sister's hand, although he was too small to walk very far and more often than not he had to be carried. The women took turns at this. Dunja was always sad when the end of the day came and it was time to go home.

Chapter twenty-six

As he stood outside the school room door holding his mother's hand, Dominik looked up at the grey concrete façade of the building that housed his school. Its only adornment was a tattered flag hanging crookedly out of an upstairs window. The austere building heightened his fear of the forthcoming day. He had spent most of the first five years of his life surrounded by extended family or in the company of his sister. Dominik felt as if his mother was there but not there. She drifted around if she was at home, rather than working as a teller at the bank. She seldom spoke and if any of her family spoke to her, more often than not she didn't answer. Tired of being ignored by his mother and given the continuous absence of his father, Dominik got into the habit of asking his sister whenever he wanted or needed something. It didn't take long for him to think of his sister as his mother.

His first day at school was the only day his mother took him there. It was too difficult for her to get to work on time if she had to take Dominik to school. From then on Dunja walked him there before she went on to her school. She was kind and for the first few months she always held his hand as they walked along the street before she kissed his cheek when she left him outside the concrete monstrosity that housed his school.

On his first day Dominik was intimidated by the class of boisterous children under the charge of a sour-faced teacher — it was all too foreign.

He had just taken his seat on a hard, wooden chair when the teacher asked him to stand up, introduce himself and tell the class about himself. As soon as he was on his feet he felt eyes ogling at him. His legs buckled, but rather than falling down, he pissed his pants instead.

'Dominik Letica!' the teacher bellowed as she pointed at him. 'Go and stand in the corner facing the wall and don't come out until I say so.'

As he cowered shamefaced in the corner, he dared to look down at his light grey shorts. Dark stains showed at his crotch and urine had run down his legs. His socks were damp and his feet were sticky as he shuffled them inside his shoes and cried in silence.

Although his first day at school wasn't a good one by the end of his first week he became friends with Vid and Mijo who lived down the road. They were inseparable twins with identical cherubic, freckled faces. He got along well with them most of the time. Although sometimes they squabbled over marbles because Vid was a cheat.

'My marble hit yours,' Vid would cry. 'Didn't you see it? Are you blind?' was always his prevalent comment. Too often he insisted that his marble had hit one of theirs when it hadn't. He owned one especially big marble with a large purple centre, which he thought was the supreme conqueror.

When Mrs Lončar, Vid and Mijo's mother offered to have Dominik each day after school because his mother worked, he was overjoyed. Mrs Lončar was his idea of a real mother. She was kind-hearted and smiled a lot. Dominik didn't care that when she did, her mouth was full of discoloured rotten teeth. She baked delicious *kolači* for afternoon tea and she seldom told Dominik off. He wasn't a naughty child, so this wasn't surprising. It didn't take long before he grew used to being at Vid and Mijo's house and often wished he could live there. The only downside was the ban on television. Children were forbidden to watch it and they were certainly not allowed to watch football. Whereas at his grandmother's house football was a popular topic and Dominik was always overjoyed if his Uncle Zoran or Damir took him to watch them play on Saturdays. As it turned out Dominik spent more time with his uncles than he did with his father who was seldom at home.

By the time Dominik left primary school the arrangement for him to go home with Vid and Mijo was discontinued. It was his sister who gave him the news on Sunday morning at the breakfast table.

'You're old enough to look after yourself after school now. You don't need to go home with Vid and Mijo tomorrow,' she said. 'And besides Mrs Lončar is ill.'

'What's wrong with her?'

'She has cancer.'

Dominik gasped and dropped the knife he was using to spread butter on his slice of white bread.

'Cancer! People die from that, don't they?'

'Yes I'm afraid they do.'

Dominik ran out of the kitchen so his sister wouldn't see his tears.

When Mrs Lončar died the following year, Dominik balled his eyes out in the privacy of his bedroom. His friendship with Vid and Mijo was never the same after that, especially when their father married for a second time. His new wife was a younger woman who was the complete opposite of his first wife. She was short and impatient with Vid and Mijo and never made Dominik feel welcome. One Saturday when he went to visit and she answered the door her demeanour shocked him.

'What do you want?' were the cold words she uttered when she opened the door and found him standing there. They were almost as cold as the look in her eyes.

It wasn't long after he started middle school when Dominik met Tonci who soon replaced Vid and Mijo in his affections. Tonci was funny. He cracked jokes often and Dominik enjoyed how Tonci made him laugh. There hadn't been too much to laugh about during the first thirteen years of his life living in the same house as his taciturn mother.

He hadn't known Tonci for long when he discovered he had a body odour problem, especially when they played football, a sport they engaged in most days after school, although by then Dominik already knew he would never excell. He played as if he had two left feet, missed the ball often and it wasn't long before he was bestowed with the nickname *Nespretan.*

On the day Tonci offered to lend him a pair of sneakers to go on a hike with their class Dominik knew he would have to learn to block his nose. Tonci's socks were crumpled inside the sneakers and both the shoes and the socks reeked. His body didn't smell too wholesome either. Regardless, Dominik didn't care, he enjoyed being with Tonci and ignored his hygiene habits because by then their friendship had been cemented and they spent a lot of time together. Dominik liked going to Tonci's house because Tonci had decided he was going to be a chef and he had already begun to cook various dishes. It wasn't that Dominik had a particular interest in food; it was more about going to Tonci's place to escape going home. He often stayed for dinner if Tonci was cooking under the supervision of his mother, especially if he was cooking roast chicken wrapped in pršut.

Chapter twenty-seven

When Dunja was accepted as a student at the Academy of Art in Zagreb University, she felt privileged. Only a select few were chosen each year after scrutiny of their portfolios. She submitted a variety of work from abstracts to a portrait of her brother and a sketch of a ballet troupe painted with pastel, water colours. More exciting was the chance to go to Paris to complete the final module on Art History at the American University.

Her teachers in the Academy of Art allowed their students to indulge in radical behaviour — smoking and wearing hippy clothes — bell-bottoms and flowing, flowery shirts with wide sleeves. It was during her time at university that Dunja took up smoking. Everyone around her indulged in it and she didn't want to be the odd one out.

She was especially proud of her mane of long-blonde hair that was all the rage at the time. It fitted in perfectly with the hippy movement in San Francisco, which she found entrancing. When she became addicted to the Scott McKenzie song *San Francisco,* which was adopted as the anthem for freedom in Czechoslovakia in 1968, during the Prague Spring, Dunja began to live life to the full.

At the time she enrolled at university, she was, of course, living at home with her parents and her brother. As young people often are, she was focused on herself and seldom gave any thought to the other members of her family. Her relationship with her younger brother suffered and they began to drift apart because Dunja developed a compelling need to break away. It wasn't that she didn't care about him anymore. She loved him as much as she always had; she just wanted to spend less time in his company.

Neither had she become any more enamoured by the apartment or the surrounding area. She coped by not thinking about it. She was busy living her newly found, radical existence, carried away by the dawning of her own self-expression in everything, particularly art. When she wasn't at university she went out with her friends. She'd met Valentina, who was also studying art, soon after her first year began. Through Valentina she met Gorana, a bio chemistry student. They hung out together often and called themselves the red, white and black trio because of their hair. Dunja's was, of course, blonde, whereas Valentina had vibrant red curls and Gorana's sleek dark hair was always worn in a ponytail.

At other times, Dunja would shut herself away in her room to study or paint or she would visit Karlo the professor at the university who had taken her under his wing. During his youth he had spent time as an apprentice art restorer at the National Museum and his knowledge about many aspects of the art world was vast.

An eccentric individual with a long beard and hair flowing back from his forehead, Karlo wore a bright-orange kaftan when he was at home in his apartment. Dunja always suspected he was gay, but hiding in the closet. It was to do with his effeminate way of walking and talking and the lack of women his own age in his life.

On the first occasion when Dunja visited his home, where dust coated many of the surfaces, she was taken aback by the interior which was overflowing with books and an impressive art collection.

'We'll have tea,' Karlo said not long after she'd arrived. 'White Russian tea. Then I'll show you some of the more interesting pieces in my art collection.'

She'd taken her first sip when Karlo asked her what she thought of the tea. Before she could answer he carried on.

'It's like sweet, tart cherries, don't you think?'

'Yes,' she said even though she didn't like it or its overpowering flavour. She could never have told him. He was kind and supportive of her artistic endeavours and she had no intention of offending him.

The most intriguing piece in his collection was a gilded triptych.

'It's an altarpiece from a Russian Orthdox Church,' he said as Dunja admired it. She had been told he was a devout Catholic and it seemed an odd icon for him to own. Yet, she imagined it was valuable. Some days, after his teapot was empty, he gave her lessons on restoration techniques and showed her the best methods of working with gold leaf.

One of his favourite sayings as they began work was, 'You never know when this might come in handy.' On Saturdays, they often spent the entire day ensconced in Karlo's cluttered workroom and sometimes she didn't arrive home until after dark. Although she'd been gone all day, her mother never enquired where she'd been. There was a gulf a mile wide between Dunja and her mother. They hardly ever talked. Dunja was locked out of the world her mother was inhabiting. On the occasions when Dunja paid her any attention she noticed how her mother, who was only in her early forties, had begun to age. Her once-pretty face was etched with fine lines around her mouth; her hair had lost it's shine and was turning grey. It seemed to Dunja that not only had her appearance changed, but so too had her personality. Nothing had the ability to put a smile on her face any more. Not even her husband's words at breakfast one morning.

'I'll be home early tonight and we'll have dinner together. It'll be a real family meal,' he said, before he left for work at the distillery where he filled bottles of alcohol on an assembly line. Dunja couldn't remember when he had last been at home in the evening and she was so looking forward to it.

Eight o'clock came and went. There was no sign of him. They took their places at the table and ate without him.

At the end of the meal Dunja was helping her mother tidy the kitchen when he burst in the door. A crooked smile suffused his handsome face and his hair was messed up.

'Did you leave anything for me?' he asked as his dishevelled appearance incited her mother's dormant rage.

'Why should I keep food for you?' Zlata shouted and Dunja jumped at the loudness of her voice. 'You never spare a thought for us.' Zlata was shaking and had to grab hold of the edge of the bench for balance. Dunja thought she had almost forgotten what she was saying in the middle of her sentence because her words sounded strange and disjointed.

'What did you say, woman?' he said as he took a step closer to his wife. Dunja was shocked at the glowering expression on his face. 'Not going to answer me as usual, eh?' As a dreadful silence imprisoned her parents, Dunja looked from one to the other. Her father continued to glare at her mother, his blue eyes were frenzied, while her mother's face was pale and her expression was stony. Dunja waited for her to say something, but she didn't.

'Well that's it! I've had enough of your sullen ways. I'm leaving! And I won't be back.' He was more than irate. He let out an ugly laugh which left Dunja dry-eyed with fear. She ran towards him and tried to grab his arm as he turned to leave. He was her father and he must stay. *What had her mad mother brought upon them?* He pushed Dunja away. Out of desperation she persisted and ran after him when he left the room.

'Take me with you,' she pleaded. She had no idea where he was going, but she loved him and she couldn't bear the thought of him leaving. It didn't occur to her then that he had an entirely different reason, known only to himself, for leaving his wife and family.

'No,' he said. 'You can't come. You must stay with your mother and Dominik.' He prised her hand from his arm and slammed the door on his way out. Dunja's legs gave way, she slithered to the floor in the entranceway and burst into tears.

Dominik had heard the commotion and came out of his room.

'What's going on?' he asked.

Dunja was quiet for a short time before she found the words to answer him. '*Tata's* gone.'

'What do you mean he's gone?'

'He's left us,' Dunja said as she looked up at Dominik. When her words sunk in, his face crumpled and he dashed back into his room. The house shook when he slammed his bedroom door.

Chapter twenty-eight

After her father left Dunja found life more difficult. Living with her mother was like cohabiting with a sleepwalker, and she was forced to take on responsibilities such as cooking and cleaning. Dominik needed a mother, and Dunja did everything she could think of that his mother should have done for him. She worried about him and did what she could to help him with his schoolwork. Several times she came close to talking to him about their parent's separation, but in the end she couldn't find the right words and it was too painful.

The only person Dunja felt able to confide in was her grandmother. One afternoon when she had no lectures and she was visiting her grandmother Dunja mentioned the deterioration in her mother.

'She was never the same after we saw the bodies,' her grandmother said as they sat at the kitchen table and Dunja helped her grandmother top and tail beans. 'That's what turned her mind; I'm sure of it. She was always fragile, but that pushed her over the edge.'

'What bodies? I don't know anything about bodies,' Dunja said.

'The sixteen antifascists who were hung. Murdered by the *Ustaše* in December 1943. We'd gone to Dubrava Street because I'd heard the shop there had flour and oil. And there they were — hanging in a row. It was the most monstrous sight I've ever seen. Some had bulging eyes, others had shat themselves and one had such a petrified look on his face that I've never forgotten it.'

'Oh my God! No wonder she's never mentioned it.'

'Then, just when I thought she was coming right, we found out that your Uncle Ivan had died,' Mara said.

'She's never told me about that either. She hardly ever talks and she's worse lately.

You can speak to her and it's as if she hasn't heard you.'

'I know. That's how she was after we saw the bodies. I couldn't get through to her. Sometimes I wanted to shake her and at times I almost did.' Mara shook her head. 'Then the final blow came when your *Dida* died. I thought she'd lose her mind then, but Nikola was there for her.'

'Can't the doctor give her something to make her better?'

'Apparently not. During the war she had to take medicine to calm her down and help her sleep and more recently I know she's been taking Valium, but nothing works. There's never been a proper diagnosis for what's wrong with her and she devours pills as though she's sucking sweets.'

'So, you don't know what's actually wrong with her?' Dunja asked.

'No. As I said it's never been given a name. Her mind's gone and no doubt that's why your father left. He couldn't put up with it and I don't blame him.'

'She drove him away, didn't she?'

'Perhaps, but you can't blame her. She's sick. You need to make an allowance for her.'

'But *Baba,* I can't … there are times when I hate her for being so inadequate.'

'No, my child you mustn't say that. She can't help the way she is. Blame the war if you must lay the blame somewhere. Come here,' Mara held out her arms and Dunja allowed herself to be held, the way she'd always hoped her mother would hold her.

Whenever her father phoned infrequently to talk to her and Dominik, Dunja was always pleased. He was bright and cheerful and Dunja looked forward to seeing him. The three of them would often go walking together in Park Maksimir or he'd meet Dunja at the Kazalište Kavana Café near the Opera House for coffee.

It was not long before Dunja found out that he had moved in with another woman. He chose not to talk about it directly; she picked up on it when he used the word *we* from time to time. In her permanent role as *mother* she chose not to tell Dominik because she didn't want him to be hurt any more than he already had been by their parents' separation. She came to the illogical conclusion that the longer it took for him to find out, the less he would suffer.

For a short time, after their father left, Dunja's godmother Marija came to stay. Dunja didn't get along with her — she found her a peculiar woman in so many ways. She wore the same black clothes every day — Dunja had no idea why. She wasn't a widow. Her long hair which was always in a bun on top of her head, was dyed to match her clothes and added to the severity of her appearance. Her thin-lipped mouth was permanently clamped and gave her a constant look of disapproval. She had a habit of glaring at Dunja with her small calculating eyes — her scrutiny made Dunja feel guilty, but of what, she didn't know as she could never imagine what Marija was thinking. On the rare occasions when she wasn't staring at Dunja, she took great delight in telling her what to do.

'Put the dinner on to cook! Fold up the washing!' she snapped.

Dunja believed Marija came to stay more out of ghoulish curiosity than to help the family — or rather help her mother, as she was *meant* to be her friend.

But without a doubt, the biggest reason Dunja detested her godmother was because she had chosen her name and Dunja hated her name. She didn't like how it sounded especially when her mother said it or rather didn't say it. It was an awkward name and she didn't feel that it suited her.

She was relieved when Marija didn't stay long. She presumed once Marija had determined to her own satisfaction that Nikola wasn't coming back, she could leave. This sad state of affairs seemed to please her, if the self-satisfied smile on her conceited face was anything to go by.

It was a dark time for Dunja when her father left. It was also when her nightmares began. The only good that came out of his departure as far as Dunja was concerned was the resumption of the bond between her and Dominik. It grew stronger because she felt a need to protect him as she had when he was much younger.

Chapter twenty-nine

At the end of middle school when Dominik was fifteen he couldn't get any sense out of his mother so he spoke to his father about his study options. On a sunny Saturday afternoon in mid-summer they were walking in Maksimir when Dominik brought up the subject.

'I want to study art Tata, like Dunja.'

'That would mean going to university.'

'Yes, that's what I want.'

'I don't have enough money for you to do that.'

'But I can draw as well as Dunja.'

'I know, but I can't afford it. I was thinking you should take metalwork or woodwork at vocational school.'

'What would I do with those subjects? I want to be an artist.' Dominik's voice had gone flat.

'I'm sure there's a trade you could get into after you finish school.'

Dominik was crushed. Instead of answering his father he began kicking the gravel at the edge of the pathway where they were walking.

'You're angry with me, aren't you?' his father said as he came to a halt and looked at his son.

'No,' Dominik said as he continued to kick the gravel but not quite so viciously.

'You don't have to hide it, you know. I'd be angry if I was you. But the fact is, there's nothing I can do about it. I'm sorry. If I had the money then it would be different.'

'You let Dunja go, so why can't I?'

'Things were different then. Your mother and I were together. Now I have more expenses.'

Dominik sighed. He had nothing left to say.

'Shall we go and get an ice cream?' his father asked.

Dominik hesitated before he answered. He was doing his best to hang on to his anger and frustration until in the end he agreed to the ice cream and attending trade school.

At the end of summer Dominik enrolled at the Crafts and Industrial Building School. The school was an old one which had been operating on various sites around Zagreb since 1882. Dominik's subjects were carpentry, stone cutting and plastering. The school in Avenija Većeslava Holjevca wasn't far from home and it was on the tram route, which was a bonus. He could catch the tram at a stop close by and the journey only took half an hour.

While he was pleased to be learning carpentry, he wasn't so sure about stone cutting or plastering. He couldn't see himself working in either of those occupations. Regardless, he did well at all three subjects and had no difficulty passing the exams. He hoped his excellent marks would be helpful when the time came to choose a career. Although that was a while away. First he had to complete his compulsory military training which he was not looking forward to in the slightest.

It was during the evening a few days after he had finished his exams when Dominik heard Dunja rummaging around in the cupboard in the hallway and he went to see what she was doing.

'What are you up to?' he asked as he watched her fiddling with the straps on an old leather suitcase. When she didn't answer him he was sure she was up to something.

'I'm going to Paris,' she said at last.

'How long for?'

'I don't know.' She shrugged.

'For a holiday?'

'No, I think ... maybe permanent.'

'Why?'

When she continued to hesitate he knew something serious was on her mind.

'I need a change,'

'From what? *Majka?*

'Not exactly, but there is that. I've had it up to here with communism,' she said as she raised her arm above her head.

'Go on,' he said. 'I'm listening.'

'I don't know how you feel, but I've grown tired of Tito cramming loyalty to the state down our throats and suppressing our freedom of speech. I don't think I can listen to anymore of his speeches. I've heard his favourite slogan *brotherhood and unity* once too often. His ridiculously high spirits don't ring true with me. And if I have to continue watching his posturing, I might regret my impulsive behaviour.' Dunja fell silent. When Dominik did nothing other than continue to look at her, she carried on. 'There's no point in complaining to *Majka* or *Tata*. They worship him as if he's the second Christ. As you know *Tata* doesn't mention him often, but *Majka* does on the rare occasions she expresses herself.'

'Tell me about it. She has told me so often that if it wasn't for Tito she wouldn't have her apartment,' Dominik said. 'We're led to believe he has the people's best interests at heart, but does he? I read the other day that he owns thirty-two official residences. How can a communist who lives like a king care about anyone except himself?'

'Precisely! His vanity does nothing to endear me to him either. Did you know he dyes his hair and uses a sun lamp to maintain a permanent suntan? He also changes his clothes up to four times a day and insists that his extensive wardrobe is kept in immaculate condition. Dispicable and so vain. I've had enough.'

'Did you read the report of the last meeting of the Comintern?' Dominik asked.

'I certainly did. He's been elevated to President of Yugoslavia for life, hasn't he?'

'That's right. We're going to be stuck with him for an awfully long time unless he dies. It's been grim enough knowing we must constantly restrain our behaviour unless we wish to end up in Goli Otok, but with this new agenda about indoctrinating the people, life could be more restrictive,' Dominik said.

'For the whole of my existence it's been impossible to make adverse comments about the state to anyone — and that includes my friends. Words uttered in jest could land me in prison because you never know who might inform on you. So far no one has reported me, well not that I know about, but I'm well aware that my outspoken behaviour puts me at constant risk. It's time to get out. I don't want to be one of those who mysteriously disappear — eaten by the night — as they say.' Dunja gave a weak laugh.

'I get why you're leaving and it's easier to get out of the country now than it used to be; just as well we don't live in the USSR. I'd come too if I could, but right now I have to psyche myself into my stint in the army. I told you I'd be called up. The letter came today. I was coming to tell you when I heard you rummaging around in the cupboard.'

'So you're not mad at me for leaving then? I was worried you might be.'

'No, of course not. I totally understand. Just don't forget to write. Oh and what about *Majka* and *Tata?* Have you told them?'

'No, not yet. *Majka* probably won't notice whether I'm here or not and I'm sorry to burden you with the responsibility of her, but you'll be gone for a while, won't you? When do you leave?'

'I'll be away for a year. I leave in a couple of weeks. Are you leaving for Paris before then?'

'Yes. The day after tomorrow.'

'And *Tata?* Have you told him yet?'

'I'll tell him first thing tomorrow,' Dunja replied.

'He won't be concerned. He has his own life now and it's not as if we see that much of him.'

'By the way, it goes without saying that we didn't have this conversation about our leader. If our views become known we'll be in trouble.'

'Trust us to be the odd pair in a silent majority,' Dominik said as he gave a sardonic laugh.

Chapter thirty

After two weeks Dunja's job hunting paid off when she answered an advert in the newspaper and found work as a live-in nanny for a family living in a grand house in Avenue Paul Doumer in the sixteenth arrondissement in Passy. It also meant she would be able to leave the scruffy room she had rented in the fifth arrondissement near the bookshops and the university.

Ivan was Croatian. He had married a French woman and they had two young boys, Adam and Louis who were not yet school age. Dunja felt quite confident about taking on the job after having looked after Dominik when he was a child. Although she hadn't found it easy explaining why she thought she was qualified to be a nanny for the first time.

Ivan, a fabric wholesaler, interviewed Dunja in his office. The coffee table in front of the sofa where Dunja sat was covered with swatches of fabric samples. He had to move them to make a space for their coffee cups.

'My mother has always worked and my father wasn't home a lot so I helped *Majka* by taking care of my younger brother,' she said. She'd stopped short of saying that her mother was hopelessly vague and distracted and had no interest in her son.

When Ivan didn't comment immediately and chose instead to light a cigarette, puff on it and watch the smoke rise towards the ceiling, Dunja was momentarily worried he would think she wasn't experienced enough with children.

'Sounds okay to me. They're good boys,' he said at length. 'I don't think you'll have too much bother looking after them. And the big plus is you speak Serbo Croat which is how I speak to them, while my wife talks to them in French. As I said in the advert it's a live-in position and you'd only be required to look after the boys during working hours, not on weekends or at night unless we have a function to attend.'

'So you want them growing up bilingual?'

'Yes, that's the idea. What do you say we go and meet the boys and their mother before we get down to the practical stuff like money and when you can start?'

'I've got the job then?'

'Yes, pending the boys and my wife getting along with you.'

When Dunja stopped in a doorway to put a match to her cigarette, the late evening sun was silhouetting her reflection in the window of a boutique. Across the road was the café where she was meeting her friends — students she met last year when she came to Paris to study Art History, the final module of her degree.

The Brasserie Lipp seemed to Dunja as if it had been there forever. She was struck by its elegance — the highly polished timber walls and balustrades, the hand-painted wall tiles with art deco illustrations more than two-metres tall and the ceiling decorated with large, nude murals. There was nowhere else quite like it. She was pleased to be back in Paris.

After one last drag on her cigarette, it was time to go inside.

She was the last to arrive. Her new friends were already seated at two tables that had been pushed together.

'*Bonjour mes amis!*' she called out.

'Ah, Diana, you're here at last.

Not long after her arrival in Paris, Dunja made her big decision. She'd always hated her name, so she decided to call herself Diana — in Paris at least. Diana Letica had a much better ring to it.

I was beginning to think you weren't coming,' Françoise said as she tucked a stray piece of dark hair behind her ear.

'As usual, I lost track of time,' Dunja replied.

'Well, you're here now and that's all that matters,' she said. 'Sit down and I'll introduce you to the newcomers.' She introduced them as Jean-Marc, her cousin, with his shoulder-length dark blond hair, and his good-looking friend Pierre.

Dunja was glad they were speaking English. She was proud of her English, which she had learnt at school, and continued to study at university. It was far superior to her French and she could converse well enough in it to have a serious, intellectual conversation.

That night, someone brought up another controversial subject for discussion — the chemical defoliant used by the United States military forces during the Vietnam War. Jean-Marc was not familiar with Agent Orange.

'What do you mean orange?' he asked. 'Does it turn you orange?' When no one laughed, he blushed and allowed his shaggy hair to obscure his face.

During a temporary lull in the conversation Dunja took the opportunity to light a cigarette. She exhaled and found herself smiling — as usual their conversation was a lively one.

The conversation took a different turn when Paul, the young man with striking green eyes, who was sitting at the far end of the table, introduced a new topic.

'So, what'll happen now that Pompidou has died? Will d'Estaing make a good leader?'

'Did anyone read his speech in the newspaper last week?' Pierre, one of the newcomers, asked. Before anybody could answer, he continued. 'It was good. No, it was better than good. He spoke with confidence about more liberal attitudes towards divorce, abortion and contraception. Seems to me he's got the right idea.' At the end of his last sentence Pierre looked down, as if he was embarrassed about his short, forthright contribution.

The conversation moved on, but Dunja wasn't concentrating. She had became conscious of Pierre sitting next to her. He was quiet, but not in a subdued way and he had made a contribution to the conversation. Not that she blamed him for being silent — it had become quite heated at one point. During another pause in the conversation, Pierre stood up and headed to the toilet. Dunja wondered if he'd come straight from his job. He was the only man at the table wearing a tie — a swirly design in several different shades of blue — her favourite colour. When he resumed his seat at the table, Pierre accidentally kicked Dunja's foot.

'*Oh pardon. Excusez moi, s'il vous plaît,*' he said.

'*Pas de problème,*' she replied in what she knew was an atrocious French accent.

'You have the most brilliant blue eyes,' he said in English. His voice had a velvety drawl.

'Thank you.' she said, blushing.

Conversations carried on around her, but she found herself drifting off. Pierre's presence had had a dramatic effect on her. Then when he moved and the overhead light illuminated his hair, she gulped. His brunette waves were tipped with the same bronze colour as her mother's hair when she was younger.

All too soon the evening ended.

The next day when Pierre called Dunja couldn't believe it.

'I hope you don't mind, but I got your number from Françoise and I was wondering if you'd have lunch with me on Sunday?' he said.

After they arranged to meet outside the Metro station at Bir Hakeim in the fifteenth arrondissement, Dunja knew it would be a long few days until Sunday.

It was late summer, the weather was settled and warm and she couldn't decide what to wear. Her Levis and a casual short-sleeved white jacket or her gypsy-style blue and white dress. In the end she chose the dress.

The sun shone softly out of a pale-blue sky as she waited outside the station. It was easy to spot Pierre waiting beside the wrought-iron fence leading on to the platform. He was tall; he stood out in the crowd and he looked more dashing than she remembered. He was laden with shopping bags from the nearby market at Boulevard de Grenelle.

After crossing the Bir Hakeim bridge they descended the shell-patterned, cobbled roadway beside the riverbank. Dunja wondered where they were going, but Pierre wouldn't say. On one side the muddy river was rushing past, while across the road, above a brasserie, were multi-storeyed, stone residences with wrought-iron balustrades as intricate as a fancy piece of knitting. She wondered if he lived in an apartment above the brasserie. She was staring up at the building, speculating which one it could be, when he told her they had arrived.

'Whereabouts is your house?'

'Follow me,' he beckoned. A few steps further on, they came to a boat.

'Isn't she beautiful?' he said proudly, gesturing towards a sleek, olive-green barge with *Marie Louise* inscribed on its bow. Dunja stared in fascination. It was enormous as well as immaculate, with a raised deck at either end. The nearest aft one, was set with a dining table and chairs beneath a cream umbrella, and surrounded by red geraniums in terracotta pots. She couldn't wait to see inside. When they descended the companionway leading to the main cabin, Dunja gulped at the splendour before her. To the left was the galley with its white porcelain sink and brass taps. She knew it must be old; regardless, the brass gleamed at her like two, golden winking eyes. The furniture combined with these old treasures and made the interior stylish and sophisticated. Dunja's glance roamed until it alighted on the blue and grey oriental carpet in the main saloon. It was plush and she couldn't resist kicking off her shoes and burying her feet in the luxurious pile.

'Gosh! It's beautiful.' To Dunja's ears her words sounded feeble — they didn't come close to expressing the luxury surrounding her.

Pierre put the shopping bags on the bench in the galley and leant against it with his arms folded smiling as though he was a cat who had polished off a bowl of sardines.

'I told you it was special.'

'You did, but I had no idea it would be this special.'

'I'll give you a tour of the other cabins later.'

'Of course! I insist on seeing everything.'

'Okay, let me pour you a glass of *Sancerre*,' he said. 'You can sit here and talk to me while I prepare lunch.' He indicated a built-in seat at the end of the galley. It was covered with striped fabric in varying shades of lavender, Dunja's grandmother's favourite colour and scent. She invariably carried a lavender-scented handkerchief, either tucked up her sleeve or in the pocket of her housecoat. When Dunja was eleven her grandmother taught her how to weave lavender cages from the bunches of long-stemmed lavender she bought at the market in Zagreb. Every summer they'd sit at the kitchen table for long spells crafting enough so they could hang at least one in every room. By the time they had finished their hands were impregnated with the beautiful scent. The heady perfume the cages gave off lingered until almost the following summer when they made new ones.

Pierre was more than competent in the kitchen and it was not difficult for Dunja to unwind and chat while he prepared their meal. Snails in a mornay sauce to begin with, and then *bar* fish and salad. Dunja had never eaten snails, but she didn't tell Pierre.

Over lunch, outside on the aft deck under a sky which was now bright blue, their conversation was laidback and centred on their families. Dunja talked briefly about her parents and how sad she was that they were separated, before she moved on to her beloved grandmother.

'You'd love her — she's the best. And I can always ask her for advice. Sometimes, I wish she was my mother. She and I are so much closer than my mother and me. But that's another story and I don't want to bore you with it.'

'I can be a good listener if you want to try me.'

'Thanks, but I'd rather not spoil today. What about your family?'

'Well, my grandparents are no longer alive. In my immediate family there's only my mother and father. Oh, and my Uncle Martin — he lives in Bonnieux, in Provence. I go there when I can. I love it because it's so different to Paris.'

'Do you get on well with your parents?' She hoped he didn't think she was being nosy, but family matter a lot — in her country.

'My parents are ... hmmm, caring and supportive is the best way to describe them. They're very generous, especially when I moved here.'

'You're lucky,' Dunja said, feeling a twinge of envy.

'Yes, I am. I have two sisters, Angélique and Hélène, who are younger than me and live at home. What about you? Brothers and sisters?'

'Only Dominik, he's a lot younger than me.'

'And you're twenty-eight, right?'

'Yes I am. How did you guess?'

'Maybe I'm psychic.' Pierre laughed.

'And you?'

'I'm the same age as you.'

'Are you?'

Her reply made Pierre laugh. 'My mother often tells me I'm becoming old before my time,' he said.

'Is she giving you a compliment?'

'Of course! Sometimes she says I'm too serious and if I don't watch out life will pass me by before I've had any fun.'

'That's true,' Dunja said and laughed. It wasn't that funny, but they were on to their second bottle of wine, the atmosphere had loosened up and Dunja's laughter was uninhibited.

'So what kind of pictures do you paint?' Pierre asked.

'Mostly abstracts. I love experimenting with texture. I often thin my paints when I'm looking for more translucent colours.'

'So tell me, who are your favourite artists? Wait a minute, we need more wine, your glass is empty. Better still, why don't we save this conversation for later and I'll take you on the promised tour instead.'

With their glasses topped up, they walked through the galley, along a short passage into the main cabin where the walls were painted the pale caramel of toffee. A black leather sofa caught Dunja's eye; it looked the perfect size to curl up on with a book. The leather was cool under her touch.

'It's called a love seat. Like the famous one designed by Salvador Dali, except that Dali's was red,' Pierre said.

'I have to try it out,' Dunja murmured as she lay on it and curled up. When she turned towards Pierre, who was watching her, his curls had swung forward and she couldn't see the expression in his eyes. She was dying to know what he was thinking, but she found out soon enough when he moved closer and trailed his fingertips along the inside of her arm. It was a delicious sensation, as if she was lying at the water's edge and her body was being lapped by soft waves. Her limbs felt languid — as if they didn't belong to her. She was quivering inside as a floating sensation overcame her. His mouth connected with hers in what began as a slow gentle kiss but was quickly replaced by one that was more urgent. She breathed in the citrus fragrance of his aftershave together with the scent of her own arousal as her eyelids drooped. Pierre took her hand and led her towards his double bunk — her euphoria remained intact.

'Close your eyes,' he said, as his hands undid the buttons on his shirt. Dunja pretended to do as he asked, but through slitted lids she watched him peeling off his clothes. Her breath caught at the sight of his naked body — well-muscled and hairless. The tip of his erect penis was glistening. He unzipped her dress down the side and tugged off her clothes. The tang of his aftershave grew stronger as he lowered himself onto her and covered her body with his. By the time he entered her, she cried out in ecstasy.

Chapter thirty-one

Dominik was almost eighteen when he started his year of compulsory military training living in the barracks outside Zagreb. From day one most of what he endured came as a nasty shock.

As soon as he arrived he was ordered to strip and put his clothes and personal effects into a plastic bag. They would be stored elsewhere for the duration of his internment. Delousing was compulsory and after they were relieved of their clothes, body after body was immersed in a murky, strong-smelling solution in an old tin bath. The Yugoslav army uniform he was issued with was made of rough fabric which scratched and chaffed his skin. His boots were heavy, poorly manufactured and uncomfortable. He developed blisters within half a day of wearing them. None of that surprised him. What he hadn't known about was the medical check-up. A doctor checked his teeth, eyes, heart and joints with a technique that was rough and quick. Dominik was naked when he thought the thin-faced, olive-skinned doctor with the unsmiling countenance had finished examining him. He jumped when the doctor barked at him.

'Bend over and touch your toes,' he ordered. Dominik jumped when he felt the doctor's cold hand prising his arse apart. *Is he looking for piles or trying to ascertain whether I'm a homosexual?* He never found out the answer, because he didn't dare ask, but thankfully that part of the examination was over with quickly.

In the raw-unfinished timber barracks with its rough, sarking ceiling, Dominik was issued with a threadbare-murky sheet complete with cigarette burns, a coarse blanket and a lumpy pillow. Beds stretched down both sides of the rectangular-shaped room, which had one door opening to the exterior, and a pot belly stove perched like a gargoyle in the centre. Without double glazing it would be uncomfortably cold in winter. Beds had to be kept in immaculate order without a wrinkle or an untucked edge in sight and on day one he learnt that if one millimetre of blanket or sheet was out of place he would forfeit lunch. By far the biggest problem he dealt with was the lack of privacy. It was non-existent in the bunk room, the shower and the toilet block. His second problem was the voices of his superiors. Orders were always bellowed out. It was as if they believed the recruits were deaf or insubordinate by nature. It took Dominik more than a week to stop jumping everytime an order was shouted at him or anyone nearby. The words, 'You soldier!' had him constantly on edge.

Lunchtime on his first day was a welcome relief. At least he could talk to the group of new recruits he was seated with, even if the conversation was an inane one where they told each other their names and where they lived, as they sat at the scarred, timber table in the mess block, while they ate their tasteless grey meal. A dollop of potato, a pile of cabbage and specks of slate-coloured meat floating in a thin gravy was dumped on to their tin plates. Everybody was dished out the same amount and there were no second helpings. At the end of the meal he was still hungry.

After lunch the recruits assembled on the barren parade ground to listen to the speech from their commanding officer given in a dull monotone, as if he was reciting from a textbook. It was August, in the height of summer as they stood in the baking heat. The officer had a large head, a bright-red face and such a short hair cut that there were bristles standing up on top of his head.

'During your time here you will follow the rules and when I say follow the rules I mean absolutely right down to what might seem to you to be a trivial order. You're here to learn allegiance to Yugoslavia and discipline. You must address all officers by their rank — sergeant, major or corporal — learn this well now or get used to spending time in solitary confinement with bread and water for company,' he said as his face grew redder and sweat ran down his cheeks and dripped onto the hard-packed earth at his feet. 'The punishment for insubordination will he handed out as often as is necessary. And make no mistake we don't tolerate disobedience in any shape or form.'

Sweat poured off Dominik as he stood at attention and feigned interest.

On his second day, he began the regular routine of drills on the parade ground as the officer in charge shouted staccato instructions — *one, two — one, two — left, left — left, right*

— Dominik could barely distinguish this word because he said it in such a weird voice — staaand at ease — quuuick march! From then on he suffered this tedious exercise three times a day. In between times he was lectured about fitness and discipline. The favoured gruelling routine was to make the would-be soldiers carry rocks from one area to another. But the forced marches at night with a heavy pack on his back were by far the worst regimen, especially when winter arrived early.

Week one had not ended when one of his fellow trainees made the fatal mistake of answering back the officer inspecting bed-making skills.

'I can see wrinkles in the blanket at the end of your bed,' the officer roared.

'My mother never taught me how to make my bed,' the recruit said as his face immediately turned dark red and sweat glistened on his forehead when he realised too late that his smart remark wouldn't be well received.

'Soldier! I didn't hear you soldier,' the officer with the shaved head and shoulders held so far back that it looked painful, bellowed in a harsher voice. 'Address me as sergeant.'

'Yes, sergeant,' the defective bed-maker shouted.

Dominik stifled a laugh, which was just as well, because otherwise he too would have been punished.

'Enjoy your stay in solitary confinement, soldier,' the officer bellowed as he stalked from the room and pulled at his jacket to straighten his immaculate uniform.

After two months of repetitive routine designed to shape the recruits into soldiers, weapons training was added to their fitness and marching drills. Dominik was looking forward to shooting a gun and was disappointed when he spent the next two months doing nothing other than pulling apart pistols, cleaning them and putting them back together. He had been in the army for six months before he fired a Russian AK47. It was crude but efficient enough with its big banana magazine. There weren't enough rifles to go around so they took turns using the ones they had. While it was an exhilarating, exacting experience shooting at a target and hitting the head or torso, Dominik could never imagine firing at a live target let alone killing a person.

At the end of every day he was exhausted. He read the letters Dunja sent every week from Paris, but he seldom found time to reply and if he did it was no more than a few brief lines to tell her he was okay. He didn't see the point in telling her how much he detested being in the army or about the severe discipline and disgraceful food. And besides, when he found out she had a boyfriend, he didn't think she'd be interested.

He never received a single letter from his mother, but he wasn't expecting one.

At night, he fell asleep as soon as he got into bed and it seemed as though he had been asleep for too short a time when he had to get up. His thoughts during this time were never profound. He had no time for in-depth thinking. His existence was taken up coping with the gruelling demands of the army routine and battling his constant hunger.

Towards the end of his training, when he'd been there for nine months, he became aware that he had changed. He was lean and fit, and he had developed a definite mindset. The diet of communist fodder at school together with this stint in the Yugoslav People's Army where communist propaganda was rammed down his throat every day had turned his thinking far more liberal. He had become an atheist. He didn't subscribe to communism, socialism and certainly not nationalism or Catholicism. He knew he was different from the usual socialist or communist youth. Being force fed an unpalatable diet had caused him to rebel. He felt sickened to the very depths of his soul and believed he was surrounded by a bunch of fanatics. Yet he dare not voice his thoughts and opinions to anyone because he knew it was unlikely many thought as he did. The brainwashing was extreme and repetitive and for that reason it succeeded quite readily. It was then that he decided to only believe in himself.

The entire year was a dreadful experience he hoped never to repeat, although he was mindful that until he turned thirty he could be called up again at any time, and if he was he felt sure he would never want to kill another human being.

Chapter thirty-two

When winter held off for a time Dunja returned more than once to her favourite places. She couldn't get enough of them. Pierre delighted in teasing her the day she said she wanted to visit the Cluny Museum for the third time. 'Maybe they won't let you in. Perhaps they'll think you are a burglar reconnoitering the place,' he said.

One Saturday morning, after the first winter storm had stripped the last of the leaves from the branches of the skeletal, silver-trunked trees in the Jardin du Luxembourg, Dunja sat on a bench sketching them, warmly wrapped in her hat and coat. The air was crisp and calm. The park was deserted and she loved it there, summer or winter. Around her, giant, rust-coloured leaves clung to wet grass. To her right a new lawn was being laid. The newly smoothed surface was pitted with indents from the previous night's heavy shower of rain. Fat worms that had escaped the freshly dug soil were slithering along the concrete nearby.

In the middle of winter, after the longest wait, the Centre Georges Pompidou was finally open — Dunja couldn't keep away. She'd been to look at it on several occasions during its construction and been intrigued by all the glass, steel and vivid colours. She had never seen a building such as this where the ducts and pipes were on the exterior of the building rather than in the ceiling spaces. It struck her as so unusual that she spent some time staring at it before she went inside.

So many of her favourite artists were represented there — Kandinsky, Klimt, Picasso, Matisse and Chagall. She was ridiculously excited before her first visit when she set out on one of the coldest days of the season. Prior to her departure, because she was fearful of getting lost, she mapped out the route. She hurried past homeless people; one man without any toes and two women carrying babies in slings. There were Afro-Carribeans and West Africans aplenty. She was not used to these people with their incredibly black skins. Diverse smells assaulted her nostrils — urine, freshly baked croissants and wet dog hair. Uncertain if she was going in the right direction she pressed on with an ever increasing feeling of claustrophobia, knowing she must find a more direct route for her return journey.

Sheltered from the cold, inside the colourful glass cage of the Pompidou Centre, she wandered from room to room lingering before the sensual feast of art for as long as possible. The spaces were huge and she must have walked miles, yet she didn't notice her tired feet. She was humbled in front of *Mit dem Schwarzen Bogen* by Kandinsky where the objects on the canvas of the arresting abstract seemed about to collide. She moved on to Chagall's *Les Mariés de la Tour Eiffel* where she stood for sometime intrigued by the mix of Russian and Parisian elements, the surreal background, and the giant white cockerel next to the bridal couple.

As well as the opening of the Pompidou Centre, the middle of winter brought bad news for Dunja. Ivan and his family were moving to New York and no longer needed her as a nanny.

She couldn't imagine not being able to live in Paris. When Ivan said he needed to talk to her about another change in plans she was sure this would be gloomier tidings because she knew for sure he wouldn't be staying in Paris. Perhaps their departure date had moved forward? On the day he invited her into his office, where colourful bolts of fabric were stacked against the walls, she was wound up.

'Please sit down, relax. Your expression makes me think your entire world has disintegrated.' Ivan laughed and exposed his crooked teeth.

Dunja wasn't sure how to react. It wasn't in her nature to complain and she was reluctant to mention how she felt, yet she had to say something. 'It's just that I enjoy looking after Adam and Louis and I'll miss them.' In her mind's eye she saw the two of them giggling when she took them to the children's playground where they chased each other around in circles and tumbled about on the springy lawn in Parc Passy. There was only eleven months difference in their ages and they looked like twins with the same olive complexions and big brown eyes, although Adam, the eldest was slightly bigger and fractionally taller than his brother.

'I'm sure they enjoy you too,' Ivan replied. 'They talk about you a lot when you're not here, you know. But listen, it isn't all bad. Something has come up and I think it might suit you.'

'A job, you mean?'

'Yes, one here in Paris.' His reply made her sit up straight and lean towards him.

'I have a friend, Mirjana who's a fashion designer. She works from home and she's looking for a live-in assistant. The position isn't available for a month, so you could take a holiday first. What do you think? I have her number here. You could call her …'

'But I've never worked in fashion before. I do appreciate you trying to help me out, but I don't imagine she'd want to employ anyone as inexperienced as me.' She slumped in her chair while Ivan stroked his small moustache and looked at her thoughtfully.

'Why don't I call her? You could give it a try, couldn't you?'

Dunja chewed the inside of her bottom lip while Ivan lit a cigarette and waited for her answer. 'But I've got no experience at all in that field.' She looked down at her black suede boots.

'I'll call her and speak to her first before I give you the phone,' he said as he reached for the telephone on his desk.

Dunja couldn't sit still. She crossed and uncrossed her ankles several times while she listened to his quietly spoken voice.

'She has a lot of artistic talent as well as a degree from Zagreb University. I believe she would grasp a new job quickly,' he said, winking at Dunja.

By the time he handed over the telephone receiver, Dunja's mouth felt as though she'd been incarcerated in solitary confinement for too long without water.

Chapter thirty-three

Dominik was relieved when he was discharged from the army. He had suffered most of his year in silence and didn't make any new friends. It wasn't that he disliked his fellow recruits. It was more that they had nothing in common. One of the pastimes he really missed during his time there was his love of reading — books of all kinds — fiction and non-fiction. He enjoyed nothing better than immersing himself in the pages of an electrifying book.

Many of the recruits would remain in the army permanently and they often talked about how they were itching to kill. He found many of them brash and overloaded with false courage. Several talked about their conquests with women too. Their language was vulgar and Dominik never took part in those conversations. He had virtually no experience with women and felt he had nothing to contribute. Regardless, he always listened to their talk. It intrigued him, though he thought much of it was exaggerated, but at least it provided entertainment.

He wasn't sure what to expect on the day he returned home. It was a Saturday morning when he was greeted by a silent house with only the loud ticking of the clock to welcome him as he let himself in with his key.

'Anyone home?' he called out. Silence greeted him. He opened the door to the living room where his mother was slumped in her green chair as though she had never left it for the entire year he'd been gone.

'Hello *Majka,* I'm back.'

When she looked up, she acted as though it was yesterday when she had last seen him. 'Where've you been?' she asked. 'You didn't tell me you were going out.'

'Well, I'm back now,' he said as he wandered off to his room shaking his head. She seemed to have lost all sense of time. During his year away he'd had a week's leave, which he'd spent at home, and she'd seemed okay then. At least his conversations with her were relatively normal — or normal for her. He was glad her brothers had been keeping an eye on her while he'd been gone. Dominik got along well with Damir and Zoran and before he'd gone away he'd made a point of asking his uncles to look out for his mother. Regardless, he couldn't help feeling bad about having left her to live by herself for so long. Had she deteriorated during his absence or had he failed to notice how confused she was before he left?

When nothing in the way of a permanent job revealed itself and because he had no other options, Dominik began working as a night-time waiter in the restaurant where Tonci, his best friend, worked as a chef. Tonci had put in a good word for him with the manager. It was a traditional Croatian restaurant, where the menu hadn't changed for years, and it was frequented by customers looking for a cheap meal. The head waiter was past his use-by date. He was so overweight the buttons on his grubby-black shirt had popped open in the region of his stomach. He had a strip of grey hair plastered across the middle of his bald scalp and he had an issue with his right foot. Perhaps it was an injury or maybe twenty-seven years on his feet had taken its toll. Over time he had become lazy too. He never pulled his weight and on busy nights, Dominik and the other staff were run off their feet while he sauntered around issuing orders as though he was their commanding officer. Dominik lasted there for three months before he became unemployed. Being treated as if he was still in the army was too difficult to tolerate.

With his sister in Paris, for the first time ever Dominik felt lonely. His mother provided no company at all; he seldom saw his father and he only got together with Tonci on his nights off. Being unemployed meant Dominik was short of money and he didn't always accept Tonci's invitations to go out. If he couldn't pay his way he didn't feel comfortable asking Tonci to pay for him.

A month later Dominik answered an advertisement in the morning paper for a company looking to hire a trainee furniture designer. Despondent about finding a job that interested him, he decided if he didn't get this one he would do as his sister had done and leave the country. Instead of France he would go to Switzerland or Germany as so many citizens from Yugoslavia were doing — thousands in fact. It was the fashion to live and work in certain European countries where job opportunities were greater and the pay was much better. However, it didn't come to that. He started work for *Stolica Dizajn* a week after his interview.

It was a large factory and considering it was state-owned it could have been worse. Stipan, Dominik's boss was lenient, with a relaxed attitude that bordered on carelessness, which made Dominik's days easy enough.

His desk was in a room along with other workers mostly engaged in different tasks to his, except for Damir Yelcić, a grey-mousy individual, who was short on words, and who worked at the same job as Dominik. The working space was cramped and the room only had a small window high up on one wall. Dominik's desk was in the back corner in front of the wall and that suited him fine. The desk beside him was vacant.

He had no difficulty picking up the tasks he was given and to begin with he enjoyed the work. His skill at draughting designs on paper was better than Damir's and within a short space of time Damir was transferred to another department because he had botched up one too many drawings. It was then that Dominik found out that Damir had no grounding that would enable him to do his job in a satisfactory manner let alone excel at it. Dominik knew this was typical of many employment situations in Yugoslavia. Unskilled workers were taken on to carry out jobs they knew nothing about and once they started work, no training was given. Dominik was pleased when Damir left. Not because he'd been competition, but because he felt sorry for him when he produced substandard work.

Stolica Dizajn primarily made dining chairs and tables and supplied hotels, restaurants and government offices as well as some party members' residences.

Although Dominik had been employed as a furniture designer his job did not entail coming up with new ideas. He was only expected to modify and improve existing designs. After he had been there for several months he became bored with the repetitive nature of his work and in an attempt to relieve his monotony he drafted a series of designs for chairs with chrome legs and bright orange or avocado-coloured vinyl seats. He would never forget Stipan's reaction.

'What the hell are these?' he said when Dominik showed him what he'd been working on.

'I thought I'd try something new.'

'What for? You know everything we produce is made from wood and we don't deviate from the colour brown.' Much to Dominik's horror Stipan screwed up his drawings and tossed them in the rubbish bin beside Dominik's desk. Speechless, Dominik stared at Stipan's retreating back and his ill-fitting jacket that was two sizes too big for him. It was then when he found out how inflexible he could be.

As soon as Stipan went back to his office Dominik took his work out of the bin and smoothed out the creases. At least he hadn't ripped it up. He wasn't daunted by Stipan's reaction and he carried on drawing new designs. He didn't have enough work and rather than ask for more he continued with what he'd started. He went on to design a love seat modelled along the lines of the one Dunja had described that was in the barge where her boyfriend lived. He wasn't foolish enough to leave any trace of his avant-garde work in his desk though. He took it home because he was certain Stipan went through his desk behind his back.

It was the evening of the day his drawings were rejected when Tonci called and invited him out on a double date. The phone had rung while he'd been lying on his bed reliving the unjustified rejection from Stipan earlier in the day and rereading the last letter from his sister. He had been hoping there'd be a new letter from her in the mail, but there wasn't. Since her boyfriend had come on the scene she didn't write to him as often.

He accepted Tonci's offer immediately. The idea of spending the evening with his sullen mother for company held no appeal.

When Dominik arrived at the Kasalište Kavana Café, Tonci, with his long, lank dark fringe that almost obscured his eyes, and who was getting tubbier by the day, was sprawled between two girls — one with dyed-red hair that was so bright it stood out in the subdued light in the cavernous interior of the café, while the other, who was draped around Tonci, had short-blonde hair. That too was dyed as was evident from the dark regrowth at the roots. As he walked towards them, Dominik wondered where Tonci had found them. Where they prostitutes? He wouldn't have been surprised. Their faces were hard and there was not an ounce of sophistication about either of them. Tonci, whose face was pitted with acne scars, never usually found women who were worth having. Any decent ones he came across were repelled by his body odour.

'Dom, my best buddie. Glad you're here. This is Nina,' he said extricating his gangly limbs from the blonde's grasp. 'And this is Tereza,' he said looking at the brooding redhead who was smoking a cigarette. 'Sit down,' he said pointing towards the spare seat next to Tereza.

'How about I get the next round of drinks first?' Dominik said noting three beer bottles on the table. 'Same again?'

By the time Dominik sat down after waiting an eternity to get served at the bar, the blonde was once more strangling Tonci while the redhead was staring into space. She looked bored. He took a swig of his beer and tried to conjure up some small talk, but all he got were yes and no answers from Tereza. He'd had no practice with women and he hadn't a clue why she was so uncommunicative. They sat in silence while Tonci and Nina snogged each other. When their carry on became too much Dominik commented. 'You gonna do it right there on the sofa?'

'Nah,' Tonci said taking out his hand from under her blouse. 'There's a party on around the corner. Thought we'd go. Are you up for that?'

'Sure,' Dominik said thinking anything would be better than sitting here next to the unfriendly redhead.

'Doesn't start for another hour though, so let's drink up,' Tonci said. 'I'll get the next round.' He stood up and so did Nina. Tonci headed for the bar while Nina went towards the toilet.

'What kind of work do you do?' Dominik asked Tereza.

'Not much,' she said after a pause.

'What's not much?'

'Just what I said.' Her voice was snappy and he wondered if he'd hit a raw nerve. Her response left him feeling inadequate and pissed off.

'Do you mind if I have one?' he said indicating her cigarette packet that was on the table in front of them.

'Help yourself,' she said in a flat couldn't-care-less voice. Dominik wasn't a smoker. He smoked the odd cigarette from time to time, usually when he was stressed, and he had a feeling he would be smoking quite a few this evening, unless Tereza suddenly came to life or he left early.

Chapter thirty-four

In vivid contrast to the new Charles de Gaulle airport, Dunja found Pleso airport in Zagreb dingy and overcrowded. On the drive into the city, the buildings were discoloured and grimy and litter clogged the gutters along the sides of the road. People, in their unfashionable outfits, were as drab and colourless as shrivelled mongooses. Inside the taxi Dunja tried to make polite conversation.

'How's the weather been?' she asked the driver.

'What? Can't you see by looking out the window?' The taxi driver, with his thin-lipped mouth and acidic tongue, was curt and rude.

It was an unfortunate welcome home; she remained silent and was glad when she reached her destination.

Dunja loved being in her grandmother's house. As she expected, nothing had changed with her family — except that her grandmother was sick — hence Dunja's arrival in Zagreb after she received her brother's letter.

If you can spare the time, I think you should come for a visit. Baba is quite down these days and I'm worried about her, his letter had said.

She had always thought of her as a strong woman who was hardly ever ill let alone confined to bed. If she thought about it consciously, Dunja imagined she would live forever. Now she had a heart condition — Dunja didn't know exactly what was wrong with her; it wasn't a topic that anyone in the family would elaborate on.

As soon as she could Dunja went to visit her. She thought she looked the same as usual, except for the dark hemispheres under her eyes, although when Dunja asked how she was, all she did was shrug.

'We'll see,' she said without looking at her granddaughter who was sitting next to her on her bed.

Dunja continued to stare at her, perturbed by her words. *We'll see* was never a good omen no matter what it referred to.

With pillows propped behind her, Mara was sitting up in bed and her wrinkled hands were on top of a snow-white sheet with an embroidered lace edge. She was stroking the lace pattern with her fingers, the same fingers that had embroidered that intricate edge many years ago, before they became gnarled and misshapen. Above her on the expanse of white wall was a large brass crucifix.

'Now, *Draga*, tell me about this boyfriend of yours,' she said as she reached out and stroked her granddaughter's hair.

How did she know about him? Dominik must have told her even though she'd told him not to tell anyone. Why had he done that? Perhaps he thought *Baba* was trustworthy. Dunja was reluctant to talk about Pierre. She would be expected to marry a man from her own country and if her family found out she had a French boyfriend, it would be met with disapproval.

'Come on, you know you can tell your old *Baba*. I've always kept all your secrets for you, haven't I?' Her grandmother grinned with toothless gums. Her faded eyes had regained their old sparkle.

'Well, his name's Pierre.'

'Is he a decent man?'

'Of course.'

'And what kind of job does he have?' she asked smiling broadly.

'He works with computers. Can you believe it? It's something new. I don't know anything about it, but he enjoys it and he's well paid. And then there's his house. It's a floating apartment — a barge on the Seine River.'

'Tell me about his family. Are they respectable? I don't have to remind you about the importance of family.'

'I haven't met them yet, but when I return we'll be having dinner at their house.'

'Good,' she nodded and patted her hand. 'That's as it should be.' She paused. 'Now, I want you to promise me that if you love him and he asks you to be his wife, you'll say yes. Here, you may not be able to choose who you marry. I want you to be happy, so you must promise me you'll do what I did and follow your heart.'

Dunja was touched by her words — she smiled. There was no way she could consider telling her she never intended to get married. She didn't want to hurt her even though her grandmother was different from many Yugoslav women. Sometimes people criticised her because she spoke her mind. Neither did she have any tolerance for chauvinistic men in a society that was full of them. So many times Dunja had heard her grandmother tell her mother she needed to assert herself.

"Tell Nikola how you feel about him coming home so late all the time. There's no reason why you should put up with that bad behaviour," Dunja recalled her grandmother saying to her mother not long before her husband moved out. It was a waste of time; her mother never broached the subject as far as Dunja knew. Her grandmother and her mother were total opposites and she often found it hard to believe they were mother and daughter. Whereas she and her *Baba* were kindred spirits in many ways and that was probably the reason why they were close.

They sat in companionable silence and because her grandmother had mentioned him, Dunja's mind drifted to thoughts about her grandfather who had died before she was born. Dunja didn't know much about why he had died. No one in the family talked about it. She would have liked to ask her grandmother what happened before he died. Instead, she asked her a different question. 'Did your parents approve of you marrying *Dida*?'

'No, but I made it plain that I wouldn't give him up and in the end they had to give in. He was a good man regardless of the fact that he was Serbian. There's good and bad in all races,' she said.

Dunja could see she was tired when her eyes closed and her head fell back onto the pillow.

It was the middle of that night and Dunja was sound asleep in her mother's house where she was staying when the phone rang. She wondered who it could be and when it kept ringing and neither Dominik nor her mother got up to answer it, Dunja decided she must take the call. Her voice was hesitant as she answered it. It occurred to her that it could be just a wrong number or a crank caller, although as far as she was aware no malicious calls had ever been received by either Dominik or her mother.

'Dunja, she gone. *Majka's* gone,' Damir stammered in a tear-filled voice.

For a minute his words didn't register and Dunja said nothing, until it hit her, but even then she couldn't speak.

'I went to check on her a short time ago and as soon as I looked at her I knew she was gone.'

As soon as he said she was gone for the second time, Dunja broke down and began to sob loudly — great shuddering sobs that left her gasping her air.

'Will you come over now?' Damir asked.

'Yes,' she stammered in an almost incoherent voice just before she put down the phone. At that moment Dominik emerged from his room rubbing his eyes.

'What's happened? Your crying woke me.'

'Oh Dominik, it's *Baba*. She's ... she's.' Her voice trailed away.

'You *mean* she's—' Dominik couldn't say the word either.

Dunja stepped towards her brother and he wrapped her in his arms as she cried her heart out. 'Uncle Damir asked me to come over. Will you come with me?'

'Of course. Should I wake *Majka?*'

'I don't think so. What do you think?'

'No, I'll tell her later. She is so out of it these days I have no idea how she'll react, and if she falls apart, we could do without having to cope with that.'

As she got dressed Dunja remained stunned. She didn't want to believe what had happened. She should have been pleased to have been with her so close to when she died, but that was no consolation. She couldn't stop clinging to the anger she felt that she had lost her.

The doctor that Damir had called was just leaving as Dunja and Dominik arrived, and after expressing his condolences he scurried away down the path that lead from the front door with his head down.

The rest of the family were assembled in the bedroom where Mara lay. Zoran and Damir were standing crying quietly when Dominik and Dunja went in. Dunja walked straight to the bed and picked up her grandmother's hand which was lying on top of the pristine white sheet. She was shocked by how cold and lifeless it was. She shuddered as she looked at her beloved *Baba's* face. Her eyes were closed and she was as pale as she had been the day before when Dunja had last seen her. Dunja stepped closer to the bed and without thinking she climbed on to the bed and wrapped her arms around her grandmother's body. Once again Dunja's body shook as she wept.

It was Damir who spoke first. 'Come, let's go into the living room. I'll make tea or we can half something stronger for those of you who want it,' he said. 'There's plenty of *rakija.'*

'Come on Dunja. Come and have something to drink. She wouldn't want you to make a fuss,' Zoran said as he stepped forward and tried to prise Dunja way from his mother's body. But Dunja refused to let go her hold on her grandmother.

'Leave her,' Dominik said. 'She'll come when she's ready.'

Damir shrugged and was the first to leave the room.

Instead of making tea, he set several small glasses and three different flavoured bottles of *rakija* on the table. There was blueberry, walnut and plum. All had been made by Mara. Once everyone was in the room Damir filled the glasses. He then picked up a glass of walnut *rakija* and raised it in the air. 'Let's drink to the life of a beautiful woman who has now gone to join her beloved husband. There was no finer woman than our mother,' he said before he emptied the contents of his glass in one go and refilled it immediately.

While Dunja stayed behind at their grandmother's house Dominik returned home to impart the sad news to his mother. Zlata was in the kitchen drinking tea when he returned and she took no notice as he entered the kitchen.

When he pulled out a chair and sat down opposite her she finally looked at him.

'It's Mara ... your mother,' he said without preamble. 'I'm afraid she passed away during the night .... a heart attack.' His voice was quiet and hesitant. 'Dunja and I have just been to see her. Dunja's still there. Do you want me to take you to see her?'

Zlata blinked but said nothing. As the seconds went by Dominik wondered if she had taken in what he'd said. The expression on her face had not altered.

'Did you hear what I said?'

'She was never there for me. She never understood me. And *Tata* would still be alive if she hadn't done what she did.'

When he heard her nonsensical words, Dominik knew his mother's mind was completely confused and he chose to ignore her remark. 'I'll take you to see her so you can say goodbye. We can go in an hour ... when you're dressed.' Silence filled the room again and Dominik assumed she was thinking about what he'd said so he said no more.

'No, that won't be necessary.'

'But she was your m—' His words dried up when Zlata stood up and left the room.

It was just as well her uncles were organising the funeral and Dunja didn't have to help because she was an emotional mess. Pulling herself together and functioning in a normal way wasn't an option. She was numb with grief. The following day she returned to her grandmother's house where she sat inert in the corner of the living room, next to the wood-burning stove, crying, blowing her nose and twisting a handkerchief in her hands. The smallest thing set her off — at lunch, when she saw *bob* on her plate, she began to cry yet again — broad beans were one of her grandmother's favourite foods.

Sveta Petra, the old stone church with only one, small, stained-glass window, around the corner from Mara's home, was full on the day of her funeral. It said so much about how well-respected she was in the community. With a heavy heart, Dunja took her place standing with her family beside the coffin in the gloomy chapel. Dominik stood beside her with his arm around her shoulders. She was nestled as close to him as she could get. Their father stood next to them. Everyone was dressed in black, including Dominik, in an ill-fitting suit borrowed from his Uncle Zoran. The family stood in a line as mourners filed past and shook their hands or kissed their cheeks. The funeral taking place around Dunja felt surreal — as if she wasn't there. She would have done anything to have her grandmother back. The anger boiling inside her began to grow worse when she witnessed her mother's apparent lack of reaction to her own mother's death. Not even this sad occasion could wake her from her somnambulant state. She was standing apart from everyone else and Dunja went over to her.

'*Majka,* are you okay?' she asked. 'It's freezing in here. Do you want my coat?' When her mother didn't answer, Dunja let out a sigh of resignation and draped the coat around her mother's shoulders before she returned to stand next to Dominik. She took his hand and her eyes glistened with tears as she looked at him.

After the events of the previous few days Dunja was reluctant to stay in Zagreb, even though she wasn't starting her new job for another two weeks. She was finding it too depressing — every second object she looked at reminded her of her grandmother.

Five days after the funeral, she made up my mind to return to Paris and stay with Pierre until she started her new job. She was packing her bag when she received an unexpected call from her father.

'Got time to meet me at our usual café for a quick drink and a chat?'

'Dunja, are you there?' he responded to her silence. 'A quick one, please, we haven't caught up for so long.'

'I'm packing, *Tata.* I'm going back to Paris tomorrow.'

'I know. Dominik told me, but there's something important I must talk to you about.'

'Can't we talk now?'

'No, I need to see you.'

His tone was pressing and although she didn't feel in the mood to be sociable, she gave in. 'Is half an hour's time, alright?' she asked.

'I'll be there.'

There were no unoccupied seats on the tram and as she stood in the overcrowded aisle, like a sardine packed in a tin of preserving salt, Dunja tried to guess what her father wanted.

Nikola had arrived before Dunja and once she was inside the Kazalište Kavana Café, with its vast almost empty interior, she saw he was not alone. Ivana, his girlfriend was with him. Her father's chair made a loud scraping noise that grated on her nerves when he stood up to kiss her cheek.

'Dunja, this is Ivana. I'll leave you to get acquainted for a minute. I'll get you a drink. I'll be as quick as I can,' he said as she sat down.

Dunja took in the sight of her bright, perky father. He was usually cheerful, but he seemed more so on this occasion. Uncomfortable in Ivana's presence, Dunja sat in silence.

Ivana was the first to speak. 'Is it tomorrow you leave?'

'Yes.'

'And you have a new job I hear.'

'Yes.'

'Are you excited?'

'Yes.' Dunja wished Ivana, who looked young enough to be her sister with her cap of blonde curls and smooth-unlined face, would be quiet. A painful silence descended upon them, when to her relief, her father reappeared with her glass of red wine.

'Hope this is okay? I suppose you prefer French wine by now.'

Dunja took a sip and without thinking screwed up her face.

Her father's laugh was hearty. 'What a face! Is it that bad? What sort of red do those frogs drink anyway?'

'I prefer *Côtes du Rhône*.' Dunja's voice was serious, but her father's light-hearted manner was infectious; it broke down her mood and before she knew it, she too was laughing. The release felt good, but it was short-lived.

'We're getting married next weekend,' her father announced without further preamble as he put his arm around Ivana's shoulders and smiled at her.

'A small wedding with close friends and family. You must come. I know it's short notice, but you know me, I love doing things on the spur of the moment.' His exuberant words infuriated Dunja. She wanted to tell him his timing was bad. Instead, she knocked back a huge mouthful of wine and stayed silent with her eyes fixed on her glass. If she looked at his face, it could have been all she needed to make her erupt.

'Do say you'll come!'

'No, *Tata*, I can't, I'm sorry. You know I'm leaving for Paris tomorrow. And it's far too soon after *Baba's* ...' *How could he be so insensitive?* When his face fell and the light in his blue eyes dimmed, Dunja felt as if her reply had been too harsh.

'I'm sorry, but my ticket is already booked and I can't change it. Will you forgive me, please?' She reached across the table, squeezed her father's hand and searched his eyes.

'You always know how to melt my heart, don't you, *Draga*? We'll both miss you, won't we Ivana?' he said, using her mother's baby name for her.

Chapter thirty-five

Dunja's days in Pierre's home passed quickly. During the day, while he was at work, she spent her time painting. She had transported more of her paints from Zagreb and she was content to work on the deck of his barge, where she set up her easel in the early spring sunshine. There were many scenes to inspire her and when it was too cold outside she couldn't stop peeping out of the portholes at the different vistas. The Eiffel Tower was close by and it caught her eye often, particularly when it changed colour at different times during the day. Sometimes it sparkled in the morning sun, while at others, if the sun was behind a cloud, it was leaden brown and stark. Another of Dunja's favourite views was the walkway beside the river with its shifting population of strollers walking their dogs. One fine, calm morning she sketched a scene with the Eiffel Tower in the background and a man walking an assortment of dogs. Splayed out from their leads, as though they were the outstretched fingers of a hand, were an elegant Saluki, a trotting Afghan hound and two miniature black poodles. A boisterous group, they pulled so strongly on their restraints that their handler looked as if he was being sucked into the eye of a hurricane. The Paris landscape was becoming familiar to Dunja and she was beginning to feel as if she belonged there.

In the evenings Pierre and Dunja usually shared the cooking, but a couple of days before she was due to start her new job he had invited Claudine, one of his work colleagues, for dinner. They had agreed that he would cook the meal. He had mentioned Claudine a lot since her return from Zagreb and Dunja was curious to meet her.

Claudine was petite and pretty with dark hair cut in a bob. Although she and Dunja were different in many ways — Claudine seemed very particular about her appearance whereas Dunja was not, yet something drew them together. Perhaps it was the way Claudine spoke her mind and reminded Dunja of her own lack of tolerance for fools. Her frank manner was a joy to Dunja's ears.

'Excuse me talking work for a minute please, but I have to ask Pierre something,' Claudine said.

'That's okay. Go right ahead,' Dunja replied.

'How's that new guy Marc's work?'

'So far not great. He's making a lot of mistakes,' Pierre replied.

'I'm not surprised. I thought he was arrogant on the first day he started and I was alarmed when Jules hired him.'

'He's only been with us for two weeks. Don't you think you're being a bit harsh?'

'No, we were told he knew his stuff and he'd teach us a thing or too. Have you learnt anything from him yet?'

'No,' Pierre replied. 'But it's early days. You're a hard taskmaster Claudine.' Pierre laughed and shook his head.

'No,' Claudine replied. 'I'm a realist.'

At the end of the evening Claudine and Dunja arranged to meet for coffee on the following day. After spending the evening in Claudine's company, Dunja hoped Claudine was about to become her first real girlfriend in Paris. Although she enjoyed her intellectual friends and their spirited debates over a glass or three of red wine, they were no more than sparring partners without the boxing ring.

The last heated conversation at the Brasserie Lipp, when Paul arrived with a surprise, was a good example of how they interact. Paul had pulled a poster from a large envelope before placing it, wrong side up, on the table in front of him.

'Hurry up, spoilsport,' Françoise said.

Paul turned the paper over slowly. 'Do you know what it is?' he asked, smirking.

'Course we do, but it's not the real thing,' Jean-Marc replied.

'Yes it is!' Paul was indignant.

'Jean-Marc's right,' Françoise added. 'It must be a copy. There wouldn't be any originals left by now.'

'Can I see it, please?' Dunja said as she picked it up and ran her hands over the words. In a recess of her mind, she knew she should know where it had come from, but she didn't. 'Where'd you get it?'

'It was in my landlady's attic.'

'Do you think it's a copy?' Françoise asked Dunja.

'It wasn't that long ago, you know,' Paul butted in.

'Ah, come on. I read somewhere that they'd all been torn down and destroyed on orders from the government,' Jean-Marc interjected.

'You're talking shit,' Paul spat.

'I think it's genuine,' Dunja chipped in.

'You would! I bet you don't know where it came from,' Paul said.

Dunja opened her mouth to speak, but then thought better of it.

'Bet you don't know what, *Sois jeune et tais toi* means?' Jean-Marc said in a mocking tone.

In a flash, it came to Dunja. 'Be young and shut up. It's from the *Mai '68* student riots,' she said as she stared at the silhouette of General de Gaulle with his protruding nose and his hand covering the mouth of a depiction of a student.

'Ha! You passed my test,' Paul said and everyone began to laugh.

These conversations told Dunja there was no way she could talk to any of them about her personal life, whereas she was sure she could talk to Claudine about almost anything.

In Avenue Suffren, Dunja's new address, the trees were already smothered in delicate pale-pink blossoms. Yet, although there were definite signs of spring, the weather was unsettled. During the last few days there had been showers every day. Dunja was hoping it would stay fine for her move the next day. Not that she had many possessions; the bulkiest articles were her canvases and art supplies. Three of the biggest ones, which she'd bought during her stay with Pierre, were as tall as she was, but that wouldn't be a problem because they were lightweight. The most difficult task would be keeping them dry.

When Dunja and Claudine arrived, Mirjana was supervising the rearrangement of furniture in Dunja's room with help from her neighbour's son. A slim woman, at least fifteen years older than Dunja, Mirjana wore her brown hair in an immaculate French roll. She was attractive, but not beautiful, with her wide-set Slavic eyes and large mouth.

Mirjana's apartment was on the sixth floor of a grand Haussmann-style building. As soon as Dunja stepped out of the clattering cage-like, wrought-iron lift, the first antique she noticed in the entrance foyer, was a highly polished, dark-timber hall table. The upstand and edges were carved in an intricate scroll pattern. The feet reminded her of lion's paws.

The three, generous-sized bedrooms all had balconies overlooking the street. The wall colours were warm shades of almond and cream. The kitchen floor tiles were black and white, similar to the ones in Dunja's grandmother's home, except these were larger and most likely far superior quality. Every room had a striking marble fireplace. She was delighted with her bedroom, especially the view over the city from the balcony.

On Sunday, she and Pierre made several short trips on the Metro ferrying Dunja's belongings. Mirjana was working in her office as they came and went. In their mother tongue, she explained she had a deadline to meet. She was abrupt. Her manner bore no resemblance to how she was the day before when Dunja visited with Claudine.

They were collecting the last of her possessions when Pierre spoke his mind. 'Mirjana's unfriendly, she's never heard of manners and *sorry* isn't a word she knows — *and she speaks a foreign language in front of me. You shouldn't work for her.*' His face was thunderous.

'You hardly know her.'

'Why do you have to leave my place anyway? I'm quite capable of looking after you.'

'She's busy. That's all.'

'A poor excuse for being rude.'

'Don't you understand she's preoccupied?'

'No.'

'You need to make an allowance for her. She's not always like this.' He glared at Dunja as if it was her fault. This fuelled her rage and she scowled at him. They continued to glare at each other in silence until there was nothing more to be said. Dunja snatched the bag he was holding and stalked off.

That night, in her new bed at Mirjana's, Dunja was wakeful. She was annoyed at Pierre for his behaviour and the night took forever to pass.

The following day her duties were light.

'Not too much on your first day,' Mirjana said. 'I don't want to scare you away. The rest can wait.'

As soon as Mirjana left to go out, Dunja called Claudine.

Dunja was the first to arrive at Le Pierrot on the corner of Avenue de la Motte-Piquet where they'd arranged to have lunch. It was one o'clock and the café was busy — she took the last available outside table where waiters dressed in formal black and white uniforms were scurrying from table to table. An older one with a drooping moustache and sad-looking eyes like a walrus, asked her if she wanted to order. In her improved French, thanks to the lessons Pierre had been giving her, she put him off, saying she was waiting for a friend. He withdrew at the same moment as Claudine crossed the road. She was wearing a cerise suit with a mini skirt and a waist-length fitted jacket with large black buttons down the front. Her lips and fingernails were painted to match her suit.

'What a beautiful bright colour,' Dunja said once Claudine had sat down.

'Thanks. It's my favourite.'

'It suits you.'

'Thanks. Now tell me about your new home,' she said, settling herself opposite Dunja.

'It's good.' Her voice sounded lame. She wasn't even fooling herself.

'I'd love to live there. My place is so tired and it needs repainting.'

'I'm sure I'll be happy there,' Dunja replied, unable to continue. The situation with Pierre had turned her upside down.

'You look worried,' Claudine said. 'You've moved into a fabulous apartment and started a great new job — I thought you'd be on top of the world.'

Sometimes, Dunja wished she wasn't so hopeless at hiding her thoughts. But then again, perhaps it wasn't all bad — it had given her the entrée she needed.

'Pierre and I have had an argument,' she blurted out.

'No! Tell me.'

'He doesn't want me to work for Mirjana or live there. We're not speaking. One part of me is furious with him but the other part, well ... I wish he'd call ... but I'm certainly not going to call him though. I'm no good at apologising, especially when it's not my fault ...' Her words ended abruptly.

'Oh dear,' Claudine said. 'Pierre's a sweetie.' She paused with her chin resting on her hands and a concerned look on her face.

'Let me talk to him. I won't tell him I know about your argument. Perhaps if I tell him how much *I* like Mirjana he'll see he's been too hasty.'

'Would you? Thank you.'

Two days went by and Dunja was starting to go crazy. During her coffee breaks, every time she walked past the telephone she stared at it. Once, she even ran her hand along the receiver. She so wanted to call Pierre. She hadn't heard from Claudine, but she didn't want to bother her. As each day passed, she grow more and more dejected.

She was on the verge of giving up waiting for the trill of the telephone, when it rang. She jumped with fright. It was Claudine and she sounded different. Her voice was flat. Her usual exuberance had gone. As soon as they got past the initial greetings, Dunja couldn't wait.

'Did you talk to him?' she stammered.

Claudine hesitated. 'I'm sorry, I tried to, but it was never the right moment and now, I think it's too late.' Silence fell as Dunja took in Claudine's words.

'Has he said anything about me?'

After another long pause, Claudine replied. 'No. He hasn't. I'm sorry.'

Dunja didn't respond. Her mouth had gone dry.

'I'm sorry I don't have better news, and I'm sorry I can't talk for longer. I have to go; I'm very busy. I'll call you again soon.' Claudine hung up. The conversation between them was so short it could almost not have happened.

As soon as Dunja put down the telephone it rang again immediately. She answered the call right away convinced it would be Pierre. It wasn't.

'Dominik!' she cried. 'What a surprise. Are you okay?'

'Yes I'm fine. But *Majka* isn't so good. She collapsed this morning and has been taken to hospital by ambulance. She's only working two days a week now and I told her ages ago it was time she stopped, but she wouldn't listen.'

'What's wrong with her?'

'They're saying it's bronchitis. She's had a bad cold for over a week and a couple of days ago she developed a cough. I told her not to go to work, but she ignored me. You know how stubborn she can be.'

'Yes, I do. How long will she be in hospital?'

'I don't know. It depends how quickly she recovers. They sent me home to pick up her things. I'm there now.'

'Should I come back?'

'No, there's nothing you can do. They've given her a drip with antibiotics. Let's see how she is in a couple days. When she comes home I'll take time off to look after her.'

'She's the same, otherwise?'

'I'd say so. Maybe a bit more reclusive. I can't remember when we last had a meaningful conversation. God knows how she manages to function at her job. Maybe they keep her on because she's been there for so long and perhaps they feel sorry for her. I have no idea how she manages to count money without making mistakes. I know she was always wizard when it came to adding, but even so.'

'I see, well you'd better go. This'll be costing you a fortune. Let me know if she gets worse, won't you? And thanks for calling.'

'Are you okay?'

'Yes, I'm fine. You'd better go. I'm worrying about what this is costing you.' She couldn't tell him that her romance, which had hardly begun, was over.

Chapter thirty-six

Zlata was home by herself. The *bora* was still blowing and the interior of her house was freezing. She felt as if she would never be warm again even when she lit the fire in the living room. After dragging her green chair closer to the blaze she shut her eyes and thought about her father.

An hour later when she woke up with a start she realized she must have fallen asleep. The fire had died down. She stood up, stirred it with the poker and threw on more wood. As she wrapped her brown-woollen cardigan more closely around herself she headed towards her bedroom.

The sea chest was in her wardrobe where she asked her brothers to put it after her mother died. She stared at it without blinking. Did it contain anything of importance, she wondered before she took the key to the padlock from her skirt pocket. It was stiff, her hands were unsteady and it took her several attempts before the padlock's mechanism finally moved.

She heaved up the lid. It crashed against the back of the wardrobe, startled her and made her jump with fright. As she dared to look inside she held her breath. The coarse dark green fabric of a WWI soldier's uniform lay folded in the bottom of the chest. She touched it tentatively, stopping short of taking it out. Neither could she bear the thought of searching the chest to see what else was in there. Fresh tears filled her eyes as she gazed at the last momento she had of her father. She took a deep breath. Could she destroy it? No, she couldn't bear to part with it. She would keep it safe. What did it matter if he was Serbian? It was of no consequence now that he was dead. When she began to tremble she knew it was time to put an end to what she'd been doing. With bumbling fingers she lowered the lid and secured the padlock.

Chapter thirty-seven

It was six p.m. on a Friday night when there was a knock on the door and Dunja went to see who was there. Pierre was standing on the doorstep holding a large bouquet of yellow roses.

'Will you forgive me?' he said as he held them towards her.

That evening they went to one of his favourite restaurants where only locals dined. *La Petite Ferme* was a small traditional bistro in a back street of the fifteenth arrondissement. It had rough, red-brick walls, red and white checked tablecloths and photos of animals — mostly farm ones, adorning the walls.

Pierre apologised again just before they arrived at the bistro. 'I'm so relieved you've forgiven me. I don't know what came over me. I get so carried away wanting to look after you; I guess I forget how much your independence means to you. I know you've told me it's one of the reasons you left Yugoslavia.' Pierre's tone was touching. Instead of answering him, Dunja stopped in the middle of the street, hugged him and kissed him on the lips.

By the time they arrived at the restaurant hand in hand, their misunderstanding had been swept away.

When a letter was forwarded to Dunja by Dominik from the Muzejski Prostor Gallery in Zagreb, Dunja was flattered by the invitation to exhibit a series of her abstract paintings. The gallery, built on the site of a former Jesuit monastery was relatively new and had the distinction of being the largest one in Croatia. It's exhibition space was as huge as its scope of work which extended from prehistoric through to contemporary. Over the next few days she contemplated it until, in the end, she couldn't keep it to herself.

'How exciting!' Mirjana said. 'Would you like to use the attic upstairs as a studio?' she asked while they were sitting having coffee on the sofa under the window in her office.

Dunja was thrilled by Mirjana's generosity. At last she would be able to paint on a regular basis. Painting was the one pleasure missing from her life since she had moved to Mirjana's.

Although the attic was small, a dormer window on one side and a larger one on the other, would provide sufficient light. The discoloured floral wallpaper was peeling away in places, while the dark grey vinyl on the floor was scuffed. Altogether, it was a shabby space. Yet, as she took it in, Dunja know it would suit her well.

The inspiration for her paintings came from the colours in Pierre's home — earthy neutrals, lavender and black. For obvious reasons, she could only paint at night once she'd finished work.

Not long after she began her artwork, Mirjana came to have a look at her progress. 'Your talent is impressive. The colour combinations are striking and they compliment each other so well. Do you only paint abstracts?'

'These days, yes. Why do you ask?'

'I was wondering if you'd like to have a go at drawing some sketches for my new collection. It would just be a matter of recreating the garments on paper.'

'In the past I've sketched or painted all sorts — landscapes, people, including my brother and a troupe of ballet dancers. So I don't see why I couldn't do that for you. At least I could give it a try and see what you think. In fact, I'd enjoy it. As you know, I love clothes.'

Mirjana was delighted with the first sketches Dunja created which meant that she was busy both day and night, and although art was her passion, she was glad the hectic phase was temporary. She knew it would be impossible to keep up such a crazy pace.

It was a Sunday when at last she had an evening off — she was going to Pierre's barge for dinner. His parents had also been invited and she was nervous. She'd had to consult Mirjana about what to wear — there was nothing in her wardrobe that seemed appropriate and she knew Pierre's parents would be formally dressed, as they had been the first time she'd met them.

Mirjana loaned her a simple black dress; the silk had a delicate lustre and a grainy texture.

Dunja was the first to arrive. When Pierre opened the door and greeted her with a kiss Dunja couldn't believe how jittery she was.

'Come in,' he said, taking her hand and drawing her to him and kissing her hello. 'You can set the table while I finish my prep. Make sure you don't spoil that wonderful dress. You look particularly beautiful.' Pierre stood back and gazed at her with a smile on his cheerful face.

When Pierre's parents showed up exactly on time, Dunja's was swamped by anxiety. Pierre's mother was elegant and poised in a black-lace dress and shiny stiletto-heeled shoes. Dunja couldn't recall ever meeting anyone that sophisticated and she immediately became tongue-tied and awkward. Her confidence plummeted further when she picked up her white linen napkin and accidently knocked her fork on to the floor. She was sure Pierre's mother must have thought she was clumsy.

When Pierre served the main course, which was boeuf bourguignon, and they were about to eat, Pierre's mother, who so far had been rather quiet, spoke.

'Dunja, you have an arts' degree, don't you? I seem to remember Pierre telling me.'

'Yes. I do.'

'Where did you study? Was it here in Paris?'

'No, I went to the University of Zagreb, although for my last module I came to Paris.'

'And was Zagreb University a good choice?'

'Yes, very much so. I loved it.'

'Pierre always said he wanted to go to university, but in the end he didn't. He was offered a special job and he chose that instead. I don't think it matters now, though. He's done so well for someone who is only twenty-five. I'm so proud of him. Well, we both are, aren't we, Henri?'

Had Dunja heard correctly? *Twenty-five*? She distinctly recalled him telling her they were the same age — twenty-eight. She remembered the conversation well. When she looked across the table at him, she was certain he was avoiding her eye.

'Diana was the top student in her year,' Pierre said without looking at her. 'She won the *Starčevica* award for the most-talented new artist.' Dunja glared at him, knowing he was changing the subject on purpose.

Dunja wasn't particularly bothered that Pierre had lied about his age. She considered confronting him, but decided against it. Now wasn't the right time. She was too busy and had too much on her mind with the upcoming exhibition. Maybe she would say something once the exhibition was over. Anyway, what would tackling him achieve? Nothing but angst more than likely.

Dunja's days preceding the exhibition were frenetic. She had to finish a batch of pencil sketches for Mirjana before her departure for Zagreb and her nights were frantic as she strived to complete the last of her artwork. It was late on Saturday night when she packed up the last of her new canvases before she flew out on the following Monday. She had finished eight and had been hoping to complete a ninth, but she had been hampered by her experiments with different paint — exterior house paint which gave a brilliant glossy finish that could hide brush strokes. Dunja had studied Picasso's techniques and was aware that he had used an exterior paint called Ripolin and she could see why. She had been able to create an interesting, marbled effect with muted edges and the odd blob or drip where she wanted them, and it dried quickly too — an extra bonus because time was an issue.

It had been a long cold winter in Zagreb and although spring had arrived, the city remained cloaked in a white blanket. Dunja knew she was lucky the airport was functioning. Snow ploughs had cleared the runways two days ago and since then there hadn't been any fresh falls. As the plane landed in the evening gloom, her view was a damp and dreary one. A blustery, grey squall of rain had blown in and the light was pale-lemony yellow. At that moment she wished she hadn't left Paris. Dirty snow and lumps of blue ice were piled along the edges of the runway and the grey sky was heavy with more snow.

The morning after her arrival, Dunja spent a long day at the gallery, supervising the hanging of her artwork. With her discerning eye, she believed she knew precisely how her paintings should be hung. After a few disagreements with the gallery director, at last she succeeded in getting them positioned to suit herself. It was late when she finished scrutinising her work from every possible angle and at eleven o'clock when she left the gallery for her mother's apartment, she was cold and tired.

She had been intending to make herself a cup of tea, but she was exhausted. Instead she went straight to bed where she fell asleep at once.

Her father, wearing a new dark suit, bought especially for the occasion, along with Ivana who was in a cornflower-blue silk dress, and Dominik were the first to arrive on Dunja's opening night.

'I've booked a table for dinner after the show,' her father said after they had greeted each other. 'I hope you haven't made other plans.'

'No, that sounds lovely,' Dunja said as she clutched her hands in front of her nervously. 'Where did you book?'

'Trilogija because it's close. Two minutes walk, I think. Is that okay?'

'Yes, absolutely fine. It has great food.'

'Can we look at your work now?' Dominik asked.

'Of course. Go right ahead. Ah, here's Karlo. I must talk to him.'

Karlo, who was dressed in a grey suit with a lavender turtle-neck shirt wrapped her in an affectionate bear hug.

'You look well, my dear,' he said. 'I trust you are.'

'Yes, I'm good and I'm so pleased you're here.'

'I had to come, after all I instigated this exhibition for you. I had to make sure your work is as good as it should be … just kidding.' He laughed. 'I can see it out of the corner of my eye and already I know it's superb. Come, talk me through how you created that interesting effect on the bigger canvas with the marbled effects. It's a new style for you, isn't it?'

'Yes. Do you like it?'

'Very much so. How did you achieve it?'

'By using exterior house paint. Imported, of course. It's French. Local paint won't do, it's too chalky.'

'Ah yes, a touch of Picasso.'

'Yes, that's where I came up with the idea.'

'Are they all painted with the same paint?' he asked as they moved around to look at a second series on the wall behind the largest one which was the first one you came to as you walked in the door. Karlo then answered his own question. 'These ones are different. They don't have the gloss of the bigger one.'

'No, they don't. Different paint.'

Just then they were interrupted by Antonio Babić, the gallery director, a tall man with a rugged face, who had come over and stood beside Dunja.

'Sorry to interrupt Dunja, if it's okay with you I'd like to speak now. A good number of people are here and I'd like to introduce you.

'Before you do, I'd like to introduce Karlo Đerek from the art department at Zagreb University.'

'Ah Karlo, we've corresponded often. So nice to put a face to a name,' Antonio said as he held out his hand.

It was a long day, but Dunja was satisfied. Three of her paintings sold during the evening and as she sipped her wine, from time to time she glanced across the table at her father and Ivana. They smiled at each other often. It was then that Dunja's thoughts turned to her mother. She had hoped she'd be here. She had called her from the gallery during a break when her work was being hung. 'I could send a taxi for you,' she'd said.

'No thank you. It's a kind thought, but I don't go out at night these days.'

'Are you sure? I'd like you to come.'

'Yes, I'm sure. I hope the exhibition goes well for you.'

Dunja knew that wasn't the entire reason she had declined the invitation. Dominik had told her Ivana would be here. She was still watching her father and Ivana when Dominik, who was sitting beside her, interrupted her thoughts.

'They're well matched, don't you think?' he said.

'Yes, they are, and I'm glad Tata is happy ... I was thinking about *Majka*.'

'Ah well, if you're about to ask how she is, she's no different. *The depression* has her firmly in it's grip and no matter what pills they give her she doesn't improve.'

Dunja's eyes welled up with tears as she pictured her mother. 'I have to be here in the morning, but I'm coming home for lunch tomorrow. Will you be there?'

'No, Tonci and I are going to a football match,' Dominik replied.

'What a shame.'

'How are things in Paris?'

'They've been hectic since I've been getting ready for this exhibition, but when I go back they should return to normal.'

'Hectic because you had to produce the artwork for this exhibition, do you mean?'

'Yes, there was that, but I've been sketching costumes for Mirjana as well as answering the phone, running errands and filing papers and ordering fabric samples. It's a lot busier than I imagined it would be.'

'But you enjoy it.'

'Yes, Mirjana is great to work for. She's so obliging. I couldn't ask for a better employer. She didn't hesitate to give me time off for this exhibition, and she's supportive too.

What about your job? How's that going?'

'Tedious is probably the best way to describe it. The guy I work for has no imagination and the stuff I churn out is dull and boring and, of course, it all has to made of brown varnished wood.'

'Why don't you find another job?'

'I'd like to, but that's easier said than done.'

'Have you been looking?'

'Yes, but here's nothing out there right now.'

'Something better will turn up sooner or later. You'll have to keep your eyes open.'

'I will, I most certainly will. So, how are you getting on with your boyfriend? What's his name again?'

Dunja glanced at her father and stepmother. 'Ssh! I told you not to mention him. No one except you knows about him and I want to keep it that way. His name's Pierre,' she said in a loud whisper.

'Sorry, I forgot. Are you still seeing him?' Dominik asked in a quieter voice.

'I am.'

'You don't sound very sure about that.'

'It's complicated.' Dunja paused. 'I found out a short time ago that he's younger than me. He lied. I can get over the white lie, but you know how we are about being in a relationship with a younger man. It's not what women do in our country.'

'Why did he lie?'

'Don't know. I didn't ask. I assume it was to impress me.'

'You can move on from that though, can't you?'

'Maybe, but then there's the other issue. He's overly protective and I'm not sure I can put up with that. Don't get me wrong. I love his company and spending time with him.'

'Are you thinking about dumping him?'

'Not at the moment, but we'll see.'

Chapter thirty-eight

Conscious that she hadn't spent enough time with her mother, on Saturday when the gallery closed at one p.m., Dunja headed to her mother's house.

Inside the silent apartment she made her way along the dark hallway accompanied by the unnaturally loud ticking of the grandfather clock. She guessed her mother would most likely be in the kitchen sitting at the table, staring into space where she had been when Dunja left after breakfast.

For once her chair was empty. Her mother was lying crumpled in a heap on the floor. Dunja gasped. Was she alive? Her waxy pallor was not a good sign. She shook her gently and called her name. She did not respond. Dunja tried to move her, but she was a dead weight and it was impossible. Dunja's hand was shaking as she fumbled with the telephone and called an ambulance. Dread engulfed her and thoughts that she was too late overwhelmed her as tears rained down her face. By the time the ambulance arrived, a few minutes later, Dunja was an incoherent blob slumped on the floor next to her inert mother.

In the ambulance she stared at her mother's ghostly face covered with an oxygen mask as she repeated the same question over and over to the ambulance attendant.

'Will she be okay?'

He didn't reply. He was busy monitoring her mother's vital signs. It seemed like an eternity later when at last he answered her.

'It's too early to say. She has a pulse, but it's weak.'

Dunja buried her face in her hands and prayed as the ambulance sped towards the hospital.

Hours passed before Dunja and Dominik, who had arrived shortly after Dunja had located him at Tonci's place, were able to see their mother. They had been sitting together in the austere waiting room in silence when a doctor finally came in. They both stood up at once.

'She's been stabilised,' he said. 'You can see her now. I'll show you the way.'

They followed him into the room where Zlata lay. Dunja thought she looked the same, with her deathly pale face still covered by an oxygen mask. She took her hand while Dominik went to find another chair. Pleased that she seemed to be breathing evenly, without letting go of her hand, Dunja sat down in the chair Dominik had pulled close to the bed. They had been sitting watching her for ten minutes when Zlata opened her eyes and mumbled something which Dunja thought sounded like, *Where am I?*

'You're in hospital. I came home and found you on the floor,' Dunja said.

When their mother didn't reply Dunja carried on. 'You'll be okay now,' she said as she looked at her brother for reassurance.

On the Monday, two days after her mother's collapse Dunja called Mirjana to ask for longer leave.

'You must take all the time you need. Family come before everything. You know that.' When Mirjana was her ever-obliging self Dunja was relieved.

A week later, in preparation for her mother's homecoming Dunja was cleaning the apartment when the telephone rang. She was astonished to hear Pierre's voice.

'I hadn't heard from you so I called in to see you. Mirjana told me about your mother. Is she okay? And are you okay?' Shocked by the sound of his voice for a few moments Dunja couldn't speak.

'We're both fine now, thanks.'

'Do you know what date you're coming back?'

'No not yet. I want to make sure *Majka* is okay first.'

'I've been thinking, why don't you come and live with me when you get back to Paris?'

Dunja lapsed into silence. 'You've taken me by surprise. I'm not sure what to say.'

'Say *yes*,' he said and laughed.

'I'll have to think about it.'

'I didn't mean to push you. Take all the time you need. I'll be here when you're ready,' he said before saying goodbye sweetly.

During the next few days Dunja's focus was on her mother. Her collapse had shaken Dunja.

When at last Zlata's condition improved Dunja had the time and the inclination to turn her mind to Pierre's proposal. It was not an easy decision and she mulled it over for some time. One minute she'd decide she would move in and then she'd change her mind. In the end she decided she couldn't move in because she was concerned about losing her freedom, although she would continue to see him.

Chapter thirty-nine

After she returned to Paris, Dunja was more than a little pleased when Karlo wrote to ask if she'd work with him on the restoration of the ceiling of the Privredna Bank in the Octagon Arcade in Central Zagreb. It was an exciting offer and one she wanted to accept, if Mirjana would give her time off ... if she had to resign, she wasn't sure she'd be able to come back to Paris without a job. The letter threw her into a panic. Karlo had asked for a prompt reply and assumed she would come regardless of what was happening with her life in Paris. *When you get here*, his letter said, *we will begin at once. It won't take you long to get into the swing of this process. We touched on the required technique in my workroom if you remember. I could see then that you had a flair for it.* She lit another cigarette, her third in rapid succession, and blew smoke towards the ceiling.

She wasn't considering Pierre, only Mirjana. She'd already had a lot of time off and she was worried about asking for more. She wished it wasn't so complicated, regardless, she couldn't put off dealing with it for any longer. She had to talk to Mirjana.

Once again they were drinking coffee at ten-thirty in the morning, sitting on the sofa under the window in Mirjana's office. Dunja was nervous and her words came out in a rush. But she was lucky, Mirjana was an excellent listener and she didn't interrupt until she had finished speaking.

'Your letter doesn't surprise me at all. You're extremely talented, as I'm always telling you. You must accept, there's no question about it,' she said touching Dunja's hand affectionately.

'But what about my job? Will you keep it for me? I know I'm asking a lot and I'll understand if you won't — or can't.'

'Business is quiet right now. It's between seasons and I'm not so busy. Now that you've set up my new filing system it will be easier for me to keep up to date with everything. I'm sure I can do without you for a time and besides I know how important this job is to you. If you don't take it you'll be miserable and so will I if I don't insist you take it.'

Dunja had always admired the arcade leading to the Privredna Bank in Central Zagreb. The floor with its inlaid mosaic tiles was a joy to walk on. The boutiques with their tall decorative doors and windows were different to any she had seen. At the end of the arcade, immediately before the bank, was a spectacular stained-glass dome — during the day the glass was a myriad of subtle reds and blues dancing in the sunlight.

It was early winter when Dunja and Karlo began work. It was already cold, in fact, it was freezing and the extra layers of clothing Dunja was compelled to wear under her overalls barely kept her warm enough. All they did was restrict her movement. But it didn't matter. When she looked at the completed sections of the restoration she felt a pleasing sense of satisfaction. She was sure she must have looked comical working on the scaffolding erected for her and Karlo at the extreme top of the building. Dressed in her baggy, paint-encrusted overalls, she had a cigarette and a small paintbrush poking out of opposite corners of her mouth. Before they started, Dunja had no idea what the job would entail and there were many times when she wished she had another pair of hands. It took her days to get a satisfactory system going. On the first day she had a close call when she almost knocked her book of gold leaf off the scaffolding. Gold leaf was extremely expensive and if it had crashed the three storeys to the ground floor, it would quite possibly have been damaged or ruined. Klimt loved working with gold leaf and as soon as Dunja started the job she knew why. There was nothing to equal the luminosity it gave off once it had been burnished, and it also lasted for an exceptionally long time without deteriorating. She had always admired Klimt's work and although she don't particularly care for his nudes, his art nouveau paintings where he used gold leaf fascinated her. *The Kiss* was her favourite. How she wished she could see the original and work out how he achieved such a brilliant effect using layers of gold leaf.

At first, Dunja was sore and tired at the end of every day and she fell asleep shortly after her head hit the pillow and slept soundly. Within two or three weeks she adjusted to the awkward positions her body was contorted into while she was working and her muscles no longer screamed and complained.

Feeling the need to have her own place, she had rented an apartment on the top floor of a block in Central Zagreb and although it was a little enclosed and clinical with so much white paint, she could look through the glass balcony doors across to the three, small manicured green parks — Nikole Zrinskog Trg, Strossmayerov Trg and Tomislavov Trg, which provided an unexpected green delight in the centre of the city.

After her return to Zagreb, much to her dismay, she hadn't been able to paint any new artwork — it was enough to be painting all day, and besides she had left most of her paints in Paris. Instead, she began taking karate lessons at SRC Šalata, the sports centre. She got on well with Marko, her teacher and once she had learnt the correct stance and the more common kicks, punches and defensive movements she began to enjoy it.

It was at the start of the lesson when Marko told the class they would be sparring with an opponent that Marko beckoned to her.

'Me?' she said.

'Yes, you,' he nodded. Her stomach did a somersault. She would have been fooling herself if she pretended she wasn't attracted to him. She had taken in his smooth, olive complexion underneath his shaggy-dark hair the first day she met him. His grin was easy-going while his eyes were dark and mischievous. It took a few seconds for it to sink in that he had chosen her as his partner. She hoped she didn't make a fool of herself.

By the end of the lesson Dunja knew she was infatuated with him and when he invited her for a drink at the Karijola Bar in Vlaška Ulica, she said yes.

It was dark when Dunja woke and the scent of sandalwood aftershave wafted over her. She took no more than a few seconds to orientate herself. In the warmth of Marko's bed it came flooding back to her.

They were still in the Karijola Bar when she knew she'd had too much to drink. Her head had been spinning when she'd gone to the toilet. She didn't care — she was having fun — a different type of fun to what she had with Pierre. When they'd lurched out of the bar with their arms around each other, there had been no question that they'd go anywhere other than to Marko's apartment.

Once he'd unlocked the door and they were inside, he'd picked her up and carried her to the bedroom. The next she knew, she had woken up without any recollection of having gone to sleep. It was still dark. Whatever had happened was a blank. She was so drunk she couldn't remember. But it definitely had happened. The sticky evidence was between her thighs.

As she lay there waiting for dawn she could have felt guilty because of Pierre — she didn't. What was done was done and there was no turning back, or any point in obsessing. Although she wouldn't be telling anyone about it.

When her head continued to pound she knew it was her punishment for drinking far too much wine.

Chapter forty

Not long after Dunja returned to Paris, Pierre booked a trip for the two of them.

Inside the station at Angers St Laud, south of Paris, Pierre waved at someone in the waiting crowd and when an overweight, balding man with a bushy-grey moustache stepped forward Dunja knew he was expecting them. The man turned out to be Pierre's Uncle Martin, who had driven all the way from Provence — a two-day journey.

'We've got about an hour's drive ahead of us,' Martin said after Pierre had introduced him and they headed towards Martin's car.

'Where are we going?' Dunja asked.

'To the village of St Clémentin. Didn't Pierre tell you?'

'No, I didn't. It was going to be a surprise.'

'Oh! I hope I haven't spoilt it.'

'No, not unless you say any more.'

'Okay, I'd better keep quiet then,' Martin said and laughed.

In the centre of Angers, close to the train station, the trees were heavy with blossom and the gardens were a mass of yellow and red flowers. On their way out of town, green fields were a welcome change from the pallid, cement-coloured city Dunja had left behind. They passed through numerous small villages; one in particular had large hanging baskets spilling over with multi-coloured flowers. Dunja counted fourteen baskets along the length of the main thoroughfare. After traversing a maze of narrow roads through the lush, ordered countryside, at last they came to the village of St Clémentin. In the centre was a small chateau surrounded by time-worn stone houses. The absence of people and the quiet was noticeable after the bustling streets of Paris.

'Are we staying here?' Dunja asked.

'A kilometre away,' Martin replied. 'Just outside the village in the mill house at Le Moulin du Pont adjacent to the river Argenton. I stayed there last night. It's quiet, except for the rushing of the river through the water races.'

Pierre and Dunja chose the attic on the third floor. Their bed was draped with a mosquito net, striped cotton rugs were scattered over the floor and double windows looked towards the river. They unpacked quickly, before joining Martin downstairs for a late lunch the owner had kindly set out on the dining table in the living room.

'How's your room?' Martin asked.

'Beautiful,' Dunja replied. 'Especially the view. The field by the river is covered with bright-yellow flowers.'

'Good. Now, Pierre, how about opening the wine.' Martin handed Pierre a corkscrew.

Diana was tired from the journey and the excitement. The bed was soft and the linen was crisp, but her mind was whirring, wondering what was on tomorrow's agenda. Earlier, during lunch, when Martin took a folder from his bag and put it on the spare wooden dining chair, she assumed she was about to find out what was going on. She was wrong. All he said was that he wanted to talk to Pierre about its contents, sometime during the afternoon. After they finished their meal, Martin suggested she went for a walk into St Clémentin. By the time she came back there was no sign of the folder.

At nine-thirty on Saturday morning when she came downstairs to the kitchen in search of breakfast, Pierre and Martin had already eaten and Martin was talking on the telephone.

'Eleven o'clock we are to be there,' he said at the end of his call. 'Diana, you'll need to wear a pair of sturdy shoes.'

First they inspected the farmhouse, a charming, nineteenth-century, stone dwelling surrounded by well-tended flowerbeds and a sprawling herb garden. The cottage alone was enough to make most people fall in love with the property. Once they moved on from the house and the garden the owner became loquacious as he talked about the rest of the property.

'There are over fifty mature apple trees and three fields planted with strawberries, raspberries and asparagus. As well as fruit and vegetables, the dairy produces a goat's milk cheese called *Chabichou*. It's an artisan cheese and we sell it and other produce at the local market. We're proud of our home, and well the entire property, which was handed down to me by my grandfather. It's been the heart and soul of our existence for most of my life. But we're no longer young and our health is declining, and we have no children or extended family to pass it on to, so with extreme reluctance we've put it up for sale.'

When he finished speaking Dunja looked at Pierre. It was then that much to Dunja's astonishment it became obvious that he was considering buying it.

At the end of their walking tour of the property, Pierre and Dunja paused and leant on a wooden farm gate while Martin and the old man walked on ahead.

'It's so beautiful here. In a different way to Provence, of course. I've fallen in love with it,' Pierre said.

'I agree, it's lovely, but I couldn't imagine living here and what about running a farm? You'd need to learn how to do that.'

'That's why Martin's here. He's offered to help me, as well as lending me part of the purchase money. I must say, I'm disappointed. I thought you'd love the scenery. And it's not that far from Paris. You could go back whenever you wanted.'

It seemed to Dunja that he had it all worked out. 'Are you asking me to live here with you?'

'Yes, if you'd like to.'

'I've always lived in the city. It's where I feel comfortable. I'd have to think about it.'

'There's so much here to inspire you. Think of the scenes you could paint.' Pierre spread his arms wide.

'Yes, I'll grant you that. But you've dropped the idea on me like a bomb.'

'It was meant to be a surprise, a stupendous surprise.'

'It's certainly that alright,' Dunja said as she set off towards the farmhouse.

Back at the mill house Dunja listened while Pierre and Martin continued discussing the farm over a light meal of French bread, paté, olives and three different cheeses, and a bottle of Gamay, one of the local wines.

'I think it's superb — better than I imagined it would be,' Martin said. 'My mind's made up. All we need to determine is how much we should pay for it. What do you say, Pierre?'

'I love it. Everything about it, especially the way the old couple have looked after it so well. What about you, Diana? You haven't said much. What do you think?'

'It's so sudden and unexpected.' Dunja felt as if she was being cornered. She was not enjoying the pressure Pierre was exerting on her. 'As I said earlier I'll think about it.'

That night in bed Pierre continued to bubble over with enthusiasm. The more he carried on about the farm, the more irritated Dunja became. Clearly he had his heart set on living there and it seemed to her that no matter what she said he kept assuming she would join him. He was not listening to anything she said.

The next day, Pierre was impatient to return to Paris and begin the process of purchasing the farm. Dunja, too, had become restless, but not for the same reason — she couldn't stop thinking about the telephone call she had received a few days before they went away. Knowing she needed someone to talk to, she phoned Claudine.

'Did you have a nice weekend away?' Claudine said as soon as she'd sat down opposite Dunja in Bistro du Commerce in Rue Commerce where they'd agreed to meet for dinner.

'It was okay.'

'Was it romantic? I was so envious when Pierre told me he was taking you away for the weekend.'

At that moment the waiter came to take their orders.

'Shall we have a carafe of *Côtes du Rhône?* And we have to have the pizza with truffle paste, rocket and parma ham,' Claudine said. 'It's the best pizza ever.'

'I'll take your word for it. What about a bowl of fries too?'

'Sounds good to me,' Claudine said as she repeated the order to the waiter. 'Now where were we?'

'You asked if my weekend was a romantic one.'

'That's right.'

'Didn't he tell you why we went away?' Dunja asked.

'No. I assumed it was just a chance for the two of you to have a break together.'

'It wasn't. He went to look at a farm that he wants to buy.'

'A farm!?'

'Yes! With goats, vegetables and fruit trees.'

'I don't believe it. Why would he want to do that?'

'No idea, but he does and because he's fallen in love with it he assumes I have too.'

'I'm shocked. I can't imagine him on a farm. Does he know anything about running a farm?'

'No, I don't think so, but his uncle came up from Provence and apparently he does. The pair of them were completely carried away with the place.'

'And you weren't?'

'Of course not. Can you see me on a farm?'

'No!'

'Anyway I have a bigger problem than that. The day before we went away my friend Valentina rang from Zagreb and offered me a job.'

'Doing what? I thought you loved your job here.'

'She designs costumes for the theatre. And I do love my job. Working for Valentina would be similar to what I do now, but it would mean I could be nearer to Mother. Her health isn't improving and I don't like leaving Dominik to shoulder the responsibility of looking after her all the time. And then there's my ambition. I want to make a name for myself as an artist and Paris isn't the place for that. I probably made a mistake coming here. If I'm going to pursue my career I need connections and I don't have any here.'

'Fair enough. But what about living in Yugoslavia again? I thought you didn't want to live in a communist country. I remember you telling me that when we first met.'

'Tito's dead now and he didn't appoint a successor, so I'm hoping Yugoslavia will move away from being a one party state and, of course, it hasn't been tied to the Soviet Union for years, so that's a help.'

'I see ... I'm not sure what to say. I'll miss you. Sounds like you've made up your mind to go back.'

'Not totally. All I've decided is that I don't want to live with Pierre on his farm and I won't be bullied into it.'

'Pierre isn't a bully. Not the Pierre I know.'

'Maybe he's not. But he won't listen when I say I don't want to live there.'

'Did he ask you to marry him?'

'No and if he had I would have said no. I don't want to get married; I want to focus on my career.'

'Costume designing?'

'In the interim yes, until I can move on to the bigger, better things with my painting. So ... what would you do if you were me? Remembering that my mentor Karlo lives in

Zagreb.'

'The answer is simple, I'd go back.'

'Thank you. I thought that's what you'd say. I needed to confirm my own thoughts.'

'What about Mirjana? How do you think she'll take it?'

'She'll understand when I explain all the reasons why.'

'And Pierre?'

'He doesn't concern me. I'm not in love with him … I can't be … I cheated on him last time I was in Zagreb.'

'Did you?' Claudine giggled.

'Yes, with my karate teacher. He's gorgeous.'

'What fun! Does Pierre know?'

'Of course not! It's none of his business.'

Chapter forty-one

After Dunja returned to Zagreb she began working for Valentina, her ebullient friend with a fluffy cloud of red hair that matched her personality. Sadly, the job fell far short of her expectations — the work was too repetitive. She'd been at her job for less than two years when she decided to resign. Every design Valentina gave her to sketch seemed to be nothing more than a variation of the last one and if she suggested making changes Valentina always said no. She had no scope to incorporate her own ideas and the work didn't provide any challenges. She got up each morning not wanting to catch the bus to work.

Notwithstanding, Dunja was conscious of not letting Valentina down. She didn't want to hurt her and she kept putting off broaching the subject of her resignation. Valentina was talented, but she was also sensitive and Dunja was nervous about how she would react. The task was becoming more and more difficult with each passing day — Valentina had told Dunja on several occasions that she depended on her and she couldn't do without her. At night in bed, Dunja could picture the freckles dancing across Valentina's nose and her cloud of red curls when she said, 'I don't know how I'd manage without you. You're a lifesaver.'

As time moved on, it got to the stage where Dunja had created a real dilemma for herself. And to make matters worse, she found she was constantly sleeping in and having to ring Valentina to say she'd be late — often almost two hours late. One morning she was about to leave for work and was struggling with the lock on the door of her mother's apartment, which had become stiff, when the postman appeared and handed her the mail. She thrust it into her shoulder bag and forgot about it.

Her day was busy — they were working on costumes for a theatre performance, starting in less than a fortnight. It wasn't until mid-afternoon, when she took a break to smoke a cigarette, that she remembered the mail she had stuffed into her bag. Sitting at her desk, she shuffled through an assortment of bills. She was about to put all the envelopes back without giving them a second glance, when the crest on a slim white one caught her attention. She ripped it open. Then, without pausing to think, divulged the contents.

'My goodness. It's a letter from the Conservation Institute offering me a job.'

'A job! But you already have one here.' Valentina's chin dropped and although her face was hidden by her voluminous hair, Dunja knew from the tone of her voice that she was dismayed.

'Listen: *We have inspected your work on the restoration of the Privredna Bank and we were so impressed by its high quality we would like to offer you a contract restoring frescoes in churches and historic buildings. Please telephone at your earliest convenience to make an appointment to discuss* ... Can you believe it?' Dunja said and then laughed as she reread the letter to make sure she hadn't got it wrong.

Valentina remained silent while she burbled on.

'I can't believe it.'

'You must take it,' Valentina said in a quiet voice.

Dunja desperately wanted to take the job, but her immediate thought was Dominik and the strain he'd already been under caring for their mother when she was in Paris. She knew she'd need to talk to him before she made her decision. Perhaps it was unfair to ask him to bear the brunt of their mother's deranged mind and difficult behaviour yet again.

They arranged to meet for a drink because she wouldn't have been comfortable discussing the issue of their mother in her home.

It was a while since Dunja had been to the Hemingway Bar in Trg Republike Hrvatske, and when she arrived first and sat down on a stylish, glossy black chair next to a small oval black table edged with gold it was obvious that the establishment had been renovated. The floor had been replaced too and was now white tiles with small black diamonds on each corner rather than the old timber floor. She'd always wondered about the name. Did the place have a connection to Ernest Hemingway?

When she saw her brother come in the door she knew he was taking in the décor.

'I wish we designed furniture like this,' he said as he sat down.

'Looks stylish, doesn't it?' Dunja replied.

'Yes, anyway, how are you?'

'Good. I've got news. But let's get a drink first, shall we?'

'Okay,' Dominik said. 'Red wine?'

Dunja nodded.

'I'll get it.' He stood up and walked to the bar.

The place was not busy because it was early on a Wednesday night and Dominik returned to their table quickly with two glasses of red wine.

'Okay, what's your news? Tell me.'

'I've been offered a job moving around the country restoring frescoes. But I wanted to talk to you first before I accept it because I'm concerned that it would mean you would have to take over the responsibility of looking after *Majka* and I am not sure if I'm happy with that and I need to know how you feel.'

'That's amazing. You must be so excited. And what a tremendous coup for you. Of course you must accept. How long would it be for?'

'I don't know. I haven't discussed any details with them yet. I thought I'd better sound you out first about *Majka*. It could be for quite a few years because I know that there are a huge number of churches around the country where the frescoes are in a sorry state.'

'Would it be good money?'

'Again I don't know until I talk to them, but I think so because it's specialised work and not many people can do it or should I say complete it to a high enough standard because it's painstaking intricate work.'

'It'd be a real feather in your cap, wouldn't it?'

'Yes, most definitely.'

'Accept it. It's far too good an opportunity to turn down. Don't worry about *Majka*, I'll cope with her. I'm so happy for you.'

'Are you sure? I feel bad and as if I'm letting you down.'

'Of course, I'm sure. Go for it.'

'Thanks.'

'Here's to your new job,' Domink said as he raised his glass.

Dunja's first assignment lasted for three years. In the city of Rijeka, west of Zagreb, her small team consisting of herself and three other workers, began meticulously restoring frescoes. The work had just begun when disillusionment struck. Two of her colleagues handed in their notice; they said the work was too difficult and laborious. That left only Dunja and Viktor. However, Dunja was certain their dedication would get them through. They were both perfectionists when it came to intricate work.

Dunja enjoyed Viktor's company. His demeanour was a constant source of entertainment. Well over six foot tall and as slim as a pencil, he wore gold-rimmed glasses sitting, more often than not, on the tip of his nose. As fast as he pushed them back where they belonged, they slipped down again.

'You look like John Lennon,' she said and he laughed. 'I think I'll call you John from now on.' From then on it became a private joke between them.

It was not long after they started working together that Dunja invited Viktor for dinner at the shabby apartment where she was staying. Using the stove, which had only one element that functioned, she cooked him a simple pasta meal with a tomato and paprika sauce. Viktor brought along a bottle of red wine and they sat at the small square table in the kitchen that was covered with a red plastic tablecloth. It was a relaxed meal, where to begin with the conversation centred on their work.

'Can't we get anyone to replace those two?' Viktor asked.

'I've asked. The work's too specific. The Institute haven't been able to find anyone. There aren't many people with the necessary skill.'

'We'll never finish it on our own. There's too much to do. The prospect is daunting.'

'It'll take us longer that's all. Look how much we've done and we've only been here a short time.'

'Maybe,' Viktor, who didn't sound convinced, said.

'Shall we move into the lounge? I've got another bottle of red wine. You can open it while I clear the table.'

'We'll be here for years at the rate we're going.'

'Of course we will. Settle down and enjoy it. It would be different if we weren't being paid and we are — quite well. Don't be so negative!'

They were halfway through the second bottle of wine when Viktor slid across the well-worn, green-velour sofa and put his arm around Dunja and drew her to him.

'I don't feel like going home. How comfortable is your bed?'

'Are you propositioning me?' Dunja laughed.

'Yes!'

Dunja didn't hesitate. She had no intention of starting a relationship with him, but the odd night in bed with him seemed like an okay idea and she hadn't been with anyone since Pierre.

To begin with she hadn't minded the lack of foreplay too much, but when Viktor was only concerned with his own satisfaction, she did mind. It was all over in a few minutes and once it was, Viktor turned over and within minutes began snoring.

Dunja lay wide awake in the dark and thought about Pierre — she missed him. He had been a wonderful lover. Tender, passionate and considerate — the best — maybe. She and Pierre had parted amicably and agreed to keep in contact, yet neither had made any effort to do so. It was then that she thought briefly about Marko. The night they'd spent together hadn't been repeated because his girlfriend, who had been way in Rome studying, returned the day after Dunja had been to bed with him.

She wondered momentarily if Viktor had any room for improvement in bed. She didn't think so. With a sigh she turned over and went to sleep.

By the time Dunja had restored the artwork in several churches in cities as far north as Rijeka and as far south as Dubrovnik she had become well known in the restoration field. No sooner had she started one project than she was asked to work on another. She was flattered to be in such demand, although she was constantly busy — almost too busy. She often thought it would be good to take a holiday, but the opportunity never seemed to arise until she received a call from Claudine. And she was also conscious that she had been neglecting her mother and her brother. It was time that she went home.

She had returned to her mother's place after finishing work at the Rector's Palace in Dubrovnik; it was after dinner when the phone rang.

'I have wonderful news,' Claudine said. 'I'm coming to your country. My mother has bought a holiday house on the island of Korčula and I wondered if you'd like to meet me there for a holiday.'

'What splendid news. When will you be there?'

'On Saturday for two weeks.'

'Is it in Korčula town?'

'No, a village about fifteen minutes' drive from there — Račišće it's called. It's a funny word with a lot of inflections. I'm not sure how you pronounce it. Have you heard of it?'

'No, but there are plenty of small villages on the islands. How do you spell it again?'

Claudine spelt out the word.

'It'll be pronounced *Racheshta*. Quite a mouthful. I'd love to come. Would it be okay if I came on the following Monday for a few days?'

'Perfect.'

After a ten-hour bus trip travelling from Zagreb to Korčula, it was a bright sunny day without a breath of wind in early September when Dunja trudged through the maze of narrow cobbled alleyways in search of a small stonehouse that she'd been told had a bright-blue door and was sandwiched between two other houses. The house was number 123. There were no street names and when it turned out to be difficult to find Dunja had to ask directions at the shop.

'I'll show you around,' Claudine said as she welcomed Dunja and led the way through the compact house. Downstairs had a combined living and dining room with a small kitchen off to one side. Dark wood panelling, which extended three quarters of the way up the walls, made the area dark and necessitated the light having to be on during the day. Upstairs were three bedrooms and a bathroom.

'We're sharing the back bedroom,' Claudine said. 'It's dark because it's got no windows, but we'll only be sleeping there so I hope it won't bother you.'

In the succeeding days Dunja had a blissful time relaxing in the sun, swimming, eating local produce such as figs and freshly caught fish from the horseshoe-shaped bay that was the waterfront at Račišće. But by far the most enjoyable part of her stay was her trips to Vaja, a secluded beach that was a fifteen-minute walk from the village. The absence of people and the clear-blue sea made for idyllic days lazing in the late summer sun as she gazed up at clouds that were as fluffy as candyfloss.

As Dunja had been expecting there was next to no nightlife in Račišće and other than enjoying a pizza and a glass of wine in one of two local cafés Dunja's evenings were quiet.

It was on one of these evenings while she and Claudine were seated outside at a rustic wooden table near the waterfront eating a superb pizza with loads of local cheese, olives and fresh anchovies when they met Pero.

'Let me buy you a drink,' he said with his round-pink face alight with a friendly smile.

'He's cute,' Claudine said to Dunja as he went inside to order the drinks.

'He has a warm smile,' Dunja replied. 'Are you going to chat him up? Because if you don't I will.'

'May the best man or should I say woman win,' Claudine said with a laugh.

Claudine's comment heralded the start of a hilarious evening. Pero joined them at their table and while the women ordered another pizza and more fries, Pero kept their wine glasses full.

'Where are you both from?' Pero asked in halting English because Claudine didn't speak Serbo Croat.

Dunja filled in the details of where they were from and how they'd met and told Pero about Claudine's mother's house.

'What about you? You obviously live here. What's your job?' Claudine asked as she admired his well-built shoulders.

'I'm a builder. I work for a stone mason who lives on the other side of the village, over there,' he said pointing to a row of houses lining the road into the village adjacent to the sea. 'We mostly alter existing houses.'

'The village is quiet,' Dunja said. 'What do you do for entertainment? Don't you get bored?'

'There's cards and music in the hotel and dancing. That's only in the summer though. The last dance of the season was a fortnight ago. What a shame you weren't here then. We could go for a drink in the hotel when we finish eating if you like.'

'That could be fun,' Claudine said. 'Shall we?' she asked as she turned towards Dunja.

An hour later they were ensconced in the hotel, a large stone building close to the water's edge, sitting on a red velvet-covered seat in a secluded booth with Pero as they listened to three local men singing as they sat at the bar drinking beer.

'I think he's mine,' Dunja said when Pero excused himself and went to the toilet.

'Yes, I think you've won. He can't take his eyes of your hair. I thought he was going to stroke it a minute ago and he keeps looking right into your eyes.'

'I know.' Dunja giggled like a sixteen-year-old.

When Pero returned they were in for a surprise.

'I have to go,' he said. 'I must pick up my fiancée from Korčula town. She's been in Dubrovnik and I must collect her from the bus station. It's nice to have met you,' he said as he kissed each of them on the cheek and went on his way.

After she returned from her holiday Dunja started a new job in Zagreb. She and Viktor had accepted a contract to restore the elaborate frescoes in the church of the Blessed Virgin Mary in Remete, a suburb on the outskirts of Zagreb. The project was huge and they expected to be working there for at least five years to complete the first stage. This was the biggest most elaborate project she had taken on, but once again she submerged herself in it. For the length of time it took — years, in fact, this job became her wonderful rewarding life. Sometimes, she was so enthralled with what she was doing she didn't hear Viktor when he spoke to her.

The church of the Blessed Virgin Mary isn't one of the better known churches in Zagreb, but it is ancient with extensive complex frescoes covering the walls, the ceiling and the inside of the dome. Relatively modest, it was built at the end of the thirteenth century from the foundations of two previous churches that once stood on the same site. It was damaged by war during the Ottoman Empire and also by earthquakes.

Viktor and Dunja began by restoring the frescoes in the dome and above the altar. Sadly, a number of the frescoes on the walls, as opposed to in the dome and above the altar, were so indistinct they wouldn't be able to repair them because in places it was impossible to discern the artwork. As they expected, progress was slow and plenty of patience was required.

Not long after they started the project Viktor asked Dunja to look at an area in the dome where he was working because he wanted her advice. She couldn't help noticing the smirk on his face and it made her eager to climb the scaffolding and see what he found so amusing.

'What do you think I should do here?' he asked. 'It's impossible to distinguish the faces on the inside of this circular fresco and I don't see how I can restore it.' He was right, the pastel-coloured faces were too faded, which was a pity, because it was the only part of the dome where the frescoes were so damaged they were almost beyond repair.

'I don't think you can finish it. It seems such a shame, doesn't it?'

'Well, I have an idea, but you might think it's crazy,' he said with a grin.

'What if I paint the faces of my nephews and nieces there, on those five we can't make out?'

At first, Dunja was shocked by his suggestion, but then she thought, who will know? 'Why not! We never get to sign our names on our work, do we?'

They looked at each other and laughed.

Later, when Dunja attended church there, she always looked at Viktor's special faces and as she recalled their secret, she smiled.

Part Three

Chapter forty-two

At the beginning of 1990, during a lull in her fresco restoration work, eager to expand her creativity, Dunja had begun designing and selling ceramic tiles, as well as painting murals on the interior of restaurant walls and decorating prayer boards with gold-leaf headings to sell at Christmas time.

Her shoulder-length hair was twisted into a knot and tucked underneath her favourite denim cap and when she glanced in the mirror of her hotel bathroom in Vienna she thought she could easily have been mistaken for a boy. It was May 1991; she was exhibiting her tiles at the Naschmarkt in Vienna, when she overheard two men discussing au unsettling incident in Borovo *selo*, near Vukovar which she knew would have repercussions. She abandoned her stand and dashed to the nearest telephone to call home. The lines must have been down because the call wouldn't connect. Blinking away tears she slammed the receiver back into its cradle. She had read in the newspapers that unrest was brewing before she'd left Zagreb and had hoped it wouldn't come to anything. Unable to wait for the exhibition to end, she packed up her car and within minutes she was driving out of Vienna, heading towards home.

South of Vienna, the motor on her battered VW Golf spluttered and moments later, it died. She turned the key in the ignition, willing the cantankerous engine to start. Again and again she tried, but it was to no avail. She was stranded on a seemingly deserted road and when a speeding car raced past; this was all it took to push her over the edge — her tears flowed. What could be wrong with the wretched car? Why did it have to let her down at a time like this?

When she calmed down and her tears stopped, it came to her. She had run out of petrol. In her haste to rush home she had forgotten to fill the tank. She climbed out of the car on unstable legs and rummaged in the boot for the empty petrol can. The trip from Vienna to Zagreb was about three and a half hours, but a frustrating walk back to the petrol station she had passed earlier, meant it would take her much longer.

With fuel in the tank, set to continue on her way, she pressed the accelerator boldly and sped up hoping to make up lost time.

The absence of traffic was apparent and she was travelling at a decent speed once she'd crossed the border between Slovenia and Croatia when she found the road blocked. A tree barred her way and the axe marks on the trunk told her it had not fallen by accident. She slowed down knowing she would have to stop. A young man with matted hair that reminded her of a bird's nest, was standing in front of the tree trunk with his shotgun pointing at her. She got out of her car and from somewhere deep inside, amazed herself as she dredged up courage she didn't know she possessed. '*Zdravo, drug*,' she said in an uncertain voice. Aware that this was the friendliest greeting she could give him, she extended her hand. The hostile-faced, young man, a Serb or more likely a *Četnik*, stared at her for a long time until he lowered the barrel of his gun.

'Where are you going?' he asked.

'Home to Zagreb.' It was then that she noticed two, older, thick-set men, also with untamed hair, walking towards her.

'What are you doing here?' the fatter of the two who had a red, misshapen lumpy nose, snarled as he raised his gun and aimed the barrel at her chest.

'I've been to the Naschmarkt in Vienna. I make tiles …' she said, before her voice faltered and her words dried up. Her eyes were glued to the threateningly close gun. The brave front she put on earlier deserted her as the fat man nudged her in the stomach with the barrel of his gun. Dunja's legs became as soft as molten candles. She had reached the limit of her endurance.

'Step away from the car,' he ordered. Terrified he would pull the trigger, she fainted.

Dunja didn't know how much time had gone by since she had passed out and when she regained consciousness she was momentarily disoriented before fear saturated her. Her hands were secured in front of her with coarse rope and she was on her back on a narrow bed covered with rank smelling bedding. The room was dim and a shutter with discoloured peeling paint was hanging at a drunken angle inside the window. She struggled in vain to sit up, but without the use of her arms it was impossible. When she discovered her left ankle was attached to the bed leg with a chain, she cried out before closing her eyes and wishing she was anywhere but here. Time passed. Minutes — half an hour — maybe — she didn't know. Her watch was gone from her wrist. Her mind went numb. She turned her head to the side as terror constricted her throat and she sobbed helplessly.

Outside raucous men's voices were laughing and shouting. She picked up profanities but no other words.

The light was fading when the door crashed open and slammed against the wall. The two older men she had encountered earlier strode in. The fat one with the unsightly nose laughed — a callous jeer that filled her with renewed terror. Then the skinnier one, with a slash where his mouth should have been, stepped towards her and wrenched the belt off her jeans. Her body went rigid as he tore open her fly and forced her jeans and underwear down with brutal hands. Dunja emitted a stifled whimper. He slapped her face and swore under his breath. When he flipped her on to her stomach, the chain reached it length and jarred her ankle, causing pain to shoot up her leg. She soon forget about it when he mounted her and she was engulfed in new pain. She screamed. Alcohol and cigarette fumes enveloped her.

'You Croat bitch,' he shouted as he forced his way into her. Unable to stop herself, she screamed again.

'Shut up or I'll kill you.' He grunted and thrust more fiercely before withdrawing and burping.

It was over. She stealed herself for the second violation knowing that the other offender must be close to the bed because his breathing was loud. She wished he'd get on with it. She bit into the stinking fabric underneath her mouth and squeezed her eyes more tightly shut.

'What's taking you so long? Are you having trouble pretending she's a boy?' the first rapist said and then let out an ugly laugh.

'Shut your mouth *kurac!*' the one hovering over Dunja replied. Her body was pushed deeper into the putrid bed cover when the second perpetrator raped her. The second time it was quicker.

'You couldn't wait, could you?' the first abuser jeered.

'I need another beer. We'll come back for more later,' his mate replied.

When the door slammed, Dunja knew they had gone. Shock paralysed her and it was a while before she could move. When at last she rolled over vomit rose in her throat and she turned her head to the side and threw up before she wiped her mouth on her jacket sleeve. A fresh outbreak of tears cascaded freely down her cheeks. Shudders racked her body like the tremors of an earthquake. Never, ever in all her life had she felt so vulnerable. The smell of the rapists' filthy bodies clung to her as she longed to wrestle her hands free and pull up her jeans. In as much as the chain allowed her to, she wriggled down the bed, turned over and curled up as best she could. She couldn't allow herself to imagine the unimaginable.

The night went by. She couldn't sleep. Drunken voices continued to laugh and shout into the early hours of the morning. She gathered from snatches of their conversation that they were playing cards. Later, as she was drifting into a restless sleep an altercation woke her. Gun shots were followed by boots stamping, the squeal of tyres and irate voices swearing. The light indicated it was almost dawn. Whatever was happening outside upset Dunja anew and she began to tremble. Not matter how hard she tried she could not keep her limbs still. And she had also developed a persistent ache in the pit of her stomach — she needed to empty her bladder. From the depths of hopelessness, she knew she had to focus on something to keep her sanity. But what? She forced her mind back to her childhood as she tried to remember a happy moment. She couldn't. Her mind refused to focus. Then her thoughts turned angry as she wondered what she'd done to deserve being raped. She was certain they intended to kill her, sooner rather than later. She hoped it would be quick and painless. But that was not the *Četnik* way. Violence and macabre killings were their trademark. Her breathing grew ragged as she struggled to suppress her thoughts. Praying was her last hope. She closed her eyes and silently recited the Lord's Prayer, '*Oče naš, koji si na nebesima da se sveti ime tvoje ...*'

Patches of blue sky were showing through the broken slats of the swinging shutter when Dunja heard men's voices again. It was a normal conversation. The shouting had ceased and they sounded more subdued. She imagined they were hungover. No doubt it wouldn't be long before they crashed open her door and assaulted her again — or worse —

came to kill her. She closed her eyes and tried not to think about it. When a glass or more likely a bottle smashed on a hard surface somewhere outside she jumped in fright. Her nerves were taut and the scraping of chair legs stretched them to breaking point. She waited for the next onslaught. A car drove away. Then came silence. She let out an uneven breath.

No more than five minutes later, the hinges on the door to her prison creaked. Her body tensed and she shut her eyes, waiting for the bang as it hit the wall. There was no bang and when she dared to open her eyes the younger Četnik who'd been stationed beside the fallen tree was standing at the foot of the bed fiddling with the chain. Dunja was too afraid to think about what he was doing when he spoke.

'Your keys are in your car. Get out of here as quickly as you can.'

Certain she was hearing things, Dunja stayed still.

'Come on!' he shouted. 'What are you waiting for?' His voice was gruff.

'Y … you're letting me go?' she stammered.

'Yes!'

When she stood up too quickly, the room began to spin. She wobbled on her feet and fell back on to the bed.

'Come on! There's no time to waste. I don't know how long they'll be gone.'

Dunja reached down and pulled up her pants. The fly was torn and the top button was missing. She clutched at the fabric and held them up as best she could.

'Are you okay?' he asked.

Instead of answering, she stared at him and wondered why was he being so considerate. There was no time for further thought when he took hold of her arm and pulled her from the room.

'Get in your car and drive,' he said as he hurried her out of the stinking bedroom into an outdoor kitchen area littered with dirty dishes, empty bottles and rubbish.

'Why are you letting me go?'

'They murdered my wife — she was Croatian.' He paused. 'You need to go now. In case they come back early.' He opened the door of her car and pushed rather than helped her inside.

'You'll need to drive back and take the last turn on the left. It's a detour that'll let you avoid the roadblock.'

'Thank you.' After slamming the door and depressing the locks, a quick glance showed her that the interior had been ransacked. Although her handbag was no longer on the floor in front of the passenger seat she was not about to search for it.

It took mere seconds to reverse before she was ready to drive on. But it wasn't that simple. Her car was in gear and she was letting out the clutch, when out of nowhere, a powerful black Audi slithered to a halt beside her. Alarmed by its sudden arrival, her foot slipped and her car lurched and stalled. Renewed panic surged through her. As she tried to pull herself together, the other driver reversed, turned at speed and powered away, clipping the side of her car as he went. Dunja was too stunned to move, let alone drive. Her heart missed a beat. Tears distorted her vision. She dashed them away with the back of her hand. The young man was chasing after the Audi, firing his weapon on the run. But the big car was too fast. It disappeared quickly, leaving the solitary *Četnik* staring after it. Who was in that car and why was he shooting at it? she wondered. Dunja knew she had to leave — immediately. Yet her reactions were pathetic. She was consumed with dread and her hands were shaking as she restarted her car. She jumped in renewed shock when the *Četnik,* who was now standing beside her car, bawled at her.

'Get out of here! What the bloody hell are you waiting for?'

Dunja's foot pressed the accelerator too hard and her car took off with an almighty leap. She gripped the wheel with sticky hands and fixed her concentration on the road ahead.

Ten kilometres down the road she had to pull over. With the engine still running she opened her door, got out and squatted beside the car to relieve herself. As she did so the stench of the vile semen the rapists had deposited inside her drifted up between her legs. She gagged and vomited bile. There was nothing in her stomach. She wasn't hungry and food was the last thing on her mind. All she felt was dirty and defiled. Something unmentionable had happened to her. A sordid secret she would never share.

Back in her car she blew her nose on the last remaining tissue left in the glove compartment. Unable to bear the thought of seeing herself in the mirror, she shut down her mind. Instead, she thanked God for her escape and prayed that he would keep her safe until she reached home.

As she was driving through the outskirts of Zagreb, it felt different. Exactly what had changed, Dunja couldn't determine. It hit her with a jolt when she spotted the flags — an absurd number, hanging from buildings everywhere. The *šahovnica* with its distinctive red and white chequered shield was ablaze all around her. She wondered if this was President Tuđman's way of saying that Croatia was only for Croatians. What a fool he was making such a provocative gesture. She was shaken up all over again and her feeling of unease heightened. His gesture was sure to have dire consequences. What had caused the situation to alter so rapidly in her absence? Dunja drove on and winced as more and more flags came into view. By then, she was more than afraid, she was terrified — war had arrived for certain. She shivered. Through her tears it was difficult to see clearly out of the windscreen. When she wandered over the centreline and her bowels turned to water, she knew she must pull over and find a toilet.

On the way back to her car she bumped into a gangly youth with unkempt straggly hair and beard. When she muttered *oprostite,* he gave her a toothless grin. Emblazoned across his black T-shirt, underneath a white skull and crossbones, were the words *freedom or death.* Without a doubt he was a *Četnik* — but why was he wandering around the centre of Zagreb? Clutching her jeans to hold them up, she broke into a run, intent on the safety of the car. Her legs were sluggish and wouldn't function properly. Too afraid to look behind her she pushed on with the sound of his footsteps pounding like a persistent drum in her head.

Minutes later renewed panic gripped her when she stopped her car outside her mother's apartment. How would she explain her dishellveled appearance? Her mind was slow to register that Dominik would be at work and her mother would more than likely be asleep in her chair in front of the television. Without pausing, she unlocked the front door as quietly as possible. The apartment was silent as she sneaked towards the bathroom. Inside she slid the bolt home and leant her forehead against the cold timber door.

With her eyes averted from the mirror, she ripped off her foul clothing and bundled it up. Later, she would burn it.

Although the water in the shower was hot as it flowed over her together with her silent tears, it didn't feel hot enough to erase the traces of the horror she'd survived.

Chapter forty-three

Dominik had begun writing a diary when he was ten. Every night before bed, he wrote about his day before he hid his diary in a cardboard box at the bottom of his wardrobe.

It was at the beginning of the war, in 1991, when he began a second diary — his war diary — where he was attempting to write a chronological record of the war and its aftermath in all the countries of the former Yugoslavia. It was a ridiculously difficult task but he was determined to stick at it.

Seven years after he started working at Stolica Dizajn he was promoted and from then on he travelled all over Croatia and sometimes further afield. Although his work kept him busy, he daydreamed often about publishing a book about the war. He was tired of reading the misrepresentations and embellishments published in the newspapers and he wanted to expose the politicians who manipulated it. Although he was aware his country had always had these issues, the outbreak of war had caused a resurgence of erroneous media propaganda.

When the war began, he couldn't wait to be called up to fight for his country. He was considering joining up when Tonci rang.

'A group of us are meeting behind the cemetery wall to talk about taking off and joining up. Are you up for it?' Tonci said.

'I'll be there,' Dominik replied. 'What time?'

'Six, can you make it?'

'Think so.' Dominik hung up and almost immediately the look on Dunja's face as she sat at the kitchen table drinking a cup of tea told him she had been listening in to his conversation.

'Where are you going?' she asked.

He paused as he tried to formulate a palatable answer. He was wondering what to say when she spoke again.

'Don't tell me you're going to run away and join up?'

Once he'd been snapped, he saw no point in denying it. 'As I matter of fact, I am.'

'You haven't heard about Vid and Mijo then?'

'No, what about them?'

'They went to Knin ten days ago and they were killed by Krajina Serbs.'

'Christ!' Why didn't you tell me?'

'I thought you knew. Are you still going?'

'No ... I ... I don't think so. That's too close for comfort.' He was content to stay put for a time — at least until he recovered his nerve.

Although he was tired, Dominik couldn't sleep. He got up and crossed the room to his desk. Old papers and discarded drafts of his manuscript littered the battered, wooden surface. He picked up a newspaper. He had hoped this tabloid would provide useful information for his writing. He'd bought copies of the first few issues earlier in the year and was pleased they were different from the usual journals published in Zagreb — the headlines and content were sensational. Many readers thought it was an appalling paper, while others including Dominik, enjoyed its controversial style. Leafing through the battered pages, he recalled his lack of surprise when the style of the paper changed dramatically within a short space of time. At first, it had been critical of the Croatian Democratic Party (HDZ) and nationalism, but after only a few issues the paper altered its stance to embrace President Tudman and his policies. He'd heard rumours that the shift took place when officials in Tudman's government began leaking sensitive information to the paper to promote government policies. He was positive someone employed by Tudman had bribed those who mattered. When the paper started promoting hate speech directed against the Serbian minority in Croatia, he found it too biased, especially when it published a list of Serbian citizens living in Croatian controlled areas who were accused of being spies and traitors.

In the end, he concluded that other sources of information such as *Vreme* — the newspaper published in Belgrade, provided a more reliable source of material.

Wide awake, he decided to reread the introduction to his book that he'd been revising. It had taken him a considerable length of time to research it because his sources were limited and he was still working on it. Not that he dared show it to anyone. He wasn't sure what reaction he would have received from his family. He didn't have an unbiased view of things. Like all his friends, he hated plenty of Serbs and *Četniks* with a monstrous passion and he too longed to kill the bastards except for one Serb who had been in his class at school — he'd disappeared when the first skirmishes broke out. Dominik didn't know what had happened to him. He was curious and when he made enquiries, people shrugged and said he'd been *eaten by the night*.

Dominik was trying to write with honesty — something he believed many people around him lacked. If he was to have any hope of publishing his work, he knew it must be a precise account of events.

Of all the people he thought about discussing his proposed book with he imagined his sister would have been the most supportive, but when he broached the subject with her he didn't get the reaction he was hoping for.

'Why are you doing that?' she asked one evening when she was preparing a meal for the three of them. 'It has the potential to get you into a lot of trouble. If you're going to persist with it then you'd better keep quiet about it,' she said as she added salt to the pot of potatoes she was about the cook.

'I wasn't planning on broadcasting it. I haven't told anyone about it except you.'

'That's good, keep it that way.'

Dominik rubbed his gritty eyes, before he stood up, stretched and walked over to the window. He pulled back the heavy brown curtain and peered outside. It was dark and the sky was black. There was no moon and no stars and his watch said it was after midnight. He dropped the curtain and returned to his bed where he plonked himself down on the navy quilted bedspread. His back was stiff and it ached. He turned his torso, this way and that, trying to relieve the cramped muscles. A shiver ran through him and prompted him to put on an extra layer — a grey-woollen jersey, one of his favourites. Autumn had passed and it was cold, especially at night. On impulse, he pulled off his thin socks, and replaced them with a pair of thick, black ones before he sat at his desk. For a time, he did nothing other than stare at the white wall in front of his desk. The chalky paint was peeling in one area and in a mindless trance he used the sharp end of his ruler to scrape off several large flakes. His concentration was lacking. Transfixed by the mess he'd made of the plaster, he blinked before putting away the ruler in the drawer of his desk and dusting the plaster off the carving of a small horse that had been given to him by his grandmother. She said his grandfather had carved it and he always kept it on his desk. It had been skilfully done; he liked it and appreciated the work that had gone into it.

His focus returned to the manuscript in front of him as he flicked through the pages. The paragraph about the beginning of the war caught his eye.

> In May 1991 at Borovo *selo*, a Serbian village in Slavonia, two Croatian policemen were fired on by Serbs and subsequently abducted. The following day, when a Croatian chief of police sent in reinforcements in the form of a busload of police to find out what had happened, the situation erupted. In the ensuing skirmish, twelve Croatian policemen and three Serb civilians lost their lives. It is the opinion of many Croatians that this was the incident that triggered the civil war.

He paused, uncertain whether the paragraph he had finished reading, which was the official Croatian version, was satisfactory. He had unearthed different versions of the events and was confused about which version was correct.

The second version, from a Serb official, suggested that two Croatian policemen had driven into Borovo *selo* for no apparent reason and opened fire on villagers, who defended themselves with old hunting weapons. Two Croatian policemen were subsequently wounded and taken to hospital. The following day three hundred policemen stormed the hospital and shot the unarmed man at the door before taking doctors and patients hostage. Three hours later one villager and twenty-five policemen were dead.

The third version, from residents in the village, suggested that the two Croatian policemen had sneaked into the village in the dead of night as the result of a bet. Their challenge was to remove the Serbian flag and replace it with the Croatian *šahovnica*. But when one of the villagers spotted them, without pausing to think about the consequences, he fired at them. There was no mention of hostages being taken, unarmed men being shot, or the village people defending themselves with ancient hunting rifles. At the end of the incident three Serbs, not residents of the village, were dead and twenty-five policemen were wounded.

Which version should he have put in his book? It would have been invaluable to have the advice of a professional author or to be able to employ an editor, as well as finding a way of ascertaining the truth. But his earnings were modest, he couldn't afford an editor and there were no writers in his circle of friends. He could count his close friends on one hand. After further deliberation, he thought most likely the first version. The phrase that most Serbs were barefaced liars — Vuk Branković's as the saying went, or brainwashed believers of falsehoods came to mind, yet he dared not commit those words to paper. He knew he'd have to give the chapter more thought.

> Croatians and Serbs who had once been friends turned on each other as hatred flared. Not even cross-cultural marriages were exempt — couples found themselves shooting at each other from opposing sides.

Dominik shivered and took off his glasses. The lenses had fogged up. When war broke out it had seemed inconceivable. He remembered thinking that if this was how he felt living in Zagreb, which was relatively peaceful, he had no conception of life in places such as Dubrovnik, Zadar, Knin or Vukovar. Cousins on his mother's side of the family had moved from Zagreb to Zadar six months before the outbreak of the war. He recalled the day he found out that his cousin Andro had died. Andro had been home alone in Arbanassi and was killed instantly when his house was hit by an artillery shell. His family had not only lost Andro, but they also lost all their possessions and everything they had spent their lives striving to attain.

Without a doubt, he knew he'd made the right decision to keep his book hidden. There were comments he had difficulty writing because he knew they would cause outrage, and any number of people could have viewed him as a traitor. Putting aside the passionate loyalty he felt for his country and writing objectively was proving much harder than he envisaged. And not only that, as he had already discovered, finding out the truth about what really happened would be more than a little difficult, particularly because he did not have sufficient resources. He knew he could never write a fully researched account of the events — he simply did not have access to the necessary information to achieve that. So often he wished he was a professional journalist — this would have meant he could interview people. He was also aware that it could most likely take him years if not decades to complete the book because it could take that long for the necessary information to surface. At the end of his night's work he finally came to the conclusion that all he could write would be more of a personal account of the war as he saw it through his eyes.

Chapter forty-four

When the air-raid siren sounded yet again, Dunja was drying the dishes after dinner. She drew aside the green velvet curtain over the kitchen window and looked out. The streetlights had been extinguished and the inky darkness outside made her anxious.

'Get the torch from the drawer in the dresser,' Dominik said. 'We need to get to the shelter.' Dunja's reactions were slow. She couldn't shake off the feelings of anguish that had clung to her since her return from Austria. She struggled to accept that her country had been plunged into war and she was finding her altered self — a consequence of being raped, more than difficult to live with.

'Hurry up, will you?' Dominik shouted.

'I can't find it,' Dunja replied.

'What? We used it a couple of days ago when the last air-raid siren went off.'

'Mother, do you know where the torch is?' Dunja asked.

Zlata was not only confused most of the time; she had become stubborn and forgetful.

Dunja wondered if she'd moved it and couldn't remember where she'd put it.

'Why should I know where it is?' her mother replied. 'I haven't touched it.'

In the candlelit room — the only light permitted during the blackout — Dominik and Dunja scrambled around in the dark searching for the torch, while their mother sat in her chair staring into space, oblivious to their frantic behaviour.

'Why are you wasting your time running around so frantically? Don't you know that if the bombs don't kill us we'll be done for by our own kind anyway?' Zlata's voice was bitter.

'Come on, *Majka*, hurry up. Can't you hear the siren?' Dominik yelled.

'Leave me here. I'm not coming,' Zlata mumbled.

'Dunja! Help me! Take her arm. She can't stay here on her own.' Dominik glanced at his sister.

Whenever the sirens sounded Dunja was used to her mother carrying on this way. She tried every ploy she could think of to stay in the apartment and it always resulted in an argument. This time Dominik ran out of patience.

'Do you want to die?' he bellowed in frustration as he stood with his hands on his hips glaring at his mother slumped in her old green chair.

'Dominik! Don't say things like that; you're tempting fate,' Dunja scolded.

'We might as well be killed by a bomb now, rather than shot as traitors,' Zlata muttered.

'Don't be ridiculous.' Dominik came to his sister's aid, and together they pulled her out of her chair.

'You won't think it's so ridiculous when they knock on our door in the middle of the night. Don't fool yourselves they don't know it's here, because they do. Don't forget, the walls have eyes … and ears.' Zlata sauntered between her children towards the front door. It was impossible to make her hurry.

'What are you going on about? Do you know Dunja?' Dominik asked in frustration.

'No idea. She seems confused about something.'

She's finally gone mad, if you ask me, Dominik thought but didn't say so.

Dominik and Dunja looked at each other with resignation as Dominik gripped his mother's arm more tightly and propelled her along the hallway to the door.

As they crossed the road in silence Dunja peered down the long dark tunnel that was Savska Cesta. It was deserted, but that didn't mean they were safe — only that the unsavoury characters who continued to frequent the area were hiding.

The concrete shelter was already crowded, hot and airless. How long would they be stuck in there? she wondered. She knew how much her mother hated it. From her seat on a rickety-wooden chair, she watched her mother sink on to an old, stained mattress and lean her back against the cold concrete wall. Her eyes appeared to be focused on a group of youngsters playing cards by torchlight on the mattress next to her. Dunja rubbed her eyes; she was tired from the stress of her mother's earlier performance. The next time she looked at her mother, her eyes were closed. She hoped she was asleep. But it was seconds later when she opened them wide and seemed to be staring at something only she could see.

'I didn't do it,' she shouted. 'I promised you I'd keep it safe. It wasn't my fault,' she mumbled.

'*Majka! Majka*! Wake up!' Dunja shook her mother. There was no point. No matter what she or her brother said or did, their mother refused to be roused.

Dunja and Dominik stared at her in consternation.

'What's wrong with her? Dominik asked. 'She's never been this bad before. Seems to me she's gone mad.'

'Stop talking about me and let me sleep,' Zlata said in a barely audible voice.

Dominik went mildly pink with shame. He hadn't thought his mother was coherent enough to hear what he'd said. For a while no one spoke.

'Do you think she was talking about the sea chest?' Dunja asked.

'Perhaps,' Dominik replied. 'That hadn't occurred to me.'

'Do you know what's in it?'

'No. I tried to open it a couple of times when I was a child and it was in the *konoba* at *Baba's* house. She caught me fiddling with the padlock and got Uncle Zoran to replace it. I was forced to give up then. It's in *Majka's* wardrobe now, isn't it?'

'Yes. She guards it as if it's full of gold.'

'Maybe it is.' Dominik laughed. 'One of these days I'm going to open it.'

Chapter forty-five

Dunja was not surprised that one of the few topics that had the ability to hold her mother's attention, when the war began, was the subject of Dominik's involvement. One morning at breakfast, when he brought up the subject again, she was relieved her mother was not in the room.

'Tonci and I are going to enlist today,' he said without looking at his sister. He was making an elaborate show of spreading butter on his bread roll and heaping on cheese and slices of *pršut*. Dunja was shocked, but she chose to ignore his remark, hoping he wouldn't pursue the subject.

'Didn't you hear what I said?'

'I did, but what do you expect me to say? You already know I think it's a bad idea, but that won't stop you from doing it. What can I say except don't tell *Majka*, please.'

Dominik's answer was to pick up his shoulder bag and walk towards the door as he crammed the last piece of bread in his mouth.

Dunja waited all day for him to return and as the hours ticked by, she became more and more concerned. Had they been accepted on the spot, as so many of them were, and left immediately for their destination?

In the evening she heard the click of his key in the door and looked up expectantly.

'Well?' she said when he dumped his cap and bag in a chair.

'Where's *Majka*?' he asked looking at her empty chair.

'She's gone to bed early. Did you get in?'

'No, the bastards wouldn't accept us. We've been given reserve status. They said they didn't want us and we'd only be called up if and when they needed us.'

'That's a relief.'

'Perhaps,' he replied, slinging his bag over his shoulder and retiring to his room.

But that wasn't the end of it. The following day, Dunja was horrified when Dominik made the fatal mistake of telling their mother what had happened. From then on it preyed on Zlata's mind day and night.

'It'll only be a matter of time before they call you up,' she said from the depths of her green chair. 'You're fit and healthy and even if you weren't, they'd take you. Once you go, you'll be killed the same as all the others. And where will that leave us, my boy?' she repeated almost every time she clapped eyes on her son.

Dunja found her mother's dismal thoughts difficult to cope with, especially when she vocalised them so often. Dominik didn't help either — he *wanted* to be called up. His desire to defend his country seemed to have resurfaced and it was only with considerable effort that she restrained him from expressing his need to murder Serbs and *Četniks* in front of their depressed mother.

'Give me a gun and I'll shoot those bloody bastards,' he said as he burst in the door at the end of his working day later in the week.

'Dominik, watch your language in front of *Majka*,' Dunja said as she looked across to where she was drooping in her chair, in front of the television.

'What do you expect me to say when I find out that there are *Četniks* living two streets away from our house? Someone has written *Četnik* in blood-red paint on their door.'

'Are you sure?'

'Of course, I am. And as for that dirty rotten bastard,' he said looking over Dunja's shoulder at the newspaper she was reading. 'It's bad enough hearing his inflammatory speeches on the radio without having to look at his ugly mug. I can't wait to have a shot at him.' He was pointing at a picture of Lazar Macura, the deputy president of the Knin town council. Macura had intense black eyes, which seemed to penetrate the depths of your soul, beneath ferociously dense eyebrows.

'Dominik, didn't you hear what I said?' Dunja thought her brother's desire to kill had become obsessive. That said, she was sure he didn't mean to hurt his mother; he just couldn't contain his patriotic yearning to go to war. When he made it clear that he wanted to continue debating the subject Dunja reached the limit of her endurance.

'Enough!' she shouted as her rape came to the forefront of her mind. When she started to shake and was fearful she'd be sick, she dropped the newspaper and ran to the bathroom.

Once she'd thrown up the entire contents of her stomach, Dunja stood up on weak legs and flushed the toilet. As she clutched the rim of the handbasin she stared at herself in the mirror above it. A white face with beads of perspiration on its forehead stared back at her. She shook her head as she stood still and tried to compose herself and blot the rape out of her mind. When she felt marginally better she rinsed her mouth with water and wiped the perspiration from her face with a towel.

The next day Dunja was on her way home after buying milk at the shop around the corner when she heard the unmistakable sound of planes flying overhead. Panic-stricken, she dropped the milk and heedless of the smashed container and milk dribbling down the pavement, she ran towards the nearest shelter. Terrified she wouldn't make it, she braced herself for the boom of explosions. By the time the shelter was in sight, the aircraft noise had diminished. From the recessed doorway of an empty house where she had taken refuge, she stepped gingerly on to the pavement and looked up. Papers were fluttering out of the sky and littering the ground like giant white pieces of confetti. She bent down and picked up the nearest one. The plane had disgorged thousands of posters from the political party, HDZ. Underneath a photo of President Tuđman were the words: *We alone will decide the destiny of our Croatia.* By the time she arrived home, she'd worked herself into an agitated state about the future of Croatia under such unwise leadership. By evening her mood had not changed and she found both her mother and Dominik irritating. It wasn't that they were behaving any differently than they usually did, but her patience had worn thin and she preferred to be on her own, in her own space. The time had come to consider finding somewhere else to live. But the question was, where, and how could she afford it? By eleven o'clock her brain was on fire. One minute she was thinking about moving and the next she was agonising about the current government. Sleep would not come easily and in an endeavour to shut down her mind, she ran a bath and submerged herself in lavender-scented water until her fingers and toes were as wrinkled as sundried figs. Unfortunately, the bath didn't help and her night was wakeful.

At breakfast the following morning she had no appetite for food or the coming day. She flicked listlessly through *Jutarnji List*, while she drank a cup of black coffee. When she moved to Paris, she was fed up with communism and she had stopped being aware of the various political factions for a long time after she returned from France, but these days she was almost consumed by it. Her interest had been rekindled when war broke out. An article on the front page mentioned that Tuđman would be giving a speech at a venue in the centre of the city near parliament that day. On impulse she decided to go. Quite why, she wasn't sure. Perhaps it was a way of stopping herself dwelling on the past or maybe it was in the hope that she'd find out Tuđman was not the imbecile she believed him to be, after all.

By the time she arrived, a little later than she intended, there were no spare seats in the hollow, decrepit city hall. She had no choice but to stand alongside others lined up at the back of the hall on either side of the doors. The president's speech began immediately after her arrival. Silence blanketed the hall, even though in her opinion he talked for far too long. She thought his speech was pompous and difficult to concentrate on. His demeanour reminded her of an irate bird. His large glasses and beak of a nose gave him the appearance of an angry starving owl. Professing to be anti-communism, he made promises to recreate the Croatian state — which sounded all well and good, until he started talking about the irregular shape of Croatia, saying it looked like an apple with a bite taken out of it. That bite was Bosnia and Herzegovina (BiH) and it must be put back. When he insisted that BiH must be part of Croatia, Dunja was staggered. And if their faces were anything to go by, many people around her were shocked and frightened by his words. When at last his speech came to an end, Dunja made her way outside in the midst of a crowd. A young man in a brown peaked cap who was walking beside her struck up a conversation.

'Never heard such rubbish in all my life,' he said, shaking his head. When Dunja failed to answer he carried on regardless. 'If you ask me, the shape of Croatia is more like the open mouth of a crocodile,' he said with a cross between a grin and a grimace.

All evening Tuđman's inflammatory speech stuck in Dunja's mind, until by midnight she was still recalling his more irrational sentences. One of his particularly stupid remarks was centred around his desire to reorganise Croatia in the same way as the attempt that had been made in 1939. There would be a Greater Serbia. BiH would cease to exist. It would be carved up between Croatia and Serbia. In his own twisted fashion, he believed BiH's Muslims would come to thank him for tearing their country apart. Dunja thought he was worse than foolish. He was dangerous and she dare not consider where he would lead his country, especially since she had heard that he and Milošević were engaging in secret meetings to discuss splitting up BiH.

During the successive days, the posters, which had fluttered down from the sky, were tacked on to walls around the city. Under cover of darkness, people defaced Tuđman's image — in many he had a floppy fringe and a moustache — like Hitler. Dunja wondered what he thought when he saw his new face.

A new pattern had established itself in Dunja's life. Many of her evenings were spent in the air-raid shelter across the street from her mother's apartment with her mother and brother and others from the immediate area. During the day, though, things were largely unchanged.

When war broke out she assumed she would no longer be offered work, but as it turned out the design work she had recently begun taking on, came flooding in. This was a productive, lucrative time. Maybe keeping busy is what stopped her from going crazy and dwelling on having been raped. Designing ceramic tiles took up a lot of her time, too, and as fast as she finished one design she moved on to the next. Her reproductions of Gustav Klimt's work were popular and she often struggled to fill orders on time.

Then, when she was least expecting it, she received a commission to refurbish the Hotel Intercontinental in Zagreb. A reception had been held there for President Tuđman during the Referendum on Independence immediately before the Declaration of Independence in 1991. Perhaps it had been decided then that something needed to be done about the tired, dilapidated state of the hotel. Or was it because this hotel was the watering hole for international media as well as the headquarters for the foreign press bureau? The middle of a war was an odd time to renovate a hotel; she believed it was part of Tuđman's pretence that everything in his country was normal.

The time frame she was given to complete her proposals for new colour schemes and furniture throughout the interior of the hotel, artwork in the public areas and selected suites, was short and Dunja was left with no time for indulgent or romantic daydreams. She was so busy she rarely looked in the mirror, but on the very day she did choose to pay attention to herself, she found that almost overnight her hair had turned white, yet it was not long since she had turned forty. She closed her mind to the disturbing reflection and once again submerged herself in what was one of the most demanding projects of her career.

It was not long after she had completed the bulk of this project when she was invited to exhibit a series of abstract paintings in the Lauba Art Gallery. She knew she was lucky because she had never been good at hustling for work. It just didn't come naturally and she was reluctant to force herself to do it. Yet again it transpired that she had Karlo to thank for proposing her for this exhibition. This was the gallery where she'd had her first exhibition, but back then it had been called Muzejski Prostor. When the war broke out she assumed that cultural activities in Zagreb would come to a halt. She was wrong.

Once again she was thrown into a panic when she discovered there were not enough hours in her day. She painted at a frantic pace. Her work wasn't her best or her favourite, but she certainly wouldn't forget it. All her canvases were painted in shades of black and white — she couldn't use colour. This was one of the effects the war had on her.

During this time the moon, which had always drawn her towards it, was seldom visible. The moonless nights provided the perfect cover for enemy planes to hide in, fly over and terrify the inhabitants of Zagreb. The blackout closed in around Dunja in a sky thick with substantial dark clouds. She felt suffocated and often woke up feeling as if she was about to scream as horrendous memories of her rape flooded her mind. Unsteady hands, set off by the wailing sirens, had also become an unwelcome part of her permanently altered being. Often, when she was working, she struggled to control them. She was ashamed that her paintings for this particular exhibition were filled with such unspeakable aggression. It would be a relief when the show was over. She intended to destroy any canvases that didn't sell. Constant reminders of this dreadful time were something she didn't need.

She had begun working on a new canvas when a different sound broke the silence — the shrill ringing of the telephone. Clicking and humming on the line told her that it was a call from another country.

'Diana! Is that you?' His words reduced her to silence. 'Are you okay? I can't stop thinking about you,' he said.

'Pierre! Where are you?' She tried to sound normal — but what was normal? She didn't know anymore. It was years since she'd heard from him and she was totally astounded that he was calling. She seldom thought about him and she was surprised that he was thinking about her. Hadn't he moved on with his life?

'I'm in St Clémentin. I've been worried about you — and your family. You should come and stay with me. It's too dangerous in Zagreb — unless you want me to come and fight for Croatia.' He laughed, but it didn't sound right and he couldn't mean it.

'I'm fine. But I can't come. I must look after *Majka* and Dominik.' She feel trapped with them, but she couldn't tell him that. They were her family and it was her duty to stay with them.

'You must all come. My home is your home.' His words were becoming less distinct and it was difficult to hear him. Even so, she was sure he knew she wouldn't come and he knew her well enough to understand she wouldn't change her mind.

'I have to go,' she said as she pictured his soft brown eyes.

'Promise me you'll call if things get worse. I'm always here for you,' he said.

Chapter forty-six

Dominik had become bolder and moved about the city more freely than he had at the start of the war. He had grown used to the droning of planes — as yet they had not bombed Zagreb. Intimidation was the game they have been playing and many people living in Zagreb had come to believe they were safe.

On his way to pick up tickets for a ballet performance at the Croatian National Theatre, because he had promised he would accompany his sister, even though ballet wasn't something that interested him greatly, he was crossing the road opposite the historic building housing the theatre, when the ominous *crump* of explosions echoed overhead. He froze as fear consumed him — there were no air-raid shelters nearby. Then, as quickly as they arrived the planes departed, leaving behind cries of people struck down by bombs. Dominik rushed in the direction of the commotion. The first person he come to was a woman sprawled face down on the cobblestones. The back of her grey coat was untouched. Her shoes had fallen off and a child was sitting beside her shaking her arm.

'Mama! Mama!' she cried over and over.

Dominik's mind was in a muddle. In the first instance he wondered if this was the only part of the city that had been attacked, then the next, he thought about contacting the rest of his family to make sure they were safe. But when common sense kicked in, he knew his first priority must be the child. He squatted down and grasped the woman's wrist and when he could not find a pulse he knew she was beyond help.

When he picked up the child he was surprised by her lack of complaint. As he carried her away from the scene he waited for her to call out to her mother again. But she was silent and lay against his shoulder limply without making a murmur.

From the safety of a doorway, where Dominik and the child were sheltering, bodies lay a few feet away in the square — some were immobile, others were calling out in pain and distress. The immediate area was chaotic.

When the child in his arms went limp, Dominik drew back his coat, which he had used to cover her, and gasped. Blood was trickling down her forehead from a wound in her scalp. Her eyes were closed and her small face was drained of colour. He was unsure whether or not the child with the luxurious brown curls was alive. All he knew was she needed urgent medical attention. He stood up and began walking. In the middle of the road, the drone of another plane overhead made him quicken his pace. That was all it took for him to lose his balance, miss his step and stumble as his ankle twisted.

Frozen in the path of oncoming traffic, clutching the child, he closed his eyes and for the first time since he was a child, he prayed as the terrifying *crump* noise assaulted his senses again. Oblivious to the pain in his ankle, he held his breath. But as quickly as it began, the second attack was over. Once again all that could be heard were the cries of more wounded. Slowly Dominik stood up, adjusted his hold on the inert child and limped towards an ambulance.

Chapter forty-seven

Dominik stepped out of the shower and dried himself before putting on his grey tracksuit. In his bedroom, he retrieved his manuscript from its hiding place and stowed it in his duffle bag.

It was November 1991; he'd been asked to travel to Lapad Peninsula, the home of many of Dubrovnik's wealthier people. Four kilometres from the old city, Lapad was the site of beautiful pebble beaches and luxury hotels. His employer had insisted he go there to look at the proposed refurbishment of the dining room in the Sunce Hotel. Dominik was well aware that Dubrovnik was being shelled by the Yugoslav People's Army (JNA) and although he complained that the trip would be unsafe, it was pointless.

'The Sunce Hotel is not in the centre of Dubrovnik, and I shouldn't have to remind you of the decree issued by the government — all workers must continue their duties no matter what the circumstances,' his boss, Petar, a dour individual who was set in his ways, said.

Dominik was not a confrontational person and did not argue further.

He would catch the train as far as Split and continue the remainder of his journey by bus. He could have stopped overnight in Split, but he decided against it. The sooner he reached Lapad and completed his job, the sooner he could return home.

As he stood on the platform at the railway station in Zagreb he looked up at the ominous sky. Low cloud, the colour of dishwater, felt as though it was sitting on his shoulders.

The train, consisting of only two carriages, was small and unheated. He kept on his coat and hat to compensate for the cool interior. In his seat by the window, he resigned himself to the journey being a long one. He knew from previous dull trips that there were forty-five stations between Zagreb and Split and the filthy, litter-strewn train was bound to stop at most of them, even if no passengers got on or off.

Once the train pulled away from Karlovac, the next station after Zagreb, Dominik began to relax. Karlovac was undamaged and functioning as normal. Nervous about what he would find on his arrival in Dubrovnik, he occupied himself by editing his manuscript.

> In August 1991, The Yugoslav's People's Army and Serb paramilitaries launched a full-scale attack against Croatian-held territory in Eastern Slavonia. The entire town of Vukovar was completely destroyed in a fierce, bloody battle that lasted for eighty-seven days. Hundreds of soldiers and civilians were massacred and another 31,000 civilians were forced to flee their homes. Vukovar had been "ethnically cleansed" of its non-Serb population and become part of the self-declared area of the Republika Srpska Krajina.

He was reading a disturbing new newspaper article which appeared to relate to this section of his writing and which had thrown his work into confusion. Yet he couldn't be sure of its accuracy. The article was about the fall of Vukovar and the reporter talked about the dreadful conditions Serb conquerors had to put up with and praised their efforts to rebuild and cope with their altered living conditions in the obliterated city. There was no mention that the destruction of Vukovar was caused by a Serbian military attack. And to make matters worse the article went on to say how inconvenienced Serbs would be if Croats tried to regain their territory. All the reports he'd read reflected this Serbian attitude. There were also constant statements that all sides were guilty and that the war was merely another episode in the history of atrocities between Serbs, Croats and Muslims. The final insult stated that outside intervention would never diminish these ancient ethnic conflicts.

But the libel didn't stop there. The next article he took from his folder cited the evil deeds of the Croatian *Ustaše* during World War II as justification for Serbia's actions. There was no mention of the Serbian Government's collaboration with the Nazis, or the *Četnik* offences during World War II. Distressed by the ugly words in front of him, he stopped reading.

For a while he contented himself with looking out of the window. His pen had become slippery in his hand. His emotions were in a torment as words leapt out at him from the page on his lap. His spirits picked up when the train passed through the dense vegetation of the Plitvice Forest. Spectacular views and lush-green trees, ranging from bright-lime green, smoky, blue-green to dark-olive green, had a calming effect on him. He settled down, turned the page and continued reading.

He was soon jolted back to reality when the train passed by the stations approaching Knin. Even though the war had begun relatively recently, already several of these station buildings had been turned into pock-marked charred shells. He assumed this would mean they were no longer functioning. He was wrong. The two men who worked at each respective station continued to show themselves and signal with their flags immediately upon the train's arrival. Dominik couldn't take his eyes off one station master in particular. The right lens of his glasses was crazed with cracks. His tattered flag was tucked under his arm as he limped out of his shattered post in his torn, soiled uniform. No doubt these workers too had been given the speech about continuing their jobs, regardless of the war.

It was at a small station close to Knin when his train was boarded for the first time by JNA soldiers. All passengers were ordered to disembark and produce their identity cards. This was an experience for which Dominik was unprepared. He grew anxious and flustered when he couldn't locate his card. He had hidden it in the dust jacket of a book in his bag. He had packed three books and in his fearful panic he couldn't remember which book he had put it in. The soldier demanding the card was impatient. When he failed to produce it quickly enough, he jabbed Dominik in the chest with the barrel of his weapon.

'Get a move on. I haven't got all day,' the soldier bellowed as he stood in front of Dominik with a menacing expression on his face. The second time the train was stopped, Dominik made sure the card was ready in his hand.

In Split, Dominik got off the train and ate a bread roll filled with cheese before he boarded a bus bound for Dubrovnik.

Close to Dubrovnik, he looked out of the bus window at the revered Arboretum of Trsteno. Severely damaged by mortars; it was a heartbreaking sight. It was then that he first began to fear for his life.

Fifteen minutes later, the bus came to a stop at the port of Gruž where Dominik intended to get off and take a bus to the hotel. The port was a more tragic sight than the Arboretum. No people were about and several of the boats in the harbour were on fire — black smoke was billowing from their burning hulls. With his hand covering his mouth, he tried to resist breathing in the putrid air. His legs were like wilted celery sticks when he ran from the bus to the shelter of the remarkably intact bus station. In the direction of the old city, dense, grey smoke was contaminating the air and loud explosions filled him with further apprehension. He shivered, turned up his collar and zipped up his coat as far as it would go. His anxiety was increasing with every passing minute and he was unable to stop himself jumping every time the explosions boomed. Cursing under his breath about the stupidity of his insensitive employer, he clambered aboard the bus. It was six in the evening and he could count the number of other passengers on one hand — he assumed they were locals carrying bags containing all their worldly possessions. The clothing they wore was stained, ripped and tattered. Their faces were downcast with sorrowful eyes. He wondered if there was a curfew in place. Did that account for the lack of people?

His arrival at the Sunce Hotel was a farce. The garden outside the main doors was a tangled mess of trampled plants and weeds interspersed with rubbish. He pushed open the shattered glass door leading to reception, eager to be under cover. Inside, the shabby unlit room was packed with unkempt, distressed humanity. Horrified by the scene spread out before him, he wanted to escape and run. Too close for comfort, a woman was re-bandaging the leg of a sobbing child with a piece of filthy cloth. A gaping hole in the child's leg stared Dominik in the face. Crusted dried blood and the jagged edges of a deep gash made him queasy. He looked the other way where an old man, prostrate on the floor, was in the throes of taking his last breath. Two women were bending over him. One, in a spotted blue dress stained with dark patches of gore, was holding his hand and murmuring endearments. When the death rattle gurgled from the dying man's throat, Dominik shuddered and hurried towards the reception desk.

'Why are you here?' the weary man on duty asked, once Dominik had introduced himself. 'I told your boss last week there was no point in you coming. Most of the hotels in the old city have been bombed. The Belvedere, the Excelsior and the Argentina are all uninhabitable.'

'Are they?'

'I said so, didn't I? People from the old town are converging on the peninsula. They think it's safer here. But they're wrong. The hotel down the road was hit last night and all along this stretch of Lapad there's no power or water, or food for that matter. We can't cope with all these refugees. Go back where you came from.' His mouth was turned down at the corners, his uniform was covered with dirt and grime and he stunk.

'There aren't any buses until tomorrow.' Dominik's voice was a high-pitched squeak.

The receptionist shrugged. 'You'll have to find a bed for the night anywhere you can. We're overflowing. See for yourself.' He gave the classic Slavic shrug before turning away. Dominik shouldered open the door next to the reception counter, where the hallway too was overcrowded with displaced people, crying babies, fractious mothers and moaning old people. The closer he looked the worse it seemed. Miserable, hungry people cowering in doorways looked towards him with fear in their eyes. The stink of unwashed bodies forced him to cover his nose with the sleeve of his jacket as he flinched at the sight of these poor specimens. There was no comfort he could give them. He felt helpless. He had never seen anything this tragic and depressing.

'D'you have any food?' a toothless old woman called out. In a trance, Dominik shook his head and sank to the floor where a young woman made space for him. He must get back to Zagreb tomorrow was all he could think about as he removed his duffel bag from his back and settled it between his legs where it could not be stolen. If only he had packed more food. It would be a long night with nothing to eat or drink. His water bottle had run dry at the bus station in Gruž and his last meal, if you could call a bread roll a meal, was at lunchtime while he waited for the bus in Split.

The night took forever to pass. He used his bag as a hard, inflexible pillow, having first wrapped one of the drawstrings around his wrist. Unable to find a comfortable position, he shuffled and shuffled as the cold emanating from the felt-covered concrete floor seeped into him. His watch said it was one-twenty a.m. when the woman beside him, with a dressing concealing her left cheek, spoke.

'Where are you from?' she asked.

'Zagreb.'

'What are you doing here?'

He was about to answer when a voice nearby erupted. 'Shut the fuck up!' an angry man bellowed.

Although he jumped with fright Dominik remained silent. Perhaps he would find the opportunity to talk to her in the morning. He turned over and closed his eyes.

When early morning dawned, Dominik had barely slept, woken often during the last three and a half hours by coughing and whimpering.

At five a.m., he set off on foot in the dark towards the nearest bus stop. He waited there for almost an hour. The first bus did not arrive until six and it was late.

The driver was irritable and short when Dominik asked to be taken to the port.

'This bus goes to the Pile Gate. The buses for Zagreb leave from there.'

Dominik sucked in a breath and grimaced. Never again would he be bullied by his boss, he told himself, as he trudged up the muddy steps of the bus. The interior was as dirty as the driver's clothes. He pushed an old newspaper on to the floor and sat down on a seat at the front.

The trip took no more than twenty minutes. When he reluctantly descended the steps of the battered bus at one of the entrances to the old city, powerful explosions made his ears ring. He recoiled with fear every time they thundered.

He found out by asking an old man with a stringy, grey beard, that the bus to Zagreb would not be there until eight. He glanced around. There was nowhere to seek cover. The bus shelter had been obliterated — no trace of it remained. He must find somewhere to hide until the bus arrived, otherwise he risked losing his life. He looked in all directions, but nowhere safe presented itself. His only choice was inside the Pile Gate, where the towering thick walls of the city could protect him. He ran across the road clutching his duffel bag to his chest, relieved that the drawbridge, which led to the centre of the city, was open. The cobblestones inside the gate were wet from a shower of rain during the night and although he noticed several puddles of rainwater, he failed to anticipate the slippery state of the uneven stones. He was too afraid and intent on his purpose. His city shoes were old and the soles had worn smooth and before he could stop himself, he slipped and fell. He landed with a thump on the base of his spine and for a minute he stayed put on the ground as pain spread through his lower back. When he plucked up the courage to sit up, he saw immediately that his wrist was grazed and beginning to swell. He had put out his hand to break his fall.

'*Jebati!*' he muttered under his breath as he picked himself up and hobbled inside the confines of the wall where he slumped down in a huddle. He pulled his coat over his head as protection against a new shower of rain that drummed on the cobblestones around him and steeled himself for the long wait.

Half an hour went by. He was restless and cold. He should have dressed more warmly. His coat was not thick enough. His lower back was on fire and when he stood up, he cried out in pain, yet he felt a need to get it moving. Perhaps a short walk might help, he thought, setting off, regardless of the continuing detonations resounding in his ears. When he reached the gigantic stone archway leading to the Stradun, Dubrovnik's main street, he stopped. Underneath the archway he lifted his knees towards his chest one after the other. The ache at the base of his spine abated a little. When a thunderous explosion made his ears ring, he knew it was time to seek cover. As he was retreating from the archway, he thought he heard a voice.

'*Pomoć, pomoć,*' the diminished voice called out. Dominik stopped. Perhaps it was his ears playing tricks on him. Then it came again.

'*Pomoć, pomoć.*' This time it was clearer. He stood still. It was less distinct the third time, but he knew for sure he had heard the cry for help. He began to retrace his steps, stopping after he dared to step past the massive, curved stones above his head. Horrified by the vista in his line of sight, he drew back, flattening himself against the cold stone wall and closing his eyes. Insides of buildings were burning; flames were leaping and dancing from gaping holes that had once been windows. A woman, running from one side of the Stradun to the other, was felled before she reached her destination; dead bodies were lying on the cobblestones along with rubbish; and homeless, hungry people were cowering in doorways nearby. Dominik squeezed his eyes more tightly shut. If only he hadn't dared to look. But it was too late. This war would be etched in his mind forever. He retreated to the shelter of the wall, but moments later wondered if he should try to help the woman lying motionless on the cobblestones. Maybe she was alive. Plucking up the courage to brave another assault on his senses, he dared to look once more into the Stradun. The woman had not shifted from where she had fallen, yet Dominik thought he saw her arm move. He took a step closer and as he did so he heard a high-pitched whistling noise. Unsure what it was, he had no time to react before an explosion, followed by a tremor, sounded too near to him. Shrapnel mixed with masonry chunks flew through the air towards him. He ducked, but his reaction was too slow. A sharp pain flared in his right leg. He looked down to see what had hit him when something struck his temple. He sank to his knees as his vision faded.

Some time later, when he tried to open his eyes, the left one remained closed — swollen shut by the injury above it. His leg and his head both ached and he was disoriented.

Chilled to his core, he tried to focus his mind and will his body to sit up. When the cold stones beneath him dug into his back, his memory returned. From a sitting position he dragged himself to the shelter of the wall. He lacked any useful strength and used the last of his reserves to struggle to a safer place. With his back against the wall he cautiously touched his head. His hand encountered a sticky substance glued to his forehead and matted in his sparse blond hair — blood. His body trembled as he was overcome by shock.

He woke up, oblivious that he had fallen asleep. The sun had already risen and it was light enough to see the face of his watch — nine-twenty a.m. — an entire day and a night had passed. He stood up slowly. As soon as he was on his feet his head began to pound. It was almost unbearable. With both eyes shut, he concentrated on blotting out the hammers beating a steady rhythm inside his brain. He licked his lips. He was so thirsty his mouth felt like he had consumed too many wafers at Holy Communion. His stomach had long since given up squealing with hunger, resigned to the fact that no food would be coming to satisfy it anytime soon. When he finally opened his eyes, his vision was blurry. He pressed his eyes closed with his fists and massaged the lids. This time when he reopened them, his vision had cleared sufficiently to enable him to look down at his body. His trousers were splotched with semi-dried, brownish blood — his blood. Through the rip in his the right trouser leg a blood-covered gash was visible. His hat was missing and his head was freezing.

How he wished he could walk through the archway to Onofrio's fountain and drink his fill before cleaning himself up. Needless to say, it would be impossible as well as suicidal to go back where he'd been when the shell exploded. There was no water in the fountain anyway. The water supply to the old town had been cut off by the JNA. At this moment he was in the best place he could be, given his circumstances.

How long would it be before Zagreb suffered the same fate? He hunkered down with his arm through the strap of his duffle bag to wait out the length of the day until the next bus arrived. This time nothing would entice him to move.

Chapter forty-eight

It was a rainy, dark night three months later; Dominik and his sister were sitting in the lounge expecting the air-raid siren to go off when she asked him what he thought was a strange question.

'Do you think you'll ever get married?'

'That's an odd question to ask me all of a sudden,' he replied.

'Do you want to, though?' she persisted.

'Not particularly. I'm not the marrying kind; I'm quite happy on my own.'

'Is that because you're the strong, silent type like *Majka?*'

'Please, don't compare me to *her*. That's an insult.' Dominik ran his hand over his head. He was almost totally bald. Most of his already thin blond hair had fallen out after his brush with death in Dubrovnik.

'Sorry, I didn't mean it that way. Perhaps you're like the grandfather we never knew. *Baba* used to say he was short on words. Anyway, that's how I see you. Usually you're quiet unless you have something important to say.'

'I suppose I am. I've never thought about it before.' It was years before he took a girl on a date. There were young women he'd been attracted to, but he never got around to asking them out. He'd psych himself up for it and then at the last moment he couldn't summon the courage. There were times too, when he looked at the women he was familiar with and he wasn't so sure he wanted a girlfriend. He used to wonder if all women were the same as his mother and his sister. His sister was bossy and controlling and his mother, well, he wasn't sure how to describe her. She'd been more or less the same all his life, at least as far back as he could remember. A long time ago, he concluded she wasn't right in the head, and he certainly didn't want to end up being married to someone like that. It was difficult enough living in a house with a domineering sister and a mad mother, without adding another woman into the mix.

'Anyway, you can't talk. I might not have a girlfriend, but you don't have a boyfriend. And besides women come with too many problems.'

'Now that is an insult. Our *Baba* was a fine woman and am I so terrible?' Dunja was angry; he couldn't fail to notice the irate tone of her voice.

'I'm not married to you so I'm not qualified to comment.' He shrugged and gave a small laugh. He remembered his grandmother well enough — and what he did recall about her personality he didn't relish even though he loved her and appreciated the love she lavished freely on others. She was controlling too, the same as his sister.

The day he met Martina everything changed. During his workday, he had developed a habit of sitting by himself at lunchtime, preferring to read rather than engage in conversation with his fellow workers. He was engrossed in a book he had always wanted to read, but had never found the time to devote to it. He had turned the page when he heard a woman's voice.

'Is this seat free?' A tall woman with bushy eyebrows towered over him.

'Sure,' he replied, wishing she'd chosen one of the other plastic chairs in the gloomy, windowless cafeteria instead. He thought momentarily about continuing to read, but decided that would be rude and closed his book.

'I'm Martina. This is my first day here,' she said.

'Welcome. I'm Dominik. What department are you in?'

'Accounts. What are you reading?'

'*War and Peace.*'

'I love Russian novels. Have you read *Anna Karenina?* The ending made me cry.'

'No. Not yet. I've just started reading them. Have you read many?' Dominik sat up straighter. Perhaps he had found a soulmate with an interest in books.

'Yes. Dostoyevsky, Tolstoy, Turgenov, Nabokov and others. I could lend some if you like.'

'That'd be great. Sounds like you're an avid reader.'

'Yes, I guess you could say I am — about a book a week on average. And I like to reread my favourites every so often.'

'I wish I could manage that. I don't seem to find the time.'

'I make time. There's nothing I like more than burying myself in a book and shutting out the world.'

'I've never thought of it that way.'

'Some people say it's a form of escapism. But I don't see it as that. It's pure pleasure for me.'

From then on, they arranged to meet in the cafeteria at lunchtime, whenever Dominik was not out of town on business.

One minute they were talking about books, and then it seemed as if no time had passed before they were married in a brief ceremony at the office of the Registrar of Births, Deaths and Marriages, with only their immediate families in attendance. Perhaps if there hadn't been a war on it might have been a more elaborate occasion.

When the ceremony began, Dominik was immediately intimidated by Martina's stature and began having second thoughts about marrying her, but by then it was too late.

Martina had hired a billowing dress and was wearing shoes with stiletto heels. The dark grey suit Dominik bought from a charity shop looked drab next to her white dress with its metres and metres of fabric and "leg of mutton" sleeves. As well as being tall with overly large hands and feet, Martina was not particularly attractive. Born in the mountains near Zagreb, her height and physical features were typical of many people from that area. Until the day of his wedding Dominik hadn't dwelt on her physical appearance. It had not been important to him. He saw it as the cover being more important than the contents of the book. He'd been entranced by the love of literature that they shared. He'd never envisaged himself as a handsome man therefore he did not expect to find, let alone marry, a beautiful woman.

It was mid-afternoon when the nine people who had attended the ceremony took their places around the table, which his sister had set with a white lace tablecloth embroidered by their grandmother.

As Dominik took his place next to his new wife he looked around the odd assortment who were gathered. His parents sat at opposite ends of the table. His father was wearing a wrinkled suit while his mother wore a glowering expression which was constantly directed at her ex-husband. Dominik was relieved she didn't vocalise her thoughts. Boris and Bela Horvat, Dominik's in-laws didn't have much to say for themselves, they, along with Martina's younger sister and brother, seemed intent on scoffing the lasagne his sister had made as the main course for the late lunch that was his wedding feast. He took in how similar in appearance Martina and her mother were, but more particularly he laughed about Martina's father's absurd eyebrows. They were so bushy they looked as though they were glued-on fakes.

No speeches were given because Dominik had insisted the entire affair was to be simple and informal. He had also insisted that they wouldn't have a wedding cake, but at the end of the meal, when it became obvious his sister had defied him, he was pleased when she produced a wedding cake and placed it in the centre of the table.

Dominik stared at the grand cake, which was covered with cream cheese icing and shredded coconut, and had a plastic bride and groom standing in the icing like two people caught in a snowdrift. 'Where did you get it? It's beautiful,' he said to his sister as he gave her a grateful smile.

'I baked it. It's an Italian wedding cake. I know you said you didn't want a cake, but it wouldn't be right not to have one.'

With hindsight, Dominik should have been warned about Martina's personality when she began to repair rips and tears and missing buttons on his clothing. At first, he thought she was multi-talented and was content to let her mend his things. Before he came to know her well, he believed she was a straightforward person, but it wasn't long before he realised she was far more complex than he would ever have imagined. Almost overnight, near the beginning of their marriage, when she started exhibiting weird behaviour and she became obsessed about the condition of his clothing and carried on about the smallest rips, tears or worn areas, it drove him to distraction especially when she insisted on inspecting him constantly. It was then that he thought about leaving her. He didn't. Instead he learnt to cope with her neurotic need to mend, repair and clean things even though they weren't dirty, but when she began to turn against his family, particularly his sister, he became distressed. It was less than a year after they were married when he finally told her he wanted out. He would never forget her reaction.

'If you leave me I'll kill myself,' she said before bursting into tears and running from the room. He couldn't take the chance that she meant what she said, so he stayed. It was at that time that they stopped sharing the same bed. Dominik bought a single bed and moved into a small room previously used for storage. He expected Martina to complain and was relieved when she didn't. He didn't think he'd ever understand her. What normal wife would accept her husband sleeping in another room? Then again he didn't find her normal with her obsessive nature. She was often grumpy and Dominik kept his head down to avoid trouble. He got up and went to work each day and worked on his book late at night when everyone else had gone to bed. Occasionally on weekends he went out with friends — the ones who hadn't been killed in the war. Tonci was still working as a chef, so there were only certain nights he was free, and even then, Dominik was frustrated in his company. He talked too much, his appalling body odour hadn't abated and his clothes smelt of fried onions more often than not. A huge amount of Dominik's spare time was spent by himself — reading and writing. With any surplus money he scraped together, he bought magazines, newspapers and books.

Early in the summer of 1993, Dominik was sitting on the bank of the Sava River on a fallen tree trunk, tossing pebbles into the water. Earlier, he had walked out in the middle of the fight Martina had tried to pick with him. He was finding it an increasing strain living with her. She had changed so much in such a short time. She was nothing like the woman he thought he had married. When he thought back over the argument he wondered what he could have done to prevent it. He'd been tired at the end of a busy week. Because it was Saturday he'd got up later than usual. Martina had burst uninvited into his room as he was about to take a shower.

'Why are you going away again? You've only just come back,' she said, making herself at home on the end of his bed.

'If my boss says I must go, then I have to. Unless I resign and I'm certainly not doing that.'

With her hands jammed into the pockets of her green quilted dressing gown, her hair straggling around her face and a seething expression on her face, he thought Martina looked demented.

'You could get another job — where you don't have to go away all the time.'

'No, I couldn't. I'm quite happy with the one I've got.' She exasperated him with her carry-on. When she spoke again, he knew it was time to leave.

'Even when you're here, you spend all your time with Dunja.'

When she started talking this nonsense and he knew he did not spend much time at all with Dunja, as fast as he could, Dominik put on his tracksuit, grabbed his cap from his desk and started for the door.

'And another thing,' she shouted as she tried to bar his way. 'You can tell that sister of yours to stop cooking *kupus*. It stinks out the house and I hate it.'

'Tell her yourself!' Dominik grabbed the door handle, elbowed her aside and left. She was right about the *kupus*, one of Dunja's favourite vegetables, although he'd never admit it. Its rotten cooking smell polluted the house for days and opening the windows didn't allow it to escape; it seemed to cling to anything and everything.

He arrived home after his walk to find Martina had gone out. He was surprised she'd left a note on the bench saying she was visiting a friend and won't be back until late. She must have calmed down. He sighed. She was so volatile and it took nothing to make her fly into a temper. He dawdled along the hallway, glaring at the loudly ticking clock. On his bed, he contemplated a short snooze, but after half an hour, he changed his mind, stood up and yawned. Sitting at his desk he turned the pages of his manuscript.

> Osijek, with its proximity to Vukovar, had no hope of escaping the war. It, too, was subjected to incessant artillery and air attacks. Because there were no military targets in Osijek, the JNA resorted to bombing apartments, schools, hospitals and churches. In September 1991, the Osijek General Hospital was hit 94 times by mortars and rockets. Reports from the hospital stated that so much blood was flowing in the emergency room it had to be swept away with a broom. After the non-stop attacks on the hospital, the operating theatres were moved. The basement was the last safe place left.

When he couldn't stop yawning and was having difficulty concentrating, he got up and headed to the kitchen to make himself a cup of coffee before he read on.

> It was March 1991 when Serb JNA forces commanded by Ratko Mladić destroyed the village of Drniš near Knin. The entire town was annihilated except for the Orthodox Church in the

centre. Knin and the surrounding villages was then under the control of Serb forces. This area of the Krajina region represents almost a third of Croatia.

Dominik wondered why Croatia so desperately wanted to retain control of the Krajina region, an impoverished area where primitiveness and aggression have been bred into the Serbs who live there. Perhaps the war would not be so prolonged if the Croats let the Serbs add the Krajina region to their territory?

He glanced at his watch. His stomach was grumbling. He'd been invited for dinner at Tonci's new house and he needed to get going. He ran his hand over his smooth head. He blinked, aware that he had been staring into space. After leafing through the new material he'd added to his folder, he doubted if he would uncover any useful information tonight.

When he first began to write his manuscript he'd left spaces and blank pages so he could go back and add extra events or expand the existing entries. Another glance at his watch told him that if he didn't hurry he would be late. He crammed the papers back inside the folder and returned it to its hiding place before unhooking his denim jacket from the back of his bedroom door and leaving. Outside in the street he looked up at the clear sky. He hoped the air-raid sirens would stay silent.

Tonci's family had moved into a new contemporary apartment not long after the JNA attacked Vukovar. Clad with zinc sheeting, it was built on a corner site subdivided from the rundown Alpine-style house behind it. Dominik had not been there before and he was looking forward to seeing it.

'I'll get you a beer and give you the tour,' Tonci said as he took off the grubby white apron he wore in the kitchen.

The apartment was over two thousand square feet. All the rooms felt enormous, including the kitchen with its island in the middle and the bank of heat lamps hanging above it. Red cube seats were scattered haphazardly around the room Tonci called the media room, where an oversize television was attached to the wall. Dominik thought the balcony doors were cool the way they slid out of sight, inside the walls. He'd never been in such a striking home.

When they were interrupted by the arrival of another visitor there was no time to look at the bedrooms or underground photographic study where Tonci's father enjoyed developing his own photos.

The other guest was an unusual one. Tom Fuller was an American doctor who worked at the Vukovar Hospital. He was an acquaintance of Tonci's father, who was also a doctor. Tom was staying in Zagreb for three days before he flew home to the United States on leave. Dominik was amused by Tom's sand-coloured hair, cut in a typically American crewcut, and his talk about baseball. His easy-going banter was entertaining. Dominik chuckled from time to time. Tom used different words and spoke with a Texan drawl, an accent Dominik had never encountered before. The way he said *kawfee* and *tomada* instead of *coffee* and *tomato,* Dominik found particularly humourous. When Tonci tried to imitate Tom's accent everyone burst out laughing.

'You're as funny as a fight,' Tom, who laughed too, said.

Tonci cooked a tasty meal. Two roast chickens wrapped in *pršut,* the obligatory *blitva* and mashed potato mixed with olive oil, garlic and lemon juice and his specialty, deep-fried onion rings. His mother had made *palačinke* and chocolate sauce for desert.

After dinner, Tom and Dominik retired to the media room, Tonci and his mother were in the kitchen clearing up and Tonci's father had gone to his *konoba* in search of more wine.

When the subject turned to the Tom's job, Dominik moved to the edge of his seat, eager to listen. 'You must be glad to have a break,' he said.

'You can say that again. This is one of the most gruelling posts I've ever had.'

'Is that because of the number of casualties?'

'There's that, but what went on in that hospital five months ago almost did me in.'

'Really? I'd like to hear about it. That's if you don't mind talking about it.'

'Well, we had this pair of Serbian doctors working there. They were a couple — a married couple. I admired how compassionate they seemed, as well as the long hours they worked. Their dedication to patients, regardless of whether they were Croatian or Serbian, was commendable. All the staff admired them. As far as I know, they were the only Serbs working there. The rest bailed out at the time of independence.'

'They didn't run away and join up?'

'If only they had.' Tom laughed. 'We caught them out one day at the end of their lunch break, when they didn't show up. I sent two of my nurses to look for them thinking they'd lost track of time, or maybe they'd been shot by a sniper.'

'And had they?' Dominik was engrossed in the conversation.

'No way. We all knew they went up to the roof to smoke. They were thirty-or-more-a-day addicts, always gasping for nicotine. Anyway, my nurses caught them in the act. From the railing around the top of the building, they were shooting at Croatian civilians in the street below. They'd stashed their rifles under some old tarpaulins that had been left there when the roof had been repaired.'

'Oh my God! That's disgusting. Did they get arrested?'

'No chance. They scarpered as soon as they were found out.'

'What a shame.'

'Yes, but that wasn't the end of it. Back in Serbia, they were heroes and welcomed with open arms to begin life in a new village.'

'How did you find out where they were?'

'They'd only been gone for three months when they had the gall to return. They wanted their old jobs back. They said the village they'd moved to was too small and life was too boring. Can you believe it?'

'Yes, easily. Many of them are arrogant.' Dominik shook his head. 'And many of them think that they're superior to the rest of us in the Balkans. At least you're rid of them now though. Things must have calmed down a bit after that.'

'Well, I can't say they've calmed down exactly. There's a war on, remember? I sure as hell do need a break, though.'

'But you do enjoy your job?'

'Yes, on the whole. The hard parts are the lack of sleep and not being able to erase the smell of blood that permanently taints me.'

'How long are you on leave?'

'Three weeks. Three weeks to blank out my mind and forget this grisly war. Some days it's one thing after another. Last week this Croatian woman came in; she'd been shot in the leg. It wasn't a serious wound and it would heal quite quickly, although her mind would never be the same again. She'd been shot by her Serbian neighbour … before the war they'd been friends.'

'I can't say that surprises me,' Tonci's father, Vlado, said from the doorway where he has been leaning his tall angular frame and listening to the conversation. 'Think I'd better pour us all another drink.'

'But that's not the half of it,' Tom said. 'When she cried out after being wounded, her neighbour slunk away unable to finish her off, so she said. The next day, she heard more shots and screaming coming from his house and by the time she plucked up the courage to look, the entire Serbian family had been murdered. Their heads were stuck on stakes outside their front door.'

'Did her family kill them?' Dominik asked.

'No, her Serbian neighbour did because they wouldn't kill their Croatian neighbours on the other side.'

'Bloodthirsty bastards!' Dominik shook head in disbelief. He would never forget this outrageous story.

When he came home from Tonci's place he couldn't sleep, so he read though some of his recent entries with a view to making them more accurate.

> It was May 1992 when the siege of Sarajevo began. Eighteen thousand JNA soldiers took up positions in the hills, encircled the city and pounded Sarajevo non-stop. They took control of the airport and cut off water, electricity and heating, but despite these unpleasant conditions imposed upon the city, they failed to gain control of it. Widespread violence was inflicted on the inhabitants by snipers hidden throughout the city streets. So many people were killed or missing, and an even bigger number were wounded. Often, people were eaten by the night and no one had any idea where they had gone …

He hoped to find out the number of dead and wounded and add it to make the entry more accurate.

It wasn't long ago that Dominik's best information sources changed when *Slobodni Tjednik*, known as the "dirty paper", ceased publication. That didn't surprise him — in fact it pleased him. He had grown tired of its biased reporting. He remembered one particularly hysterical issue that was displayed openly on the newspaper stands — photos of dead people with their throats cut, pulverised faces and gouged-out eyes, under the headline *Victims of Wild Beasts*. It was as if the paper had been written by Serbs who were often depicted as victims of Croatian terrorism, even though no Croat had harmed them. He recalled other headlines too, *Bloodbath at Dawn* and *Massacre of Innocents*.

He flicked through the pages of his manuscript until he came to a different topic.

> In January 1993, Bosnian volunteers began to dig the Sarajevo tunnel. When it was completed in mid-1993, food and humanitarian aid were at last able to be ferried into the city. The tunnel was 1.5 metres high, 1 metre wide and 960 metres long, and it also allowed people to escape. It is estimated that about a vast number of people used it — speculation was in the region of one million while millions of tons of food were transported through it. The tunnel became the besieged city's lifeline …

Chapter forty-nine

Dominik had never considered himself a lucky person and the letter that arrived in the mail on the last day of July proved it. He had been recalled to the army. His reserve status had been activated at the last possible moment. He knew before he reported for duty that he was being posted, even though the letter didn't say where he was being sent.

As he reread the letter he thought about the unpalatable task of informing his family. To begin with, he considered hiding it from them. But if he lied and said he was going away for work and then failed to return, that would be catastrophic. He also briefly considered disappearing into thin air and letting them think he'd been eaten by the night. At least with regard to his mother it would save the scene he knew she'd create when he told her.

During dinner on a sweltering midsummer's night, Dominik was quiet. He still hadn't figured out how to impart the news to his family.

After dinner, when he didn't know how to deal with it, he began pacing around his bedroom like a tiger in the zoo at Maksimir.

It was then that Dunja knocked on his door and came in.

'What's up?' she asked. 'You were out of sorts at dinner.'

He opened his mouth to speak, but then closed it, unsure what to say.

'Something's bothering you. Is it Martina?'

'No.' He paused. 'I've been called up.'

'No! When did you find out?'

'A couple of days ago.'

'Do you know where you're going?'

'No. But I have to report early tomorrow morning.'

'Oh, Dominik,' she wailed as she clung to him.

'Such bad luck. I'll be thirty-one in a few days. Then I'd have been exempt. I was so keen at the start of the war, but I'm not now … and I'm reluctant to tell *Majka*. It'll only upset her.' Dunja let go of him and stepped back. For a time they looked at each other in silence until Dunja stifled a sob and blew her nose.

'Perhaps you're right. What she doesn't know won't hurt her. Then, with a bit of luck, when you come back she won't know you've been gone.'

'But what if I don't come back?'

Their conversation hit a lull.

'What about Martina? Will you tell her?'

'She'd be worse then *Majka.*' No, I can't face telling her either.'

'Do you want me to tell them?'

'No, tell them I've had to go away on an urgent job. I'll be leaving very early so you can tell them at breakfast. Are you okay with that?'

'Yes. It's for the best. But you'll come back. I know it.'

'I like your optimism. I wish I felt the same way.'

Sleep for Dominik was a long time coming. His room was airless and even if it hadn't been humid he couldn't have dropped off. In the morning, he would have to leave the house ridiculously early. He'd sneak out. If his mother got up early to go to the toilet, as she often did, and she saw him in the old uniform he had unearthed from the bottom of his wardrobe, he didn't know what he'd do.

The sun had risen over the horizon and was creating a pink glow across the sky on 4 August 1995, when Dominik shifted his weight from one foot to the other in a group of restless men outside the barracks. A sea of soldiers stretched before him — many were as young as eighteen while others were over forty. Something was brewing, there were far too many recruits congregating for an ordinary intake. While they waited for their names to be called, the smell of unwashed bodies and uniforms enveloped Dominik. It was a long wait before he was herded into the group that made up the 137th Home Guard Regiment, whose mission was to protect the flanks of the Zagreb corps.

Dominik's platoon commander was younger than him and his accent told Dominik he was not from Zagreb. On board the troop train heading south to Karlovac, Dominik learnt that he came from the village of Blato on the island of Korčula. At the age of twenty-six, he was considered a veteran fighter having fought in the sieges at Dubrovnik and Mostar. His surname was Gavranić. Dominik had no idea of his christian name. They were all addressed by surnames or at times, because there were so many of them, as "Soldier". In his mind Dominik called his commander Liquid Amber. His large expressive eyes were a freaky amber colour and when he became agitated they lit up making him look almost deranged. His face was weathered to deep brown and he had more than a week's beard growth. Dominik was seated opposite him staring at Gavranić's pink lips. They were so full it was as if he had been stung by a bee.

Their destination had not been disclosed and Dominik was surprised when they were ordered to get off the train at Karlovac — the first stop after Zagreb. From there he travelled south by truck on a dirt track to an area where the Home Guard was gathering. The trucks lurched from side to side as they hit potholes until they came to a clearing surrounded by secondary growth and beech trees where they set up a makeshift-tented camp.

Crates of weapons were already on site and Dominik was issued with an American rifle. It used a different bullet to the AK47 and seemed more well made. It had a plastic stock and foregrip, and because of the metal it was made of, it was lighter than the Russian gun. There was a type of carry handle on top with the rear sight set in it and the magazine was long and straight unlike the curved one on the AK47. The recruits were given an hour of instruction to familiarise themselves with the new weapon and that was it.

'We're waiting on more to come from the Americans. They're being trucked up from

Split. They'll be better and newer than these,' one of the sergeants said. Dominik had heard about a shipment of arms delivered to a Serbian stronghold in Bosnia near the beginning of the war that had been labelled "bananas", and he wondered what the labels on these crates would say. But the origin wasn't the same, so maybe the Americans would be more honest than the Russians even if the weapons were being flown in under cover of darkness while the airport was closed to all other flights.

Dominik found it a dangerous prospect holding the trigger down and firing round after round non-stop. As he handled his lethal weapon, his current predicament hit home. He wasn't brave. But if he had to kill to stay alive, he wouldn't hesitate.

Dinner was a plate of cold beans and two-day-old bread. Campfires were not permitted in case the smoke was seen by the enemy. For the rest of the evening Dominik was free. The men in his platoon played cards by lamplight while Dominik sat nearby and stared into the darkness trying not to think about the following day.

At eleven-thirty p.m. they received their orders. They were the second part of four sectors of *Operacija Oluja,* the push to liberate the Serbian enclave of Kraijina.

The soldiers leaning against an assortment of war machines in the semi-darkness before dawn were a motley collection with tattered uniforms and irregular head gear — bandanas, knitted caps and beanies. The absence of helmets was noticeable. The eerie pre-dawn, grey-blue light was alive with glowing cigarette tips. Everyone smoked and when Dominik was offered a cigarette he accepted hoping it might quell his agitation. The taste was bitter and he threw it away after a few puffs.

When Gavranić discarded his cigarette, Dominik knew they were about to move out. Sheltered behind the would-be machines of destruction, Dominik adjusted his black beanie and gripped his new rifle, carrying it by the top handle. His left hand was free. The spluttering of engines starting up and gears gnashing assaulted his ears.

He marched in the thick of the band of soldiers for several hours until well after the sun had risen. It was blazing in a sky the colour of faded blue ink. In the distance the thump of artillery and rocket fire was constant. When noise boomed nearby and smoke was visible, Dominik expected to encounter the enemy. Instead they came upon a ghost town with nothing other than burning buildings, charred rubble, burnt-out, overturned vehicles, discarded piles of bedding and clothing. The inhabitants of Obravac were nowhere to be seen. Gavranić and his men had arrived too late. Another platoon had done the job for them. Dominik was relieved. Maybe he wouldn't have to use his rifle after all. When a cheer started up somewhere ahead it provided confirmation that the Serb population had already departed. Over the brow of the next hill thousands of Serbs were clogging the road in cars, on tractors or horse-drawn carts. The caravan of humanity extended for miles.

As soon as Gavranić ordered his men to stop, they halted. For several minutes they stood idle in the hot sun while Gavranić talked on his radio. The men around Dominik lit up. He declined the offer of another cigarette.

Dominik thought he was given the soft option when he was asked to accompany Gavranić and a dozen others on a foray through the surrounding buildings. They moved from house to house and it soon became obvious they were not the first soldiers to have been there. Four men from another platoon were lounging in a courtyard next to a windowless house, drinking beer. After engaging them in minimal conversation Gavranić ordered his men to move on. In the adjacent property, washing was hanging on the clothesline and a fly-blown, unfinished meal of *ćevapi, tikvica* and *krumpir* had been abandoned on the dining table. On the living room floor a set of red and blue plastic soldiers were lined up facing each other, ready for battle. Dominik left without disturbing them. His hand was clammy on the butt of his rifle and his uniform was stuck to his back with sweat. He dared not imagine what would happen if one of the dwellings was inhabited.

After they checked three more houses and found no one, he had begun to believe it was all over when a sporadic burst of machine gunfire hit the stone wall of the courtyard behind him. Chips of stone flew in all directions. The man beside Dominik was hit and fell, unable to get up. After they had retreated to safety Gavranić ordered his men to surround the house. Dominik and Gavranić stayed where they were while four others crawled down the side of the house to the back of the property. Gavranić's rifle had a grenade launcher attached to it and once he had given the others time to reach their destination he used it and launched one into the courtyard. Dominik crouched behind the substantial stacked-stone wall and waited for the grenade to explode. Gavranić reloaded quickly and fired a second one through a window. Once the explosion had cleared, Dominik followed Gavranić as he charged ahead in a fearless fashion with his amber eyes on fire. The courtyard was empty except for splintered timber from a wooden table blown up by the grenade. Gavranić kicked open the door to the living room. In the centre of the room another table had been shattered by the blast, a dresser had fallen over and shards of crockery were spread everywhere. On the floor an ancient machine gun was lying inert next to its owner — an aged *baka,* dressed in black and coated with blood. Gavranic strode over and kicked her. When her leg twitched, Dominik turned away as Gavranić shot her in the head at point-blank range.

Chapter fifty

Every morning over breakfast Dunja continued to read selected articles in *Jutarnji List*. It was Friday when she came upon an interesting one written by a reporter in Sarajevo.

When the war ended in 1996 with the signing of the Dayton Treaty, Dunja hoped no more innocent people would be killed, but according to the article, in Sarajevo that hadn't been the case. Snipers had remained active and people were continuing to die. With the news that BiH was under EU supervision Dunja hoped the situation would soon become peaceful.

Another article highlighted other problems. This time in Serbia, where the future remained uncertain as Milošević continued to harass Kosovo and shelter the two men most wanted by the International Criminal Tribunal for the Former Yugoslavia (ICTY) — Mladic and Karadžić.

Dunja felt fortunate to be living in Zagreb because most of Croatia had become stable. She was not often prone to thinking back over the war years, but as she lingered over her second cup of coffee, in her pyjamas on her own in the kitchen, she become reflective. Many Croatians were disappointed with the terms of settlement under the Dayton Agreement. When Croatia occupied areas of BiH where Croatians were living, numerous Croatians expected Croatia would be granted those areas as part of its territory. Large scale disappointment followed when this did not come about. Regardless, Dunja was grateful there would be no more senseless slaughter of her fellow human beings in Croatia at least. Events such as the diabolical happenings of *Operacija Oluja* at Knin in August 1995, would be etched in her memory forever. Although Croatia declared victory there and reclaimed its land, she could not condone the horrifying massacre of so many innocent civilians, regardless of their ethnicity. She also felt sorry for her brother having had to participate in it. She would be eternally grateful that he was unharmed.

After her country was turned upside down by the war, it should not have surprised her that Zagreb had become a different city. Displaced people converged on the city and took up residence not long after the war started and they were continuing to make their way there from other regions such as Slavonia and Krajina and also from BiH. Zagreb had not been bombed heavily during the war and Dunja imagined they were under the impression it would provide refuge. She accepted that these unfortunate refugees needed new homes, but she was distressed by how drastically they had changed the face of the city. Zagreb had once been the cultural centre of Croatia, but culture and etiquette were breaking down as the city filled with a cosmopolitan mix of people. Perhaps she would get used to it, but she was not enthralled by it. She felt as if she was losing her identity and certain changes that were taking place were making this unbearable, if not confusing. She used to think of herself as Yugoslavian, but now everyone had new labels — Serbian, Croatian or Bosnian.

It was only last week when she had been looking forward to dining in Nokturno, one of her favourite Italian restaurants in Central Zagreb, with Gorana and Valentina when the evening turned sour before it started. They were being shown to their table in the recently renovated interior, dominated by red and green, when Gorana spoke to two men seated at a nearby table. Their accents told Dunja they were Serbian.

'Do you know them?' Dunja asked, after they had sat down.

'Yes, but not well. They're pharmacists from Belgrade. Although I don't know the woman with the short dark hair who's joined them.'

Dunja wouldn't have given them any further thought, if she hadn't overheard their conversation with the waiter. Dressed in immaculate black attire, he was efficient and friendly.

'You tosser,' the Serb with a nose so big it looked as though it had been transplanted on to his face, said. 'I ordered red wine, not white. Get me red now, or better still get me another waiter.'

'There's no need to speak to him like that,' their female companion said. 'It was an honest mistake, caused by you being indecisive in the first place.' The Serbian pair laughed.

'Don't you know he expects to be treated that way,' Big Nose replied.

'Why are you always so embarrassing?' the woman asked. 'Every time we go out, you make an ugly scene.'

'He can't help himself,' the other Serb with the rimless glasses, who had so far been quiet, said. 'He was born that way. And who gives a shit about a waiter from Macedonia anyway?'

The conversation was too much for Dunja and her companions. They stood up, cancelled their orders and left.

Chapter fifty-one

Dunja wanted to ignore Tuđman's voice, yet she could not. She was in the middle of preparing grilled fish with garlic sauce and rice for dinner, when she heard his voice on the television. Sucked in by curiosity, she sat down in her mother's green chair. It was then that Dominik walked in and joined her. The news programme showed a clip of Tuđman giving an address earlier in the day. He was announcing a new plan he had devised, designed to assist Croatians with readjustment after the war.

'What ridiculous nonsense,' Dominik shouted. '*Confiscation of Memory*, I've never heard a more stupid name in all my life.'

'Ssh! I'm trying to hear what he has to say,' Dunja said. Tuđman's monotone voice went on to say how removing any reminders that Croatia had once belonged to the state of the former Yugoslavia, would help Croatians return to normality. Dunja believed his absurd notion was nothing more than an attempt to secure allegiance to his political party, HDZ. Dominik jumped to his feet and turned off the television.

'What a load of rubbish,' he said. 'Who needs to listen to that drivel?'

'The pompous fool loves the sound of his own voice,' Dunja said.

'How the hell he imagines he will make us forget about the war, when hundreds of bodies are discovered in mass graves every day, I can't begin to guess. God, that man is a moron.'

'He's more than a moron, he's dangerous.'

Dominik gave a sigh of resignation, followed by a shrug.

Watching Tuđman's sermon has not been a good start to Dunja's evening. The next even greater irritation came when she called her mother for dinner and she refused to leave her room.

'I'll bring your dinner in then,' Dunja said, but Zlata wouldn't have it.

'Leave me alone. I'm not hungry.' Her voice was flat and she was already in bed. Her face was as pale as the white pillowcase underneath it.

'Are you not feeling well?'

'I'm not hungry. Don't worry about me.'

'Let's see how you are a bit later on. Maybe you'll feel like eating something then.'

In answer Zlata closed her eyes and turned away.

In the dining room, Dominik had set the table with Dunja's new placemats. Last week she had bought six inexpensive bamboo ones and painted them with sprigs of lavender and sprays of green leaves. They were quick and easy to decorate and they turned out so well she was considering creating more and selling them.

She had served dinner for the three of them when the third annoyance of the evening came in the form of Martina. She was surly and anything Dunja said she answered with a curt one-word response.

When Dunja asked how her job was going all she said was okay and when Dunja asked if she was busy all she said was no. She was not interested in elaborating. It was bad enough that her mother was out-of-sorts but what Martina's excuse was, Dunja couldn't imagine.

'Dominik, what about coming to Sarajevo with me for a weekend?' Dunja asked, determined to ignore Martina's sullen mood.

'What for?'

'Well, I've been reading about what's been happening there since the war and I'd like to have a look.'

'Sounds like a good idea. When do you want to go?'

'A couple of weeks' time?'

'Why do you want to go there? It's dangerous,' Martina said.

Dunja watched her glare at her husband. 'Not now, surely,' Dunja interjected.

'What about me? Aren't I invited?' Martina cried, as if she was a spoilt child.

'Of course,' Dominik said.

'Do you think I have a death wish? You shouldn't go there either,' Martina said as she shoved back her chair and stormed out of the room, slamming the dining room door as she went.

'She seems to have forgotten the war is over,' Dominik said quietly.

The following morning Dunja remained keen to go to Sarajevo to see the recycled art crafted out of war ruins, despite Martina's outburst. Objects such as burnt ceiling beams, broken chairs and glass fragments, were being re-fashioned into striking art forms. She'd also read that theatre groups, often underground, had popped up and were producing plays about the war. As yet she hadn't been able to pluck up the nerve to travel to Sarajevo on her own. Travelling any distance alone by car was no longer a palatable option. She was hoping Dominik would accompany her, because he would provide security and he also knew his way around, but after Martina's outburst it was not looking likely.

Dunja was delighted when she finally bought her own apartment in Remete on the outskirts of Zagreb. She had spent so much time in this quiet suburb while she was restoring frescoes in the church of the Ascension of the Virgin Mary that she never forgot how much she loved it there. When an almost new apartment came up for sale, she knew it was meant for her.

At the end of a quiet street, on the border of the city limits, her apartment was the top one of three with an outlook over a vineyard owned by the university and beyond to the mountains. She'd been yearning for her own space for so long and on her first evening there she envisaged sitting in solitude on her terrace with a glass of wine. Her dream of peace and quiet, combined with the spectacular rural view, had at last become a reality.

She planned to divide the living room in half using sliding doors and set up one half as a studio. The light streaming through the windows would be excellent for painting, provided she didn't become distracted by the spectacular mountain landscape.

Every spare moment she had, she'd been shopping. She'd bought furniture, linen, curtains, kitchen equipment and a large work-table for her studio.

On the morning of the day she was moving in she was bubbling over with excitement. She couldn't wait to live there.

Chapter fifty-two

It was 1998, two years after the end of the war when Dominik was asked to assess a refurbishment project at the Astra Hotel in Sarajevo.

He had always been a night owl and even though he was leaving early the next morning, he was spending a couple of hours going over part of his manuscript, which he thought needed rewriting. He'd bought himself a takeaway cheese *burek* for supper and he had taken his first bite before he begin reviewing a section near the end of his manuscript.

> At the beginning of May 1995, Croatia launched *Operacija Bljesak* to liberate the Serb-controlled areas of Slavonia and Krajina. Seven thousand Croatian soldiers took part in the

offensive, which lasted for less than 48 hours, crushing the resistance put up by approximately 5,000 rebel Serbs.

Immediately after the *Operacija Bljesak* offensive, Serb planes attacked Croatia's capital Zagreb, dropping cluster bombs from a height of 1000 metres above civilian populated areas of the central city. There were only two attacks, in which seven people were killed and almost 200 injured. Following the attacks, the inhabitants of Zagreb lived in a state of fear while they waited for more lethal bombs to be dropped on their city.

He would never forget how terrified he'd been by the bombs detonated on the day he went to pick up the theatre tickets. He and Dunja never did get to see that ballet performance.

In July 1995, more than 8000 Bosnian civilians were slaughtered by Serb forces under the control of General Ratko Mladić in Srebrenica. By the time NATO decided to bomb Bosnian Serb tanks advancing on Srebrenica, it was too late. The visibility was too poor.

In early August 1995, Croatia launched *Operacija Oluja* to gain control of the Knin area. One hundred and twenty thousand Croatian defenders gathered to take Knin after five days of fighting, before raising the *šahovnica* chequered flag from the top of the 13th-century castle that dominates the town.

Although Dominik had played a small part in *Operacija Oluja,* as yet he had not been able to ascertain the truth of what really happened. Most of the reports he'd read talked about how many Serbs were slaughtered by Croatian defenders when, in fact, for several days preceding *Operacija Oluja,* prolific radio announcements had urged the Serbian population to leave and escape rather than be killed by the *Ustaše*. The exodus from Knin and other areas was orderly. Serbian inhabitants left with shirts on their backs and vehicles loaded with possessions. Dominik knew that was true. He'd witnessed the departure of a huge number. Apart from losing their homes, the worst fate they suffered was having sticks and stones thrown at them as they departed. The fighting in Knin could not have been fierce because the only people who remained in Serbian houses were the old *Babas* and *Bakas* who refused to abandon their homes. They stood no chance of survival even though some were armed with machine guns like the one Gavranić had finished off.

As he re-read what he'd written Dominik knew he'd be condemned by both Croats and Serbs if any of them chanced upon it. As to who might consider publishing it, as yet he had no idea.

After he left Mostar, Dominik drove through the lush Neretva Valley. From then on the terrain became more mountainous. He encountered several tunnels, the altitude began to increase and the temperature inside his car dropped. He had borrowed his sister's old VW Golf. The ventilation system didn't function well enough and the windows misted up.

From time to time he passed clusters of derelict village houses. Several were burnt out and many had weather-beaten, crooked *For Sale* signs stabbed in their front lawns. Cemeteries too, became a familiar spectacle — vast numbers of white columnar headstones told a wretched tale.

Twenty kilometres before Sarajevo, when Dominik was so cold he couldn't feel his toes, he stopped in Jablanica. A bowl of hot lamb and vegetable soup inside a rundown café soon warmed him up.

On the outskirts of Sarajevo grim scars from the war greeted and outraged him — deserted ruins and buildings riddled with bullet holes and smashed windows.

When rain set in, the temperature fell below ten degrees. When he arrived in Sarajevo, it was submerged in dense cloud. In the centre of the city too many cars parked at drunken angles and blocking driveways, which meant he had difficulty negotiating his way into the hotel car park.

After unpacking his meagre bag, he declined the offer of an evening meal in the claustrophobic, hotel dining room. Dressed in a new, heavy coat with a fur-lined hood, he headed out on foot. Around the corner from the hotel, at the end of a confined alleyway he stumbled upon a Turkish restaurant. Handmade meatballs, onions stuffed with rice and capsicum and a basket of pita bread provided an inexpensive, alcohol-free dinner.

The following morning, a watery sun was rising. From his hotel room window he took in his first view of the hillsides surrounding the city. As the enormous leaden cloud bank rolled away it revealed an imposing cemetery — more white headstones than he had ever seen before in one place. The giant, burial ground was on the site of the stadium of the 1984 Olympic Games. The headstones stood out like soldiers on parade. He couldn't take his eyes away from the startling sight.

Before breakfast he went for a brisk walk in the cold mountain air. While crossing the Latin Bridge over the Miljacka River, he was accosted by a beggar with a tin cup in one hand and a stick in the other. Her toothless, weather-beaten face with its crisscrossed wrinkles reminded him of the grill on the radiator of an old car. He dropped a handful of coins into her cup. Further on, a pack of mangy wild dogs with jutting bones rushed past him, intent on their search for food. By the time hunger drove him back to his hotel, the sun was glinting off the tombstones and had turned them an ethereal shade of gold.

At ten o'clock it was time to get down to work. Dominik toured the hotel with the manager and made notes. He'd seen plenty of peculiar hotels over the years, but nothing with such cramped spaces and small rooms. It would be a difficult task finding furniture compact enough to suit. To make matters worse, the ceilings were low and all the wood was varnished dark brown. He wouldn't have been surprised if it had been more than forty years since any redecorating had been done. The entire hotel reeked of the communist era. By the end of his inspection he had at least decided cube seats, like the ones in the media room in Tonci's house, could work well in the bar.

After lunch, Dominik's time was his own. He wandered through the labyrinth of narrow lanes close to his hotel, passing craft markets where the tick, tick, tick of hammers was constant. He bought a beaten-copper Turkish coffee pot from a man with one leg because he was enchanted by the rosy-gold copper and the intricate pattern carved on the metal handle. He walked on along the busy streets until he reached the Markale Market Place. He'd written about the massacres here. But the chapter was incomplete. Yet again, he had struggled to discover the truth. He was aware of the statistics. In February 1994, 68 people were killed and 114 injured, while in an identical attack in August 1995, 37 were murdered and 90 wounded. From the information sources he had available it was unclear who fired the mortar shells. At the time of both incidents, Serbian authorities denied responsibility and accused the Bosnian government of shelling their own people in an attempt to incite international outrage. Dominik didn't subscribe to that theory. He was sure the incidents were both carried out by the Army of Republika Srpska, but as yet he hadn't been able to unearth any written reports to substantiate his view. Around him, in the bustling food market, customers queued for plentiful supplies of dairy produce and vegetables. He leant against a wall and shut his eyes as he took in the smells and sounds around him. When a child cried out in a shrill voice it reminded him of the child he had rescued near the National Theatre in Zagreb and he found it easy to imagine terrified bewildered shoppers screaming and running for their lives as mortar shells exploded. When the light grew dim, he shivered, recalling the earlier carnage in May 1992, on the spot where he was standing. In a similar incident, known as the bread-queue bombing, 16 people died. Once again confusing statements were issued immediately after this bloodshed — some continue to believe that Bosnian Muslims attacked their own kind to draw international attention and sympathy to their plight, while others maintain that those who died were Serbs, killed by Muslims to force the United Nations to impose sanctions on Serbia. Dominik was sure the reaction to the last outrage in August 1995, proved Bosnian Serbs were responsible.

On August 30, 1995, Operation Deliberate Force, set in motion by General Smith, without the initial approval of the United Nations, destroyed many of the Bosnian Serb artillery positions in and around Sarajevo. This was the beginning of the end of the siege of Sarajevo.

As he dwelt on the past, Dominik failed to notice the silver-grey, low cloud that had descended around him until wet mist shrouded him, blotting out his vision. His coat was damp. He pulled his hood over his head and turned back towards his hotel.

The following day, as he had no work, he decided to drive from Sarajevo to Pale and then on to Foča. Not only was this the heart of Karadžić territory, but it was also a known haven for war criminals. He was hoping that this journey would provide material for his book, but as to what form that would take he had no idea. He also hoped Dunja's car was up to it. He knew the territory across the *vukojebina* would be rugged.

It took him over an hour to drive to Foča along winding roads through dense forest. At times the road was so narrow the journey was hazardous and he constantly worried about vehicles coming from the opposite direction.

Foča was nestled between the hills and his first impression was of a sleepy village with everyone quietly going about their business. It was at the entrance to the town that he came upon a monument to Serbs killed during the war. He found this laughable considering that in 1992, Serbs exterminated Foča's entire Muslim population of twenty thousand by torture or execution. Many of the bodies were tossed into the Drina River. Most of the women had been held in Partizan Hall where they were repeatedly raped before being murdered. As few as three thousand Muslims had returned to resettle here. Who could blame them? Dominik knew he certainly wouldn't want to came back and live in a place where such horrific brutality had taken place — that did not include the extermination that had taken place there during WW II.

When his stomach told him it needed food, he parked the car and walked along the street until he came to the nearest restaurant — an unremarkable establishment with drab-colourless walls and cheap-plastic chairs and tables. He didn't care, all he wanted was a quick meal before he took a look around. When a couldn't-care-less waitress came over, he ordered a steak and fries. Considering the place was not busy it took forever for his meal to arrive and when it did, the steak was as tough as the leather on the straps of his duffel bag and the fries were over-salted and over-cooked. He ate as much as he needed to satisfy his hunger and washed it down with a beer — *Prima Božićno*, a local lager he hadn't tasted before.

After his meal, he went exploring. He greeted the locals, but most ignored him and eyed him suspiciously. He knew his accent would be noticeably different and maybe he was too well-dressed to fit in. He wasn't quite sure what he was hoping to find and he had sat down in a café bar thinking he would order another beer. But he changed his mind about staying when he was greeted by a surly waiter.

'What do you want? Why are you in our town?' the waiter said rather than asking what he'd like to order. The look on the waiter's face was hostile and without replying Dominik walked out. On his way down the street he passed three people grouped together. Because they were staring at him, he knew they were talking about him. As he passed them, one spat on the pavement. He walked more quickly. His car was parked around the corner and once he was in it, as fast as he could, he headed out of town. A threatening feeling had engulfed him. He knew he shouldn't have come.

Once he hit the winding road leading through the forest he felt safe. However, that feeling didn't last. In his rear view mirror a dented, VW Golf came powering up and tailgated him. Not once but several times. Each time the angry driver hit his car, Dominik struggled to stay on the road. This continued all the way down a steep slope as the angry driver played cat and mouse with Dominik who kept accelerating whenever he could as he tried to get away. The maniac repeatedly thumped the back of Dominik's car, trying his best to push him off the road. Several times Dominik tried to speed up and lose him; however, the narrow vertiginous road made it impossible. The chase went on until the enraged driver grew tired and tried to overtake Dominik on a tight corner. As Dominik gaped in horror at the approaching corner he knew that if a vehicle came the other way, they'd both be done for. When his pursuer swerved in front of him, Domimik slammed on his brakes. They were both travelling fast and Dominik smashed into the other car and inflicted new dents on the already pock-marked wreck and caused it to slew around. He was trying to gather his wits when his pursuer got out, stormed towards his car, waving his arms and shouting obscenities. When he ripped open Dominik's door he was still bellowing.

'We know why you're here, foreign fucker, get out and don't come back!' he shouted as he grabbed Dominik's shirt front and shook him.

Dominik, who was usually mild mannered quickly became incensed with rage tinged with fear. He'd had enough of the strange, resentful people in Foča. He lashed out with his fist and caught the madman with a blow that glanced off his jaw.

'So you want a fight, do you, *kurac*? Well I'll give you a fight alright,' he yelled as he lunged at Dominik aiming a punch at his stomach.

The blow wasn't powerful enough and Dominik stood his ground then struck again, this time with his foot. His assailant dropped to the ground as his feet were swept out from under him. Dominik took a couple of steps towards him and kicked the man as hard as he could between the legs. His opponent yelped, drew his legs towards his body and slithered backwards. Dominik stepped back when he saw the would-be tough guy move too far. Seconds later, he screamed as he plummeted over the edge of the precipice.

Dominik was breathing heavily, trying to pull himself together when he heard an odd sound behind him. Was his attacker's car inching forward or was he imagining it? He stared at the dented vehicle. The sound of tyres crunching on gravel confirmed that the car was indeed moving. Seconds later it picked up speed and travelling at a walking pace. *Shit! It's coming straight for me.* Without hesitation he moved out of its path and watched as the front wheels ran over the lip at the side of the road. It teetered on the edge and there was a creaking, groaning noise as the muffler and exhaust system were ripped off the chassis. Then the body of the car followed its owner and plunged into the ravine below. Dominik shuddered when it hit the valley floor with a sickening thud and the graunch of metal. *That's what happens when you leave it out of gear and don't pull on the handbrake.* Dominik had no desire to look into the ravine. Instead he walked over to the exhaust system and contemplated it. *I'm in the shit — no I'm not — there won't be any evidence.* As calmly as he could, he kicked the car parts in the same direction as the car.

Dominik hastened into his car, closed the door and quickly depressed the lock. For a brief moment he sat slumped in his seat as he allowed his breathing to return to normal. *What if his mates are following him? I'm out of here.* He started the engine and gravel shot out from under the front wheels as his foot exerted too much pressure on the accelerator. *Slow down or you'll end up where that blockhead is.* Clutching the steering wheel firmly, he kept driving and didn't look back.

The following day he had to leave. He was too shaken up. He would drive south to Mostar. He wanted to satisfy the hankering he'd had forever to visit a mosque, but it couldn't be any mosque. His choice was the Karađoz Bey mosque, built in the sixteenth century. It had been damaged during the war and he doubted that there had been sufficient time to rebuild it.

It was an ominous sign when he drew close to his destination and couldn't see the minaret. When a parking space suddenly materialised, he took it.

From close by he stared at the pile of rubble. The hat-shaped dome was partially intact but it had gaping jagged holes where it had been struck by artillery while the tall minaret had been decapitated. A barrier had been erected to keep people out and there was no sign of any restoration. The dreadful destruction brought tears to his eyes. He had no particular interest in the Muslim religion, but it had been an iconic structure that was clearly important to the devotees.

Before leaving Mostar, Dominik had one last stop to make. He had promised Dunja he would visit a particularly famous spice shop. He asked a passer-by for directions and was pleased to learn that it was only two streets away.

The interior told him the old-fashioned shop had been there forever. Cobwebs dangled from the ceiling, the paintwork was so old and dull he couldn't determine whether it was brown or red and the lighting was inadequate, but it didn't matter. The spices were contained in small, pull-out drawers and their aroma was sweet and strong. He breathed deeply and savoured the mingling of cinnamon, turmeric, coriander, garam masala, cardamom and more. He choose a selection for Dunja and he couldn't resist a large slice of *Halva* from the glass-topped container on the counter to eat on the way home. The sticky, local confectionary made from tahini, honey and pistachio nuts was a real treat.

As he headed off, he thought back to the events of the previous day. He'd been deep in the territory of Radovan Karadžić, one of the war criminals on the ICTY's most wanted list and he had to admit he was disappointed not to have found anything new to add to his book. Had he been dreaming that something would just magically drop into his lap? The truth of the matter was he hadn't actually encountered anyone he could have talked to who could have added to his existing knowledge. Perhaps he should have stopped in Pale, but he couldn't face it after what happened in Foča.

Chapter fifty-three

It was October 2008, when Dominik caught the bus to the centre of Zagreb for his appointment with Ivo Pukanić, the editor-in-chief at *Nacional*. He was elated at the prospect of his work being published by such an influential paper. He admired Ivo Pukanić, especially in 2003 when he had the nerve to interview Ante Gotovina, one of the war criminals sought by the ICTY. At the time of the interview, Gotovina had been on the run, his whereabouts unknown. Dominik wondered how Pukanić managed to contact him, or taking into account Gotovina's arrogant personality, maybe it was the other way around. Pukanić said he had interviewed Gotovina in an EU capital. He was amused when Pukanić declined to specify which one.

He was due to meet Pukanić at six, but as soon as he saw the queue of traffic from the window of the bus, he was anxious that he'd be late. At six-fifteen he knew he'd be late. The bus was moving at a crawl. He asked the obliging driver to let him out and he jogged the rest of the way.

He had reached Palmotićiva Ulica, when he couldn't go any further. That street and others nearby had been cordoned off. Police were swarming like vultures around a carcass.

'Could you let me through please?' he asked the nearest officer, a mean-looking character with a number-one haircut.

'No,' the policeman replied at he stared at Dominik's cap.

'I have an appointment at *Nacional.*'

'Do you now? And who might you be?'

'I'm Dominik Letica. I had an appointment with Ivo Pukanić at six o'clock. I'm late.' He was beginning to feel concerned.

'Well, whoever you are, you'll be coming with me.'

'What for?'

'I'm taking you in for questioning.'

'Why?'

'*Slušati!* Shut up if you know what's good for you. I'll ask the questions, not you. Have you got that?' He drew his pistol from its holster and waved it at Dominik. 'Get a move on, *kurac*!'

It was then that the carnage came into view. The wreckage of at least one car, maybe more, was close by. An ambulance was in attendance and more police were stationed there too.

Dominik stopped and stared at the police officer until his eyes begin to water.

'Do you mind telling me what's happened?'

The policeman took a step closer and eyeballed him. 'Are you trying to tell me you don't know?'

'I have no idea!'

'I find that hard to believe.'

'Look, I've never been here in my life before,' he stammered.

'I suggest you tell that to someone who gives a shit.' The policeman came to a halt adjacent to a squad car. 'Get in the back,' he ordered, gesturing with his gun.

'Where are we going?'

'As I said before, I'm taking you in for questioning.'

'What for?'

'Shut the fuck up. How many times do you need to be told?'

Dominik cowered in the back of the police car, next to another equally sour police officer, unable to believe what had befallen him.

Inside the police station, his identity card, wallet, telephone and watch were confiscated, before he was pushed into a windowless room containing two battered chairs and a desk. When the door slammed, leaving him alone, he slumped on to the nearest chair. His heart was pounding, he'd broken out in a sweat, and sooner rather than later he needed a crap. What the hell was going on? Then, because he was in a police station, he began to feel guilty, but of what he had no idea. No doubt he would find out soon enough what was going on.

He crossed and uncrossed his legs. The seat was hard and uncomfortable. He stood up, walked around the minuscule room, blew his nose on his handkerchief and wiped the sweat from his forehead.

Twenty minutes later, the door opened and admitted a different police officer. Judging by the insignia on his jacket, he held a higher rank.

'What's going on?' Dominik blurted out as soon as the officer sat down behind the desk and placed a notepad in front of him. The officer ignored his question and continued with one of his own.

'Did you know Ivo Pukanić?'

'Look, I've never met the man, let alone been to his office. I'm a furniture designer.' Dominik was pissed off and spat out his words.

'I know that. What were you doing in Palmoteciva at six-twenty?'

'I had an appointment with Ivo Pukanić.'

'What about?'

'I've written a book and I was hoping he might publish it.'

'A bit difficult now that he's dead.'

'Sorry?'

'You heard what I said.'

'So, why have you detained me?' He looked his interrogator directly in the eye and began a staring-out contest. As the seconds ticked by, Dominik refused to be beaten. His eyes watered, he dared not blink and he was not the first to look away.

'We have footage of a man running away from the scene of the crime and you fit the description.'

'What! This is nothing to do with me.'

'We'll see. I'm going to let you spend the night in a cell until we make further enquiries, unless of course you'd prefer to confess now?'

'Confess to what?'

'Murdering two men.'

'I've already told you, I'm not guilty.'

'So you say. We'll see what happens in the morning, shall we?' The officer stood up and left the room.

Dominik spent a rough, wakeful night sitting up, leaning against the wall on a hard bed smelling of urine, in a cell with five other detainees. He was awake the next morning at half-light. Unaware of the time, he kept still and stared at the concrete ceiling above him and the graffiti on the wall adjacent to the bed. He read, *Ivo je bio ovdje* and *Jebem ti sve po spiskul*.

He hadn't been allowed to call home the previous night and he couldn't imagine how his wife would have reacted when he didn't come home. He had omitted to tell anyone about his appointment with Pukanić.

As he shuffled forward to the edge of the bed, he kept his eyes on the floor at his feet. He had no desire to talk to the other ruffians in his cell. He remained sitting where he was, immobile for what seemed like forever. His bladder was bursting, but he couldn't face walking over to use the communal bucket in the corner.

He looked up when he heard the rattle of keys in the door.

'You, Letica, out!' a short, physically intimidating officer he haven't seen before shouted.

'Get your stuff from the front desk on your way out,' the policeman said.

'Are you letting me go?'

'That's what I said. Are you deaf?' As soon as he was outside the police station he scurried into a narrow alleyway that ran beside the building and with much relief took a piss. Then he went in search of a bus stop, which he found without too much difficulty. However, there was a wait of over half an hour before the bus to take him in the direction of home arrived. The journey took him thirty minutes because the morning traffic was heavy.

By the time he arrived, it was seven-thirty and Martina had already gone to work without so much as leaving him a note or a message on his phone. Didn't she wonder where he'd been all night? Dominik sighed with resignation as he picked up the telephone and dialled his sister. There was no reply. He assumed that she was away. He glanced at his watch. After he'd had a shower he'd watch the television news at eight o'clock and then call his office and tell them he would be late.

The headlines told him all he needed to know. Ivo Pukanić and his marketing manager had been murdered by a bomb planted on a motorcycle parked next to Pukanić's Lexus in the car park around the corner from their office. It was detonated as the two of them were about to get into the car. A man described as thin-faced, in his early thirties, who was wearing a baseball cap, was seen running from the scene of the crime. The news item suggested that Pukanić's outspoken reputation and no-nonsense style of reporting, particularly in relation to a cigarette smuggling operation, had cost him his life.

As Dominik set off for work it was then that he recalled how shaken up he'd been six weeks ago by the murder of Ivana Hodak, in broad daylight, in downtown Zagreb. Thought to be pregnant at the time of her death, she was the daughter of a prominent lawyer defending a client accused of stealing 3.5 million euros worth of diamonds, allegedly used as collateral during the war, to secure arms' deals.

He was falling into despair about the fate his country. Despite independence, there was still no freedom of speech. After these sickening incidents he was beginning to believe there was no chance that his manuscript would ever be published. Ivo Pukanić was the only man he could think of who would have been bold enough to print what he'd written. But what would the repercussions have been if he had? Thankfully Dominik would never know.

That evening after he returned home from work, he retreated to his room. He was not in the mood for any form of conversation with his wife and he certainly didn't want to tell her where he'd spent last night. He was still struggling to understand why she hadn't asked where he'd been. If he did tell her about what had happened, she would never understand that he was a victim of circumstance. More than likely she would blame him regardless.

Restless and not feeling ready for sleep even though he was tired after last night, he opened his manuscript until he came to one of the most abhorrent passages in his manuscript.

It was March 11, 2006 when Slobodan Milošević, 'The Butcher of the Balkans' as he had become known, died.

Dominik felt no pity rereading his words.

> Milošević was found dead in his cell at the United Nations Detention Centre in The Hague, near the end of his trial for war crimes. The results of an autopsy confirm he suffered a heart attack. It was common knowledge he had been suffering from a heart condition and high blood pressure. He was a crushed man. Without his wife, who was in Moscow, he was alone and miserable. When his request to travel to Moscow for treatment was declined, it is thought he stopped taking his medication, thereby causing his own death. This did not stop speculation by his supporters that his heart attack had been deliberately caused by the ICTY. In April 2001, Milošević was arrested and indicted by the ICTY on charges that included genocide, deportation, murder, racial and religious persecution, inhumane acts, extermination and torture. Following these charges, he was further indicted for ordering the murder of former Serbian President Ivan Stambolić and the attempted murder of the leader of the opposition, Vuk Drašković.

Dominik's book was shut and he'd pushed back his chair, when he noticed he'd inadvertently dropped a page of notes. He yawned yet again; it was time for sleep, but he couldn't keep his mind off Milošević. He picked up the page and read.

> Milošević's entire family were believed to be unbalanced. His mother, father and uncle had all committed suicide and it looked as if he had inherited their insane behaviour. Some said that instead of taking his own life he had instead killed his own nation.

Once he'd slotted the page in its rightful place inside the book cover, he moved to his bed and lay on his back, fully-clothed with his hands behind his head and stared at the ceiling as he pondered his amateurish attempt at writing. Would he be able to find anyone who would publish it?

Chapter fifty-four

Two years had gone by since Dominik had been detained for the suspected murder of Ivo Pukanić. For several months his manuscript lay dormant. It seemed pointless working on it. He couldn't think who else might want to publish it and he knew there were glaring gaps in it where he hadn't been able to verify what he'd written. Then much to his delight a new avenue presented itself when he succeeded in setting up a meeting with the editor of *Aktual*, a new weekly that had gone into circulation two months ago. He had high hopes this newspaper would agree to publish his book, perhaps in instalments. After he sent them a sample chapter, they invited him to come and discuss it.

The drab newspaper office with dirty, grey walls adorned with nothing other than fly dirt was busy. Staff rushed in and out of various offices visible down the corridor leading away from the reception area. Dominik's appointment was behind schedule. He had been waiting for almost an hour. He glanced across at a man with a prominent nose and a mane of overgrown, grey-brown hair — the only other person left in the waiting room. The man was sweating profusely as he fiddled with a pen, clicking it, and tapping it on the CD he was holding in his other hand.

Dominik broke the silence: 'Is it always this frantic in here?'

'Yes! Do you have an appointment?'

'Yes. It was almost an hour ago. Have you been here before?'

'No, but I've heard it's always busy.'

'Are you a writer?' Dominik asked.

'No. I'm a photographer. I've made a documentary, which so far I've had no luck selling. I'm hoping someone here will be interested.' The individual was chatty and friendly. Dominik was sure he too must have been bored and frustrated by the endless waiting.

'Is it about the war?'

'No, it's about Jasenovac. But no one will touch it. They all say the subject is too sensitive. Can you believe it, after all this time?'

'Seems rather strange.'

'I can't get anyone to so much as look at it when I tell them it includes an interview with one of the former inmates. They shut the door in my face. I wouldn't be surprised if I get the same reaction here. I'm Dario by the way.'

'Dominik. Pleased to meet you. What's that picture on the cover of the CD?' Dominik had noticed it earlier and couldn't take his eyes away from it.

'It's a carving done by one of the inmates,' Dario said as he held up the CD so Dominik could see it more easily.

'Where did you find it? If you don't mind me asking.'

'On the internet. I copied it.'

Before Dominik could comment further, the conversation between them came to an abrupt end when the receptionist told Dominik he could go through.

'Good luck,' Dario said as Dominik stood up to make his way to the journalist's office.

'Not quite our thing,' said the editor, sliding Dominik's writing sample across his untidy desk towards him. He paused to light a cigarette before going on. 'To tell you the truth, what you've written would tread on too many toes, if you know what I mean. The war's too recent and I'm not sure people, especially politicians, want their noses rubbed in it.'

'That's disappointing and not what I was hoping to hear.' Dominik sighed.

'I'm already copping a huge amount of flak for the stuff I publish here and if I printed in full what you've written, then I'd really be putting my neck on the chopping block. We could tone it down, of course, but I don't see the point — neither do I want to end up dead at the hands of the mafia, like Ivo Pukanić.'

'I see.'

'What you've written is strong stuff though … it'd probably be better to wait another five years, maybe more, until things have calmed down a bit. Then we might run it. Come and see me then,' he said, standing up and walking around the other side of his desk.

'Keep writing!' he added as he held out his hand.

Dominik left the newspaper office and trudged along the street staring at his boots. The fierce sun was beating down on his bare head. It had taken him so long to get up enough courage to show his work to anyone else after the Pukanić debacle and to find out that it had all been a waste of time was not only frustrating, but it was also a real piss-off.

He put the book out of his mind. He'd already waited for the duration of the war plus several more years and he would have to search for yet another publisher.

He turned his mind to his encounter with Dario in the waiting room of the newspaper office. The picture on the CD cover had disturbed him. He lengthened his strides. He needed to get home as quickly as possible.

The wooden horse on his desk looked so similar to the one on the CD cover, he couldn't stop staring at it as he turned it over and over in his hands.

That night in bed, different scenarios filled his head. In the early hours of the morning, he got up and went to his desk. Once his computer was up and running he brought up a website about Jasenovac. It was not a topic he knew a lot about.

He begin to read. Known as the Auschwitz of the Balkans, the concentration camp had been set up by Ante Pavelić, the fascist dictator of Croatia beside the river Sava, near the village of Jasenovac, close to the border between Croatia and BiH. Run by the *Ustaše,* it was said to be one of the cruellest death camps imaginable. Between 1941 and 1945, between 750,000 and 900,000 Serbs, Jews and Roma were murdered, often by bloodthirsty cut-throats using a *srbosjek*. Dominik paused. The article he was reading was not well written and seemed biased towards Serbs. He decided to check out other sources. The next one he read was worse and said Jasenovac was a symbol of *Ustaše* genocide. He read on. Serbian propaganda claimed that over a million Serbs were slaughtered there. The next website he found appeared more accurate and put the figures at 30,000 – 60,000. That included Gypsies, Jews, Serbs and Croats. It went on to say that the behaviour of the *Ustaše* was one of the reasons many Croats and Bosnians joined the Partisans. Although Dominik understood why that may have happened, he was mystified by the discrepancies in the number of victims. It looked as if each ethnicity had twisted the figures for their own ends; individually hoping that their particular version would become history.

In 1945, the last thousand or so prisoners still incarcerated there, staged a jailbreak immediately before the camp was overrun and liberated by Tito's Partisans. He glanced at his watch. He had run out of time. If he didn't hurry, he'd be late for work.

All morning Jasenovac claimed his attention. By lunchtime he'd worked out that if he was to solve the riddle he would need Dario's help. He had memorized Dario's surname, which was Babić, from the CD cover and it was not difficult to find a listing for him in the telephone book. After a brief conversation, they agreed to meet at the end of the day for a drink.

As soon as they were seated in a booth at the back of a poorly-lit bar, Dominik produced his carving and placed it on the table. Dario sucked in an audible breath.

'Where did you get that?' he asked, picking up the horse.

'My grandmother gave it to me. It was a present; my grandfather carved it. I didn't think anything about it at the time; then I saw your CD cover.'

'It's remarkably similar, isn't it?' Dario said.

'It sure is. It's a puzzle — an absolute puzzle. It caused me to spend half the night reading about Jasenovac. I tried to look for a list of inmates' names. But I couldn't find a complete one. I thought maybe my grandfather had been sent there because no one in my family has ever said much about him. When I drew a blank, I tried searching for a list of survivors, thinking that he might have been on that, despite the idea being far-fetched. I drew a blank there too.'

'Do you think your grandfather was imprisoned in Jasenovac?'

'Yes, quite possibly. He died under unfortunate circumstances and no one in the family wants to talk about it even if I ask. Not even his wife when she was alive. I know he was part of Tito's inner circle until he supposedly fell from grace. He served in the war with Tito. All I recall is my grandmother saying how unfair his death was that after he'd suffered so much during and at the end of the war. She said it was cruel and unjust.'

'What did he die of, if you don't mind me asking?'

'He killed himself in prison after they accused him of spying for the Soviets.'

'I guess that would have been around the time that Hebrang was caught for alleged spying?'

'Yes, I think so. Although my grandfather's body was returned to his family, whereas Hebrang's was never found. To this day his son is still trying to find out what happened to it — without success.'

'Yes, I know about Hebrang.' Dario paused. 'I might be able to help you. I have a list of inmates who died in Jasenovac and a list of the escapees. It's in my computer.' Dario opened his briefcase and pulled out his laptop.

'Okay, let's see. Here we go. What was his name?'

'Anđa Milić.' In the ensuing silence while Dario scanned the list, Dominik picked anxiously at a hangnail on his left thumb.

'Let's try the deceased list first,' he said as scanned the names that were in alphabetical order. I've found an Ivan Milić. Any relation?'

'Christ! My uncle. He was arrested by the *Ústase* near the beginning of the war and no one ever found out what happened to him.'

Dario let out a low whistle, as he turned the computer screen towards Dominik.

When he stared at the screen, Dominik's eyes filled with tears.

'Good God! No one ever knew how he died. My grandfather wouldn't tell anyone, not even my grandmother.' His voice faltered. He felt as if he'd run into a stone wall. His head drooped and he closed his eyes as he tried to stem the grief welling inside him.

'The list of survivors is here too. I'll try that.'

'I have a feeling you'll find him there. From what I know my grandfather witnessed Ivan's death, but he refused to tell anyone where it had happened. All he ever said was that he died a hero.'

'You're right,' Dario said. 'Here he is, Anđa Milić. Once again Dario turned the screen towards Dominik who stared at it in astonishment.

'So where does the carving come into it then?'

'No idea. Maybe he carved it while he was in Jasenovac. *Baba* had other things he carved when he was young and I know he was good at it. Or maybe someone gave it to him.'

'I guess we'll never know and there's no way we can find out after all this time.'

For a short time they sat in silence.

When Dominik heard the clicking of Dario's cigarette lighter he turned towards him. Dario was flipping his cheap plastic lighter over and over in his hand while he stared across the room.

'What are you staring at?' Dominik asked when he saw Dario's eyes were fixed on something or someone on the other side of the room.

'That character over there. The one with the shaved head. Every time I look up he's staring at me. I've seen him before, but I can't think where.'

When a mild feeling of panic spread over Dominik, he forgot about his grandfather, his uncle and Jasenovac.

'Perhaps we should leave,' Dominik said.

'If you don't mind, I think we should go straightaway. 'Can I drop you somewhere?'

'Are you going anywhere near Savska Cesta, the opposite end to where the old prison used to be?' he asked as he wiped the sweat from his face with his handkerchief.

'Yes. I live around the corner.'

They left the café with Dario striding ahead. A few steps away from the café door, Dominik looked back, but the man didn't appear to be following them.

'My car's across the road.' Dario's speech was as rapid as his footsteps. Inside the car he turned and glanced towards the café.

'Can you see him?' Dominik asked.

'I don't want to alarm you, but he's crossed the road and he's hurrying towards us. I'm certain I'm being tailed.'

'But why would he be following you?'

'No idea. Shades of the secret police, isn't it?'

'Yeah, but they don't exist anymore, remember?'

'That's what's worrying me.' Dario pressed the accelerator and they speed away into the darkness.

Later, hoping to distract himself from the events earlier in the evening, Dominik opened his book at the beginning.

Later that year, in October 1991, the city of Dubrovnik, which was by now crowded to overflowing with 55,000 refugees seeking safe haven within its city walls, was surrounded from all sides, including the sea, by the JNA and their allies the Montenegrin reservists. From their positions in the surrounding hillsides, the JNA did their best to destroy the historic core of the old city into which more than 2000 artillery rounds were fired ...

He was satisfied with that section, but the beginning of his book now seemed inaccurate. Doubt was creeping into his mind about why the war began. He'd been reading articles from the archives of *the Guardian*, *the Los Angeles Times* and *Helsinki Watch* and listening to the *Voice of America Radio* more frequently. He had come to believe that the major event, which brought about the conflict, happened when the Slovenian and Croatian Communist Party delegates walked out of the Yugoslav Communist Party Congress in January 1990. Following this, the first multi-party elections were held in Slovenia and Croatia. The Yugoslav Federal Government viewed this as a breach of the Yugoslav Constitution and subsequently ordered their army to attack. First Slovenia, then Croatia and subsequently BiH.

He also discovered that Croatia had been bankrupt when it declared independence. What money it had was in banks in Belgrade. Immediately after Croatia seceded, Belgrade confiscated all Croatia's money. The new Croatian Government was forced to rely on financial support from Croatians living overseas and the sale of Croatian athletes abroad. More than 1,500 player contracts for footballers and basketballers were signed, yielding millions of dollars.

After the election, when President Tuđman failed to pacify the fears of the minority Serbian population residing in Croatia, they began to rise up, thus causing the first skirmishes in different areas of Croatia.

Croatians were not looking for, or prepared for war when they were attacked by an army with weapons of modern warfare such as planes, artillery and cluster bombs. They were forced to build an army from scratch to defend their homes and families. At the beginning of the war, weapons and ammunition were almost non-existant.

Dominik had read so many different theories about why the war started he was becoming perplexed. Getting to the heart of the matter was a frustrating experience. Some articles agreed with each other and some did not. *Helsinki Watch* stated that the war in Croatia was not as many choose to believe — namely the result of age-old hostilities by repressed communists. Instead it was the product of a relentless propaganda campaign aimed at stirring up these old tensions engineered by Serbia's irresponsible, power-hungry leader Milosević. After all his limited research this was the view Dominik preferred to believe. He needed to give the beginning of his book greater thought and consider rewriting it.

Chapter fifty-five

Dominik had spent the last hour tidying his desk. All his old newspapers were stored in a box underneath his bed and he had moved books he had yet to read to the bookcase at the head of his bed. For the first time in ages the surface of his desk was clear. All that remained was a stack of unused paper and several pens on the right-hand side. He didn't expect it to stay uncluttered for long. He was an untidy person by nature, and it wouldn't be long before it became chaotic again. But at the moment it felt good.

In the kitchen he dumped the rubbish he'd collected from his room into the bin and heated water to make coffee. He was glad Martina had gone out for the evening. He preferred his own company.

Back at his desk, he began writing. Half and hour later, he paused to reflect on what he'd written. He found Serbia's attitude towards Kosovo astounding; although there were no reliable statistics on the population of Kosovo, he believed that of the two million people who lived there only five to six percent were Serbian. He couldn't understand why Serbia would not let go of Kosovo, especially when they persistently insulted not only the Albanian people but also the Serbs who lived there by calling them primitive and medieval. He had never visited Serbia and had no desire to go there.

Putting aside his book, he opened the atlas he'd recently bought from a second-hand bookstore. When he assessed the respective sizes of the countries surrounding his own, he had difficulty coming to terms with squabbles over land until his eyes were drawn to the archipelago of islands off the coast of Croatia, one in the north and the other in the south. There were more than three hundred islands in total. He would be travelling to one of these, the island of Hvar, the following week. Villa Dalmacija, in the old town of Hvar, had requested a quote for refurbishment.

It was six in the morning when he caught a coach from Zagreb to Split. The journey would take him six hours and he would get there in time for lunch with his sister who was engaged in touch-up work at the Diocletian Palace.

They had arranged to meet at *The Black Cat,* a restaurant in a back street, close to the bus station that neither had been to before.

'Did you know it serves burgers and curries?' Dominik asked after they'd sat down in the shady outdoor courtyard.

'No, the people in my hotel said it was different, that's all. Do you want to go somewhere else?'

'No, let's give it a go.'

Dominik ordered a BLT while Dunja chose a vegetarian wrap. Their meals took a while to arrive and they had plenty of time to chat.

'How are you enjoying your new place? I bet you're loving the peace and quiet,' Dominik said.

'I sure am. So much so I didn't want to leave to come and do this job. But now that I have a mortgage I need to make sure I can pay it. How's things between you and Martina? Any better now that I'm not there?'

'No, just the same. We more or less live separate lives. I try to keep out of her way. And since she's no longer working at the same place as me it's better. We don't have to travel to work together any more.'

'I didn't realise she had a new job.'

'Yes, she started work in the accounting department of a plumbing company after you moved out. I was relieved. She goes out a lot more than she used to as well and spends more time with her family. In the evenings we often eat separately, although she usually makes a meal for *Majka*. Strangely enough they seem to get on well enough. I can't understand why.'

'Do you mean they talk to each other?'

'Not particularly. I think it's a case of like attracting like.'

'What do you mean?'

'They're both a bit strange in the head.'

Dunja laughed. 'You mean depressed?'

'*Makja* certainly is. As to what's wrong with Martina I couldn't say, but something must attract them to each other.'

'What are you going to do about you and Martina?'

'You mean am I going to stay with her?'

'Yes. You can't be happy.'

'Not particularly. I try not to think about it and focus on other stuff and take it one day at a time. Also there's *Majka* to consider. I think she'd be upset if Martina and I parted.

'She must know your relationship isn't good.'

'I don't think she's noticed. You know how unobservant she is. She lives in another world most of the time, in fact, almost all of the time now.'

'Yes, sad isn't it? She's been like it for years. Although sometimes I have a feeling she sees more than she lets on.'

'For most of my life she's been odd,' Dominik said and shook his head sadly.

After an unremarkable meal, they threaded their way towards the Diocletian Palace through streets crowded with tourists. Dunja was in the process of regilding one of the figures outside the cathedral of St Duje. Dominik shaded his eyes with his hand and looked up at the gleaming yellow gold glinting in the sun while Dunja climbed the scaffolding. Once she was standing close to the statue Dominik took a photo of her before they went inside to look at the frescoes near the altars. This was the first time he had seen his sister's work and he was awestruck by its intricacy. He lingered, enthralled by the painstaking effort she put in to restore the astonishing frescoes.

After saying goodbye to his sister, an hour later he boarded the catamaran to Hvar. From the nearest porthole, he looked across to the island. The coastline was steep with perilous paths leading to several gravel beaches while the spine of the island was dotted with pine forests. When there was no sign of vineyards, olive groves or lavender fields, Dominik assumed they must be somewhere in the middle of the island that wasn't visible from the sea.

A room had been reserved for him at Villa Dalmacija and after checking in, he went for an evening stroll. In the harbour were several imposing superyachts. He moved on, unimpressed by their obscene opulence. He followed the path around the edge of the waterfront until he come to a restaurant and nightclub sited on a small headland overlooking the sea where he stopped for a beer.

The next morning, during breakfast in the dining room, he sat by a window overlooking the bay as he scanned the local paper. An exceedingly local one it was too, nothing like the newspapers in Zagreb. The front page featured a photo of a prince he'd never heard of, dancing the night away at the night club he'd seen the previous day. Apparently, his gold superyacht was moored in the marina. It was then that one of Hvar's nicknames came to mind — *the Party Island* as opposed to *the Lavender Island.*

At ten-thirty he had an appointment with the hotel owner to discuss the refurbishment. First and foremost on the agenda was the restaurant and the reception area. Much to Dominik's relief, the owner, a portly balding man in his mid-fifties, was well aware that both of these areas were dated and needed to be refreshed and brightened up not only by repainting the walls throughout, but with new modern furniture. The owner produced a chart with paint colours as soon as they began to discuss doing way with the drab once white walls which were now a dirty yellowish-brown. Together they chose pale, egg-shell blue for the walls which would be complemented by cushions and curtains of ultramarine blue to fit in with a nautical theme that the owner had in mind. Dominik was pleased with the outcome of their discussion and also with the furniture order he had secured. Once the meeting was over he walked to a pizzeria he'd noticed yesterday, close to the water's edge.

After enjoying a well-made tasty *crni rižot* plus a bowl of fries for lunch, he wandered further afield until he come across a small park. For a time, he chilled out on a wooden bench under the spreading branches of an old tree. Behind the park he stumbled upon a crumbling ruin. The doorway was intact and out of curiosity he wandered into the interior. It was cool; sheltered by the tree where he'd been sitting. He stepped over fallen blocks of stone and picked his way across to the one graffiti-covered wall that was still standing. A caricature of Stjepan Mesić, a former president of Croatia, had been stencilled over the entire wall. There were dozens of black images. Underneath were the words *cro juda*. Dominik had never seen this ugly representation before. He was shocked. He admired Mesić, a founding member of the Croatian People's Party (HNS), but clearly whoever created this abomination did not.

After dinner, he felt in need of a little light relief and headed for the night club, but when he got there, it was deserted.

'Where are all the people?' he asked the waiter in the adjacent restaurant.

'The tourist season ended on the last day of August.'

'But today's only the second of September.'

'Yes, when it ends here, it ends.'

Chapter fifty-six

It is early December 2011, when Dominik exercised his right to vote in the parliamentary elections. He was up early and at seven-fifteen he walked to the nearest polling booth. It was a bleak day and light snow was falling when he set out in his fleecy-lined overcoat, deerstalker hat and woollen gloves.

At lunchtime, he ate leftovers from the fridge — a pork casserole with broad beans that Martina had made. Although the meat was full of flavour, he wasn't hungry. He picked at the food, eager to turn on the television in his room to watch the election results.

Much later, reclined on his bed with his pillow propping him up, Dominik waited anxiously for the votes to be counted. He crossed his fingers in the hope that change would come. HDZ, the centre-right party, had been ruling Croatia almost constantly since independence in 1991, except for the period between 2000 and 2003. HDZ had recently been exposed as a hotbed of state-organised corruption and embezzlement on a massive scale. Its former leader, Ivo Sanader, who had been charged with corruption, was arrested while attempting to flee the country. His trial had begun and he had pleaded not guilty, attempting to dismiss the charges against him as a fabrication. Another former deputy prime minister and other senior party figures had also been charged and HDZ itself was at the centre of a slush-fund scandal. If these corrupt politicians were convicted, he hoped it would set an example to others, although he doubted it.

He slid to the end of his bed and sat up straight, when much to his relief, HDZ was soundly beaten at the polls. The *Kukuriku* Coalition, a centre-left party led by Zoran Milanović, had a resounding win over HDZ. Dominik laughed and cheered at the strange name of the victorious party, which was named after a restaurant in Kastav, a historical town ten kilometres north-west of Rijeka, where members of the party had first convened. The new coalition was made up of four parties: the Social Democrats, the Croatian's People's Party, the Croatian Party of Pensioners and the Liberal Democrats. He was looking forward to watching how the new government would deal with the calamity it had inherited — a disastrous economic legacy with national debt soaring to extreme levels, unemployment at twenty per cent and a depressed national mood.

He had been impatient for the day when Croatia became independent, but he had to admit that the changes he hoped would come, had not. Perchance, he'd been hoping for a miracle to extract his country from the communist way of thinking. It was more than twenty years since independence and Croatia was still struggling with its new identity. Communist traditions clung like soil to the roots of a *maslina* blown over in a storm. He wondered how many years would it take for his country to find itself and adopt a better, more democratic existence.

In the newspaper he'd read an article stating that in July 2013, Croatia would become a member of the European Union. The EU Commission's report on Croatia's progress towards EU accession in October 2011, stated that Croatia needed to intensify its fight against organised crime and corruption, increase judicial and administrative reform, boost protection for its minority population and encourage the return of war refugees. After the report was released, President Ivo Josipović announced he was pleased that Croatia had made a significant step forward, but Dominik doubted that the people of his country would respond well to joining the EU. So many were against it and stuck doggedly to their old ways. Some were even calling the EU, *the New Yugoslavia*. He also doubted corruption and organised crime could be stamped out in the foreseeable future.

It was three a.m. when he turned his book over in his hands and stroked the grain on its leather cover. *Surely there must be someone out there who will publish my work. It's a story of human suffering that needs to be told.*

Chapter fifty-seven

Dunja was becoming increasingly concerned about her mother's health. She usually went to visit her every Saturday morning, but she'd missed the last two because she'd been inundated with jobs and her work had fallen behind. Her latest project was designing a new logo and marketing material for a beauty spa. It was proving to be demanding because the owner kept asking for changes.

When she'd been too busy to see her, Dunja had rung her mother, but the conversation was filled with long silences and she found her mother vaguer than ever.

At the end of the last call she phoned Dominik at work.

'*Makja* seems worse,' she said. 'What do you think?'

'Yes probably. She's lost weight and she's hardly eating anything. Only enough to feed a bird.'

'Has she seen the doctor recently?'

'No, I asked her if she wanted to and she said no. When I tried to argue with her she became hostile, so I gave it up.'

'I'll cancel my Friday morning appointment and come to see her then. Could you tell her please?'

'Of course. Let me know how you find find her.'

By the time Dunja got to her mother's apartment on Friday morning, her temper was frayed after she got stuck in a traffic jam for three-quarters of an hour. She became angrier when she discovered the front door was locked. Using her own key to let herself in, she hurried along the hallway and pushed open the kitchen door.

As if it was a rerun of a scene from an old movie, her mother was lying on the tile floor — Dunja knew by looking at her that she was too late.

When the day of her mother's funeral arrived Dunja was battling to blot out the sight of her dead mother — her chalk-coloured skin, staring eyes and gaping mouth.

She wasn't surprised when the mourners did not fill half of the small church — the same one where her grandmother's funeral had been held. The two funerals couldn't have been more different. Zlata had almost no friends. She had shut herself away in her own dark, silent world years ago.

Dunja gave her father a wintery smile as he and Ivana took their places next to her. She was touched that he had brought along a wreath of red and white flowers and an old, framed photo of her mother where she looked young and beautiful. It was not a photo Dunja recalled seeing before and because it was black and white it did not show Zlata's amazing hair colour — striking auburn with golden tips that Dunja recalled so well. Tears hurried down her father's face as he placed the photo on top of Zlata's coffin.

Dominik stood quietly composed on the other side of his father. Dunja was not surprised he expressed little emotion. He had never been close to his mother. Yet when he turned his head and their eyes met, Dunja saw pain. Her heart went out to him and that was all it took for her to break down. She wept — shuddering and gasping and if it wasn't for

Ivana, standing next to her, she would most likely have keeled over. When they left the church Dunja covered her grief-stricken face with her handkerchief and kept her head down in the hope that no one would engage her in conversation.

After the funeral, she went straight home to Remete. The thought of attending the wake at her mother's home was too distressing. She couldn't face her family let alone anyone else who might have turned up.

Later that day, she thought she was sufficiently recovered to read the letter she'd found propped up against the sugar bowl on the red Formica bench, on the day her mother died.

She took it out of her bag and turned it over in her hands. In her mind's eye she saw her mother's pill bottles in disarray on the bench after she'd phoned the ambulance. One by one, she'd picked them up — each one was empty. Had they all run out at the same time, or had she taken an overdose? Her hands had been shaking as she swept the bottles off the bench into the rubbish bin and jammed the letter into her bag where it had remained until now.

Sitting on the sofa, inside the doors that opened onto her terrace, she unfolded the sheet of paper, with her mother's wonky, sprawling handwriting and read.

Dear Dunja,

> *When you read this you will have found me. I make no apologies for you being the one to come upon me, because there is no one else who I would want to see me now. It is my way of punishing you for what you did to me all those years ago. If it wasn't for you I would still be married. I can never forgive you for taking away my husband. You thought I never knew what went on between you and him when you were a child. But you were wrong. I heard him creeping into your bed and the two of you engaging in things which should have been meant for him and me alone.*
>
> > *That's all I have to say as my final farewell and although there are now only the two of you left to keep your ugly secret, you will have to live with what you did to me for the rest of your life.*
>
> *Majka.*

The letter slipped from her hands and fell to the floor. Her body followed as she slithered off the sofa and collapsed. After she retrieved the paper, she tore it into shreds and screwed it into a ball. With as much force as she could she threw it at the opposite wall, before she buried her face in her hands and she sobbed. *How could her mother say such horrible untrue things? Dominik was right, she must have been insane.* She cast her mind back, remembering the occasional night when her father had put her to bed and how he had sometimes got into bed with her when he came home late. Had she blocked out something she didn't want to remember? She didn't think so. The letter was the ravings of an unbalanced mind. She wasn't guilty. How she wished she could bury her mother's nasty accusations along with her body.

The room was in darkness when she picked herself up from the hard floor. The ball of paper had bounced off the wall and was lying beside her — a small pale glow in the dark. Dunja's extremities were cold and numb with pins and needles. She shivered. Her legs had seized up and her eyes felt as if she'd been caught in a sandstorm. She stumbled into the kitchen and flicked on the overhead light. With frozen fingers, she dropped the ball of paper into the empty stainless-steel sink after teasing out a small end — enough for the flame to take hold. It burnt quickly. Seconds later it was nothing more than a pile of feathery ash. With a burst of water she flushed it down the drain.

An hour later, Dunja was in bed trying to block out the world when the telephone rang. She didn't want to answer it, yet the ringing persisted.

'Hello,' she groaned.

'It's me, Dominik. Did I wake you?'

'No. I can't sleep.'

'Are you okay?'

'Yes. Tired after today, that's all.' She couldn't tell him about the letter.

'We should open that chest,' he said in an excitable voice. 'Can you come over tomorrow?'

'I'm sorry. I'm not up to it right now. Do you mind if we wait? Today's been more difficult than I thought.'

'We've waited this long I guess a bit longer won't matter. Call me when you're feeling better, okay?' Dominik failed to keep the disappointment out of his voice.

Chapter fifty-eight

Dominik had been working on the end of his manuscript when he became firmly convinced that all three sides involved in the civil war were guilty of atrocities, just as they were equally to blame for embellishing and misreporting the truth about many of the incidents that occurred during the war. Be that as it may, it was his considered opinion that the majority of the blame for the outbreak of war lay with the Serbs, fuelled by Milošević's greed for a Greater Serbia. He had no difficulty writing the following passage because it was a statement of fact.

The ICTY — the United Nations court of law dealing with war crimes committed during the civil war in the Balkans in the early 1990s — was set up in 1993. Based in The Hague, the ICTY calls to account those individuals from every ethnic background who are suspected of bearing the greatest responsibility for atrocities committed against humanity. As at November 2011, the tribunal had so far indicted 161 persons; among them were Ante Gotovina and Mladen Markić for their parts in *Operacija Oluja*. Both were found guilty, and on 15 April 2011 they were sentenced — Gotovina to 24 years and Markić to 18 years in prison. These decisions were in effect an indirect verdict against Franjo Tuđman, the first president of Croatia, who died in 1999, when prosecutors were planning to have him indicted.

He remembered well the day he went by himself to listen to the verdicts on the giant screens set up in Trg bana Jelačića. The square was crammed with thousands of expectant patriots disgorged by the trams — locals and visitors alike. The *zastava* was displayed prominently along with huge, blazing banners of Gotovina and Markić. To begin with the atmosphere had been jovial and party-like. Revellers stood around reading the special edition of the newspaper with the generals pictured on the front page as wondrous heroes. A musician played a song on his accordion dedicated to Gotovina — *Ante Gotovina, Ante Gotovina, like the golden hay, eyes like the blue sky, like our homeland Croatia.*

Dominik had just bought a bottle of Karlovačko when a voice behind him shouted, 'If they are human, they will release him. He's not guilty of war crimes.'

Dominik moved away, but wherever he went similar comments were being voiced.

'He must be set free. He is a true man as well as a Croatian war hero. He liberated our country and now we are free.' He tried not to listen, but the voices penetrated his brain and made him feel guilty because he didn't share their views. He could never condone Gotovina's actions.

The jeering began immediately after the guilty verdicts were announced. He was staggered by the strength of the population's denial. All around him, comments were uttered about what a fitting victory *Operacija Oluja* was, and what a powerful affirmation it was of the country's identity. Their status as heroes had prompted the government to pay Gotovina's and Markić's legal bills. The prime minister was quoted as saying the verdicts were *unacceptable* and the government would apply to overturn them. Appeals against both sentences were filed as soon as possible.

Judges at The Hague tribunal ruled that Gotovina was part of a criminal enterprise along with Tuđman, his defence minister, and the army chief of staff, all three of whom are now dead and cannot be held accountable for their actions.

Recently, the European Union put pressure on Serbia to pull in war crimes suspects. In May 2011, Ratko Mladić, who had been indicted for genocide, was arrested after 16 years on the run. The charges against him relate to the massacre at Srebrenica of more than 7000 Bosnian Muslim men and boys. Mladić refused to plead; he went so far as to express deep pride for his wartime actions and stated he felt no remorse. When Mladić left the courtroom after the charges had been read, the victims' families in the gallery, were heard to shout out in Bosnian, 'Butcher.'

Dominik was making his second trip to Sarajevo; he intended to travel to Pale where he wanted to find Ljiljana Karadžić's famous pink house. He asked Dunja to accompany him.

'What a shame, I can't go. I have too much work on,' she said when he called her.

'Next time,' Dominik said. 'And you'll have to come. I won't take no for an answer.'

Late morning, as soon as he had completed his business at the Hotel Astra, he caught the bus to Pale. Silver and white clouds were hurtling across the pale sky, but from time to time the sun made a brief appearance and when it did the the light changed instantly from gloom to glare as if a switch had been turned off and on in rapid succession.

It was a half-hour trip to the mountain town where the ski events for the 1984 Olympic Games had been held. The terrain on either side of the road was mostly steep. The surrounding hills were a vivid green and the rugged country looked inhospitable.

Immediately after his arrival in Pale, he asked the first person he came upon for directions to the pink house. It wasn't difficult to find. The colour was so vicious it stood out like a lime in a bowl of oranges. It looked as if she had got carried away tinting her own paint. He stood and stared at it for some time until a burly man emerged and barked at him.

'What d'you want?' he demanded.

'Nothing. I'm having a look around.'

'Not today, you're not. Bugger off.'

Dominik left quickly; afraid the ugly apparition with cauliflower ears would set upon him.

In Pale, when he found a café grill called Kladionica, he pushed open the door and looked inside. The wooden tabletops were charred by cigarette burns, tall-backed adzed chairs were scattered around the room like guards at attention and in the far corner of the room the *Kladionica* machine had a steady stream of optimistic gamblers.

He ordered a bowl of thick vegetable and bacon soup. It was spring and even though it wasn't warm, he decided to eat outside, rather than inside where the atmosphere was congested with cigarette smoke. He choose a seat at a glass-topped table close to the street in a courtyard bathed in watery sun. As soon as the waitress brought his bread roll he tore off the crusty end and began to chew. What did the rude thug at the pink monstrosity mean about it not being a good time to look at the house? As far as he was aware, Karadžić was still on the run.

When he spotted a copy of the local paper lying on a nearby table, he reached across and picked it up. The front page article caught his attention at once and explained why the bodyguard was so touchy. Two days ago, soldiers had blasted their way into a priest's house in Pale where they believed Karadžić was hiding. The priest's family received life threatening injuries even though there was no sign of the fugitive.

Dominik was ravenous and he ate his soup quickly while he listened in to the conversation at the next table.

'They've set out already,' a young woman with dyed black hair and harsh crimson lipstick said. 'We'd better hurry if we want to join them.'

There was more talk, which he overheard too, but he couldn't fathom it and had no idea who *they* were.

When the waitress came to clear his table, he ordered coffee. He'd brought his manuscript with him and it seemed like a good time to add to his chapters on Sarajevo. As he was about to begin a woman perched herself on the vacant chair opposite him and asked if he had a light for her cigarette. Her hand was shaking. Dominik's eyes settled on her face. A scar in a rough triangular shape stood out above her left eyebrow. Her green eyes were slanted. He knew he was staring at her, but he couldn't take his eyes away.

'Sure,' he said, pulling a matchbox from his pocket.

'Would you like one?' she held the packet towards him with her unsteady hand.

'No, thanks. Not at the moment.'

She gave him a quizzical look.

'Are you wondering why I carry matches if I don't smoke?'

'Well, yes.'

'I do occasionally. I picked them up yesterday at the market in Sarajevo. The design on the box caught my eye.' He turned over the box of Red Devil matches and showed her the image of a chubby Satan-like character dressed in red.

She laughed.

'Am I interrupting you? Are you working?'

'Not exactly.'

'You're not a journalist, by any chance, are you?'

'No. I'm a furniture designer.'

'Are those your drawings?'

'No.' He laughed. 'It's a book I'm writing in my spare time.'

'That's cool. What it's about?' she stammered.

Dominik was hesitant to answer, but the light in her cat-like eyes drew him to her. They were the most unusual eyes he had seen. Then there was her hesitancy — it made her seem ultra-polite. He was sure she wasn't a local yet her accent didn't reveal her roots.

'It's about the war,' he replied.

She leant back in her chair, as if she was shrinking away from him. 'But you're not a writer?' she said at length.

'No, just pretending to be.'

Their eyes met.

'Do you live here?'

'No. In Zagreb.'

'What brings you here?'

'A refurbishment project at a hotel.' He continued to stare at her until it occured to him that it would bother her and he looked away.

'I must be going,' she said.

'Must you?'

'I need to leave or I'll be late for work.'

He looked into her eyes again, reluctant to let her go. When he spoke he was astounded at his words. 'Are you free tonight? Could we have a drink together or maybe dinner?' He looked down, embarrassed by his forthright questions put to a woman whose name he didn't know.

She studied him in silence. 'I don't finish until eight. I'm free after that. But I work in Sarajevo though, not here.'

'That's okay. I'm staying at the Hotel Astra in the centre of Sarajevo. Do you know it?'

'Yes.'

'There's a quaint Italian restaurant around the corner. Do you like Italian food?' he said.

'Yes. I could meet you outside the Astra just after eight. My name's Sofija by the way.'

'Wonderful! I'm Dominik. See you then,' he replied as Sofija stubbed out her cigarette and stood up. He watched her leave. She was thin and as she walked she looked around with an anxious air as if she expected him or someone else to be following her.

Dominik paid his bill. He was intending to wander around Pale before he caught the bus back to Sarajevo.

It was around the next corner that he heard the noise without knowing what it was or where it was coming from. He spun around and stared down the street — mesmerised. Then before he knew it, he was surrounded by a seething mass of Bosnian Serbs marching up the street. Their faces were shielded by masks and they were waving the Serb tricolour. They assumed he was joining them and when he tried to elbow his way out, someone punched him in the face. A glancing blow landed on his cheekbone before a psycho abused him for not wearing a mask. A third person shoved a mask towards him and ordered him to put it on. It took him no more than seconds to recognise the caricature. He dropped the mask and pushed his way out of the horrifying group of fanatics until he stumbled clear.

His cheek was hot and his fingers found a lump which was swelling by the minute. Shaken by what he had been through, he decided to go back to the café for a drink before he set out for the bus stop.

In the restroom of the Kladionica Café he sluiced his face with cold water. The mirror told him that he had only sustained a graze and the skin had not been broken. He returned to the outside table where he had been sitting earlier. He had ordered a *Sarajevsko pivo* and a shot of *rakija* when a man sitting at the next table asked him for a light. He smiled. How did people know he was carrying matches? Or was it that they assumed everyone was a smoker?

'Sure,' he said reaching into his pocket for his box of red devils. 'Take the box,' he said.

'Thanks. Don't you smoke?' a pale-skinned man with a full head of dark-curly hair and a black leather jacket replied. He had an unmistakably English accent.

'Now and then, but not right now.'

'What about a drink in exchange for the matches?'

'There's no need for you to do that. I've already ordered anyway.'

'The next round then,' he said.

'Okay.'

'That's quite a lump you've got there. Are you okay?'

'Yeah, I'm fine. In the wrong place at the wrong time. That's all.' He was reluctant to say where he'd been.

'Did you join the march?'

His response surprised Dominik. 'Not by choice. Some guy slugged me when I refused to put on his Karadžić mask.'

'I can imagine. Those bloody fanatics are obsessed.'

'So I discovered.'

'Are you here on holiday?' Dominik asked. He was friendly and Dominik saw no harm in continuing the conversation.

'No we're journalists from London on the trail of Karadžić. But don't shout about it. We're not welcome here.' Just then they were interrupted by the arrival of their drinks.

'Pull up your chair and join us if you like,' he said gesturing towards a woman who Dominik thought looked Muslim. Her complexion was olive and large dark-framed sunglasses hid most of her face while a scarf covered her hair.

'Have you had any luck tracking him down?' Dominik asked once he had moved his chair.

'No, all we've found is a bunch of angry villagers out in the *vukojebina*.' Dominik laughed at his use of that word. He enunciated it so well he knew he must speak Bosnian or Serbo Croat at the very least. Dominik knew all about being in the *vukojebina*, but he didn't want to bore him with that story.

'Where are you headed now?' Dominik asked.

'Probably to the airport to get the next plane out of this godforsaken place.'

'There's nowhere else you can look for him, then?'

'No. You seem interested. You're not in the same profession as us by any chance, are you?'

'No, I'm merely curious. I figure he must be around here somewhere, mustn't he?'

'Probably,' he said before lowering his voice. 'Karadžić cut a deal with the

Americans, Holbrooke and Co in ninety-five. They agreed to stand aside and leave him alone for ten years while peace was being established. After that he'd be free to come back. Nobody will find him unless he wants to be found, though. And he doesn't because he knows that regardless of his deal with the US, the ICTY want him.'

'Are you serious?'

'Deadly. I interviewed Karadžić and his brother back in 1992. They told me about the deal they'd been offered by Holbrooke. I probably shouldn't be telling you this, but what the hell.'

'Christ! So, the West are effectively helping to hide him. Is that what you're saying?'

'Well, that's one way of putting it. When the ICTY get a tip-off about his whereabouts no one tries too hard to find him.'

'Like the incident four days ago at the priest's house?'

'Yes. There's been a few of those.'

'Have you written about this stuff?'

'Yes, my articles are online. Easy enough to find. You seem to have quite an interest in you-know-who yet you don't look like you live here.'

'I'm from Zagreb. I've been writing a book about the war in my spare time. I'm not a writer though. I just want to write a true account of the war, not a biased one, if you know what I mean.'

'Totally, one exposing the propaganda,' the woman added.

'Yes.' Dominik nodded.

'Look, if you want any help, I'm Ed. Here's my card and this is Barika. She used to live here until she was driven out by the war. She was the wrong ethnicity, if you know what I mean.'

'I certainly do. And thanks, my name's Dominik. I might email you, if that's okay.' Dominik stood up and held out his hand. If I don't hurry I'll miss the bus.

'No problem. Pleased to meet you. Anything I can do, just ask,' Ed replied.

Dominik hurried away eager to get out of Pale, but equally as eager to open his computer and look up the journalist's website.

Back in his hotel room he had difficulty concentrating on his computer screen. He kept thinking about the coming evening. Was he mad or desperate or maybe both inviting a woman he didn't know out for dinner? He'd never done anything so impulsive.

There were five pertinent articles written by Ed. They were hard-hitting and it seemed to Dominik, truthful. But he couldn't know for certain. He bookmarked the page and when he got back to Zagreb he would email Ed with the list of questions he'd scratched out on the hotel notepad.

The Italian restaurant turned out to be a great find. The interior was more charming than Dominik could have imagined. Plaited garlic and bunches of dried chillies hung from the structural beams and jars of preserved lemons sat on a shelf high up on two of the walls. There were no more than a dozen rustic-wooden tables and in the centre of each chianti bottles held slender beeswax candles. They were given a secluded table in the corner near the window. The lights had been dimmed and were barely sufficient to see what they were eating.

After much deliberation, they decided to share a lasagne and a spinach and gorgonzola ravioli, and, of course, a bottle of chanti. Sofija seemed more nervous than she had been earlier in the day and he wondered if she was as shocked by his impulsive behaviour as he was. He poured them both a glass of wine and decided to clear the air.

'In case you're wondering, I don't usually invite strange women out only a few minutes after I meet them. I don't know what came over me …' Unsure where his sentence was leading, his voice petered out.

'I'm a strange woman, am I?' Sofija was flirting with him.

He smiled. For a minute he was worried he had offended her.

'No! I don't go out with strange women.'

'Well that's nice to know.' She laughed and once again their eyes locked.

After Dominik gave her a scant outline of his life he was keen to know about hers, yet he sensed her reluctance to talk. She played with the molten wax stuck on the side of the wine bottle, picking off pieces and crumbling them in her fingers. Silence fell between them for a time before she spoke.

'Mine's not a pleasant story,' she said.

'Neither is my failed marriage.'

'My story's much worse.'

'Are you sure?'

'I'm certain.'

They lapsed into silence.

'Come on. Fair's fair. I told you my secret, so you have to tell me yours.'

'Okay, but don't say I didn't warn you … I was born in Goritsa, a small village in

Bulgaria, about an hour's drive from the capital. My sister Katja and I lived there with my mother. My father walked out when my sister was a baby. We never saw him again. Mother had never been a strong person and I was sixteen when she was diagnosed as terminally ill and had to give up work. We were poor and it was then that she suggested Katja and I should go to Bosnia and find jobs. Mother said she knew this friend of a friend who helped people relocate there. I didn't want to leave her and I thought Katja was too young to work, but mother was insistent, so I gave in.' Sofija paused, pulled a tissue from her sleeve and blew her nose.

'The trip took hours. We had to drive all the way across Bulgaria and then through BiH. We were in the back of an old van. The windows had been painted over and we couldn't see where we were going.'

'Weren't you worried?'

'Yes. I never had a good feeling about any of it, least of all about the man who'd organised it. He was sleazy. Anyway, he'd organised passports for us which he said we'd have to pay for when we started working in the bar. He kept them and showed them to the officials at the border crossings we went through.'

'Were there only the two of you in the van?'

'No, there were seven of us altogether.'

'And what happened then?'

'Do you write about stuff that happened after the war?' When she changed the subject her voice was hesitant.

'I could. It depends on what the relevance of it is, if you know what I mean.'

'Yes, I think I do.' She turned her cigarette packet over in her hand, tearing nervously at the outer cellophane cover.

'I could show you something I'm sure you'd want to write about.'

'Now?'

'No. Tomorrow, if you have time.' She looked at her watch. 'I can't talk about it any more.' She wiped her nose on a tissue before she stood up and hurried towards the toilet. Although Dominik was desperate to find out what happened next, he knew he couldn't press her. She was upset and when she returned to the table, despite the dim light, he could tell she had been crying. He would have to bide his time. Maybe wait until tomorrow to find out more.

In the middle of the night Dominik woke up. For a moment he was disoriented until he saw the red shining numerals gleaming on the face of the clock on the bedside table. A long-stemmed lamp with a tulip-shaped shade was within reach and he switched it on. It bathed his hotel room in soft-yellow light. He pulled back the bed cover, stood up and walked over to the window where he drew back the beige curtain and looked out. There were no street lights, but a small circular moon was illuminating a pale lavender elongated cloud formation that was swirling slowly across the purply-black night sky.

Dominik kept seeing Sofija's oriental eyes. They had left a lasting impression on him. He was attracted to her, yet it was not all about her eyes, it was to do with her quiet demeanour. She was the opposite of all the women in his life. He knew it had taken her a while to pluck up the courage to talk to him about something that was clearly significant to her and he couldn't imagine what she intended to show him. Another part of him felt sorry for her because of her anxiety. Her fingernails were chewed and the tremor in her hands was non-stop. Regardless, he found her sensual. Maybe in the morning reality would bite and he would see it was nothing other than lust that he felt for her.

'Put your bag in the back,' Sofija said through the open window of her decrepit once-white Yugo. 'And mind the flowers.'

Dominik stowed his backpack on the floor to avoid crushing the bunch of yellow chrysanthemums wrapped in brown paper that were lying on the back seat.

'Where are we headed?' he asked once they had got past greeting each other.

'You'll see.'

When he looked across at Sofija, her eyes were concentrating on the road ahead. Not long after they left Sarajevo she turned right and they headed down a rough-unsealed road with tall, thin trees on either side. He wound down his window to let in fresh air and caught a whiff of rotting vegetation.

'We're nearly there,' she said after another fifteen minutes. They continued on in silence. Sofija kept her eyes on the road while Dominik took in the passing scenery. They were travelling through a small forest. The rustling of the rust-coloured leaves was audible through his open window. There were no houses anywhere. He didn't know where they were in relation to Sarajevo because he'd lost all sense of direction, but clearly Sofija knew where she was going.

When at last they came to a halt, it was outside a derelict-stone building in a clearing on a small hill. Sofija turned off the car engine and stayed put. Dominik opened his door and got out.

'Have a look inside. I'll wait here,' she said.

Dominik entered the building through a doorless opening. A scuffling noise erupted as rats scurried towards the dark corners. The light inside was dim. Filthy windows were blocking it out. But it is sufficient for him to see that it had once been a bar. Broken tables and chairs were strewn about and behind the bar, empty bottles and glasses had been smashed and scattered. It was a dirty shambolic hovel smelling of damp, decay and shit. After a quick glance around he'd seen enough. He walked outside into the sunlight and sucked in a breath of clean air. Sofija was leaning against the side of her car. When he came closer, he saw that she was crying.

'Have a look in the other building, through the grey door.' Her voice was subdued.

He pushed open the rotten wooden door with his foot, stepped through the doorway and stared. It was a small chamber with concrete walls — a prison cell, complete with bars on the window. Burnt rotting rags in the middle of the room attracted his attention. A rusty bowl in one corner was coated inside with dried brown scum. The room smelt stale and musty. He sneezed. Something about the place gave him the creeps. The air felt dead. He hurried out. Sofija had not moved from beside the car, although she was no longer crying.

'We lived in that room,' she said. 'There were twelve of us. That bowl was our toilet and we slept on three filthy mattresses. They gave us a meal once a day and we did shift work in the bar.' She lapsed into silence.

Dominik stared at her drooped head. 'And your sister?'

'I'm coming to that. Every time we worked in the bar we delivered drinks to the male customers. That was the cover for our real occupation. We were bought like cattle in a market place and abused on a regular basis.'

'By local men?'

'Serbs mostly and sometimes American servicemen — peacekeepers.' Sofija stifled a sob and rubbed her eyes.

'And Katja?' Dominik dared to ask.

'She was fourteen. On our first night here, she was raped by Ivan, the owner of the bar. From then on she couldn't cope. Whenever they told her to go to the bar she would scream and scream until they marched her there with a gun pointing at her head. Then one day she vanished. Nobody would say where she was or what had happened to her. I'd heard that girls who didn't do as they were told were sometimes shot, but I hadn't seen it happen. I thought she might have run away, but I knew she would never have left without me. We were more than sisters. We were best friends.'

'Was there no way to find out where she was?'

'No. Three weeks after she disappeared I began pestering the hell out of anyone who might know. And when I asked too many questions, Ivan smashed my head with the butt of his pistol.' Sofija ran her finger over the scar on her forehead and fell silent.

'We have to leave soon. But first, I need to scatter her flowers. Will you come with me?'

'Of course.'

Sofija retrieved the bunch of flowers from the back of the car and set off on foot towards the tall, thin-trunked trees nearby. Dominik walked beside her, too stunned to speak.

On the edge of a ridge overlooking a small clearing, she stopped and untied the string on the bouquet. One by one she spread the flowers in the clearing while he stood and watched her.

'I try to imagine she is somewhere peaceful like this,' she said, coming to stand beside him. 'Every month I bring her flowers. Always yellow, because it was her favourite colour.' Dominik stepped towards her and wrapped his arms around her.

'Have you thought about going home?' he asked.

'I did for a while after the rest of us were set free when the place was raided by the authorities. But I knew Mother would no longer be alive and the rest of her family were non-supportive. They sat in judgement on her when my father left.'

'That's harsh.'

'In the end I decided it would be better to stay here and start a new life. I prefer to be where Katja is.' Sofija's breathing came in uneven bursts.

Dominik didn't know what to say and he fell silent.

Sofija whimpered and pressed her head into his chest.

'What can I do?' he asked at length.

'Be my friend, and promise you'll tell our story.'

Chapter fifty-nine

It was Friday night — the radiators were on, her apartment was warm and Dunja was relaxing on the sofa with a glass of wine. She'd left the curtains open on purpose; the full moon was illuminating the outline of the Medvednica mountain range in the distance. She could make out the outline of Sljeme, the highest peak. As the minutes passed, she watched the outline fade until it became indistinct and all that was left was a crimson line low in the sky. Earlier in the evening, before the light began to dwindle, she'd braved the cold air outside and ventured onto her terrace, wrapped in her fur-lined coat, to enjoy the panorama of the vineyards and the lower mountain slopes with their stunning array of autumn colours — the leaves were hues of saffron and blood orange.

Dunja thought about her mother often. She was having difficulty moving on. Unsure how to deal with the aftershock of her death, she began spending more and more time on her own. There was no one she could talk to. She considered sharing her grief with Valentina or Gorana, but their families were normal and well-balanced and she doubted they would understand what she was feeling. Some days, she sat and stared at the wall unable to occupy herself. She'd lost her focus. In her darkest moments, often in the middle of the night, she wondered if she'd ever be able to put her mother's death out of her mind.

Two days later when she was feeling more depressed than ever, she decided to go to the doctor.

It had been more than two years since she'd seen him and he said she needed a full medical examination including blood tests. He began with a breast examination.

'Okay, put your arm above your head. That's good,' he said as his fingers moved in a circle around her left breast. 'Uh huh,' he said, as if he's talking to himself.

'Can you feel this?'

'Yes. It's a lump, isn't it?'

'Yes.'

The next half-hour passed in a whirlwind. Afraid and tearful, Dunja cringed in the chair in front of his desk while he made telephone calls. His office was drab, confined and too hot — she broke out in a sweat before she lapsed into a stupor, staring at his glasses with the round black frames. Rather than thinking about the medical issue unfolding before her, she thought about the doctor's face and how it reminded her of a falcon — his unusual yellow eyes, slicked back blond hair and pointed nose. When he interrupted her thoughts by speaking in a raised voice, she was jolted back to reality.

'Please sign these admission forms after you've read them,' he said as he slid papers across his desk towards her. She was beyond caring by then and turned the pages mindlessly, signing her name in the appropriate places. In her confused state, she was relieved someone else was looking after her. The following day, she would be admitted to hospital; the doctor would investigate the lump to see if it was malignant.

She left his office feeling shattered. She couldn't take in what had happened — not only the bad news about the lump, but the speed at which everything was moving.

The first sensation she became aware of was a dull ache in her left side. Her left arm was heavy, she couldn't move it and if she tried to lift it, stabbing pains radiated down her arm into her hand. Anxious about what had been done to her, she reached across her body with her right hand and traced the bandages around her chest and discovered that her left arm was strapped to her body. When she was unable to bear her uncertainty any longer, she touched her left breast. It felt alarmingly flat. She cried out and dissolved into tears — unsure which was worse — the pain or the shock. She pressed the buzzer to call the nurse. When there was no response, she panicked and pressed it non-stop.

'What has he done to me?' she wailed at the nurse who finally turned up.

'You're fine. Right now, there are other patients who require urgent attention,' she said in an indifferent manner.

'But I'm not fine ...'

'You must wait for your doctor. He'll explain everything to you.' She turned and rushed off in the direction of a commotion nearby. Loneliness enveloped her — she couldn't recall ever feeling so helpless.

Hours later, her doctor confirmed her worst fear — her left breast had been removed.

'Was there cancer?' She struggled to make herself heard through her tears.

'I don't know. The results of the biopsy will tell me. I removed it to be sure.'

'Couldn't you have waited for the results first?' She was angry and disappointed by what he'd done.

'Well, perhaps, but that would've meant two operations. I prefer to do things this way. Anyway, in two years' time you can have a breast reconstruction. The cost will be covered by your pension.'

'I wish you'd told me what you were planning before the operation.'

'Have you forgotten you signed an authority giving me permission to do what I considered necessary in my professional capacity?'

'But ...'

'I couldn't tell you beforehand what was involved because I didn't know the exact size or nature of the tumour until I operated. You're suffering from shock. Once you've had a good night's sleep you'll feel better — I'll prescribe you some sleeping pills. Tomorrow you're scheduled to begin physiotherapy to strengthen your left arm.'

'When can I go home?'

'You'll need to stay for seven days until the biopsy results are back. I'll see you again before then.' He left without so much as a backward glance.

Everything had happened so quickly she hadn't had a chance to let anyone know she was going into hospital. And besides, yesterday she was under the impression she'd only be there for a day while she underwent tests and a biopsy. She wouldn't be home until the twenty-fourth of December, the day before Christmas. Eager to leave, she called Dominik.

After she'd explained to him where she was and why, he was so silent she thought he'd hung up.

'Why didn't you tell me you were going into hospital? I can't quite take in what you've told me. Are you okay?'

Dunja paused. 'As okay as I can be I suppose. I'm so shocked that he removed my ... I can't say it. I thought he was only doing a biopsy.'

'I'll come and visit you tomorrow after work. What time is visiting?'

'Seven till eight.'

'Do you need anything?'

'Yes, could you get me some nightdresses — two if you can please. There are no gowns here and I didn't bring anything because I didn't know I'd be staying. Oh and a towel, some soap and toilet paper. They don't provide those either.'

'No problem,' he said. 'See you then and I'll bring you home on the twenty-fourth too.'

Dunja ended the call. In her despondent mood, she closed her eyes to the discoloured peeling paint overhead. She hated being in the hospital. The food was awful — grey and tasteless and always served in aluminium bowls left over from the war. And she desperately wanted to turn over. An impossibility with her arm, of course. And even if she could, the bed was too narrow and hard. Instead, she pulled the sheet higher. It, too, had seen better days and was punctured with cigarette burns. Needless to say, it didn't provide any warmth and she had not been given a blanket.

At the end of an uncomfortable sleep she woke without feeling at all rested. She stared at the phone until, out of desperation, she dialled her father's number.

'You need to stay in bed and rest,' he assured her after she told him what had happened.

'What are you doing on Christmas Day?' she asked him.

'We're off to Ivana's cousin's place. I'd suggest you come with us, but we already have a full car.'

The thought of spending Christmas alone upset her. She had never spent it by herself. She had wanted to ask Dominik about spending it with him, but Martina would put a stop to that.

Outside her living-room window, feathery snowflakes floated to the ground turning the landscape vivid white. It was going to be a splendid white Christmas.

Dominik and *Tata* had called her earlier in the morning to wish her *Sretan Božić*. Since then the hours had passed slowly. The snow was a clean white blanket on her terrace.

By mid-afternoon she hadn't eaten anything. The previous day her father had sent over a Christmas food parcel — a chicken, some *kulen* and Ivana's homemade traditional sweets, *kroštule, arancini* and *fritule*. It was a kind thought, but she couldn't summon the energy to cook the chicken, when there was only her to eat it. In the depths of despair, she picked at the sweets.

By evening, she'd sunk into hopelessness. In bed, she buried herself under a mountain of bedclothes and shut out the world.

Chapter sixty

Dunja threw out her double bed. It was time for a change and she was having a cleanout. She bought a new single one with a ledge on the side for her books. The frame was cane and it was more like a daybed. Her old bedding had also been consigned to the rubbish and she had treated herself to new lavender-coloured linen and a duvet cover with sprigs of lavender inside dark-mauve squares. She was amazed at how cleansing it was to redecorate her bedroom. Her finishing touch was to stack her unread books on the ledge ready for reading at night-time, *The Road Less Travelled* by M. Scott Peck was on the top of the pile.

As part of her new regime, she began each day with a brisk walk. Every few days while she was out walking, she collected drinking water from the stream in the woods because she believed it was purer than the town water and she was convinced it was also healthier. Her diet had also undergone a radical change after she enlisted the help of a naturopath who designed a macrobiotic diet for her. Giving up smoking was the most difficult decision she'd made. She used to smoke thirty cigarettes a day and there were times when she thought she would go insane for want of one.

Soon, she knew she must consider returning to work. Although it was ten months since her operation, she had taken a long time to come to terms with the loss of her breast. She had been devastated by the cancer scare and her confidence had evaporated. The wrinkles on her face were bad enough, but she found the jagged scar where her left breast had been sliced off much worse. Unless she had to, she didn't look in the mirror.

Last week she'd had an appointment with a cosmetic surgeon to discuss the reconstruction of her breast. 'The waiting list is two years,' he said with a kindly smile on his long-thin face.

'That's not good news,' she said as she sat opposite him in his drab office. She had never been in a doctor's office in Croatia that was light and bright or well decorated. All buildings that related to health were old and unsightly. Many didn't look as if they'd been redecorated for fifty years. Not only did she find them dismal and depressing, but they also offended her artistic eye.

'It's not injured people that the hospitals are full of these days. It's ex-soldiers and civilians with Post Traumatic Stress Disorder. I'm afraid you'll have to wait. There's nothing I can do about it except apologise — I know that's no consolation.'

The interview left her feeling low, especially as she'd read in the newspaper that people with PTSD were allocated one counselling session per year. It didn't make sense that these patients would have an impact on the waiting list for reconstructive surgery. Without a doubt the health system had failed her. To begin with her breast had been removed in its entirety before the doctor had established whether the lump was malignant. As it turned out, the results indicated it was benign. Then there was the surgeon's comment about her other breast and how if she had the left one reconstructed it wouldn't match the right one. Her right one had drooped with age. If she wanted that lifted, she would have to pay. At the end of the day she was not surprised by the appalling health system. Her mother had been a victim too.

Dunja's motivation was completely gone and her creative juices had dried up. It was just as well she had a pension and she'd saved enough money so she could continue to pay her mortgage without being forced to work. At least she didn't have that to worry about.

Her mood fluctuated — one day she was fine on her own, and the next she was lonely and miserable. Valentina and Gorana visited from time to time and they both told her she spent too much time by herself and that she should get out more. Maybe they were right, but most of the time she was content to sit on her terrace and take in the view.

It was late afternoon, the sky was clear, and the moon was visible — a pale transparent grey. With a cup of dandelion tea, Dunja was reclined in the cane chair given to her as a present by Dominik when she moved to her new home. She felt unusually clear-minded. Perhaps she was coming right.

She must have known something when she put off searching for a new job — it was a Wednesday morning when she received an unexpected letter from the Croatian Ministry of Culture, offering her a painting sojourn in Paris for three months. She knew she had Karlo to thank for this. At the end of the war she had been inducted into the Croatian Association of Artists after being proposed by him.

As she reread the letter in her hand her excitement grew. Six artists had been offered a place. Accommodation would be provided in ateliers near Les Halles. Her only costs would be for day-to-day living. She couldn't believe it — they had chosen her. What an honour. The letter went on to say that if she didn't want to go, or if she didn't reply within seven days, her space would be offered to someone else. There were no conditions attached and it would be up to her whether or not she chose to paint.

Paris made her think about Pierre. If she accepted the invitation, she would be close to him — assuming he was still living south of Paris. She considered telephoning his mother for news of him. He had been a sweetie. It was a shame she'd met him at the wrong time in her life.

The following day, she woke up to a clear-blue sky. She was feeling much happier and impatient to get on and organise her trip. Immediately after breakfast, she made the call to the ministry and accepted their invitation.

Later, while she was packing her bags, it dawned on her that a change of scene in

Paris could be exactly what she needed to complete her recovery.

Dunja was hesitant to admit she was dismayed by the minute size of her atelier, but at least she had own private workroom. Her work table was against the wall; above it a small window overlooked the street. It could have provided a view of the street, if the glass was clean. It didn't matter though; the light bulb in the room was bright and perfectly adequate. She gave herself a talking to about not complaining. She was impatient to get started and begin planning her first project.

Overall, Paris had not changed; it was almost as if no time had elapsed since she had been there in the 1970s. She was glad to be back. The only downside was the area around Rue Rambuteau where she was staying. There was a scruffy edge to it and as she explored it on her first afternoon she came across seedy characters loitering in the entrance to the Metro and in the recessed doorways.

Her days established a pattern. Between eight and nine in the morning she treated herself to coffee and a croissant at a traditional café, a few steps from her atelier, while she worked in her diary. It wasn't the usual kind of diary — she didn't write in it; she drew sketches inspired by whatever was happening around her. Paris seemed to be the city of small dogs. Everywhere she turned she saw them. The inspiration for her first sketch came from a wire-haired brown terrier and his master in olive-green corduroy trousers, sitting a few feet away from her. She drew a pencil sketch of the two of them, with the dog lifting his leg to pee against the table leg. Her sketch reminded her of Egon Schiele's work.

One of the first museums she visited was the Musée Picasso, which was close by. It had not been there when she lived in Paris previously, having only opened in 1980. She was overwhelmed by emotion as soon as she went inside. She lingered before work that astounded and excited her — *The Death of Casagemas* in particular. She knew it had been painted during Picasso's blue period and depth of feeling and tension she felt as she studied it shook her.

Dunja's afternoons were for working. She couldn't say painting, because not everything she created was a painted canvas. Often, she took photos and created a series of say, six images. She had completed one of the Eiffel Tower. Not the usual tourist-type photos, but up-close black and white macro shots taken from underneath the tower, looking up into its framework. They were unique and bold and she intended to enlarge them for an exhibition.

The next project she had in mind would be different — photos again, but this time with the focus on texture and movement, making use of the River Seine.

When Pierre kept coming into her mind she decided to ring his mother, but no sooner had she made the decision when she couldn't summon the nerve to make the call. All she succeeded in doing was convincing herself that his mother wouldn't want to know her after all this time. She was afraid of being rebuffed and didn't think she could cope with that. She was still fragile. After dithering about and lingering over more coffee, in the end she set off to visit her old haunts.

The market at Boulevard de Grenelle hadn't changed; it was only the vendors who had grown old or been replaced by new ones. With a *tarte au citron* in her hand, Dunja ambled past the stalls recalling the happy times she and Pierre had spent there. One thought led to another and she returned to the Metro with a yearning to find out what had become of his barge.

From the window of the train she searched the river for his boat. Much to her annoyance, the train was crowded and too many heads obscured her vision. But it didn't matter, it was only a five minute walk from the station.

The barge was derelict and unloved. The paint was flaking and the metal gate leading onto it was locked with a rusty padlock. She was shocked at the state it was in. It looked as though nobody lived there anymore. She turned away, thinking she shouldn't have come.

On another whim, she trekked up the incline to Ivan's house in Passy. It had been a beautiful house and she hoped it had remained the same. She was out of breath by the time she reached the top of the hill, although it was not particularly steep. She was rewarded by a more pleasant sight. The stately old home was as well loved and majestic as ever. Outside the black, wrought-iron gate, as though she was a monkey in the zoo, she stared through the bars into the flower garden. Lost in the past, she didn't hear the young man who walked up behind her, until he spoke.

'*Puis-je vous aider?*' he asked.

Embarrassed to be caught ogling at what she assumed was his home she turned as pink as the roses in the garden. 'Oh, pardon,' she mumbled. The clanging of the gate rang in her ears when the young man closed it and gave her a fleeting smile.

Lunch, back at her atelier, was a salad. Not long after she had finished her meal, she was overcome by tiredness — her morning immersed in the past had worn her out. Instead of working, she lay down for an afternoon nap.

Three hours later she woke up with a start. She'd had a dream about Pierre. It wasn't a bad dream — she wasn't distressed — simply feeling nostalgic. They were on a motorbike riding at speed along the road from Zagreb to Vienna. She was clinging to his back, with her long blonde hair streaming out behind them. The dream was so vivid, it revived her courage to call his mother.

The phone rang just once before she answered it. For a second Dunja thought about hanging up, but something urged her on.

'Hello, Maxine, it's Diana Letica. Do you remember me?'

Maxine's breathing was loud and as the seconds passed Dunja feared Maxine had forgotten who she was.

'Of course I do, my dear. How lovely to hear from you after all this time. Are you in Paris?'

'Yes, I'm here for three months, painting. How are you?'

'I'm well, but growing older by the day.' Her voice was a soft sigh. 'But, then again, I suppose we all are. I was thinking about you only the other day and wondering how you were. Would you like to come for coffee if you're not too busy? It would be lovely to catch up.'

'I'd like that very much.'

'What about Thursday morning?'

Dunja accepted her invitation gladly, almost unable to contain her excitement.

It had been so many years since she'd seen Maxine, and though she'd aged she looked younger than her years. She'd kept herself slim and she was, as always, immaculately groomed with her long-silver hair in an upswept style. Dunja found herself drawn to Maxine's thick-lensed glasses which magnified her already large eyes. Pierre had her eyes and Dunja found it unnerving looking at them even after all this time.

Maxine was friendly and talkative as they sat in her sunroom, surrounded by healthy green plants. They were about to have coffee and Dunja was dying to ask about Pierre, but she felt too apprehensive to bring up the subject. She needn't have worried, though. Maxine began by telling her that Henri had died ten years ago. She then went on to update Dunja on her daughters' lives with their respective husbands and children.

'And then, there's Pierre — darling Pierre,' she said. 'Such a caring, devoted son. You do know he got married, I suppose.'

'No, it's quite a while since I've heard from him.'

'Oh, I see.'

'He rang me during the war,' Dunja said, recalling the conversation she'd had with him as if it was yesterday.

'Ah yes, he told me he had called you, hoping he could persuade you to come back to France. He was terribly disappointed when you didn't.'

'Was he?'

'Oh yes. My poor dear Pierre. It took him so long to find someone to marry, and then in 1998, he surprised us all by marrying Antoinette, just when we all thought he would be a bachelor for the rest of his life.'

'I'm glad for him, and for you too, of course.'

'She already had two grown-up children from her previous marriage, you know.'

'Oh, a ready-made family then?'

'Now, I've just remembered, I've found some photos. I hunted them out last night.' She picked up a handful of shots from the mahogany side table next to her and passed them to Dunja. The sight of Pierre choked her up. His hair had turned silver the same as his mother's and he was wearing glasses with tortoiseshell frames. He hadn't really changed that much although his hair was much thinner.

'They're taken outside his house in St Clémentin,' Maxine said.

That night in bed Dunja replayed the conversation she'd had with Maxine over and over. *Did she notice I don't have a wedding ring? And did she see I still wear the pearl ring Pierre gave me?*

At Gibert Joseph, Dunja bought art supplies for her next project before she headed to the Seine with her camera. Using indelible markers, she'd drawn large pink circles on pieces of transparent waterproof paper. Her intention was to float the sheets of paper in the shallow water at the edge of the river, where they would twist and turn as the current and the wind took them. She would photograph them dancing on the surface of the water above the smooth, round pebbles on the riverbed.

At the end of her day's work, not only was she exhausted, but she was also wet. She accidentally fell in the river when she was in too much of a hurry to take a shot before the current altered the angle of the floating paper. She had overbalanced in shallow water at the edge of the river and although her jeans were soaked through up to her thighs, she clambered out without dropping her camera or getting it wet. She wasn't concerned — she was ecstatic with her results.

Chapter sixty-one

Back in Zagreb, with her creative ability awakened after her time in Paris, Dunja accepted a daunting new assignment. She would be restoring frescoes in Castle Miljana, the original summer house of the Rattkay family near the village of Velikog Tabora, seventy kilometres from Zagreb in the direction of the Slovenian border. The original construction of this four-winged baroque castle began in the sixteenth century and took a further three centuries to be completed. It had recently changed hands, and its new owner, Dr Franjo Kaifež, was renovating it because he intended to open a small number of rooms to the public.

It would be Dunja's task to uncover the rococo frescoes originally painted in the eighteenth century by either Anton Lerchinger, or Ivan Ranger who also painted the remarkable frescoes in the church in Remete. She was offered the prestigious job at Castle Miljana after the new owner viewed her work there.

The project was complex — the most difficult one she had tackled yet. It would be an arduous, delicate process where she would need to use a scalpel to uncover the frescoes without damaging them. As she expected though, she was in her element and thoroughly enjoying a new challenge. Viktor and her team of six men were professionals and she had no problems organising and assigning their tasks. When they first began work, with the exception of Viktor, the others were astounded that their supervisor would be a woman. However, Dunja soon gained their respect.

The castle has been vacant for many years and as it was unfit for habitation, Dunja and her team were staying in the nearby town of Velikog Tabora. On their first free weekend, four of them went on a daytrip to the village of Kumrovec, where Tito was born. It was a mere ten kilometres away and none of them had been there before.

Tito's home, originally built in 1860, has been preserved and restored to how it would have been at the time he and his family lived there when he was a child. The largest house in the village, it was the first one to be built from brick. The others had been constructed from timber and earth.

For many Slavic people this is a revered place. Dunja had never been a Tito disciple and although his house and the displays were interesting, she was not moved to tears as many of her fellow countrymen are when they go there.

She was however, drawn to the bronze statue of Tito in its prominent place outside the house. Crafted by Antun Augustinčić in 1948, it was a towering sculpture of Tito wearing a greatcoat. As imposing as it was, the longer she admired it, the harder it was to accept the exorbitant amount of money it cost to create it. Viktor was emotional as they stood side by side, studying the monstrosity. There were tears in his eyes and after lengthy contemplation, he spoke. 'It was such a tremendous loss for the country when Tito died. He was a great man. He gave us so much.'

His words didn't surprise Dunja. She had always suspected Viktor was a faithful communist caught up in Tito's cult following. She'd kept quiet when he'd spoken about him on other occasions, but it was at this moment when she recalled a phrase she'd read recently describing Tito to perfection as *one of the greatest magicians of self-promotion*.

Perhaps one could argue that Yugoslavia would not have disintegrated ten years after the death of Tito, if he'd been succeeded by another communist leader, but that wasn't how Dunja saw it. Surely it would only have been a matter of time before many Croatians and the other peoples of the Balkans would have craved independence. If Croatia had continued as a communist state, war would have been inevitable, if only because of Milošević. His quest for nationalism, and his greed to create a Greater Serbia by forcefully taking land from his neighbours and murdering innocent people, had been insatiable. Dunja knew nationalism had already begun to rear its ugly head during the 1970s, when it was suppressed by Tito and his secret police.

While Viktor continued to go on about communism, Dunja took her leave and wandered away, knowing for certain that nothing could ever have come of the relationship between him and her. Their political points of view were so far apart that if they ever sat down to discuss them, it would end in an argument.

On one of his regular visits to assess the progress of the restoration, Mr Kaifež brought along a reporter and a cameraman from one of Zagreb's main newspapers. Dunja was thrilled when he said they wanted to interview her. Progress was going well and she knew they would be impressed.

The following week when Viktor appeared ready to begin work he had a broad smile. 'Look, we're famous now,' he said, spreading out the newspaper. The photo showed all eight of the team wearing their white coats. They were clustered in front of one of the frescoes as though they were a team of surgeons. Dunja laughed. Underneath the photo was an article about the restoration. The mention of Dunja as the leader was written in glowing terms. She was proud and a warm glow stayed with her for the rest of the day.

So far, they had completed a large part of the cleaning and scraping process and Dunja was almost ready to start repainting the first of the frescoes. Most had clear contours, which she could follow without too much difficulty, but it was meticulous work. So many of them were elaborate. The most detailed Dunja had come across. The scenes comprised several landscapes, the four seasons, and depictions of the lives and customs of eighteenth-century nobility. To begin with, Dunja worked on a pastel-coloured fresco she adored. A musician playing a horn for a group of aristocrats who were leisurely lounging on the grass around him. It was a fresco she loved restoring and she was oblivious to what was happening around her while she gave it her total attention.

At the end of the Miljana contract, Dunja believed her work restoring frescoes was over. She suffered too much contorting her body into unnatural positions in freezing stone buildings. It was time to concentrate on design work, which she had no difficulty picking up since she had become well known in the art world in Zagreb.

Every so often she exhibited her artwork at various galleries around Zagreb and she would have liked to exhibit more, but most of the time she was too disorganised. The series on the Eiffel Tower and the River Seine, which she had been so excited about, remained untouched in her drawer. Whenever she came across them she made a new resolution to get them ready for an exhibition.

When she returned from Castle Miljana she was pleased to be back in Remete. She had missed her home. On her first day back she wandered from room to room enjoying the sense of freedom she always felt in her own space. She was still delighted by her lavender-themed bedroom and her living room with its view towards the mountains. While she was in Velikog Tabora she had bought a new throw and three cushions at the market. A dexterous *baba* had crocheted them out of fine white wool and they were a homely addition to her sofa.

She was in the bathroom opening the skylight when she smelt a lingering stale smell. On closer inspection, she discovered that the pipe behind the toilet had cracked and water was dripping onto the floor. She would have to get it fixed before the timber was damaged. There was also another puddle in the centre of the room and water was leaking in around the skylight. The surround had perished. It was just as well she hadn't stayed away any longer.

That evening she was looking forward to painting again and she was tidying up her paints when the telephone rang.

'Hello, Dunja, it's Ivana.' Her voice sounded serious. 'I'm not interrupting you, am I?'

'No, not at all.'

'I'm calling about your father. He's in hospital having tests. He hasn't been himself for more than a month now and yesterday I finally persuaded him to go to the doctor.'

'Is he alright?'

'Well, he's tired all the time and he's lost weight, even though he's eating well.'

'Oh!'

'Anyway, he's having blood tests and the doctor wants to keep him in hospital for a rest and to monitor him. I know you'll want to visit him. Visiting hours are from three till four.'

Dunja could tell by the tone of her voice that Ivana was worried. It was the first time she'd heard her sound so solemn. She glanced at her watch — it was almost two o'clock. 'If I hurry I can get there by three.'

'Good. He'll be pleased. I'll see you there, *Draga* — and thanks.'

Ivana's news overwhelmed Dunja. She couldn't imagine life without her father. He had always been such a vibrant person. She thought he too would live forever. There was one consolation though. At least she was back in Zagreb, so she could spend precious time with him.

Three nights later, in a morbid mood, she was slumped on the sofa in her living room with a glass of white wine, attempting to get up the enthusiasm to cook herself a meal, when the phone rang.

'Hello!' a hollow-sounding voice said.

'Claudine! Oh my goodness.' Claudine had moved away not long after Dunja left Paris and although they exchanged letters from time to time they hadn't spoken for many years.

'How are you?' Claudine asked.

'I'm well. It's lovely to hear from you. Where are you?'

'New Orleans. My mother's unwell. That's why I'm calling. I'm coming back to France to be with her.'

'I'm sorry to hear that. I hope it's nothing serious?'

'Well, it is I'm afraid. She has cancer.'

'You'll never believe this, but my father does too and I only found out this morning.' Dunja's eyes glazed over with tears. This was the first time she'd mentioned her father's illness to anyone and it was difficult putting it into words.

'Oh dear, it sounds as though we're both going to be in for a rough time. Listen, I'm calling about her house on Korčula. It has to be sold and she's asked me to contact you to see if you want to buy it.'

'She has?'

'She says she wants it sold to someone who'll love it, and she thought of you because all those years ago when we were there you seemed to be taken with it.'

'That's sweet of her.'

'The key's with a real estate company in Korčula. You could look at it, if you want.'

'I'm flattered your mother has remembered me, but it's not a good time right now, and to be honest with you, I'm not sure I could afford it. How much does she want for it?'

'Maybe fifty thousand euros, but honestly I've no idea what it's worth.'

'Can I call you later when I've had a chance to think about it?'

'Sure. There's no hurry. If you don't want it, I'll understand and I'm sure my mother will too.'

In her kitchen, Dunja poured another glass of wine, filled a pot with water and put it on to boil. She was intending to cook herself a pasta dish with tomatoes and herbs from the planter on her terrace. While she mulled over the phone call from Claudine, she was frying onion and garlic absentmindedly when the phone rang yet again. This time it was Valentina.

'Dunja! I'm beside myself. Something amazing has happened and I'm going to need your help.' She was fizzing with enthusiasm.

'Slow down!' Dunja laughed.

'You'll never believe this, but I have to go to China and you must come with me.'

'China?'

'Yes, I've been offered a job designing costumes for *Aïda*. It's being performed in Beijing in November. I only found out a few minutes ago. We'll have to leave very soon, there's not much time. Do say you'll come. I can't do it without you.'

If she thought the first call was startling then she didn't know what this one was.

'I'm happy for you. Congratulations!'

'Do say you'll come.'

'I'm afraid I can't. I've just come back from the hospital. My father's unwell … it's cancer. It wouldn't be right for me to leave right now, I'm so sorry.' There was also another reason she didn't want to visit China. It was a communist country. Yet she couldn't say that to Valentina. She knew Valentia supported communism, and as Viktor did, she often said that life would be far better if their country returned to communist rule. Dunja was well aware that the brainwashing continued even though Tito was no longer alive.

Dunja couldn't help wondering why opportunities in her life were often piled inconveniently one on top of another — these events were no exception.

Chapter sixty-two

A month later, eager to see her father again, Dunja wasted no time climbing the concrete steps to his front door. He and Ivana lived in a small old-fashioned apartment bequeathed to Ivana, an only child, by her mother. Although Ivana had done her best to make the interior cheerful, whenever Dunja went there she found it cramped and depressing. Not even the new red, white and green terrazzo tiles she'd had laid on the kitchen floor to match the existing terrazzo sink, or the fresh coat of white paint on the walls, had succeeded in brightening it up. Nothing could detract from the gloomy varnished wood which dominated the décor.

Lounging on the brown and white striped sofa in the living room, her father looked perky, more perky than he had a few days ago. In fact, he looked so well she'd like to have believed the doctor had made a mistake with his diagnosis. Ivana brought in a pot of Turkish coffee, but when she placed a cup in front of Nikola he baulked.

'Don't you drink coffee any more?' Dunja asked him.

'It gives me palpitations.'

'Have you told the doctor?'

'It's nothing to worry about. I'm fine.' He shrugged off her question.

'It's the opening of your exhibition tonight, isn't it?' he said. 'You must be excited. I wish I could be there. I'm so proud of you, you know.'

'Thanks, *Tata*. I'm looking forward to it a lot.'

At long last Dunja was exhibiting her Eiffel Tower series. Eight of her photos had been enlarged to prints one-metre square. The new prints came out more as sepia than black and white. The outlines were clear and the saturation level had exceeded her expectations. As she had hoped, the overall effect was bold.

It was eight o'clock when Dunja arrived at Moderna Galerija in the Vraniczany Palace with Gorana. She had chosen to wear her favourite black and white jacket with the zany abstract design on the back. She was so excited about the evening ahead her stomach kept somersaulting.

At the start of the evening, she was elated when a photographer from the morning paper took shots of her standing in front of her artwork. But from then on the evening deteriorated. The attendance was disappointing and only two of her pieces sold. This shouldn't have surprised her. She had waited too long. Her idea was no longer original. A French artist had already exhibited a similar collection.

Dunja and Gorana were partaking of one last drink before they went home when Dunja's mobile rang. She almost didn't answer the call, until she saw it was Ivana.

'He's gone,' Ivana sobbed. 'Your father's gone.'

'What? Have you called an ambulance?' Dunja's words were garbled. 'What happened? He seemed so well today …'

'It was so sudden.' Ivana had become fractionally calmer. 'I don't think he knew what was happening. It must have been a heart attack because by the time I called the ambulance, he was gone.'

'I'll come over right away.'

Dunja was in no state to drive and was relieved when Gorana offered to drive her. On the way she stared out of the windscreen without talking, unable to take it all in, praying it was a ghastly mistake and that she'd see her father sitting on the sofa, smiling, as he had been earlier. But that was not the case. After tearful greetings, Ivana left Dunja to be with her father while she and Gorana retreated to the kitchen to make tea.

Nikola had been moved and laid out on his bed below a copy of his favourite artwork, Da Vinci's Last Supper. He was already cool in death. When Dunja touched his hand, reality set in. Gone were the wrinkles on his face, smoothed away by death's final hand, the same hand that had closed his brilliant blue eyes for the last time. Dunja sat alone with her sorrow trying to remember happier times, but all that welled up inside her was the memory of her mother's dreadful letter. Her breath came in gasps and she let out a broken sob. She was certain her beloved *Tata* could never have been guilty of her mother's accusations. She was glad she'd never told him about the spiteful letter. She had thought about showing it to him immediately after she'd read it, but dismissed the idea. It wouldn't have achieved anything except to have caused him undue distress.

It is unusual for Croatian people to make wills. More often than not it's understood the eldest son will automatically inherit everything. Nikola was an exception to this unwritten rule. His will came to light the day after his death. He had given his wife a letter to be opened only in the event of his death. His assets were to be divided between Ivana, Dominik and Dunja. Ivana was the recipient of his pension. Dominik received a small amount of money, the family bible and other family heirlooms. He had not been left anything else because he had inherited his mother's house when she died. According to his letter, Dunja was to receive the bulk of her father's money, in recognition of her care of Dominik when he was younger. She had no idea that had been her father's intention and she was taken by surprise.

The last stipulation in his will related to his funeral. He had requested burial in

Groblje Mirogoj; the final resting place for a large number of Zagreb's residents — including many renowned ones. He had also stipulated that his funeral service was to be held in the chapel at Mirogoj.

On the morning of his funeral when Dunja arrived early at Mirogoj, its tranquillity was tangible. Enclosed by a high wall designed to block out noise from nearby traffic, the park-like setting was magnificent. Fresh snow covered the ground and all noise was hushed. She meandered along the shingle paths among mature maple, spruce and chestnut trees until she came to the pastel-coloured arcades designed by Herman Bollé in the nineteenth century. When she stopped on the path a giant bronze statue encrusted with verdigris towered above her. The statue's arms were outstretched from rolled-up shirt sleeves. He held a hat in his right hand. Over two metres tall, the green man's name was Adolfu, the same as Hitler. Dunja shivered.

When the hearse glided through the beautiful domed entrance to the cemetery, Dunja buttoned up her coat and walked towards the chapel.

She found the service harrowing. In the poorly lit chapel, a draft forced its way under the door. She was cold — too cold. Before long several of the candles alight on the sideboard adjacent to the altar were snuffed out when the wind began to howl. Without a doubt, the weather was closing in.

Ivana, Dominik and Dunja sat holding hands in the pew closest to the coffin. Dominik was quietly composed and Dunja was proud of her younger brother when he walked with his head held high to the pulpit in front of the altar where he delivered a short heartfelt eulogy.

When the time came for them to attend the graveside, the weather had indeed deteriorated. It was snowing heavily; star-shaped crystalline flakes floated down from the solid mass of cloud in the white sky. Thankfully the wind had dropped.

Once it was over, Dunja gave her apologies to Ivana for not coming back to the house until later saying she wanted to go to Park Maksimir.

'I'll come with you,' Dominik who was walking on the other side of Ivana, said.

The car park was empty and the snow had temporarily ceased falling when they set out on foot. Plodding through wide-open spaces, sometimes ankle deep in snow, they were quiet as they thought about the times they'd been there with their father.

'Do you remember what huge strides *Tata* used to take and how I was always telling him to slow down because we couldn't keep up,' Dominik said.

'Oh yes, it was as if he was on a mission.'

'Yes a mission to nowhere. That's what I used to say to him, wasn't it?'

'Uh huh. And the time I sprained my ankle when he went on ahead and I ran to catch up.'

'He was often in a hurry.'

Maksimir was almost always busy, winter and summer, but on this occasion it was not. The cold had kept people indoors. They stopped briefly and surveyed the vast expanse around them.

'It looks like icing on a giant cake. What a shame our footprints have blemished it,' Dunja said.

'They'll soon be gone when the next snowfall comes,' Dominik replied.

Chapter sixty-three

The relationship between Martina and Dominik hadn't improved despite a short holiday in

Split and a truce at Christmas time. When his mother died and his sister moved out, Dominik thought life with Martina might improve. It didn't. In fact, she had begun to treat him as she used to treat Dunja. Nothing he said or did satisfied her. One night after dinner they were sitting in the lounge in front of the television when she started on her favourite topic.

'Why do you have to go away so much?' she whined.

'That's the nature of my job. You knew that when you met me.' Dominik wondered why she hadn't figured out that their marriage was dead and nothing could resurrect it. They didn't sleep in the same bed, they hardly spent any time together and yet she had this fixation about him going away. What did it matter and why did she care? He'd never understand her. She was altogether too weird.

'You're never here.'

'What do you expect me to do about it?'

'Why can't you get another job?'

'Because there's nothing wrong with the one I have and I'm quite happy with it.'

When her next sentence began with, 'But you never consider me …' he interrupted her. He had reached the end of his tether.

'I don't understand you. You go on and on about my job. Why does it concern you? We live separate lives and we have done for some considerable time. All you ever do is nag me about the same old subject. I can't listen to this anymore.'

'It's your job that has caused the rift between us.'

'Don't talk nonsense. You know perfectly well it's nothing of the sort. I can't sit here and listen to your senseless talk any longer. I've had enough. Do you hear me? I've had enough.' Shaking with rage he stood up, knowing that if he didn't leave he'd most likely say something he'd regret. He was seriously angry — she had almost succeeded in pushing him over the edge. He put on his hat and coat and left in a hurry.

Spending time with Dario filled a void in Dominik's life. They'd been getting together every couple of weeks since the night they uncovered the mystery about his grandfather. He had arranged to meet Dario later, but not until nine o'clock.

Knowing he would be more than an hour early he fastened the top button of his coat and turned up the collar against the cold. He'd have a beer on his own while he waited for Dario. He had considered going for a walk, but the air temperature was zero.

On the corner of a one-way street he paused before crossing it. A few steps further on, a hard object whacked his right shin. He stumbled, lost his footing and fell. Straightaway, he was set upon by three thugs dressed in black. They kicked him mercilessly and as blows descended upon him, he tried to protect his head by covering it with his arms. He was momentarily thankful for his thick hat and heavy coat until searing pain broke out all over his body. He felt as if he was being stabbed by hot knives.

'*Za dom spremni, kurac,*' the bastards shouted over and over as they pulverised him with their boots. When the agony became unbearable, he passed out.

Chapter sixty-four

When Dominik woke up, it was a struggle to open his eyes. The first person he saw was his friend Dario sitting on a chair beside his bed.

'Thank God you're awake,' Dario said as he leant towards him.

'How are you feeling?'

'Ghastly! Where the hell am I?' His voice was hoarse and his throat was parched.

'In hospital. You've been in a coma.'

'Have I?'

'Yes. Two weeks, you've been out of it.'

Dominik groaned.

'Your sister's been here all morning and your wife's coming in this afternoon. Dunja's gone to get something to eat. She'll be back in a minute.'

'Christ almighty! I can't believe I'm alive.' He licked his dry lips. 'I must look bad.' He struggled to raise his right arm but couldn't.

'I guess you could say that. A bit like a mummy with all your bandages.'

Dominik tilted his head and looked down the length of his body.

'Do you know who they were? Did you get a look at them?'

'No, they chose that part of the street near the Retro Caffe, where the lights are out. There's no light there.' Dominik coughed. It hurt to breathe.

'I'd better call the nurse. They'll want to know you've woken up and you might need something for that cough.' Dario turned and started towards the nursing station in the corridor.

'Wait a minute,' Dominik spluttered.

Dario stopped and turned.

'I might not have seen their faces, but I heard their words clearly enough — *'za dom spremni.'*

'The nationalist slogan. The very one the *Ustaše* loved to spout whenever they got the opportunity.' Dario shook his head. 'It's my fault,' he said as his face coloured.

'What d'you mean?'

'Well, last year I spoke out rather forcefully about how I detest nationalism. It was at a photography exhibition where I thought I was among friends. Clearly I wasn't. A number reacted aggressively. One guy took a swing at me. At the time, I laughed it off. We'd all been drinking. I never thought they'd try to extract retribution and certainly not on one of my friends. I'm so sorry, Dom.'

'Don't blame yourself. Please. I shouldn't have gone into that murky street.'

'I can't help feeling responsible.'

'Well you shouldn't. It's too late for that. We can't turn back the clock. Besides, how do you know it wasn't someone who'd got wind of my book?'

'It's possible, I suppose. I hope that's the end of it. I had no idea these bloody nationalists were becoming so violent. It seems to me the movement is escalating.'

'God! I hope not.' Dominik shuddered as fear took hold of him.

It was six weeks before he was released from hospital. His left arm was broken and his right kneecap was damaged, and he'd sustained so many bruises it was impossible to count them. His kidneys had taken a pounding and he walked with a limp, which would probably be permanent because of the injury to his kneecap. It would be at least another month before he could contemplate returning to work.

Recuperating at home was boring and he spent most of his time emailing Sofija, who needless to say was vastly relieved when he made contact with her again after he'd come out of his coma, reading books and newspapers or watching the news on television and from time to time going over his manuscript. Yesterday he finished reading *Good People in an Evil Time* by Svetlana Broz, Tito's granddaughter. During her time in Bosnia working as a cardiologist, she had collected over a thousand testimonies from survivors of the Homeland War from all three ethnicities. It was a credit to her. Dominik knew Tito would have been proud.

One of the last entries in Dominik's manuscript started his mind whirling.

> In October 2011, Radovan Karadžić, the wartime president of the so-called Republika Srpska and also the most senior official apart from Slobodan Milošević, went on trial for various crimes in relation to the siege of Sarajevo. He refused to plead, saying the tribunal had no right to try him.

Dominik had read about Karadžić being arrested while he was hiding in Belgrade disguised as a new-age healer with a knot of hair tied on his forehead to lure energy from space. He was overjoyed that he would no longer be able to function as either a charlatan psychiatrist, a talentless poet or a mass murderer. However, would he get away with his crimes? Much to Dominik's horror, many of the high-ranking suspects who had been convicted by the ICTY, had had their convictions overturned. In his opinion too many of the appeals were upheld. Included in the reversals were Gotovina and Markić. The tribunal had for some reason enacted an about-face. The appeals appeared to have succeeded because of a *loophole* in the threshold of proof required for conviction. Many who had been sent to prison had already been set free — released after serving only two-thirds of their sentences. Dominik believed something, or maybe someone, had frightened the judges and they were running scared. He was devastated by their gutless actions, and saw their decisions as a pitiful end to the war, with no justice for either the victims or their families. All hope of it had been buried along with the bodies of the dead. The entire scenario left him feeling apprehensive. He was certain something was brewing. What was the point of the ICTY? Everything he'd seen and heard made him well aware that nationalism was not only on the rise in Croatia, but nationalists were in denial of the war. They preferred to talk about the people they said they had saved, rather than the people who had been murdered, or the war criminals and the ICTY.

After looking over that chapter of his manuscript Dominik couldn't settle down. He needed to read to shut down his brain. He would make a start on a novel he had bought last week. Set in Yugoslavia in the 1980s, *Miraculous Chronicles of the Night* written by Radovan Karadžić was an autobiographical tale that spanned the time the author was arrested for fraud in 1984. Only 1200 copies had been printed and these had sold out instantly at the Belgrade International Book Fair. The publisher said if he'd had 50,000 copies he believed he would have sold all of them. Dominik was eager to see if it was worth reading or not.

It was very late when he put down the book. He read the first fifty pages and so far he was not impressed. He believed he was reading the ravings of fanatic; however, he would persevere. Perhaps it would improve.

Chapter sixty-five

It was a Saturday morning when Dominik woke up early. Since he'd met Sofija he'd thought about her often — her green eyes glistening with unshed tears, and her ceaseless habit of twisting a lock of her chestnut hair round her forefinger.

They were now corresponding daily by email. He told her that Martina had wanted a reconciliation, which had failed, while Sofija confessed how nervous she was about the escalating unrest brewing in BiH. She had been sure she wanted to continue living there, but was having second thoughts, especially after Republika Srpska passed a referendum to celebrate their own national day in defiance of the constitutional court.

I think this is their first step to becoming part of Serbia, she'd said in her email.

I'm inclined to agree with you, he had replied.

Sofija had been working as a waitress in a night-time restaurant, but she was eager to obtain a job that would earn her a better income. To that end, during the day she'd been attending a computer skill's course.

When Croatia announced it was bringing back compulsory military training, he didn't tell her. The statement issued by the minister of defense said it was a new national security strategy because of geopolitical and regional threats. Dominik was perturbed by this news. Which neighbouring country was threatening Croatia? It could only be Serbia.

Dominik was lying in bed thinking about her last email. She was due for a week's holiday and she had emailed asking if she could visit him. He hadn't replied yet because he was uncertain where she could stay.

His house was out of the question, unless he plucked up the courage to confront Martina and tell her he wanted not only a separation, but for her to move out immediately. He could have asked his sister if Sofija could stay there, but he was reluctant to pursue that possibility. Although it would not be her intention, his sister could trample on Sofija. Dunja was forthright whereas Sofija was quiet and relatively shy. He wasn't sure they'd be compatible.

His last choice seemed to be the one that made sense. Once, he would never have contemplated this option, but times had changed. He would book a hotel room for the two of them. He had sufficient money saved and he would book a suite in the Hotel Intercontinental — the one that his sister had been employed to renovate during the war. It was in another part of Zagreb therefore the chances of him seeing anyone he knew were remote. He knew the hotel still looked good because he'd been there recently to supply new furniture for one of the restaurants. He booked a superior room which was €115 per night — an extravagance, but he didn't care. As far as he was concerned it was an investment in his future. And as for

Martina, he'd just tell her he was going away for business and he would be vague about his destination unless she pressed him.

Sofija had borrowed a Volkswagen car from a friend and driven from Sarajevo to Zagreb. The 400-kilometre journey had taken her six hours. Dominik was already waiting for her at the hotel when she arrived after lunch. He'd been eager and excited for days before her arrival and since the morning he'd been nervous. He'd only ever been to bed with one woman before — Martina. And that was neither a satisfying nor rewarding experience or one he wished to repeat.

Outside the entrance to the hotel they indulged in a long embrace. When they parted all Dominik wanted to do was look at her. In the silence that followed they held each other's gaze before he took her hand and led her inside towards the lift the would take them to their room — a tastefully decorated one with yellow and caramel decor on the sunny side of the building.

Inside the room Sofija covered her face with her hands. 'Tell me I'm not dreaming,' she said. 'Hold me. Please hold me,' she said softly.

'My darling, do you know how much I want you?' Dominik said as he pulled her close.

In reply Sofija tilted her head towards him and he covered her lips with his. She trembled as he kissed her. When his longing for her body became too much he began to undress her and when she was naked she stepped into his arms again before he lifted her up and carried her over to the bed and lay her gently on it.

It was evening when exhausted by the depth of their love Dominik and Sofija finally fell asleep.

Chapter sixty-six

It was a tiresome, twelve-hour trip on the bus from Zagreb to Korčula and by the time Dunja arrived the real estate office had closed. Fortunately, they had left the key for her in the café next door. Another bus ride took her to Račišće. Along much of this twenty-minute trip the road snaked beside the seafront before changing direction and turning inland for a short distance. There, the red-brown soil looked rich and fertile; she passed well-tended olive trees and grapevines separated by crumbling stone walls. Nestled among the trees, close to the road, she glimpsed a group of rusty sheds propping up each other. In front of them, two wizened *baka* were sitting on once-white chairs offering advice to a man in green overalls tending a fire under a still. Dunja couldn't suppress a smile and almost shuddered as she thought about some of the fiery spirits these old people still made.

Although the journey had left her overheated and tired, she felt compelled to look at the house belonging to Claudine's mother as soon as possible. After a short walk along the paved waterfront, up the steep cobbled street, past the gigantic stone cross, she was there.

From the outside the tiny house looked the same, but the inside came as a real shock. Claudine had not prepared her for that. Had anyone been there in the last twenty years? As she shied away from dense, grey cobwebs, reminiscent of a horror movie, which were hanging from the ceiling in the living room, she saw mould covering every surface. The disagreeable smell of dampness assaulted her nose and she knew further horrors would be lying in wait upstairs as she made her way up the steep, narrow staircase. She had only taken two steps when the handrail came away in her hand. She continued on up, more slowly on the spongy stair treads. The floor on the landing was in a much worse state than downstairs and she was afraid it would give way under her feet. In the bedrooms, the bedding was rotten and the curtains were hanging in shreds. But that wasn't the worst of it. When she entered the room where she and Claudine had slept, the floorboards gave way and she nearly fell through a gaping hole. She had planned on staying there, but that was not an option. Shocked and disappointed, she retreated downstairs, hoping the treads would hold her weight. Her disenchanting experience had left her in desperate need of a stiff drink and something to eat.

A rustic pizzeria on the waterfront was the only place open. After taking a seat in the courtyard outside at a table covered with a shiny, red-vinyl tablecloth, she ordered a four-cheese pizza and a glass of *mali plavac*. She knocked back the wine as soon as the waitress put it on the table. She was halfway through her second glass when her meal arrived and she demolished the entire pizza together with a third glass of wine. Once she had cleared Dunja's table, the owner, a plump curly-haired woman of about fifty, came over for a chat.

'Are you here on holiday?' she asked.

'Yes, for a few days.'

'Where are you staying?'

'I don't know yet. Can you recommend anywhere?'

'I have an apartment upstairs that could suit you.'

Although it was small and over stuffed with furniture, it was clean and tidy. Dunja told her she'd take it. The living room opened onto a narrow terrace overlooking the sea and once she'd unpacked her bag, she ventured outside. As she stood on the terrace and looked out to sea, her thoughts returned to the depressing condition of the unloved house. Before long, she was shivering in the cool evening air. She retreated inside and crawled into bed. When her head hit the pillow, she fell asleep at once.

The next morning she woke up feeling refreshed and hungry. The only establishment serving breakfast was the hotel on the waterfront where the menu was displayed on the wall beside the door. To her dismay, the one and only meal on offer was tripe — not her favourite — the smell alone put her off. She bought a ham and cheese roll at the small supermarket and back in her apartment, made a cup of instant coffee.

Over her meagre breakfast on the terrace under a promising clear, pale-blue sky, she turned her attention once more to the house. Could she face having another look at it, or should she forget about it and go home? In the end, she choose to brave it — surely it couldn't be that bad or, if it was, maybe it could be repaired. It was then that she remembered the young man she and Claudine had met when they were here — a builder who lived close by. Maybe she could ask his advice.

It didn't take her long to find his house. She could never forget the mermaid sitting beside the front door. He'd told them it was one of his first stone carvings — but it certainly wasn't the last — several others were now keeping it company. Most notable were a seal, a seahorse, a giant fish and a turtle. Dunja knocked on his door, hoping for the best.

Pero hadn't changed. Sure, he'd grown older and fatter, but his cheeky-blue eyes had not dimmed. He didn't remember her. She didn't expect he would. It was a long time ago and she knew she looked much different. Once they got past their initial reacquaintance, Pero was more than willing to give his opinion on the house and, even better, he agreed to look at it at once.

As he wandered from room to room in silence, his face gave nothing away. Upstairs in the main bedroom, he forced open the door onto the terrace and at last he spoke.

'It's not so bad. It's been closed up for a long time. That's what's caused all the mould, but the inside's dry.' He ran his hand down the nearest wall. 'That's a plus. A lot of these old stone houses have permanently damp walls because of the seepage from the bank behind. They built them too close to the earth. But this one is good. Of course the floor on this level is a bit of a problem — it's rotten and the entire area needs replacing, but it's not a big area.'

'So, you think it looks worse than it is?'

'Yeah. I mean, don't get me wrong, there's a lot of work that needs doing, but it could be done quite quickly. How much does she want for it?' he asked on his way down the rickety staircase.

'Fifty-thousand euros.'

'Offer her twenty-five and I'll do the work for you.'

She thanked him for his time and he went on his way. She had plenty of thinking to do. She'd never thought about owning a second house before. She meandered through it again, trying to picture it clean, repaired and painted in her favourite colours. She recalled it used to be cute and cosy, if a little dark, and there was probably no reason why it couldn't be the same once more. In the process of imagining the redecoration, she came upon a glass-fronted cupboard recessed into the wall of the living room. Out of curiosity she opened it. On the shelf inside sat a surprise — her mauve sunhat. It too, had suffered and was spotted with patches of mould, especially the lavender band around the crown. Picking it up and turning it over was all it took for her to decide to buy the funny little house and make it her own.

Her decision demanded a celebratory glass of *Grk*, the famous dry white wine from the nearby village of Lumbarda and a plate of seafood risotto at the hotel. And that was when she met Filip. He wasted no time sitting down at her table and introducing himself; it was as if he'd been waiting for her, or perhaps he saw her arrive the day before.

Filip was a local, born and bred in Račišće. Tall and slim with dark hair and a heavy five-o'clock shadow, his forearms were covered in dense-black hair, as was the base of his neck where his shirt was unbuttoned. She wasn't sure what to make of him, but at least he was friendly — so far, he was the only person in the village, other than the woman who owned the pizzeria, who was welcoming. Immediately after he introduced himself, he asked where she was from and why she was here. She saw no harm in telling him she intended to buy the rundown house. He sat next to her, chatting, but when her risotto arrived, he jumped up and rushed away without any explanation. She thought he had gone, but minutes later, he reappeared carrying a bundle of photos. He laid out snapshots of himself taken ten years ago when he was exploring the inside of a cave in the nearby bay of Samograd. He was proud of the photos and she had to admit he did look handsome in the enlarged colour photographs.

'Do you want to walk with me to Vaja, later on?' he asked before they parted company.

Vaja looked the same — it could easily have been yesterday when she was last there. The air was warm and wispy-white clouds were drifting across a washed-out, blue sky. It was no surprise that Filip and Dunja were the only people on the beach. It was autumn and the tourist season was over. They ambled along the shoreline. Dunja picked up interesting-shaped stones, driftwood and small pieces of coloured glass worn smooth by the sea, while Filip stayed quiet, walking with his hands clasped together in a clumsy fashion behind his back. He was an odd character and Dunja wasn't sure what to make of him. Perhaps he was just lonely. Once he began to open up Filip told her his father had died a long time ago — he was an only child and he lived with his mother. Although he wasn't particularly forthcoming, he did tell her he was divorced and keen to remarry. Back in the village, he offered to buy her a drink at the hotel. She declined. She'd only met him a few hours ago and already he was becoming clingy — she didn't mean he was too forward or behaving inappropriately, but he was invading her space. When she'd first met him she had wondered if he could be a potential partner, but it didn't take her long to decide that wasn't an option. And besides ever since she'd been raped she no longer wanted a permanent man in her life.

Back in Zagreb, Dunja called Claudine.

'I had no idea Mum had let the place get in such a state. You're probably not interested in buying it then,' she said.

'Well, I was shocked by the condition it's in, but then I spoke to Pero the builder, remember him?'

'Did you?'

'I did and he hasn't changed that much. I mean he's older and fatter but you'd recognise him easily. Anyway, he had a look at it and we talked about the cost of repairs. I'm interested in buying it, but I couldn't afford to pay more than twenty-five thousand euros.'

'Sounds fair enough if it's in such bad condition. I told you we have no idea what it's worth. Let me talk to Mum. I'll call you back later tonight.'

The evening passed and she failed to ring back.

When the telephone rang the next morning she knew it would be Claudine. When she said her mother had accepted her offer, Dunja allowed her excitement to grow.

A month later, mail was exploding out of Dunja's letterbox at Remete. She assumed it would be the papers relating to the purchase of her new property. It wasn't. The French stamps gave her a clue. Without further pause she ripped it open and read.

> *Dear Diana,*
>
> *I am so worried about Pierre that the only thing I can think of doing is to write to you. It is two weeks since I came back from his wife's funeral in St Clémentin and as the days go by he seems to be sinking further and further into depression. I have never seen him so dejected.*
>
> *Anyway, because he was so depressed I stayed with him for a few extra days. Before I left we had a heart to heart. I was shocked by his words. At first I thought he was confused but when he kept talking about you until I realised that he is still in love with you. For a while I didn't know what to say. I tried to persuade him to sell up and move back to Paris and live with me — my house is so big that we could both live here without getting under each other's feet, if you know what I mean. He said he'd think about it, but he didn't mean it and I'm sure he was only trying to humour me.*
>
> *I took that opportunity to suggest he go to Zagreb to see you, but he said no, he couldn't do that because it was too late. I brought the subject up again the next day and this time he was a bit more receptive and said he'd think about it, but he needed time. I couldn't help asking him how many more years he needed! Anyway, I'm hoping I've got through to him because yesterday when I rang him, without me bringing up the subject, he said he was considering going to Zagreb, but first he would come and spend some time in Paris with me.*
>
> *I hope you don't mind me writing to you, but if he does come to see you, since it was my idea, I thought I should warn you. Of course, my dear, if he contacts you and you don't want to see him, please don't be afraid to tell him.*
>
> *I do hope my letter isn't too much of a shock to you and that it finds you well.*
>
> *All the best,*
>
> *Maxine.*

The letter drifted from Dunja's hand on to the kitchen table. She was stunned. Poor Pierre.

How sad for him. Fancy him being in love with her after all these years. But more to the point, what would she do if he came to see her?

After another exhausting trip from Zagreb to Račišće, this time driving her new baby Renault van, Dunja was exasperated to discover that the power and water had not been connected — still she couldn't stay there. She had hoped Pero would have begun work, but when he explained that without power it would be too difficult, she understood, even though she was left with no option but to rent the apartment above the pizzeria again. Resigned to this latest setback, she retired early, hoping tomorrow would be a better day.

The next morning Pero arrived at her house earlier than she did. It was nine o'clock when she found him, crowbar in hand, standing outside her front door, organising a group of boys from the village as they cleared out the decaying timber and old furniture.

'Your job is to drive into Korčula and see what you can do about getting the power connected,' he said not long after her arrival. 'The water will be on later today. I've arranged it with Vodavod.'

After a long wait to talk to the man in charge at Elektrojug, Dunja came away with a promise that he would sort out the paperwork this week. When she dared to ask which day, he shrugged. She left before she said something she'd regret.

During the morning the boys made good progress. Upon her return from Korčula a huge pile of rubbish was stacked on the walkway waiting to be taken to the tip at Lumbarda. Pero had opened all the doors and windows and already her house was smelling fresher.

Later in the day, Filip turned up on her doorstep as she was sweeping out the living room. It didn't take him long to find out she had arrived; no doubt word spread fast in such a small village. He didn't stay for long, but before he left they agreed to go for a walk later, along a seldom-used track through the olive groves between Račišće and the neighbouring village of Kneže.

Winter was not far away and before she set out Dunja put on two extra layers underneath her jacket. As usual Filip was short on words and their walk was punctuated with long silences until once more Dunja brought up the subject of his family.

'What happened to your father?' When he didn't answer she wondered if she'd hit on a delicate subject. She was about to give up on receiving a reply when he spoke.

'I don't like talking about my father's death. It's embarrassing.'

'We can talk about something else if you want.'

'No, I'll tell you, but you must keep it to yourself.'

'Of course.'

'He had a heart attack.'

'Why does that embarrass you?'

'Because of what happened to him. It was ages before we noticed he was missing. We searched everywhere, but we couldn't find him until someone pointed out that the door to the outside toilet — you know, the hole-in-the-ground type — was open. He'd fallen in headfirst and they had terrible trouble getting him out.'

Dunja had a strong urge to laugh. She didn't, in case he was offended.

'How awful for you and your mother. Was your wife there then?'

'No, I was a child. I was still at school. It happened years before I met my wife. I didn't get married until I was thirty-seven — then my wife left me two years later.'

'I'm sorry. That's sad. Why did she leave?'

'She came from Žrnovo and I don't think she liked living in our village.'

'What was she like?'

'Pretty. She had long dark hair … but that's over,' he said quickly. 'I'm looking for a new wife now.'

'You'll find someone.'

Filip made no comment.

They were almost back in the village and about to go their separate ways when a flurry of words poured out of his mouth.

'It's my Saint's Day tomorrow and I wondered if you'd come to my house for coffee in the afternoon?'

She accepted his invitation because she felt sorry for him.

The following afternoon, there was no reply when she knocked on the door of Filip's house. She banged more loudly a second time, but there was still no response. Then, as she was about to walk away, a weathered woman with hairs sprouting from her chin opened the door.

'What do *you* want?' she barked, looking Dunja up and down.

'Hello, you must be Filip's mother. I'm Dunja.'

'I know who you are.' She glowered at Dunja. 'I suppose you think you're going to take my son away, the way that other one did.'

'No …'

'Well, he's not here, so you can go away. I know all about women like you.'

'Filip invited me for coffee to celebrate his Saint's Day and I've brought him a small present. When will he be back?'

'He won't be. What've you got in there?' She snatched the paper bag from Dunja's hand.

'Huh! Fruit! Do you think we're penniless and he can't support us? Go away and take your fancy city ways with you. You're not welcome here.'

Five minutes later, at three-fifteen in the afternoon, Dunja flopped on to a chair in the pizzeria and ordered a glass of *rakija* and a glass of red wine. Nikitsa, the owner, came over and sat down at her table; she had seen the look of distress on Dunja's face.

'What's the matter? Your face has gone white.'

When Dunja told her what she'd been through, expecting her sympathy, Nikitsa laughed.

'Why is it so funny? She was horrible, so horrible. Why does she hate me so much?'

'Because you're the talk of the village.' She pushed her salt-and-pepper curls out of her laughing eyes.

'Me! What have I done?'

'Every night you go walking with Filip and the entire village, including his mother, has seen you, and now he's telling everyone he's going to marry you,' she said with a chuckle.

'Marry him! Are you joking? He's twelve years younger than me and we're nothing other than friends. I've certainly never said or done anything to make him believe otherwise.'

'That's not what he thinks. You'd better stop going for walks with him if you don't want to be talked about — but you know, even then, that probably won't shut them up. It's exactly the sort of juicy gossip they love here.'

'I can't believe it. He seems lonely and I was only trying to be his friend, but marry him. We have nothing in common. What happened to his marriage anyway?'

'His mother caused problems. She never wanted him to get married in the first place, and when he did and his wife moved in, which is normal here, of course, she made life intolerable for her. She criticised everything she did and she kept at it, until in the end, she drove her out.'

'No!'

'Filip should've left with her, but he's tied to his mother's apron strings so there was no chance of that happening. No doubt you noticed she'll do anything to keep her son at home.'

'How sad. Filip told me his wife didn't like living in this village, which I gather wasn't quite true. If he loved his wife why did he let his mother drive her away? He must be very weak.'

'Weak is not the word for it. Can't you tell he's slightly simple? His nickname is Half-bake. Oh, and his wife, sure she was attractive, but she was also simple — probably more so than him.'

'No, surely not? You're being unkind. I can see he's a bit shy, but *simple*. Are you sure?'

Her remark made Nikitsa laugh harder. 'Look, if you know what's good for you, you need to start pushing him away otherwise he'll cause you bigger problems. He tries to latch on to almost every new woman who comes to the village,' she said, shaking her finger at Dunja in a good-hearted way.

By the end of the conversation, Dunja knew Nikitsa was giving her sound advice. But the next day, when she tried cancelling her walk with Filip, he turned up regardless, wearing a wretched look on his face. And though she couldn't bear to look at his hangdog expression she didn't have the heart not to go. From then on, he took to ringing her on her mobile several times a day. He never wanted anything in particular, but she couldn't hang up on him.

Meanwhile, no progress had been made on her house; she found it frustrating, to say the least. By the time she'd paid another depressing visit to the power company, and with the constant calls from Filip, she was fed up with the village. It was time to return to Zagreb.

Her bag was packed and she was on her way up the hill for one last look at her house when Pero turned up unexpectedly. He wanted her to meet the young man he intended to hire to work on the house.

'Goran is a skilled stonemason and tiler, but he's young and I want to make sure you're happy with him because I know how particular you are,' he said handing her a piece of paper with Goran's phone number written on it. 'I told him you'd give him a call.'

She wanted to leave, but she knew it was important to meet Goran otherwise she would worry about the standard of his workmanship.

With the notion in her head that she'd cook a tomato risotto for him using the spirit burner she bought in Korčula yesterday, after she'd called Goran, she walked to the village shop and asked the proprietor with his in-need-of-cutting grey hair and jowly-unshaven face, for six of his best *paradajz*.

'Why are you speaking *that* language here? We don't use that word. In fact, we've never used that word. If *rajčica* are what you want, then say it.' He scowled. 'You're not Serbian, are you?'

'No, certainly not. I was born in Zagreb.'

'Well, we've never spoken Serbian here. Not even during Tito's time. And anyway, don't you know that the official language of Croatia is now Croatian?' His voice was not only sarcastic, but he also had a know-all arrogance about him. In silence, she watched him weigh her tomatoes on his scales.

'By the way,' he said, 'I hope you're not going to ask me for any of that *Arab* food.'

Dunja gaped at him, horrified, guessing he meant couscous, but she was not about to use that word in his shop, because clearly, it too was a dirty one.

'I don't sell *Arab* food and I don't serve *Jews,*' was the next obnoxious remark to gush out of his mouth as he pushed the bag of tomatoes towards her. After his last remark, she recovered her senses along with her voice. 'Do you have a problem with Jewish people?'

'Don't you know they caused the financial crash in 2008 by controlling all the world's banks?'

Dunja shoved the tomatoes towards him and stalked out of his shop, slamming the door behind her. She would buy her tomatoes from the blue van parked on the waterfront. It was owned by a friendlier local.

The atmosphere in front of the van was tense. The quietly spoken man with a grey crew-cut, who was buying vegetables couldn't be a local. The village inhabitants were largely unresponsive towards him — almost aggressive. When he turned to walk away Dunja recognised him as a man she'd heard other customers talking about in the pizzeria. Although he had been born in this village, it was of no consequence, because at the outbreak of the war in 1991, he became commander of a tank battalion in the JNA, while during the course of his life in Serbia he married a Serbian woman. Every summer, he returned to the village for a holiday and stayed in his family house, but whenever he did, he was the subject of gossip. Some thought he was a hero because he refused to fire on Croatian villages in Slavonia, whereas others said he was a traitor because he had joined the JNA and married a Serbian woman. He was shunned by many of the village inhabitants who ogled at him from afar. It was unsurprising that he kept to himself.

It was not Dunja's lucky day. The vegetable truck had no tomatoes for sale.

The next day she did the best she could to make her living room habitable for her first guest. Pero had given her two wooden crates for seats and a third one served as a table. The blue linen she had brought with her from Zagreb came in handy to cover the crates.

Over a pizza and a bottle of *Pošip* red wine, she learnt that Goran, a slight young man with a shaved head and red and blue tattoos running the length of his arms, had only been living in the village for a few weeks. He had left his hometown of Slavonski Brod in northern Croatia because he could not find ongoing work. Dunja spent some time asking him about his qualifications before they wandered around her house and discussed various areas, particularly retiling the bathroom. Tiling was Goran's specialty and he had brought along a book with photos of jobs he had completed.

'I take great pride in my work,' he said as Dunja flicked through the pages.

'Yes, I can see that. You are meticulous. The photos make that obvious.'

'Thank you,' he replied as he blushed.

Once Dunja was satisfied that Goran was the right man for the job their conversation moved on to subjects other than the work to be carried out on her house. She found it refreshing to discover a young person so well informed about his country. In addition to being an avid reader, he also kept up with the news and current affairs on television. When the conversation turned to politics, Goran had plenty to say for himself.

'Croatia would be much better off with a change of government,' he said as he lit another cigarette.

'Do you think so?'

'I know so,' he replied. 'Mesić is a traitor. He implicated our army when he testified at the Hague by spouting nothing but lies. Him and those SDP party members talk shit. What this country needs, is a leader from HOS. Then we might get some action.' He knocked back half a glass of wine in one swig and held out his glass for a refill before extracting his crumpled cigarette packet from his jeans' pocket. His words startled Dunja, yet she shouldn't have been surprised he was a supporter of Hrvatska Odbrambene Snage — the fascist party — many young people in Croatia were. She didn't comment that she'd once met Mesić, let alone say she liked and respected him.

'What about Tuđman? You must have thought his nationalist policies were okay,' Dunja said.

'No, he wasn't hard line enough. I mean, he was into driving other races out of Croatia, but in my opinion they need to be more than driven out, they need to be exterminated

— in case they think about coming back.'

'I couldn't abide Tuđman, but exterminating them, that's being far too harsh. I did cheer the day he died though.' Dunja was horrified by the anger pulsating out of Goran. It was simmering on the surface and she could see it wouldn't take much to make him explode.

'Too right. Bloody oath!' Goran said.

'Yes, it was the same as it was with Tito,' she said. 'We couldn't get rid of Tuđman until he died.' For several moments silence fell between them, until Goran changed the subject.

'I was seven when the war broke out. It stole my childhood, and it stole too many of my family and friends who were killed by those bastards. I'll never forget it. I was nine when I tried to steal a gun. I wanted so desperately to kill those fuckers.' His voice was tense and he was speaking quickly, winding himself up like a mechanical toy.

'You sound like my brother.'

'I hated the bastards back then and I hate them now. My mother suffered from depression because of what she went through during the war and she'll never recover. She's dependent on sleeping pills for life. And we were lucky my father wasn't killed. He's a mess too. He can't work. He lost his right leg fighting in BiH.' Goran's gaze seemed fixed on nothing. His skin had gone pale. He was no longer the jovial young man she had met a short time ago. He was bitter and disturbed. Sweat had broken out on his forehead and a glistening sheen of it coated his shaved head. Damp patches were showing around the underarms of his black AC/DC T-shirt and his body odour was drifting towards her.

'What a terrible time you went through. I'm sorry to hear it. Zagreb was a haven by comparison.' When Goran didn't comment further, she continued burbling on, trying to fill the uncomfortable silence. 'Perhaps you should try to forget the war and move on . . .'

'Forget it! Are you joking? Not a day goes by when I don't think about it. I'll never be the same again. How could I be? And it's often the small things that bring it all back. Like every time I eat. Look at my teeth — what do you see?'

Dunja flinched. Goran's voice had become loud and had a desperate edge to it.

'Well, I ...'

'They're yellow and full of holes. I've already lost more than half of them. I got scurvy during the war because our diet was so bad. And I can't look at a terrace any more without remembering my neighbour. He was standing on his balcony next to our house when I saw him get his head blown off.'

'Oh no! I had no idea. I just can't imagine it.'

He didn't hear her and carried on. 'I was ten. Since then, I can't remember what it's like to sleep through a whole night — I can't silence the noise of the guns. Sleeping pills are useless.' He reached into his pocket with a trembling hand and pulled out a sheet of what she assumed were sleeping tablets and thrust it under her nose. 'I'm dying for another war to break out.'

'You can't mean that. We can't go through another war. Don't say such terrible things.'

'I mean it alright. I can't wait to kill as many of those bastards as I can. I'm ready and waiting. I've got an AK47 and some RPGs hidden under my mother's bed. And you know what? I don't care if I die as long as I kill as many of those fuckers as possible before they kill me.' Goran's outburst left him trembling as if he was a blithering idiot.

There was nothing more Dunja could say. She hoped his state of mind was okay enough that it wouldn't effect his work. She'd have to get Pero to check on him regularly.

Chapter sixty-seven

It had been more than ten years since Dunja had worked on the restoration of the frescoes in Castle Miljana, when she received a request asking if she would restore new ones. Mr Kaifež had died and his widow had sold the castle to Mr Kolaric, a builder, who was intending to open another room. Dunja was surprised to receive the call and about to dismiss the idea, but she had no design work on and another year of work at the castle would be convenient, so she agreed to it. When they discussed her start date though, things did not go well. He wanted her to start work immediately whereas Dunja wanted a break of a couple of weeks. She knew for certain that there were few people with her skill who could restore these delicate pieces of art, and with that in mind, she tried to push for the date she wanted, but he wouldn't budge. By then she had already mentally committed herself to the job, so she reluctantly agreed to start in a few days' time.

Next, she tracked down Viktor.

'Oh no. I couldn't do that work again. I'm too old — and I must say I'm amazed you're taking it on. Surely you have better things to do.' She was taken aback by his reaction. She'd been counting on being able to work with him; she had made the mistake of assuming he shared her passion for restoring frescoes.

All too quickly it dawned on her that she was on her own. After pondering her predicament, a possible solution came to mind. She would contact the Institute of Conservation. As it turned out, they were extremely helpful and within a few days she had organised Anton, Miljenko, Andrija and Danijel — four, young, enthusiastic specialists.

As soon as they arrived at Miljana all four were eager to see Dunja's previous restoration work. Had it stood the test of time or deteriorated over the years? She was a bundle of nerves and suffered palpitations immediately before they opened the doors to the room where she had spent so much concentrated time. What would she do if her work had broken down and degenerated into an unrecognisable blur, or if the walls were covered in mould?

As she stood in the centre of the room she looked around and smiled. The frescoes encircled her as though they were long-lost friends. She felt as if it was only yesterday when she had restored them with all her love and care. What a relief it was to find they had remained perfect without a stain or a blemish. She moved from one to the next, admiring them. Her team was full of praise for her work, particularly when they came to her favourite fresco, the horn-playing musician and the aristocrats.

The new room that was opened was about fifty square metres. Dunja's initial probe with a scalpel told her the frescoes have been covered by several ancient layers of chalky paint. It would be a slow process removing these dense layers of lime wash before she could think about restoring the frescoes underneath. On day one, she discovered water damage in one corner of the room and damage to a wall where heating ducts had been installed by the previous owner. This had not helped to preserve the frescoes. She hoped the contours of the designs would be visible enough to guide her through the restoration process.

She had been working away steadily and the job was on schedule when her age began to make itself felt — her sixtieth birthday had been and gone. The arduous scraping was taking its toll and it was proving much more difficult than she anticipated removing the lime wash. Her right hand was suffering, her fingers ached much of the time and a lump was developing on the heel of her hand where it pressed against the wall. Not to mention the muscles in her upper arm that were stiff and sore from the exacting work.

It was a Friday, when the owner told her they didn't have to work during August. It was the hottest month of summer and he suggested they took a holiday.

Dunja decided to travel to Račišće and give her weary limbs a chance to recover before she resumed work in September. If her hand continued bothering her, she would have to delegate more of the scraping to the others while she made a start on painting.

With two free days before she left for Korčula, Dunja set aside an afternoon to deal with an issue that had been bugging her for too long. She intended to change her name legally. Armed with the necessary papers, she arrived at the office of Births, Deaths and Marriages, where the registrar directed her upstairs to room 106.

She knocked on the door before sitting down to wait on an uncomfortable chair in a cold corridor. After a long delay the door was opened by a sour-faced individual with wispy strands of hair sticking up from his almost bald head. He admitted her to a stark cubbyhole furnished with nothing more than an old wooden desk with steel-pipe legs and two rickety-wooden chairs.

'What do you want?' he barked.
'I want to change my Christian name please.'
'Why?' he demanded as he tapped his pen on the edge of his desk.
'Because I don't like my name. In fact, I hate it.'
He stared at her with disagreeable eyes. It was none of his business why she wanted to change her name and she certainly was not about to divulge why she wanted to be called

Diana. If she told him it meant Goddess of the Moon, or that she was fascinated by the moon, or that she was known in France as Diana, she was certain he would ridicule her. With an irritated expression on his tart face and an intentionally loud sigh, he picked up her application and her birth certificate and studied them. In the silence that followed, he screwed up his face until his down-turned mouth made him look like an ugly fish.

'We'll see,' he said, fiddling with the keyboard on his computer.

'Why do I need to justify changing my name?'

'Because it is your birth name and there's nothing wrong with it.'

'I only want to change my Christian name, which I'm perfectly entitled to do. We are no longer a one-party state you know.' She looked him in the eye. For a time neither of them spoke.

'How long will it take?'

'Who knows? I can't say. I've got more important things to do.' He shrugged. Once he'd scooped up her papers carelessly, he shut them in his desk drawer, slammed it closed and turned his attention to his computer screen.

Outside in the street, Dunja was fuming. She thought being treated like that was a thing of the past. All she could do was hound him until he completed her request.

Back at Miljana, with a paintbrush no thicker than a pencil, Dunja began work on a handsome minstrel with a beer tankard in his hand. He wore bright-red pantaloons, a blue jacket, and a jaunty hat that had a plume tucked into the band and which was adorned with flowers. Dancing in slippered feet, his smile was boundless. How she adored restoring him to his former exuberant self. As she painted the finishing touches to his rejuvenation, she knew without a doubt that he was indeed a unique fresco.

Chapter sixty-eight

She hadn't been back from Castle Miljana for long when the postman delivered a letter for her with a crest on the envelope. It was another offer to spend time in Paris, paid for once again by the Ministry of Culture. Did she want to go? Of course she did.

Dunja's arrival back in Paris was not without drama. First of all, she was shocked by the condition of the once avant-garde airport. It was shabby and poorly maintained. The peeling discoloured paint, missing tiles and unclean toilets were distressing. Eager to be on her way, as soon as she had collected her bag she went outside, but her path was barred by policemen carrying submachine guns. An incident had occurred and part of the terminal had been cordoned off. She didn't know her way around the airport well and it wasn't long before she became lost looking for an alternative route to the bus stop. Everywhere she turned she encountered more police. Paris had changed. She knew these were new measures put in place because of terrorist issues in Paris and other parts of France during the last twelve months, even so it had changed the face of the city and given it a frightening atmosphere. The presence of so many law enforcers had made her fearful. She knew it was the guns that caused it. She tried not to look at them because everytime she did her heart began to thump. She was glad when at last she boarded the bus.

    She was disrupted a second time after she got off the bus and boarded the Metro. The train came to a longer than usual halt at one of the stations on her route. The air smelt of gunpowder. The train remained motionless. Unsure what was going on, she fought off panic. Desperate to know what was causing the delay, in English, she asked the man standing next to her.

    'It's a *manifestation*. Our democratic right.' He shrugged. New passengers with streaming red eyes clambered on board. Dunja overheard an English speaker say that police had fired tear gas to control a demonstration and probably prevent it from turning into a riot. More coughing distraught passengers pushed their way into her carriage until it was packed with bodies.

    'Democracy is the right of every Frenchman,' the angry bald man she had spoken to earlier, spat.

    When fear grabbed hold of her, she tried to shrink into the corner of the carriage, but she was unable to get away. He looked worked up and ready for an argument. She felt out of place in a foreign country. Around her raised voices babbled. They spoke too quickly and she couldn't understand enough to get the gist of the conversations. By the time the doors banged shut and the train departed she was trembling. There were just too many people crammed into the small space and the air was infused with tension. Claustrophobia overtook her — she wanted to get out — it was impossible.

Despite the previous day's events she was thrilled to be back in Paris. On her first morning, she resumed her former routine — coffee and a croissant for breakfast while she sketched in a new diary sitting in Terres de Café, a new café which seated six people inside and four outside. She wouldn't have spotted the café if it hadn't been for the tantalising smell of chocolate coming from inside it. It was an authentic café where they roasted their own coffee beans and baked food on the premises. Her first espresso and the chocolate brownie accompanying it were so good she indulged in a second round of both. As people buying takeaways came and went she lingered over her coffee, while her eyes searched for inspiration for a new sketch. Sooner or later an attention-grabbing scene was bound to tickle her imagination. It wasn't long before a unique apparition appeared. Dunja smiled when a stylish old woman with her Siamese cat trotting behind her on a lead, walked past. The woman wore a red tartan skirt and shiny flat-heeled shoes with gold buckles on the toes. Her attire matched the red and gold studded collar on the sleek cream cat.

When her sketch was finished she listed all the places she'd like to visit during the next three months.

A month had gone by the time she returned to the Musée Cluny. She had a longing to feast her eyes on the medieval Lady and the Unicorn tapestries that she fell in love with so long ago. The tapestries were every bit as special as she remembered them and it came as no surprise that she had difficulty tearing herself away. The unicorn's trusting eyes drew her towards them with a mystic power. Before she left, she bought a memento from the shop — at least, that was the excuse she came up with for buying herself the luxurious red and gold silk scarf patterned with a reproduction of one of the tapestries.

After a spell of window shopping in the Boulevard St Germain Dunja found herself at the Jardin du Luxembourg where she strolled in the autumn sun enjoying the gardens and the statues. By mid-afternoon the sun was low in the sky and the air was growing cool when she sat on a sunny bench beside the small lake where sailboats floated in the erratic breeze. She had not been there long when a man with untidy silver hair sat down on the other end of her seat. There were plenty of empty seats available and she was irritated that he chose to occupy that one in particular — he was too close for comfort and he seemed to be staring at her. Every time she looked the other way she was sure he was watching her. It was time to leave.

She gathered her belongings and hastened towards the exit and the bus stop. Outside the gates a bus pulled in. She leapt aboard — the only passenger to get on. The doors closed behind her as she made her way to a seat at the back, sat down and stared out of the window.

The man had been left behind at the bus stop. His eyes were huge in his gaunt face — magnified by his glasses which had tortoiseshell frames. A look of desperation haunted them. She blinked and stared at him. Their eyes met. Could it be Pierre?

When the bus glided away from the kerb, it was as if the man was caught in its slipstream. Dunja rushed from her seat. Her hand was unsteady as she reached to press the buzzer for the next stop.

Chapter sixty-nine

'Us Croats love our red wine, but it doesn't taste as good as the blood of *Četniks* from Knin,' the man with the bright-red, sunburnt face shouted. The men gathered around him saluted — the salute executed by the Croatian *Ustaše*. Dominik sidled away. He had no desire to be associated with a group of inflammatory fools.

He had travelled from Zagreb to witness the celebrations in Knin. The journey was tedious and suffocating. Every available seat was taken and as usual the air conditioning was not working. The train stopped at every station, regardless of whether passengers were alighting or coming onboard. In his seat next to the window he dozed, unable to sleep because of the oppressive heat and the noise created by other passengers. He was restless. Sweat trickled down his back. It was five o'clock in the morning when he arrived at the fancy new station in Knin — his checked shirt was wrinkled and clammy. Glad to be more comfortable in the cooler outside air, he took in the scene. Throngs of people were everywhere. Snippets of conversations told him they had come from Croatia, Bosnia and Herzegovina, Serbia and as far afield as Australia.

The proceedings began at dawn when doves were released into the clear blue heavens as a symbol of peace. Dominik gazed at the birds' snow-white bodies and hoped for a day without ugly incidents.

The government had labelled the event, the twentieth anniversary of *Operacija Oluja*, a country fair. A laughable name in view of what had taken place.

He listened to President Kitarović, with disdain. With her bleached blonde hair and her penchant for being photographed in a skimpy bathing costume, her voluptuous image was often splashed across the media. She spoke at the unveiling of a statue of Franjo Tuđman, the very man who authorised the *Operacija Oluja* campaign. From one extreme to the other — bikini to butcher's babe.

'We pay homage today to the *Operacija Oluja* defenders who fought bravely for our freedom. They were indeed patriots who liberated us from oppression. We will be forever grateful for their courageous protection of our homeland, Croatia.' Dominik was unprepared for the stupidity of her misleading, provocative words. Watching his fellow countrymen behave inappropriately embarrassed him. Secreted beneath the dense, drooping branches of an ancient *maslina*, still he could not escape.

His thoughts remained fixed on Kitarović. If her speech was anything to go by she appeared to be following in Tuđman's footsteps — an individual Dominik detested. In his eyes Tuđman had committed too many crimes. The most heinous being his justification of

Operacija Oluja. Dominik was appalled by Tuđman's statement in 1991, that slaughtering Serbian families had been necessary to liberate Croatia from evil.

The sun had reached its zenith when a crowd of boisterous revellers surged towards Dominik and his shelter beneath the three-hundred-year-old tree was no longer his own.

'Our men fought like heroes while those Serb bastards murdered innocent civilians in cold blood and raped our women,' the man, a few paces away from him cried as he swigged on a bottle of Karlovačko beer. Dominik moved to the other side of the tree to avoid any more obstreperous scandalmongers with too much to say for themselves.

'No one ever gives a damn about Knin except on this bullshit day. It's a poor excuse for a celebration if you ask me,' another drunken reveller spewed.

Throughout the day merrymakers had been singing and dancing in the streets. A band was playing one song over and over — *Evo zove, evo dana*, sung by the Croatian *Ustaše* during WWII. *Here comes the dawn, here comes the day,* replayed itself in his head as despondency enveloped him.

He pulled his threadbare Red Star Belgrade cap more firmly onto his head and thrust his hands into his jacket pockets. He'd overheard one too many unpalatable remarks and the heat was becoming unbearable — at least thirty-five degrees in the shade — maybe hotter. After one last glance at the cloudless, cobalt-blue sky, he hurried away in the direction of the train station. Weaving his way through the intimidating crowd, he was intent on making himself as inconspicuous as possible. He kept his tired eyes focused on the ground at his feet. When he lifted his gaze for a moment, he was relieved to see the station was directly in front of him.

When the hordes closed in around him, he stepped to his right to avoid being hemmed in. His leg was still weak. It wobbled and did not bear his weight well and he came close to falling. Instead, he collided with yet another inebriated visitor.

'I'm not surprised they're celebrating an empty victory because they scored next to none of them twenty years ago,' the man lectured the individuals clustered around him before he spat on the ground and stepped backwards, landing on Dominik's toes. He flinched, but not from the pain in his foot. He'd landed in the thick of a party of Serbs. What the hell were they doing here? It was time to go home.

Exhausted at the end of a draining day, Dominik collapsed in his preferred brown chair in the living room. It was close to midnight when he turned on the television, intent on watching other *Operacija Oluja* commemorations that had taken place around Croatia that day. He tried to remain positive, but he was dismayed by the first footage he saw. In front of the Croatian Embassy in Belgrade the president of the Serbian Radical Party was burning the Croatian national flag.

'We will always remember what is rightfully ours. Krajina and Kosovo will once again belong to Serbia.' The president's voice was filled with bitterness.

Dominik hit the off button on the remote in disgust. Anger and despair remained simmering under the surface of too many Croats and Serbs. The media propaganda was as effective as ever. With each passing week the outlook for stability in the Balkans was growing darker. He stumbled towards the bathroom with leaden feet. He knew it would only take a small incident to reignite the war.

It was three months after the twentieth commemoration of *Operacija Oluja* when Dominik finally uncovered the secret hidden in the sea chest in his mother's wardrobe.

He wanted to tell Dunja that he was intending to open the chest, but she was in Paris. He was debating what to do when coincidentally she rang. It was eight o'clock at night and he was by himself staring at the television in the lounge without seeing what was on the screen when the call came.

'Dominik, it's me,' Dunja said in a perky voice.

'Gosh, what a surprise. I was just thinking about you, wondering when you were coming back.'

'Good timing then,' she said and gave a small laugh. 'That's why I'm calling. I'm extending my stay. I'm not sure when I'll be back.'

He thought about asking her why but didn't. It was enough that she sounded the most cheerful she had for months — perhaps years. 'So you're having a good time?'

'Better than a good time. The time of my life,' she replied and laughed again.

'I've been thinking about the chest. Do you mind if I open it? Or would you rather I waited until you are back?'

'That old thing. I'd forgotten about it. Go ahead. It probably doesn't contain anything of value. I know you'll let me know if it does.'

When Dominik ended the call he was still marvelling at the sound of his sister's voice and he wondered what it was that had made her so cheerful. No doubt she would tell him when she was ready.

Ever since he had arrived home from work he had been impatient for Martina to go out. That morning she'd said was going to a movie with her girlfriend, yet she seemed to be taking forever to leave.

By the time he began sawing the padlock off the cupboard door, he was hyped up. The padlock was strong and he was exasperated when he broke the first blade. He'd always hoped the chest would be full of money, but his sister had laughed at this suggestion saying she had an idea what was in there. When he pressed her, she refused to say. When at last the padlock broke and he pulled open the door, he was sweating. The rusty sea chest lay in the bottom of the cupboard. The lid was secured by another padlock, but this one was smaller and not so robust.

The stench hit him as soon as he lifted the lid. The grey-green coarse cloth smelt musty and was covered in spots of foul-smelling mould. When he pulled it free, it released a cloud of putrid air.

He covered his nose and took a step backwards. It stunk. While he waited for the dust to settle he stared at the pile of rotting fabric until curiosity got the better of him and he spread a WW1 Serbian soldier's uniform on the floor. The legs had been rolled up and crudely hemmed to fit a man with shorter legs. In an instant, he know it had belonged to his grandfather. He went back to the chest and rummaged around inside it. The last remaining item was a steel helmet, which had once been painted khaki, but was now a dirty, greenish-brown with spots of rust dotted all over the dome. Dominik stared at the insignia on the front and touched it with his fingers. It was a stylised eagle that was almost square in shape. When he picked it up a wad of discoloured paper fell out. He opened it. The document explained why his mother had a fixation about the chest. He remembered her saying more than once that if *they* found it his family would all be done for. Why didn't she dispose of it years ago? he wondered. It wasn't such a big deal, yet she carried it around forever as though it was a hair shirt. He dumped everything back in the chest and slammed the lid. There wasn't sufficient time to deal with it now. It had taken him too long to get into the chest.

Chapter seventy

'War is coming!' Sofija said in a panic-stricken voice when Dominik answered his mobile. 'Have you watched the news tonight?'

'No. Is there something I should see?'

'Yes. Ivanić, the Bosnian-Serb politician, is mouthing off about an appeal lodged by Izetbegović against the 2007 decision that cleared Serbia of genocide. You probably know that Izetbegovic is a Muslim Bosniak.'

'Was that the United Nation's ruling?'

'The International Court of Justice.'

'That's not good. I take it he doesn't like it.'

'Of course he doesn't, he's a Serb. He was fired up and angry. He said the appeal violates the constitution and it will threaten peace and stability not only here, but in all of the Balkans. He says it will lead to the gravest crisis in Bosnia since the war.'

'I wouldn't be surprised if he's right.'

'I don't know what to do. I'm afraid to stay here.'

'Don't panic. Nothing will happen overnight. Let me sort a few things here first. I'll email you. No, on second thoughts I'll call you in a couple of days.'

'Okay. I'll be waiting to hear from you. I'm frightened.'

'I know, don't worry. I'll ring you as soon as I can … I love you.' He vocalised the words that were always in his head.

'Thank you. I'm so glad I met you,' she said and then paused. 'I love you too … forever,' she said in a soft voice.

He disconnected the call with his mind in a turmoil. On yesterday's news there was footage of radical Serbian politicians protesting against Frederica Mogherini, the chief of European diplomacy. Their placards said, *Serbia doesn't trust Brussels; We don't want the EU.* Dominik had purposely omitted mentioning this to Sofija.

In view of Sofija's call, he must tell Martina their marriage was over. He'd been procrastinating. He'd told Sofija that he'd end his marriage when they'd spent their week together at the Hotel Intercontinental. Martina would have to move back to her parent's house, but first, he must destroy the contents of the chest.

It was her father's birthday and the subject had come up at breakfast that morning.

'Will you come to Tata's birthday celebration tonight?' Martina asked as she stirred sugar into her coffee.

'I can't, I have drawings for a new line of tables with wooden tops and stainless steel legs to finish — sorry,' he lied.

'Can't they wait? You haven't visited my family for months.'

'No, they can't they were due last week,' he said as firmly as he could hoping the conversation was not about to turn into an argument. It didn't. Martina sighed loudly and stood up abruptly.

'I'll stay the night then.' She gave him a black look and stormed out of the room.

During the early evening while he was waiting for her to leave, he picked up his Red Star Belgrade cap from on top of the pen holder on his desk. He ran his finger over the insignia. People all over the Balkans had always supported this team and many were not Serbian. Dominik had worn the cap for years, but at the beginning of the war he felt compelled to hide it because Željko Ražnatovich, the leader of Arkan's Tigers had become the spokesman for the Red Star supporter's group. Although he had continued to watch Red Star's matches, Dominik had shut his ears when the crowd shouted their support of Milošević with, *Serbian Slobo, Serbia is with you*. Later, he was amused when Milošević suffered defeat over Kosovo and Serbia was bombed by NATO, and the chant changed to, *Slobodan, kill yourself and save Serbia*. After Arkan's death, when the Red Star fans defected, Dominik recommenced wearing the cap. He replaced the cap back on top of his pen holder.

When he heard the front door slam, Dominik lit the fire in the living room. At first it sulked, but when he squatted in front of it and feed it with pieces of dry olive wood it was soon burning fiercely, throwing out tremendous heat. He stirred the blaze with the poker and stared at the yellow flames leaping towards the ivory-coloured mantelpiece. The fire was ready and so was he.

With unsteady hands, he ripped the pages from his journal. The only part he would keep was the cover given to him by his father. From then on, he intended to press wildflowers between the new pages he would insert inside it. Page by page, he fed his book into the inferno. It was a slow process — he didn't want any trace left. When his eyes glazed over, he dashed away the unshed tears on the sleeve of his denim shirt and carried on feeding more pages into the pyre.

Next, he opened the chest, took out the uniform and threw it into the flames — first the jacket and then the trousers. When he heard a momentary whoosh, he became concerned that the cloth was about to smother the flames, but he need not have worried — the embers were red hot, the putrid fabric burnt quickly and all that remained was an unwholesome odour. Intent on his task, he went back to the chest and picked up the helmet with its Serbian insignia. It appeared to be made of lightweight steel and he wondered if his inferno would be hot enough to melt it. He tossed it in anyway, pushing it into the embers with the poker. He lingered over the birth certificate, giving it one last look, running his fingers over his grandfather's name before consigning it too into the fire. He wasn't superstitious, like so many of his fellow countrymen and women, but somehow it was a final gesture. He watched it crumple in the flames and in his heart he knew he was doing the right thing. If war broke out again no one would find these incriminating relics.

While the fire continued burning strongly he checked inside the chest in case there was anything else he needed to destroy. He couldn't imagine he had missed anything. What else could there be? Bending down, he grasped the lid of the chest and pulled with all his might. It was too heavy and he couldn't shift it, let alone remove it from the cupboard. He rubbed his rust-covered hands on his trouser legs while he glared at the chest in frustration. It would have to stay there for the time being. He crouched next to it and reached inside for the last time. As he suspected, there was nothing left. He was about to remove his hand when his fingers encountered something in the base. He shone his torch inside and saw what his fingers had touched. Under accumulated dust was a dull metal stud set in the oiled fabric lining the chest floor. The stud was small, almost invisible. He contemplated it for a moment. *What other secrets could this damn thing hold?*

He pressed the stud with his fingers. It didn't move. He put his thumb over it and pushed harder. Still nothing. He was about to give up and then he tried pushing it sideways. He heard a click. A panel in the chest floor lifted.

The bundle was heavy. He stood up and carried it to his desk. He knew what he'd find before he unwrapped the cloth. He lay the object beside the papers accompanying it.

Sitting at his desk, he unfolded the papers and begin to read. Page by page, he looked through what appeared to be records — though of what he wasn't sure. He settled in to study them.

Sometime later, he was still staring at the papers in shock. Typed and yellowed with age, most of the transcripts were illegible. He scanned the pages until he came to a letter with an almost indecipherable signature at the bottom. The ink had faded and it took him some time to discern it, but with the aid of his powerful desk lamp and a magnifying glass, he came to an unspeakable conclusion. The letter, which was partly legible, was addressed to his grandfather and dated in early 1946. It was signed by Aleksandar Ranković, the man who was often referred to as Tito's executioner. He switched on his computer and typed Aleksandar Ranković into the search engine. Before long, his unsmiling face, with a countenance remarkably similar to Dracula, was on the screen. He began to read.

> Ranković was born in Draženac, Serbia, on 28 November 1909 and died in Dubrovnik on 20 August 1983. At the end of World War II, he was responsible for sentencing to death thousands of so-called traitors. He was in charge of UDBA — which by the mid-1960s had files on the private and political lives of millions of Yugoslav citizens.
> In July 1966, Ranković was stripped of all his official functions after it was discovered he had plotted against Tito in a power struggle. He was convicted of bugging Communist Party meetings and also Tito's private conversations in a bid to oust him.

Dominik stopped reading and stared at the wall above his desk, piecing things together. To begin with, Ranković and his grandfather had both been born in Draženac, and according to the letter his grandfather had been employed by Ranković and UDBA. Why had no one ever told him? Perhaps they'd been too afraid. He knew many people continued to live in fear of its once far-reaching tentacles, believing they could still be arrested, tortured or imprisoned.

He sat staring at the fire until it was nothing more than ashes. The papers were burnt and all that remained was the charred, blackened helmet. It had shown no sign of melting and he was not surprised that the insignia remained visible. Using the poker, he dragged it out of the fire and wet it in a bucket of water before throwing it into an old sack, which had contained firewood. He tied it securely with a heavy piece of string.

After returning to his bedroom he turned his attention to the other object tainting his desk. The pistol was a dull, blue black with black-plastic grip panels. There was a five-point star in a circle in the centre of each grip. The automatic had obviously seen much use because in places the finish had worn to show the silver of the steel from which it was made.

He sat and regarded the pistol without moving for a long time. Then almost unconsciously he picked it up. At least he knew enough about firearms not to shoot himself, or anyone else for that matter. There was a button beside the trigger guard. He pressed it and the magazine dropped out on to the table with a clatter. The topmost bullet was sitting ready to be chambered. It had remained bright despite the years it must have been hidden away. The casing of the cartridge was the shiny gold of polished brass. The projectile at the head of the brass casing was gleaming reddish copper. A gaping hole in the projectile's tip alarmed him. He knew the hole was designed to cause the maximum damage to the target. He also knew these hollow-point bullets were illegal in many countries.

His hands were trembling when he pulled the pistol's slide back to check that the chamber was empty. It wasn't. Another bullet flew through the air and fell to the floor beside his chair. He gasped. The weapon had been loaded and ready to fire the moment the trigger was pulled. He put the gun on his desk and stooped to retrieve the cartridge from the floor. He placed it on the table beside the gun and the magazine and sat staring at the deadly tableau in front of him.

When his thoughts focused on his grandfather and how many people he had killed with the gun, he made his decision. Who knew what his or his country's tomorrow would hold? He loaded the magazine back into the pistol and took the leather cover of the book he had destroyed and hid the gun inside it before stowing it in the bookcase at the head of his bed. He had one bullet left. He rolled it around in the palm of his hand while he debated what to do with it. In the end, he slipped it into his pocket. Would he toss it into the river, or wouldn't he?

He donned his heavy coat, woollen hat and sturdy boots, lifted the sack over his shoulder and ventured outside.

There was no moon to light his way, but he didn't need one. He had walked this path many times before. Half an hour later, he was nearing his destination when the clouds opened for a brief time and the moon illuminated the way. He stepped off the gravel path and the grass crunched under his feet — a frost was beginning to form. He shivered and increased his pace, hoping to warm up. At the edge of the Sava River he stopped. For a moment or two he was stricken with guilt — it dissipated.

Darkness shrouded him as he took a deep breath and filled his lungs with icy air. He lifted the sack from his shoulder and flung it with all his might into the river. To begin with, it sank below the surface before reappearing further down river, bobbing up and down until it settled and floated away on the swift current. He glued his eyes to the murky blob until he could no longer make it out.

'Flow, river, flow,' he chanted aloud over and over, willing the river to take his grandfather's helmet back to Belgrade where it belonged.

Acknowledgements

In my attempt to adhere to the correct timeline for historical events I would like to acknowledge the following publications that were of invaluable assistance to me in writing Eaten by the Night:

Milovan Đilas *Wartime*; Julian Borger – *The Butcher's Trail*; Misha Glenny – *The Fall of Yugoslavia*; Misha Glenny – *The Balkans*; Robert Greenberg – *Language and Identity in the Balkans*; Rebecca West – *Black Lamb and Grey Falcon*; Wilson Centre Digital Archive; Vladimir Dedijer – *With Tito Through the War 1941 – 1945*; Vladimir Dedijer – The War Diaries Volumes 1 – 3; Richard West – *Tito and the Rise and Fall of Yugoslavia*; Brian Hall – *The Impossible Country;* Igor Vukić – *Labour Camp Jasenovac; Tito* – Milovan Đilas; *The Yugoslav Auschwhitz and the Vatican* – Vladimir Dedijer.

Printed in Great Britain
by Amazon